"I want you," she whispered, shivering in anticipation.

His hand closed over hers. "If we do this, there are bound to be repercussions."

There was a warning there, but she ignored it, her desire for him overpowering common sense. "I don't care," she said, the fire inside her building to a fever pitch.

"But I do." He sighed, a shadow crossing his face. "And there are things we should talk about, things I need to—"

"Later." With a soft, slow movement, she kissed his palm. "We'll talk later. Right now, I just want you. *Please.*" She raised her hand and ran it along the curve of his jaw, then trailed her fingers across his lips, pleased when she felt his body tremble at her touch.

With a moan of pleasure, he pulled her into his arms, crushing her to him . . .

ALSO BY DEE DAVIS

Dark Deceptions
Dangerous Desires

DESPERATE DEEDS

DEE DAVIS

FOREVER

NEW YORK   BOSTON

If you purchase this book without a cover you should be aware that this book may have been stolen property and reported as "unsold and destroyed" to the publisher. In such case neither the author nor the publisher has received any payment for this "stripped book."

This book is a work of fiction. Names, characters, places, and incidents are the product of the author's imagination or are used fictitiously. Any resemblance to actual events, locales, or persons, living or dead, is coincidental.

Cover design by Diane Luger
Cover photo by Franco Accornero
Book design by Giorgetta Bell McRee

Forever
Hachette Book Group
237 Park Avenue
New York, NY 10017
Visit our website at www.HachetteBookGroup.com.

Forever is an imprint of Grand Central Publishing. The Forever name and logo is a trademark of Hachette Book Group, Inc.

Printed in the United States of America

First Printing: August 2010

10 9 8 7 6 5 4 3 2 1

For my friend Cecily, the personification of strength and grace.

This is the way the world ends . . .
T. S. ELIOT

PROLOGUE

Southeastern Colorado

So are we in any danger here?" Lieutenant Roger Mather asked.

"As long as we don't hit any big bumps, we should be fine." Tyler Hanson glanced over at the young soldier driving the van, feeling a twinge of guilt as his fingers tightened on the steering wheel, his knuckles going white. "I'm kidding," she assured him, swallowing a smile. "The detonators are totally harmless without a payload attached."

"So then what's with all the precautions?" His fingers relaxed, but his frown lingered. "I mean, since when is an outsider called in to handle a routine weapons transfer?"

"I'm not exactly an outsider. I come from an army family."

"Ah," Mather nodded, "an army brat."

"Exactly. I bounced around from base to base following my father. And I enlisted as soon as I was old enough. Did my basic training at Fort Hood."

"The armpit of Texas," Anthony Gerardi commiserated

from his perch in the back of the van. "So why'd you opt out?"

"Let's just say I found a higher calling—or maybe I should say it found me. Anyway, here I am."

"Doesn't change the fact that your being here marks something bigger than just a run-of-the-mill transport," Anthony observed, his eyes narrowed speculatively as he cut a glance at the crate holding the detonators.

"Look," Tyler said, turning so that she could see them both, "the detonators are prototypes. Microelectromechanical systems. Technically advanced devices that aren't available on the open market."

"Come again?" Roger asked, eyes on the road.

"They're nanotechnology. Part of a drive to miniaturize nuclear weapons."

"So why are we shipping them to the Brits?" Anthony asked.

"Because they helped develop them. And shared in the cost. It was a joint effort, and now that this phase of development is completed, each country will continue working on its own. Anyway, our job is to make sure that the devices make it safely to Colorado Springs."

"To the Air Force base." Roger nodded. "And from there?"

"They'll be transferred to British control."

"You still haven't explained why you're involved in all of this," Anthony prompted.

"In my unit, I'm the expert in munitions." She shrugged. "So when we drew the mission, I was the obvious choice to go."

"And by unit—you mean A-Tac." Roger and Anthony exchanged glances.

"I see you've done your homework."

Anthony smiled. "A little. When we heard you were going to be involved, we did some digging. Still seems odd, though, that you guys would be called in."

"Yeah, well, I had the same thought. But the order came from the top. CIA brass. And when my bosses call, I listen."

"Doesn't sound that different from the Army," Anthony said.

"You said you were military." Roger turned slightly, his brow furrowed with confusion. Then recognition dawned. "You're General Hanson's daughter." His eyes widened, fear mixing with respect. It was always like that. Her father was an icon. A soldier's soldier. He'd fought in three wars and worked for five administrations. Most recently as an undersecretary at the Pentagon. Even in his retirement, he'd kept his finger on the nation's military pulse. Until a new enemy had surfaced, threatening to rob him of the very essence that made him who he was.

"Guilty as charged," she said, turning her head to look out the window. Forest lined the road on either side, the trees looming black against the midnight sky. An occasional light blinked in the distance, but for the most part the area was uninhabited, which was exactly why they'd chosen this particular route.

"Wow." Anthony whistled. "Talk about connected."

"From my point of view, it's mainly a pain in the ass," she said.

Roger sighed. "And I know just what you mean about relatives."

"Sounds like there's more to that story," Tyler said, not

really interested, but grateful to move away from discussing her father.

"Yeah." Anthony grinned. "He married the base commander's daughter."

"Hey, you can't help who you fall in love with." Roger shrugged.

"Maybe," Anthony said, "but if I thought getting married would mean sitting behind a desk for the rest of my career, I'd seriously reconsider."

"I take it your father-in-law isn't keen for you to see any action?" Tyler asked.

"Exactly." Roger nodded. "I was all set to ship out with my unit to Afghanistan. But when we found out Mary was pregnant, she got totally freaked. Wanted me home. So her father pulled some strings. Said it was better for the family. And here I am."

"Totally screwed," Anthony said, commiserating.

"How far along is your wife?"

"Six months. She's stopped throwing up. But she's started with the mood swings. You have any kids?"

"No way," Tyler said. "I'm not interested in any kind of commitment. My job doesn't allow for it. And even if it did, I'd pass. No offense intended, but most relationships just aren't worth the effort."

"Now who's got a story?" Roger smiled.

"Nothing worth telling," Tyler said, folding her arms as she looked out the window again. "And for what it's worth, I wish my father had been home more. Might have made things a hell of a lot easier for all of us. So enjoy the time you've got. There'll be time for deployments later."

"Not if General Fisher has anything to say about it," Anthony teased.

"Shut it," Roger warned, but he smiled. Clearly the lieutenant wasn't as displeased with his situation as he pretended.

Tyler stared out the window, wondering how it would feel to be part of a family that really worked. Hers had been as dysfunctional as it got, although in later years she'd come to understand her father better. Or at least why his marriages hadn't worked. And why he'd left her on her own so much of the time. Duty was a bitch. Along with loyalty to country. They always came first. *Always.*

If she ever married, she'd wind up taking the backseat. Expected to fulfill the traditional role—the little woman, just like her mother. Justin's defection had only proved the point.

She swallowed as memory reared its ugly head. She'd loved Justin with every ounce of her being—and he'd betrayed her in the worst kind of way, expecting her to give up everything for him. His career over hers. And when she'd refused, he'd walked away—and some part of her had died. Which frankly, suited her just fine.

She had all the family she needed. Her brother Mark. And her unit at the CIA. She'd been with A-Tac for almost ten years now. A lifetime, all things considered. And the friendships she'd forged meant everything. She shook her head, banishing her rambling thoughts as she looked out at the starswept night. She'd always loved the mountains. There was something majestic about them, even now, in the dark, when their profile was little more than a shadow beyond the line of the trees.

"What's that?" Roger asked, slowing the van as a shape loomed out of the darkness.

Tyler leaned forward, squinting as the van's headlights

caught the gleam of metal. "Looks like a motorcycle," she said.

"What the hell is it doing here?" Anthony asked, already reaching for his gun.

"I don't know," Tyler said, her eyes locked on the fallen bike. "Maybe there's been an accident."

"Or maybe someone's trying to block the way." Anthony frowned.

"Not likely." She shook her head. "There's no way anyone could know that we're here. Besides, it's really not much of a blockade. I mean, we could get around it if we needed to."

"So maybe that's what we should do," Roger said as he pulled the van to the side of the road.

"Someone could be hurt," Tyler said, reaching into her coat pocket for a flashlight. "You guys stay in the van. I'll check it out." She opened the door and hopped out, her senses on high alert. "Keep close watch," she cautioned. "And if anything happens, get the hell out of here. Don't wait for me." She didn't honestly think there was any danger, but she'd learned a long time ago not to take chances.

Except for the soft whine of the van and the wind in the spruce, the road was quiet. No signs of life—just the discarded chassis of the motorcycle. From its angle, she guessed it had been abandoned in a hurry, probably to avoid oncoming traffic. She moved the beam of her light, her eyes following the line of a skid, the mark seeming to confirm her hypothesis.

To the left of the road, the mountain rose straight upward, the rocky face impassable. To the right, behind a shattered guard rail, the scree-covered shoulder sloped sharply as it dropped down to the forest floor.

Tyler leaned down to feel the engine of the motorcycle. Whatever had happened here, it hadn't been recent. Still, she needed to make certain that no one was stuck out here without help. The county road was an old one, the pass less traveled than the newer highway to the east. They'd chosen it on purpose. But the very reasons they'd decided on the route made it a danger for anyone in trouble.

Careful to keep an eye on the road and the woods beyond, she walked back over to the van. "The engine's cold. Which means that the bike's been here a while. But I need to make sure no one is stranded or injured. So I'm going to check over there where the guard rail's broken."

"I'll move the bike," Anthony said. "Might as well make it easy on us."

"Just keep your eyes open," Tyler said. "Roger, you stay with the detonators. And as before, if there's any trouble—"

"I know. I know," he said, lifting his hands. "Pedal to the metal."

"Dude, you watch too many old movies," Anthony said, as he jumped down to the pavement, a rifle slung across his back.

The two of them walked back to the motorcycle, and then as Anthony leaned down to pick up the bike, Tyler headed to the far side of the road and the guard rail. One of the wooden support posts had been knocked down, the metal railing bent and twisted. She knelt, the flashlight beam illuminating the rocky scree and the pine needle carpet stretching out into the forest.

At the foot of a gnarled old spruce, the light caught on something blue. Tyler frowned and stepped over the railing. Moving the beam slowly across the ground, she tried to make out what it was she was seeing, but the distance was simply too great. So after signaling her intent to Anthony, she began to make her way down the steep incline.

The darkness, combined with the loose rock, made it rough going, her tumbling thoughts making the descent even more difficult. It had been her mother's scarf, caught on the bridge's railing, that had first alerted a passerby of something amiss. But they'd assumed it was flotsam. Nothing worth worrying over.

Tyler shook her head. She wasn't going to make the same mistake.

As she reached the bottom of the incline, the woods closed in around her, the damp smell of earth and vegetation filling her nose. From this angle she couldn't see the highway above her. And thanks to the overhanging trees, she couldn't hear much either. Sweeping the flashlight beam over the ground, she located the flash of blue she'd seen from above.

After making her way over to the base of the tree, she bent to retrieve the swatch of material, her fingers tightening reflexively around the oblong piece of silk. Her mother's scarf had been blue, too. The coincidence was enough to send chills racing through her, followed by a wash of suspicion.

Tyler didn't believe in coincidence.

She pulled her gun and turned slowly in a circle, the flashlight's beam fading as it shot out into the forest. The pines shimmied and aspen leaves rattled, the hollow sound swelling as the wind swept through the trees.

"Is anyone out there?" Tyler called, her voice swallowed by the wind. "Hello?" She frowned and turned slowly again, still clutching the scarf. "Anyone?" Leaves swirled at her feet and behind her rocks skittered down the slope. She swung around, her instincts moving into overdrive. Something was wrong.

She started back up the slope just as a shot rang out from the road above. A burst of adrenaline sent her scrambling upward, but in her haste she stumbled, falling to her knees, the scarf whipping out of her hands, the wind carrying it back into the forest. Another shot broke through the night, this one followed by several more.

She pushed herself to her feet and clawed her way back up the steep embankment. At the top, she dropped down behind the guard rail, gun at the ready, while she tried to assess the situation. The van was still parked on the far side of the road, its headlights cutting through the dark, illuminating the motorcycle, now safely on the far shoulder. And just beyond it—a body.

Anthony's.

Anger mixed with bile as she fought to maintain control. Another round of gunfire erupted from somewhere behind the van. Roger rounded the front of the vehicle, firing behind him. Without stopping to think, she popped up, providing cover. Roger turned in her direction, running full out as bullets exploded at his feet. Two gunmen came around the van from the back, both firing.

Tyler moved closer, using a fallen tree branch for cover. Roger was only a few hundred feet away now, crouched low and moving on a zigzag. She fired in the direction of their assailants, knowing that she was too far away to kill them but praying that she was close enough to keep them from finding their mark.

At first it seemed to be working, and then just as Roger reached the guard rail, he fell forward, clutching his side. Springing to her feet, Tyler moved so that she was between him and the gunmen. Another man had emerged from behind the truck, which meant that now there were three of them. All armed, and closing fast.

Not the best of odds, but she'd be damned if she was going down without a fight. Still shooting, she knelt beside Roger, feeling for a pulse, her heart dropping when she realized there was none. Scrambling backward, she leaped over the guard rail, using the rusty metal to provide a modicum of protection. She fired twice more at the approaching men, then pivoted when she heard gravel crunch behind her.

A fourth gunman appeared through the gloom, his gun leveled at her gut. She fired, but he was faster, the force of the bullet knocking her backward to the edge of the embankment. For a moment she teetered there, trying to hold her balance, and then another bullet slammed into her and she fell, tumbling down the steep slope, her gun going flying as rocks clawed at her skin, the world seeming to move in slow motion as she slammed to the bottom, hitting her head first against a tree and then against the sharp edge of a rock.

She struggled to hold on to her thoughts. Thinking of Roger. His wife. Their baby. And Anthony laughing about old movies. She'd faced death more times than she cared to admit. But this time it seemed as if maybe her luck had run out.

From above her, she felt more than saw the bright beam of a flashlight. And she tried to sit up, to find some kind of weapon, but her limbs weren't working, her mind going fuzzy. She stared up at the gnarled limbs of the old tree, surprised to see the oblong piece of blue silk.

The color seemed brighter than before. Like a doorway, beckoning.

And as she gave in to the peaceful bliss of unconsciousness, she realized that, like her mother, she was probably destined to die alone.

Someone was trying to strangle her. She could feel fingers around her neck, and pressure against her chest. Summoning every ounce of strength she had remaining, Tyler struck out, satisfied to hear a grunt of pain. These bastards were going to pay for what they had done to Roger and Anthony.

Shrieking like a banshee, her hand closed around a rock as she rose to her knees and raised her arm, trying desperately to focus on the dark shapes of the men surrounding her. Fighting against nausea, she squinted her eyes as she swung her fist.

A steely hand intercepted hers, fingers locking on her wrist like a vise, a pair of eyes so blue they were almost black boring down into hers. "Never a good idea to kill the medic." The voice was British, refined. "He was just trying to make certain that you were all right."

"He was trying to choke me." Tyler frowned, her head spinning as she fought against his hold. "I could feel his fingers."

"He was taking your pulse." The man lifted an eyebrow, waiting. And Tyler shook her head, her vision finally clearing. A man with a medical bag and a medic's insignia stood off to one side, eyeing her warily. Beyond him, she could see the others, military men, working the scene.

With a sigh, she relaxed her arm, allowing the man with midnight eyes to take the rock.

"I didn't know." Her gaze locked with his, and she blew out a shaky breath. He nodded, releasing her wrist, the sudden lack of contact oddly disarming. "I thought they were still trying to kill me."

"Who was trying to kill you?" A beefy-looking man with a general's star stepped into the light, his voice tight with anger.

"I've no idea," Tyler said, instinctively flinching away, searching for her blue-eyed stranger, disappointed when she realized he was gone. "I only saw them from a distance."

"And why exactly was that?"

"I was down here. Looking for a body." The minute it came out, she knew how stupid it sounded. Especially in light of all that had happened. She'd been duped. But she wasn't about to let this man know the full extent of it. "There was a motorcycle in the road. We thought that someone had been hurt. So I checked it out."

"Where were Mather and Gerardi?" the man asked, making notes on a small pad of paper.

"With the transport." She blew out a breath, trying to clear her head, but everything was going hazy again, her beleaguered brain pulling out the images of Roger and Anthony's bodies. "Are they..."

"Dead?" The man glared down at her, and she felt a wash of nausea, the taste of bile bitter in her throat. "Yes, they are," he said, his voice laced with contempt. "But then you already knew that."

"I tried to help," she gasped, struggling for breath, her lungs feeling as if they were collapsing. "I was too late. What about the detonators?"

"They're gone." His mouth tightened as he said the words. "Stolen."

"Pardon me, sir," the medic frowned, interrupting as he moved closer. "She's injured and I need to make certain that she's been stabilized."

"Yes, well, my men are dead. So I think she can handle a few more questions," the man said, waving the medic back.

"You're Roger's father-in-law," she whispered, everything suddenly making sense. This man thought that all of this was her fault.

"I am—or should I say *was*." The word hung between them in the air.

"Sir, I—," the medic tried again, as Tyler fought against another wave of nausea.

"Gerardi was found by the motorcycle," the general continued, ignoring the medic, his eyes boring into hers, even as his voice became less emotional.

"Right," she nodded, trying to keep her mind clear. To remember everything that had happened. "I forgot. He was moving it out of the road. So that we could pass."

"While you were down here in the ravine," the man repeated, still eyeing her dubiously. "Looking for a body."

"I wasn't sure what exactly I was looking for," she said, anger flashing. "I just knew that something wasn't right. And when I saw that the guard rail had been compromised I thought that someone might be down here. Hurt. Only it turns out it was a set-up."

The general shot her another disgruntled look.

She struggled to sit up, but her head had other ideas, the world going wonky again.

"General Fisher," the voice of her Englishman carried across the clearing, even though she couldn't see him. "She needs medical attention. There'll be time for questions later."

The general sucked in a breath, as if to argue, but turned away as the medic dropped down next to her.

"Who was it that was talking just now?" she asked, eyes searching the slope for some sign of the stranger. "The Englishman?"

"Don't know his name," the medic said. "But he's with British Intelligence. Must be a pretty big deal, because the general doesn't give in to anyone. Anyway, I heard that the stuff you were transporting belonged to him—or more accurately, his government."

"MI-5," she nodded, wincing as he tightened a pressure bandage. "He must be the guy I was supposed to be meeting. What time is it?"

"Almost three." He opened a packet of astringent, cleaning an abrasion on her face.

She's wasn't sure exactly what time they'd stopped, but it had been close to midnight, which meant she'd been out a couple of hours at least. No wonder her head was hurting. "How'd you know to come look for us?"

"Standard ops." He shrugged. "When you didn't turn up, they tried to raise you on the radio. And when that didn't work, they figured something had to be up."

"Or down, as the case may be." She tried for a smile, but coughed instead, wheezing with the effort, pain radiating down her side. "I feel like my chest is on fire."

"You've bruised your ribs," the man said, his fingers gentle as they explored. "The body armor saved your life. But between the bullets and the fall, you're pretty banged up."

"I've been shot before." She sighed, her strength waning. "It was a close call, and I kind of developed a thing about protecting myself."

"Understandable," he said, bandaging the abrasion on her forehead, then lifting his hand to call for a stretcher.

"Too bad you didn't think to share your caution with Mather and Gerardi." The general was back, his gaze pinning hers.

"You think I had something to do with this?" she asked, fighting against both anger and pain now.

"Lady, I don't know what to think," he said, as the medic and another man loaded her onto the gurney. "All I know for certain is that my men are dead, and you're still alive. And, considering the circumstances, that seems a bit too convenient."

CHAPTER 1

Ambassador Hotel, Colorado Springs—twelve hours later

I'm okay, Avery. I've got bruises on my bruises but nothing seriously wrong. I swear." Tyler sank down on the bed in her hotel room, cradling her cell phone while she tried to make herself more comfortable. Avery Solomon was A-Tac's commander and one of Tyler's oldest friends. The two had met when she was in the Army. It was Avery who'd recruited her to the CIA.

"I'm sorry I couldn't be there." Even with the distance she could hear Avery's regret. "You shouldn't have had to go through that alone."

"It's part of the job." She shrugged, the gesture hurting more than she was willing to admit. "Missions go bad."

"I'm not buying any of this, Tyler. I saw you, remember?" Avery had insisted on being present for her debriefing, and since there was no way for him to be there physically, he'd settled for videoconferencing. "I know how much this cost you."

"I shouldn't have lost them. I should have seen the signs and gotten us the hell out of there."

"But you didn't," Avery said, his tone probing. "Which tells me that something else happened. Something you omitted from the debrief."

Tyler sighed. Avery knew her too damn well. "There *was* something. But I don't want to talk about it over the phone. Not even a secure one."

"That sounds ominous."

"Maybe. I don't know. Maybe I'm overreacting. But it seemed like someone was playing us—or more specifically, playing *me*. Anyway, I'll tell you everything when I get there. Thanks for clearing me to come home."

"There wasn't anything more you could tell them. I can understand Fisher's need to probe. I'd feel the same if it was my people that had been lost. But he was pushing too hard. Barking up the wrong damn tree."

Tyler smiled. "Thanks for that. It's nice to know someone has my back. Have you got any leads on who might have stolen the detonators?"

"Nothing concrete. It's too early. Hannah is working on it as we speak." Hannah Marshall handled intel for A-Tac. If there was anything to provide insight into who'd stolen the detonators, she'd find it.

"So does everyone know what happened?" It wasn't that she wanted to keep it a secret, but there was part of her that hated having her failure paraded about—even among her friends.

"As you know, word travels fast in our circles," Avery said. "So the whole team knows that the detonators were stolen. And that you almost died in the process. But beyond that I figured it was best to keep the details need-to-know. So Hannah's up to speed. And Nash, of course. He threatened to fly to Colorado if I didn't tell him everything." Nash Brennon was the unit's second in command.

"And if he knows, then Annie knows," Tyler said. Annie was Nash's wife, and there were no secrets between them.

Avery laughed. "Sometimes I wonder how they made it all those years apart. It's like they're two halves of a whole. Anyway, I knew you wouldn't mind if I filled them in."

"Of course not." Nash and Tyler were close. And she and Annie had hit it off almost from the beginning—except for the part where Tyler had thought Annie was a traitor. But that was water long under the bridge.

"So you're sure you don't want one of us to fly up there?" Avery asked.

"No. Honestly. I've got a flight out first thing in the morning. So I'll be home for dinner. And we'll talk then. Right now I just want a stiff drink," she sighed, realizing that it was going to take more than one.

"It wasn't your fault, Tyler."

"Intellectually, I know you're right," she closed her eyes, seeing Gerardi's body on the roadside, "but emotionally I just keep replaying it, trying to figure out what I could have done differently."

"Hindsight and all that," Avery said, his pragmatism calming her in way nothing else could have. "And you can rest assured that we're going to hunt down the bastards that did this."

"I'm counting on it. And when we find them, I want first crack. But right now, I just need to decompress. You know?"

"I do. So I'll let you go. But I'll be here if you need me. Nash and Annie, too. In fact, I'm sure they'll be calling."

"Thanks. But I'll be fine." She sucked in a calming breath, ignoring the resulting pain that laced through her chest. "I'll call you when I get to New York." She terminated the call, and then turned off the phone. Avery was right. Nash would call. And tomorrow she'd be glad to hear his voice. But for now, she was tired of talking. She needed quiet. And she needed that drink.

Pushing off the bed, she walked over to the minibar, and pulled open the little refrigerator door. Inside, lined up as neatly as soldiers, were a platoon of tiny liquor bottles.

She pulled out two bottles of Wild Turkey and poured them into a glass. When she'd turned eighteen her father had taken her to her first grown-up dinner party. The host, a longtime family friend, had asked her what she wanted to drink. She'd hadn't actually had much experience with cocktails, so she'd asked for a strawberry daiquiri. And she'd thought herself very sophisticated drinking the icy pink beverage.

It was only after she got home that she learned that the host had actually left the party to go to a nearby market to get the supplies needed to make the drink. Her father had been furious, and he'd informed her that she was never to ask for something so complicated again.

He'd taken a bottle of scotch and a bottle of bourbon from his liquor cabinet and poured a stiff tot of each. And then he'd told her to pick one. Scotch or bourbon. The scotch had tasted bitter, with a hell of a bite, and the bourbon, by contrast, had been smooth, almost sweet.

She'd drunk bourbon ever since.

She downed the glass in a single swallow, closing her eyes as the heat slid down her throat, expanding through her chest. She could almost feel the tension coiled inside her loosen as the warmth filtered through her body.

But it wasn't nearly enough.

She opened the refrigerator door again, sorting through the little bottles, but to her dismay, there was no more Wild Turkey. And somehow, in light of the events of the last twelve hours, she didn't think that a thimbleful of Bailey's Irish Cream was going to suffice.

She turned to the telephone, searching for the room service number, and then abruptly replaced the receiver, deciding instead to head downstairs for the bar off the lobby. She'd find a dark corner and nurse a couple of really good drinks. She'd be less likely to let her emotions take over in a crowded bar. And besides, misery was supposed to love company.

She grabbed her keycard and headed downstairs via the elevator. The bar was small. Like a thousand other hotel bars. Nondescript in a high-concept, designer kind of way. Huge vases of flowers had been placed strategically throughout, dividing the space into even smaller alcoves. The perfect place to unwind—or to hide.

Ignoring the curious stares from a couple of businessmen sitting at the bar, she made her way to the far corner and a table with two large wing chairs. An electric fire flickered behind a glass screen, the lack of warmth and sound only adding to the sterile feeling of the place. After ordering a Maker's Mark, she settled into the chair facing the room. It would be more peaceful to stare into the pretend fire, but old habits died hard. Better to keep watch.

One of the men at the bar smiled and lifted his glass, and Tyler shifted the chair so that she could more easily avoid his gaze. The waitress brought the bourbon and retreated, leaving Tyler to her thoughts as soft music swelled in the background. Just what she needed—a soundtrack.

Gerardi and Mather weren't the first people she'd lost during a mission, but that didn't change the depth of her regret. And even though Avery was right and it wasn't her fault, she still felt as if she should have done something different. Something that would have kept both men alive.

She blew out a breath and took a sip of bourbon. Usually, when an operation went south, she had backup. People to decompress with. This was the first time in years she'd handled an op on her own. But as she'd told Girardi and Mather, she was the expert in munitions. So the assignment had fallen to her. And since there'd been no need to involve more personnel, it had been deemed a routine operation.

But the mission had turned out to be anything but routine, and now, because of her mistakes, two good men were dead.

She tipped the glass and finished the contents.

"Way I've always heard it, Maker's Mark is a sipping bourbon."

"Didn't know you Brits ran toward bourbon at all," Tyler said, looking up into the dark blue eyes of her MI-5 agent, although for the life of her, she couldn't think why she'd think of him as "hers."

"We do get shipments from across the pond." He shrugged, signaling the waitress for more drinks as he slid into the chair next to hers. "I didn't get the chance to introduce myself before. Owen Wakefield."

He held out his hand, and Tyler sucked in a breath, not certain that she wanted to touch him. Another irrational thought. Maybe he was right and she should have been sipping. With a tight smile she reached across to take his hand in hers. "Tyler Hanson. But considering the circumstances, I suspect you already know that. You're MI-5, right?"

His hand tightened for a moment, his grip strong, his fingers engulfing hers. Then he sat back with a crooked smile. "How did you know?"

"The medic at the scene. He told me. And if he hadn't, the accent would have given you away. I guess I was supposed to be bringing the detonators to you."

"Well, I was just a courier. Same as you. But, yes, I was at the base when we heard about the ambush."

"Yeah, well, sorry I couldn't have done more about that." She sat back, waiting as the waitress brought their drinks. "If it matters at all, I was just sitting here replaying the whole thing."

"Haven't you already done enough of that? Looked to me like you were getting a pretty thorough debrief."

"You were there?" she asked, with a frown.

"Yes." He nodded. "At least in spirit. I was listening in via computer. At the base. Reciprocal courtesy and all that. After all, technically, the stolen detonators belonged to us. My government put a lot of money into their development. They're not going to be happy about losing them."

She tilted her head, studying him. He was just this side of devastating, his dark eyes framed by lashes that would have made Revlon cry. His hair was perfectly cut, and she'd wager a month's salary that his suit was hand-tailored. He carried himself with the assurance of an aristocrat and the stealth of an operative. James fucking Bond with a five o'clock shadow.

"I suppose that's understandable," she said, feeling somehow violated just the same. "How did you know I'd be here?"

"I didn't. We just happen to be staying at the same hotel."

"Government rates." She lifted her glass in a mock salute. "So I guess I've made a real mess of things for you. I'm sorry."

"Why?" He frowned. "It's not as if you knew what was going to happen."

"Yes, but it was my job to see the signs. Recognize the threat. And instead, I fell for their ruse lock, stock, and barrel."

"Which only means that they were good."

"Or I was bad." She took a long sip, letting the burning liquid soothe her jangled nerves. And guilty conscious. "Bottom line, your detonators, and those men, were my responsibility. Which means that everything that happened is, at least in part, on my head."

"You're letting Fisher get to you."

"No. I'm not. I'm just calling it the way it is. I realize that I had no way of anticipating what would happen. But the signs were there, and instead of seeing them for what they were, I let my judgment get clouded." By memories of her mother, but she wasn't ready to share that part of the story. "And because of that two men are dead."

"And the detonators are missing."

"Tell me something I don't know." She frowned at him over the rim of her glass. "Like who the hell you think might have walked away with them."

"I've got nothing," he said, spreading his hands wide. "It's still too early. No one is taking credit, if that's what you're asking. And any number of parties would be interested in the detonators for any number of reasons. They're state of the art. So if nothing else they'll fetch top dollar on the black market."

"That's exactly what worries me. If those detonators fall into the wrong hands…" she trailed off.

"It could go very badly," he finished for her.

"Exactly. And it's not just that they're state of the art. It's that they're designed for nuclear weaponry. We have treaties that guarantee our countries are not engaged in increasing our nuclear stockpiles. Particularly new technology. If word gets out that we've been secretly pursuing advance—well, I don't have to tell you what the political ramifications will be. Not to mention the possibility of someone actually using the devices."

"Spoken like someone who knows her way around ordnance," he said, his eyes probing.

"What can I say?" She shrugged. "I've always liked things that go 'boom.' I studied engineering in college. And then joined the Army where I spent five years defusing everything our enemies deployed. And another ten working for the Company."

"Still dismantling?" The question was casual, but his stillness signaled his interest in her answer.

"Let's just say I can handle both sides of the equation. Whatever's called for. My unit isn't the kind politicians trot out when they want to look PC. What about you?

Ordnance turn you on?" She hadn't meant to use those exact words, but the bourbon was doing its job.

"Not bloody likely."

The retort was unexpectedly sharp, and she frowned. "I'm sorry, did I say something wrong?"

"It's me that should apologize." He shook his head. "It's just that I've seen too damn many people hurt by little boys playing war. Anyway, once upon a time, the answer would have been 'yes.' I studied nuclear physics at university. Graduate work at Oxford. And then Number 10 Downing came calling. Patriotic duty and all that. I worked counterterrorism for longer than I should have."

"And now?" she asked, instinct telling her there was more to the story.

"Like I said, I'm a courier."

"Well, I suspect you're more than that. But since we've only just met, and since my follies are bound to have caused you one hell of a political headache, I won't probe. And besides, I came down here to try to forget about it all for a little while."

"Except that there really is no way out, is there?"

She stared over at him for a moment, trying to judge his tone. But there was no condemnation. Just a world-weariness that she was more than familiar with herself. "Not really. At least not without a lot of this." She raised the glass and took another long sip. "So where in England are you from?"

"The northern coast of Cornwall," he said, accepting her change of topic without comment. "Small village called St. Ives. My father was a fisherman."

"I thought that usually ran to families."

"It did—for something like five centuries. Until the

waters were fished out and there was no way to make a living. Anyway, it was never my cup of tea. I've always been more interested in the intricacies of fission than in trawling for fish. Although I suppose I did inherit a bit of the sailor's need for adventure."

"An adrenaline junkie."

Again his expression tightened. "Maybe once upon a time. Not so much now."

"And your father?" she asked, again moving purposely away from probing too deeply.

"Still in St. Ives. Although these days he spends more time in the pub than he does in a boat. He likes talking about the old days."

"Sounds like my dad. Only he's retired military. And not one to take to retirement easily."

"Rather be out there on the front line."

"Exactly. He's not the rocking chair type. With him action has always been more relevant than reflection." A trait they shared. That's exactly why she'd joined A-Tac. Maybe if she was a little less of an adrenaline junkie, she'd have made different choices. Maybe she'd never have been called on to guard the shipment.

But then she'd never have been in a hotel bar drinking with a real-life James Bond.

Hell, maybe there was a silver lining to this nightmare after all.

"So which state do you come from?" he asked.

"Technically, none of them. My dad was stationed in Germany when I was born. But I've lived in quite a few. We moved around a lot."

"Army brat."

"You're the second person to call me that today," she

said, sobering as Lieutenant Mather's words echoed in her ears. "Anyway, it's an apt description."

"Sounds like a colorful life." He lifted his glass to his lips, then swallowed, the muscles in his throat contracting with the motion, and she found herself wondering what his skin would feel like.

"I suppose, looking at it with hindsight, it was," she said. "Although at the time I hated it. Every time I'd get myself settled enough to have some sort of a life, my dad would come home from wherever and announce that we were moving again."

"Hometowns aren't all they're cracked up to be. I promise," he said, unaware of the shifting direction of her thoughts. "What about your mum? How's she handling the nonretirement?"

"She's dead." Tyler tried to keep her tone casual, to keep the memories from surfacing. She'd already been down that road, and once in twelve hours was more than enough.

"I'm sorry." The regret that flashed across his face was real.

"It's nothing really. She's been gone since I was a kid. My dad remarried, a couple of times actually. An active career in the military doesn't really promote happily ever after. Or maybe it was just my father. Anyway, suffice it to say I've had a parade of stepmothers. All of which went into making my life—what did you call it—colorful?"

"Well, I suppose we should drink to it." He lifted his glass. "I mean after all if your father had settled down, you might not have chosen the path you did. Which means that I'd be sitting here drinking on my own."

She smiled, thinking how much his words mirrored

her earlier thoughts. "Or you'd be back at that pub in St. Ives, lifting a pint and celebrating the successful delivery of the detonators."

"The obvious negatives aside, I think I much prefer being here with you."

His flattery was probably meant to disarm her. And the truth was—it did. She hadn't been with a man in longer than she cared to admit. It was just too damn complicated considering her occupation. And she'd never shared a drink with someone as alluring as Owen Wakefield. Maybe it was the accent. Or the cleft chin. Or the way his hair brushed back from his forehead.

Or maybe it was because he was part of her world— albeit halfway across the ocean. Hell, maybe *that* was the appeal. A chance for a brief encounter with no worries about future entanglements. MI-5 worked within the United Kingdom, for the most part. Chances of her ever crossing paths with him again were slim to none.

"How about another drink?" he asked, hand already half raised to signal the waitress.

"Maybe we should have it upstairs," she suggested, her gaze colliding with his, the suggestion surprising her almost as much as it did him. She finished her bourbon with a gulp, not sure where exactly she was headed, but certain, in the moment, that it was the right direction. "I've got glasses in my room."

CHAPTER 2

As the elevator doors slid shut, they moved together with a familiarity that belied the fact that they'd only just met. It was as if she'd made love to him before. As if she knew every inch of him by heart. His lips were hard, his kiss demanding, his hands moving over her body—teasing, exploring. His whiskers scraped against her cheek, the friction sending heat spiraling downward to pool between her legs.

A part of her wanted him to take her here and now, but she knew that neither of them wanted to explain to their respective bosses why they'd been caught in an elevator in flagrante delicto. So instead she pushed closer, relishing the feel of his body against hers, the motion of the elevator enhancing the friction.

She opened her mouth, welcoming him inside, reveling in the thrust of his tongue against hers. They parried and dueled, using touch as a silent language, neither advancing nor retreating but instead joining together in a tempestuous dance of emotion and sensation.

He tasted like bourbon and toothpaste, the discovery at once seductive and familiar. She twisted her fingers through his hair, the black strands wiry and strong. Like the man.

He cupped her breast, his thumb circling her nipple through the cotton of her camisole, and she swallowed a moan, the action only heightening her desire. His mouth moved to her cheek, then her ear. Waves of pure physical pleasure washed across her as his tongue found the soft whorl. This time she couldn't stop her cry, and he pulled back to look at her, his smile slow and sure.

She jerked away, embarrassed at her lack of restraint.

"Are you having second thoughts?"

"No." She shook her head, her breathing still ragged. "It's just that I'm usually not into public displays of affection."

"But we're alone," he said, a twitch of amusement touching the corner of his mouth.

"On an elevator," she whispered, sotto voce, glancing suspiciously around the paneled space. "What if there's a security camera?"

"There's not," he soothed. "I checked when we got on. Occupational hazard."

One she should have been thinking of instead of focusing solely on what it would feel like to have him moving inside her. She fought for breath, licking her lips, the skin sensitive from his kisses.

"I can go if you want." His dark eyes met hers, the passion there making her heart stutter.

"No." She shook her head, reaching for his hand as the elevator doors slid open. "I want you to stay." Hell, she wanted him to take her right here and right now, but considering there was an elderly couple waiting to get on, it didn't seem the most opportune of times.

They walked off the elevator, fingers entwined, their bodies touching as they walked down the hallway. As soon as the doors behind them dinged shut, Owen swung her around into his arms, her back against the wall, his mouth demanding as he swallowed her protestations with his kiss.

It was as if he were sealing a bargain she'd no idea they'd made, his mouth at once tender and possessive. A shiver of worry rippled through her, but was gone before she had time to think about it, replaced by the sensual pleasure of his touch. His heat invaded every part of her, a raging fire that she had no desire to extinguish.

She splayed her fingers across his chest, feeling his heart beating wildly against her fingers, her own beating in tandem. He pulled her closer, her hands trapped between their bodies, raw physical need overriding all other thought. She ground against him, rewarded by his muffled groan, and he cupped her buttocks, their bodies rubbing together in an age-old dance.

Tyler let conscious thought go, intent instead upon riding the wave, finding release from the glorious pain building inside her. Release that only he could give her. Then from far away she heard the elevator ding.

"Oh, God," she whispered, her voice thready with desire, as she pressed her face against his chest, "you're turning me into an exhibitionist. I thought the English were supposed to be repressed."

"I'm afraid you've been sadly misinformed," he answered, his breath hot against her cheek. "And unless you want me to take you right here in the hallway, I suggest we go to your room. Now."

She nodded, unable to pull together a string of words. She couldn't remember the last time she'd wanted someone this badly. It was as if she'd been waiting for him all her life. Which was a ridiculous notion, but one that nevertheless, in this moment, seemed oddly irrefutable.

With a last hot kiss, he swept her up into his arms and strode down the hallway, releasing her at her door, her body sliding against his as she dropped to her feet. "Where's the key?" he asked, his voice tight with need.

"Here," she said, pulling it from her pocket.

He grabbed it and slid it through the slot, the light turning blessedly green. In seconds they were inside, the door swinging shut as he pulled her back into his arms, everything that was hard and unyielding about him coming together in the moment, hot and demanding. And she opened her mouth to his, relishing the feel of his tongue as it tangled with hers, each of them taking and giving, their movements a prelude of things to come.

He pressed her back against the wall, and she wrapped her leg around his hips and twined her fingers through his hair. His hands found the smooth plane of her back beneath her camisole, massaging her skin, the friction from his calloused palms arousing her heightened senses even more. She pressed closer, feeling him hard against her, and knew he was aching for her as much as she longed for him hot and ready inside her.

"I want to see you," he whispered, his hands closing around the hem of her camisole.

She smiled and leaned back, lifting her arms, and in one fluid movement he stripped away the cotton chemise.

"Jesus Christ," he said, his eyes narrowing as he took in the dark purple bruises that spread across her chest.

Between her desire and the bourbon, she'd almost forgotten her injuries. "They're just bruises. From where the bullets hit the Kevlar. It could have been much worse."

"And the scar?" he asked, reaching out to gently trace the jagged line running between her breasts.

"That's what happens without the vest. I've been really lucky," she said, resisting the urge to cover herself with her arms. "Twice."

His hands moved to her shoulders as he moved closer. "I'm sorry."

"It's just part of the job." She'd tried for flippancy, but choked on the last bit instead.

"If it helps," he said, his voice still gentle, "I understand." He pulled off his jacket and shirt. His right shoulder was covered with scar tissue.

"A bomb?" she asked, recognizing the telltale signs.

"Wrong place. Wrong time." He nodded.

"So you were lucky, too," she whispered, splaying her fingers across the damaged skin.

"I'm not sure I can agree with that." He shook his head, his hand covering hers. "But I'm alive. And it's moments like this that make me glad of it."

She nodded, and they stood for a moment, eyes devouring each other. Then with a groan of impatience, she reached for him, hungry to feel his skin hot against hers.

Velvet and steel.

Following her lead, he pulled her close, his kiss devouring as he sucked her tongue and then bit her bottom lip, the gesture halfway between pleasure and pain,

the sensation traveling first to her belly and then trailing
fire to the wet place between her legs.

God, she wanted this man.

With a blatancy that surprised her, she pulled down
the zipper of his pants, her hand slipping between white
cotton and the hard, smooth skin of his abdomen, her
fingers closing around his penis, the heat seeping into her
as she moved her hand rhythmically up and down.

With another groan, he swung her up into his arms
again and moved to the bed, setting her amidst rumpled
sheets. She shimmied out of her jeans and then arched
her back, her hands on her breasts, their gazes colliding
in a heat that was palpable. She let her hands trail slowly
down her stomach to the apex of her thighs, teasingly
running a finger across the crotch of her cotton panties.

His eyes darkened, the deep blue turning black. She
shivered in anticipation, watching as he pulled down his
pants, his penis springing free, hard and solid, and one
hundred percent male. With a smile that would no doubt
melt icebergs, he straddled her, two fingers hooking into
the elastic at her waist.

He slid the panties off, and she opened for him, her
body humming with a life of its own. Dipping his head,
he found the tender crest of one breast, drawing the
nipple into his mouth, sucking it with a strength that sent
heat rippling from breast to groin. She tipped her head
back, her mind spinning away, anticipation building.

His hands moved lower, stroking her stomach and
then the soft flesh of her inner thighs, while he teased her
nipple with his teeth. Then in one swift move, his thumb
unerringly found the soft skin of her labia, and quickly
laid her defenses to waste, his fingers sliding deep inside

her, his tongue still stroking her breast. She swallowed, the delicious tension inside her ratcheting up to levels beyond anything she'd ever experienced.

His thumb flicked against her, and she threw back her head and moaned, the sound guttural, coming from deep inside her. Then his tongue replaced his thumb, the hot, moist pressure making her buck against him, then struggle to escape the finely drawn pain he was creating.

But his hands circled her hips, cupping her bottom, effectively holding her in place, his tongue moving faster and faster, heat streaking through her with each and every touch. She wanted more and yet she wasn't certain that she could stand the exquisite torture.

He sucked then, pulling her tight, and she climaxed, sensation sending her over the precipice, spiraling out of control, her contractions so powerful she fought to breathe. As her body spasmed, he moved to pull her close, the two of them lying together, body to body. And she reached up to press her lips against his, the kiss softer and deeper than before, but no less wanting. This time she explored the hot crevices of his mouth and the smooth surface of his teeth, feeling the heat rising inside her again.

With a slow smile, she pushed him back, rolling over so that she was on top of him. He reached for her breasts, the feel of his fingers against her skin like kindling on a fire. He rubbed her nipples until they were hard and throbbing. And she tightened her thighs, holding his penis tight between her legs, the tiniest wriggle sending pleasure rippling through her.

"Take me," he urged, his eyes hooded with passion, his voice so low it was almost a growl. "I want you. Now."

Her lips quirked, and she enjoyed the moment of

control, knowing full well that if he chose, he could change their positions in an instant. Still smiling, she lifted up, and with the help of his guiding hands, impaled herself upon him. He filled her completely, her slick passageway stretched tight.

She closed her eyes and slowly began to move. Up. Down. Up. Down. Caressing him, her internal muscles tightening and releasing as she moved, pleasure building with each slow thrust. In and out, deeper and harder. The tension inside her building as she concentrated on the rhythm, the only reality now the sensation between her thighs.

His hands tightened on her hips, and their eyes locked as they moved faster and faster, the connection beyond physical. Then there was nothing but the feel of him moving inside her and the pounding need for release.

She reached for it, twining her fingers with his, sensation blotting out every other thought, until the heat inside her exploded into tangible joy, shudders shaking her body as she banished all the darkness and let herself fly free.

Later—much later—she sat on the bed watching as Owen bent to peer into the minibar.

"It seems you've drunk all the bourbon," Owen said, still looking into the little refrigerator.

"There were only two," she protested. "And I needed them both. Medicinal purposes." It was hard to believe that the two of them were having such casual conversation, in the nude, no less. She was far from a prude, but she'd known the man less than twenty-four hours, and yet, somehow, it felt like the most natural thing in the world. "We could order something from downstairs."

Owen glanced over at the clock. "I think it's too late

for that. So, I guess we'll just have to make do." He turned around holding two bottles of Bailey's Irish Cream.

"Seems a bit, I don't know, *tame*—all things considered? I wouldn't have picked you for a liqueur kind of guy."

He grinned, walking over to drop down beside her on the bed. "Let's see, first you accuse me of being repressed."

"No, no..." she said, waving her hands. "I think you've successfully proved me wrong on that count. Which is all the more reason why I'm surprised at your choice of beverage."

"It's not my fault you polished off all the bourbon," he reminded her, twisting the lid off the first Bailey's bottle. "And besides, it's not what you drink, so much as how you drink it." He waggled his eyebrows suggestively, his heated gaze skimming over her naked body.

"Surely you're not," she protested, scooting back on the bed, "I mean..."

"Now who's repressed?" he asked, moving closer.

"I wasn't...I didn't..." Tyler's heart was beating so fast she thought it might jump right out of her chest. "I just..."

Owen covered her lips with a finger, then straddled her, tilting his head to one side. "I'm just looking for a little dessert. Surely you wouldn't deny a man something so sweet." He lifted the bottle and drizzled the liquid between her breasts. She shivered, more from anticipation than cold, as it ran across her skin, pooling in her belly button.

He lowered his head, his tongue caressing the scar between her breasts before tracing the sticky liquid's path downward, moving across her stomach to the soft indentation in her belly. Sucking lightly, he sipped the contents, then drove his tongue inside, the contact making her writhe against him, wanting more. Needing more.

He continued to probe, driving in and out and then letting his mouth trail lower, flicking against the soft skin between her legs.

"Wait," she whispered, struggling to maintain control. "You're not the only one who's hungry."

His smile was slow, his eyes echoing her desire as he rolled over, his penis springing turgid against his stomach. With shaking hands, she opened the second bottle and trailed the sweet chocolaty liqueur along the line of hair that grazed his abdomen.

After licking the sweet liquid off his stomach, she closed her mouth around his penis, the wet heat getting an instant response. Circling her hand just below her mouth, she gently squeezed and sucked, using her tongue to tease him as he grew harder.

She felt his fingers in her hair, as his groans of pleasure urged her on. She started to move faster, to take him deeper, but he pulled back. "I want to be inside you," he said, his voice hoarse with passion.

"Now?" She smiled up at him, licking the last of the Bailey's off her lips.

He nodded, still struggling for words. "If you do that one moment longer it will be too late."

"Well, we wouldn't want that," she said, containing a smile.

"No, we wouldn't." He stared at her a moment, and then with a growl of pure passion, flipped her over, his big body covering hers as he took control, sliding his fingers deep inside her, his thumb flicking against her clitoris. Desire surged and her laughter faded, her thoughts centering on the delicious sensation coursing through her.

She pushed upward, taking him deeper, and then bit

at his lips, forcing her tongue inside his mouth, finding the same rhythm as his fingers, her action reversing their roles yet again, the tortured becoming the temptress.

He moved his hand and lifted his body, sliding into her with one smooth motion. She arched her back, spreading to accept him, her mind screaming now for release. He drove deep, and she tightened around him in welcome.

Then he held so still, she could feel their hearts beating together as she reveled in the simple pleasure of connection, the binding of his body to hers. Then, as if unable to stand it any longer, he began to move, first withdrawing, and then driving deep and then deeper still.

She rose to meet him, thrust for thrust, their bodies moving in mirror image, up and down, thrusting, parrying. A dance that drove her to the brink. Her body tightened in anticipation, tension stretching as she strained against him, wanting to be closer and then again closer still.

Tyler arched against him one last time, thrusting upward, pulling him deeper. And then the world exploded into a symphony of sound and light, the release beyond pleasure, beyond pain. For one perfect moment, there was no future and no past. No expectations. No responsibilities. Just the two of them. Man and woman. Explosive and elemental.

It was a fantasy and she knew it. But that didn't change the power of the act, or the magic of the man.

Morning light streamed through the window and across the bed. Tyler buried her head underneath a pillow, craving more sleep. It had been a long night. The thought brought memory to the surface, and, blushing, she sat up, pushing the hair out of her eyes.

The room was empty. Which, although not unexpected, was surprisingly disappointing, the only signs that she hadn't spent the night alone the two empty bottles of Bailey's and the used condoms in the trash.

She smiled, remembering. And then frowned, wondering when she'd become so desperate. Picking up men in bars wasn't exactly her usual mode of operation. But then winding up on the losing end of an operation wasn't the norm either. So maybe the one thing had led to the other. And it wasn't as if she'd ever see the man again.

The thought wasn't as comforting as she'd have expected, and she swung out of bed, heading for the shower, her body stiff and sore in places she'd forgotten all about. Which brought on another smile. She'd say one thing for Owen Wakefield. He was a hell of a lover. In one night he'd single-handedly managed to debunk the idea of the stuffy Englishman.

James Bond would be proud.

Still laughing at her own ridiculous musings, Tyler stepped into the shower, letting the hot water pound away her aches and pains. The bruises had intensified overnight, the coloring more vivid than before. Her body's way of healing. She'd had worse. And survived. In the end she'd been lucky.

Or maybe Owen was right. Maybe there wasn't such a thing as luck. Maybe things happened the way they did for a reason. Either way, it was time to face reality. No more flights into fantasy, bourbon-induced or otherwise. She tipped her head back, letting the water wash away the last vestiges of her night with Owen.

It had been wonderful. But like all good things—it wasn't meant to last.

CHAPTER 3

Owen walked into the restaurant, automatically assessing the place for danger. He wasn't expecting anything out of the ordinary, but it was always best to stay on the alert. The place had been chosen for its obscurity—a hole in the wall Mexican joint on the outskirts of Colorado Springs. Logan Palmer sat in the back, the obligatory basket of tortilla chips and salsa sitting half eaten in front of him.

"You're late," he said, frowning as he looked up at Owen.

Palmer worked for the NSA, as part of a cloak-and-dagger division tasked with policing America's intelligence agencies—spying on the spies, as it were. In the old days, Owen would have considered a man like Palmer reprehensible. Beneath contempt. But at the moment, he merely represented a paycheck.

And a way to get through one more day.

"I've been waiting almost half an hour."

"Missed the turn." Owen shrugged as he slid into the booth. "Even after four years of living in your country, I still look for signage on the left. Anyway, I'm here."

"So what have you got." The older man sat back, waiting.

"Not much, I'm afraid." Owen reached for a chip, dipping it into the fiery salsa before popping it into his mouth. "At least beyond what's official. I did everything you asked. Went to the scene and to the base for her interrogation. I even followed her to her hotel. We shared a couple of drinks. But if there's anything beyond the official version, Tyler Hanson's not telling. She's a professional. She knows the drill."

Except that she'd risked opening herself up to him. Sharing her bed and a little piece of herself. If he'd been any other man he'd have felt guilty for what he'd done in taking advantage of her when she was hurting. But anything decent about him had died a long time ago in an explosion in Mayfair.

"So you're saying she's innocent?" Palmer asked.

It was tempting to concur. Maybe he owed her that much. But in truth, everyone had secrets, and if Tyler's had anything to do with the stolen detonators, he wasn't helping anyone by lying. "I can't say anything definitively. Like I said, she's not the type to give anything away. Still..." He paused, trying to order his thoughts.

"Go on," Palmer prompted, eyeing Owen over the rim of his iced-tea glass.

"It's not anything specific really," he said. "It's just that if I'd been in her situation, I'd never have left my team alone on the road. Not unless there was something really compelling to pull me away."

"The motorcycle?"

"Not enough. There was damage to the guard rail, and she mentioned something about thinking there might be a body down in the ravine. But the motorcycle was in the middle of the road. So the logic doesn't follow. Unless there was something else."

"Something she's choosing to keep secret," Palmer mused. "But considering the questions surrounding her survival in the wake of the deaths of the rest of the team, you'd think she'd be more willing to talk. So maybe her only reason for going down into the ravine was to get the hell out of the way. She was wearing a vest, right?"

"Yes. But she'd been injured in a previous operation." He'd seen the scars, but he wasn't about to share that information. "So it's possible she was just being cautious."

"Maybe. Or maybe she knew what was going to happen, and she wanted to make it look good. Get shot without risking any real damage."

"You've never said why you're gunning for Tyler Hanson," Owen said, reaching for his water glass. "I mean, you called me in before the transport left the base, which meant you suspected something might happen even then."

"We had intel. Nothing concrete, but it seemed to indicate there might be problems."

"With Tyler?"

"Not specifically, no. But when A-Tac was made a part of the transfer it raised a red flag."

"I'm not sure I'm following." Owen shook his head. "Why would their involvement sound an alarm? Aren't their missions sanctioned from the top? I'd assume they're above reproach."

"Not in this political climate. In fact, they're exactly the kind of unit the politicians are targeting. Especially after this latest round of revelations regarding CIA turncoats."

"You're talking about the guy from Colombia?" A former operative had been running arms operations out of South America, his inside knowledge allowing him to avoid detection. He was responsible for bringing down an entire black ops division, jeopardizing U.S. security in the process. The U.S. Congress had had a field day. "But he was stopped, and from what I've read his operations were dismantled."

"Unfortunately, there was more to it than that. He had help, and from what we've been able to gather he'd managed to infiltrate the organization at the highest levels."

"But I still don't see the tie-in to Tyler Hanson and the detonators."

"It was a team from A-Tac that managed to bring the traitor's actions to light. Tyler was part of that team. And we believe that the insider helping with the arms deals also originated with A-Tac."

Owen let out a low whistle. "So that's why we were called in. But couldn't the traitor have come from somewhere higher up in the chain of command?"

"It's possible. But the fiasco in Colombia wasn't the first time A-Tac's had problems. There's been a string of apparent sabotage. Communications problems, jammed guns, cut ropes."

"Care to elaborate?" Owen asked.

"Pretty straightforward stuff. On a mission in the Far East the communications system cut out. It was a new one and at first the failure was considered a fluke. But then on a second mission, this one stateside, a jammed gun almost cost them the mission. And then during an operation in Cyprus, a climbing rope broke during an ascent almost taking out four operatives."

"All conceivably accidents."

"Yes. Except on further examination, the gun proved to have been tampered with and the rope was severed. And explosives the team took into Colombia to eliminate an arms stash had also been tampered with. And no one had access to the equipment but members of the team and their ancillary staff."

"So it had to be an inside job."

"It would seem so." Palmer nodded. "Of course none of this would have come to our attention if not for the revelation that the man they were hunting in Colombia was in fact homegrown. But when you take it all in combination—especially adding in A-Tac's role in the detonators theft—the potential connection can't be ignored."

"And since Tyler was the only A-Tac member on site in Colorado—she's moved to the top of your list," Owen said, his mind churning as he considered the possibilities. "What about the other incidents? Was she present? I know from her dossier that she was medevaced out of Colombia early in the mission."

"Actually, it puts her in the perfect position to ferry information to the traitor," Palmer said, propping his elbows on the table and steepling his fingers. "For exactly the reasons you state. After surgery in Ecuador, she came back to the States, with full access to everything necessary to keep the information flowing. And when you add that to the fact that there's no real reason for her to have been part of the transport team, it starts to look pretty suspicious."

"What do you mean no reason?" Owen asked. "I thought she was an expert with ordnance."

"She is. But the detonators weren't exactly high-risk. Without a payload they're harmless. So why the need to bring in someone with her credentials?"

"Maybe there's something about the payload we don't know? I mean the CIA and Homeland Security aren't exactly known for playing nice together. Could be they're holding out on you."

"I'd agree except that this wasn't a CIA operation. It was military all the way. And to hear General Fisher tell it, they were as surprised as anyone to find out Hanson had been assigned to the transport. Orders appear to have come from the top at Langley, but things like that are easily doctored."

"So you're thinking that someone within A-Tac, possibly Tyler Hanson, fabricated the assignment?"

"I wouldn't go that far. At least not yet. But my bosses believe it's worth investigating. Especially when you factor in Ms. Hanson's miraculous survival. It just seems a little too convenient that she just happened to be wearing a vest, and then managed to be out of direct range when the attack occurred."

"You sound like General Fisher."

"I read his report. He seems even more convinced than I do that she's responsible for what happened."

"Well she appeared genuinely upset about losing Gerardi and Mather." That much he was certain of. Although it didn't clear Tyler. It simply made things more complicated.

"Doesn't mean anything except that she isn't a cold-hearted killer," Palmer said, his words echoing Owen's train of thought. "Or maybe she didn't expect them to be killed. At this point anything is possible. But I don't think we can ignore the possibility that she had something to do with what happened out there."

"Agreed. It's all circumstantial, but that doesn't make it any less damning. Anyway, I'm sorry I couldn't get you more." He probably could have, too, if he hadn't allowed himself to get distracted.

"Not to worry." Palmer shrugged, his tone a little too nonchalant. "You just need a little more time."

"Using what possible cover? It was one thing for me to go in for a day and pretend to be MI-5. It's quite another to pull it off for any extended amount of time."

"I have faith in you." Palmer's smile lacked any trace of humor. "Besides, I called in a favor and you're now officially back with her majesty's secret service."

"On what planet? There's no way they'd take me back. Not to mention that I'd never agree to it. Not willingly."

"Relax. It's all just semantics. If someone calls and inquires about your status, you'll appear to be on assignment here."

"But I'm not."

"Actually, you are. Or at least it's going to look that way. Seems that your superiors at MI-5 are as concerned about the disappearance of the detonators as we are. And as part of their attempt to get to the bottom of what's happened, they've assigned you to work with A-Tac to find answers."

"That must have been some kind of a favor," Owen said, frowning. "I find it hard to believe that the suits at Thames House are going along with this."

"As long as they believe their interests are being served," Palmer said, "they'll do as they're asked. Although

I'll admit we didn't tell them you were actually involved. More that we were just borrowing your name and background for the operation."

"All right, so you've wrangled MI-5. But what about A-Tac? More specifically Tyler Hanson."

The truth was that there was a hell of a lot about his reappearing that wasn't going to sit well with her. Chiefly the fact that she'd thought she was sleeping with a one-off, not someone she was going to have to work with on a daily basis. He'd couldn't even contemplate how she'd react if she knew he was secretly trying to prove that she'd committed treason.

"Trust me, Tyler won't be a problem. She obeys orders. And Avery Solomon is on board with the operation."

"He knows the truth?" It was Owen's turn to frown.

"No." Palmer shook his head. "He believes what he's been told."

"So why would he agree to letting an outsider work with his team? Did you pull strings with him as well?"

"Actually, no. Avery Solomon isn't the type to be coerced. He's cooperating because he believes, first off, that you are who you say you are. Which under the circumstances makes perfect sense."

"And secondarily?"

"He knows there's a problem with the unit. And he knows that it's going to take an outsider to help find that problem and eliminate it. He just doesn't know that you're working for me."

"And if he did?" Owen asked, feeling a lot like he'd just stepped from the frying pan into the fire.

"Then your life wouldn't be worth a damn."

*   *   *

Tyler walked through the airport garage fighting against irritation. Her flight had been delayed. Weather in Denver. And then when she'd arrived she'd discovered her luggage was lost. Not that there was anything she couldn't live without. It was just one more thing added to an already horrible couple of days.

Well, there'd been one highlight, but she wasn't going to think about that, at least not here in the middle of a concrete box while she was trying to remember where the fuck she'd parked her car. Pushing her backpack over her shoulder, she sighed and turned in a semicircle trying to find the Isuzu. In a sea of SUVs it wasn't exactly standing out.

She glanced up at the numbered bay and shook her head. C-35. She'd parked in D. Clearly she needed to concentrate. Mumbling under her breath, she adjusted the backpack slung over her shoulder and moved onto the ramp leading to the next level.

It wasn't as if she didn't have things on her mind. Hell, what she needed was a good long rest, preferably with a nice bottle of bourbon. Although last night's adventures had begun much the same way. Maybe she'd skip the booze and go for Ben and Jerry's. Fudge Brownie. Annie swore by the stuff.

Tyler smiled, thinking of her friend. Annie, of all people, would understand if Tyler wanted some down time. In fact, no one would blame her for calling it a day. All she had to do was head home and lie low for a couple of days. Give herself time to process on her own. Of course that'd mean ducking Nash and Avery's calls, which wouldn't be easy to do considering that they were both neighbors.

And besides, it wasn't as if she actually had anything to hide. It was just that she hated screwing up. Her father had always been quick to remind her that "there was no fiercer hell than failure." She hadn't discovered the original author until college. Keats. *There is not a fiercer hell than the failure in a great object.*

Keats's words might be more eloquent, but the sentiment was the same. Failure wasn't an option. But here she was, returning from a fiasco of an operation, and the blame lay squarely on her shoulders. She'd failed, and two men were dead, their family's lives changed forever. There was nothing she could do to bring them back, but she could sure as hell man up and make sure that the bastards who'd killed them paid.

And the best way to do that was to tell Avery everything. All of it. And then get back to work. The detonators were out there somewhere, and she had to find them and bring the perpetrators to justice. It was the only way Gerardi and Mather were going to rest in peace. Or maybe it was just the only way she'd be able to let it go.

Either way this wasn't the time to run for cover.

She sighed, rounding the corner just as a car whipped around the curve, brakes squealing as it swerved to avoid her. Flattening herself against the wall, she reached for her gun, cursing when she realized it had been packed inside her now-lost luggage. The car wheeled around the corner, but not before the driver flipped her off and Tyler bit off another oath.

There was no reason to think anyone was following her. And even if they had been, she'd taken precautions—scheduling her flight at the last minute and flying under an assumed name. Still, she was edgy and grateful suddenly that she didn't have the gun. In all honesty, her instinct had been to fire first and ask questions later. But last she checked, shooting the bird wasn't exactly a reason to blow someone away.

She fought against a bubble of laughter, surprised to find herself capable of emotion, although considering the night she'd spent with Owen, she wasn't sure why she had any doubts. The man had definitely called forth her baser reactions. Most of them pretty damn satisfying.

She shook her head, clearing her mind of her cascading thoughts, and focused on the garage, scanning for the silver Isuzu. It was in the far corner exactly where she'd left it. And with a sigh of both relief and exasperation she started across the driving lane heading for the SUV.

From behind her something rattled and she spun around, searching for the source of the disturbance. Nothing else moved, the only sound the low humming of the fluorescent lighting. Shadows extended from the back wall across the row of cars. She waited a beat and then, satisfied that she was alone, pressed the unlock button and headed for the car.

In front of her, the pavement exploded as a bullet bit into the garage floor. Diving for cover, Tyler moved between two cars, trying to locate the shooter. Another round cut into the bumper in front of her, and she rolled underneath the car, holding position.

A third bullet slammed into the cement about six inches in front of her, and she scrambled back, slipping out into the space between her car and the one next to it. Yanking open the door, she slid inside, reaching across the seats for the glove compartment and the gun she had stashed there.

The gunman fired again, this time shattering the rear window. Tyler's fingers closed on the butt of the Sig-Sauer and she jerked upward, turning to shoot, her finger tightening on the trigger—only nothing happened. The chamber was empty. There were no bullets. Frowning, she looked for the extra ammo she kept stashed under the dashboard, but the pack had disappeared.

Cursing, she ducked back out of range, just as the shooter fired again—this time taking out one of the rear tires. Heart pounding, she shoved the key into the ignition, the gunman, reflected in the rearview mirror, closing the distance between them now. She turned the key and the engine sputtered, then refused to start, the grinding sound of the starter underscoring the hopelessness of her position.

Scrunching down in the car, she moved across the floorboard, intent on escaping from the far side of the car. But as her fingers closed around the door handle, the shooter appeared in the space of the still-open door, gun leveled, his dark eyes ambivalent.

She sucked in a breath, reflexively covering her face with her hands, and the gun exploded, the sound of the report echoing through the garage. In front of her the gunman frowned, and then slumped to the floor, his silenced gun clattering against the pavement.

"Tyler?" Nash's voice rang out from across the lot. "You okay?"

She popped up, gasping for air, her mind still trying to make sense of the latest developments. "I'm here," she called, relief making her voice sound husky. "I'm fine." She slid out of the car and kicked away the gunman's weapon, then bent to check his pulse. "He's dead."

Nash moved out from behind a car in the row across from hers, followed by Emmett Walsh, the team's communications expert. "You're sure you're okay?" Emmett asked, his dark eyes concerned. "You weren't shooting back."

"Someone took the bullets from the gun in my car," she said, nodding at the Isuzu and the abandoned Sig on the seat. "And the airline lost my luggage."

"Sound like you're having another bad day." Nash grinned as he reached her side, holstering his gun.

"An understatement. But I'm still alive. That's got to count for something, right? How'd you guys find me?"

"GPS," Emmett said, bending down to search the dead man for ID. "We just followed the signal to your car. Nash had a feeling something might happen. So we figured it was best not to take a chance."

"Well, thank God for your instincts." She smiled at them both. "I was running out of options fast. If you hadn't gotten here when you did..."

"You'd have figured something out," Nash finished for her. "The guy have any ID?"

"Nothing." Emmett shook his head, turning the body over.

Tyler let out a gasp. "Oh, my God, it's Alexander Petrov. I didn't recognize him at first. The hair's different. But it's him, isn't it? One of the guys who was tracking Drake in Colombia?"

Nash bent down for a closer look. "I think you're right. We'll need to get a forensics team out here to verify it, but I'm pretty damn certain that's Petrov."

"I'll call Avery and get things started," Emmet said, moving away as he spoke into his cell phone.

"So what does this mean?" Tyler asked, frowning down at the body. "I wouldn't have expected Petrov to still be after us. Especially not me. I mean, how the hell would he have known I was in Colombia?"

"Same way he knew where to find Drake," Nash said. "Someone's been feeding him information."

"Information that almost cost me my life." Tyler sighed. "So you think he had something to do with the detonators being stolen?"

"I think it's impossible to know for certain. But the facts seem to point in that direction. Although I doubt he was in on the actual theft. Petrov's more of a clean-up man. Someone you call in to get rid of loose ends."

Tyler repressed a shiver, lifting her gaze to meet Nash's. "And by 'loose ends,' I'm guessing you mean me."

Tyler stood in the college courtyard, her mind still in turmoil. Nash and Emmett had driven her home, then obligingly left her to her own devices when she'd re-quested some solitude. For the past thirty minutes or so, she'd been wandering around campus, trying to order her thoughts as she ignored texts from Avery. As much as she wanted to avoid a debrief, she knew she couldn't put it off forever. Better to just get it done.

Squaring her shoulders she headed up the steps leading to the Aaron Thomas Academic Center, the heart of A-Tac's operations. A part of Sunderland College, the Center had been created fifteen years ago by the CIA in response to the increased threat of terrorism. The nationally renowned think tank was home to a dozen or so of the best minds in the country, Ph.D.s who also handled some of the nation's most dangerous counterintelligence operations.

There were eight permanent members of the American Tactical Intelligence Command (A-Tac), all tenured professors with expertise in both academia and espionage. And from time to time, as missions demanded, they were joined by other experts in their fields, the think tank acting as cover for their association and affiliated operations. The Center literally covered the intelligence complex underneath, students attending classes without any knowledge of the A-Tac headquarters beneath their feet.

A passing student waved, and Tyler pulled herself from her thoughts, returning the gesture. She loved her teaching job almost as much as she loved ordnance. Books had always called to her, and as a child she'd often escaped the reality of her messed-up world for various writers' imaginary ones. Her father hadn't given any credence to the habit, going so far as to call it a waste of time. And when she'd chosen English as a major, he'd almost blown a gasket.

But she'd minored in physics. And then, driven by some part of herself that she hadn't even known existed, she'd joined the Army, again to her father's dismay. But it was only with A-Tac that she'd gotten the chance to combine her talents. Literature and explosives. An unusual skill set to be certain. But for the most part she'd been happy here.

The trees above her shivered in the wind, almost as if they were reacting to her racing thoughts, copper-colored leaves whirling as they drifted to the ground. The campus was bustling, students hurrying to class, coats buttoned tight against upstate New York's October chill. The afternoon was fading, lights flickering to life as twilight moved toward darkness.

"Tyler," a breathless voice called as Adam Brennon hurled himself into her arms. "You're back." Adam was

Annie and Nash's son, a whirlwind of energy who loved life with the abandon only a child can achieve. "Mom said you were coming home today."

She hugged him tight, holding him close, breathing in the scent of little boy. "Good to see you, champ." He wriggled free, just as Annie caught up to them.

"Hey, glad to have you back," Annie said, her brow furrowing with worry. "You okay?"

"I'm fine now." Tyler grinned down at Adam. "So what level of Dragonflight are you up to?" Adam was a Nintendo enthusiast—more specifically a Wii game involving dragons.

"Level eighteen," he sighed. "I can't get past the wizard's guards."

"We came out here for a bit of a break," Annie said, ruffling her son's hair. "Sometimes it's nice to remember there's a real world out here."

"Ah, Mom." Adam frowned. "There's nothing wrong with video games. They improve my hand-eye coordination."

"I suspect you've already got that covered," Tyler said. "After all, you do put in a lot of hours."

"Only 'cuz I want to win. And I've been doing other things, too. Like playing ball."

"So how's the soccer team?" Tyler asked. "You still playing goalie?"

"Yeah. I'm getting pretty good."

"But they're not going to let you start in the game if you're late for practice. So we need to get going." Annie shot Tyler an apologetic look. "We'll talk later?"

"Count on it. And when you've got some time, I need some help with level fourteen," Tyler said, smiling down at Adam.

"Not a problem. The key is using the sword of Shim-rah. You should have picked that up in level four. I'll show you what to do."

"Sounds like a plan." Tyler nodded. "Have fun at practice." She watched as mother and son headed out into the fall afternoon, the picture of normalcy. The thought lifted Tyler's spirits and she pushed through the doors of the Center.

"Hey there," Nash said as he joined her in front of a bank of elevators. "Wondered when you were going to show up."

"I figured it was time. Avery's texts were growing more insistent."

"I'll admit he can be a bit on the persistent side. But only because he's worried about you. It's been a rough couple of days." He shrugged, inserting a key into a slot next to an elevator marked "professors only." "Was that Adam I saw outside?"

"Yeah, he and Annie were on their way to soccer practice."

"He's really good at it," Nash beamed. "But I guess I'm a little biased."

"Just a little." Tyler smiled. "But I can see why."

"So how are you feeling?" Nash asked, pulling the conversation back to the situation at hand. "Physically, I mean?"

"Sore. But okay. Doc said I had a couple of bruised ribs. My chest has gone Technicolor. But it could have been a hell of a lot worse if you hadn't found me when you did. So'd we get verification on Petrov?"

"Yeah, they lifted prints and Hannah verified that they belonged to Petrov. We're still waiting for DNA, but it's just a formality. She's working now to try to figure out who he was working for. But so far there's nothing concrete. Not that I expect her to find anything. Petrov isn't the kiss-and-tell type."

"Too bad we didn't get him alive." Tyler walked into the elevator and as the doors slid shut she moved the little Otis Elevator plaque and inserted another key. The elevator lurched and then headed downward. "Maybe he'd have been able to give us something more."

"There wasn't a choice. If we hadn't taken him out, he'd have killed you."

"I know. And I'm grateful, believe me. I just wish we had a better handle on how all of this fits together."

"I hear you," Nash said. "Avery's been on the phone with the brass for most of the day."

"I'm guessing they're not happy campers."

"They're never happy." Nash grinned. "So there's nothing new in that. And the good news is that I think Avery's convinced them to let A-Tac officially be in charge of the effort to get the detonators back."

"I'm surprised. After my debrief with General Fisher, I figured they'd balk at letting me stay involved."

"I think that's where the raised voices came in." They stepped off the elevator into the austerely appointed reception area.

The room served more as a buffer than as a real welcoming area. From time to time students tried to gain access to the elevator. Usually they wound up in an upper-floor lounge, but just in case there was ever a breach to this level, the reception area was designed as a decoy and, without proper identification, the precursor to a not-so-pleasant meeting with Avery—who also happened to be the dean of the college—and a one-way ticket out of Sunderland altogether.

"Well, I'm glad Avery triumphed," Tyler said, slapping her hand against a bust of Aaron Thomas, the cool marble concealing a biotechnical scanner. "I would have worked to find out what happened whether we were officially sanctioned or not, but it'll be a lot easier with Langley behind us."

A panel in the rear wall of the reception area slid open, and the two of them continued into the hallway on the other side, the panel closing behind them with a whoosh.

"Avery's waiting for us in the war room." Nash cupped her elbow as they made their way down the hall.

"You didn't run into me by accident, did you?" she queried, frowning up at him as they walked. "Avery sent you to find me."

"He was worried," Nash said. "Hell, so was I."

She sighed, at once grateful and annoyed. "No need, but I appreciate the sentiment. The important thing now is to get this show on the road. I need to find the bastards who did this."

"Totally understandable," Nash said, "but before we dig in, you should probably know that there were a couple of conditions to our being allowed to take over the investigation."

"Such as?"

"I'll let Avery tell you," Nash said, waving her through the door of the war room.

The big man was sitting at the conference table in front of a computer console. He rose to his feet when he saw her, his dark eyes concerned. "Glad you could join us. I was starting to wonder if maybe you've jumped ship."

"Hardly. Just needed a little time to get my bearings.

Almost getting killed two days in a row can be a bit disorienting. Anyway, there was no need to send a search party," she said, her fondness for the man mixing with annoyance. "I was on my way."

"Well, I worry."

"That's what Nash said." She smiled, unable to hang on to her irritation. It was good to be back among friends. "He also said that we've been given the green light to find the people who stole the detonators."

"I figured you'd be pleased."

"But there are conditions?"

"Actually, only one, and it was more of a request," Avery said, tilting his head toward Hannah huddled with someone at her computer station in the far corner of the room. "One that we were more than happy to accept under the circumstances."

Hannah turned first, her spiky hair highlighted with magenta today, the color a contrast to the turquoise frames of her glasses. "Glad to see you're all in one piece," she said with a smile. "Hate to think I'd have to deal with these guys on my own."

"I wouldn't do that to you," Tyler answered, her attention still on the man standing next to Hannah. He'd had his back turned as he bent to study the computer screen, but now he was facing her, his lips quirking with an irreverent smile as his dark blue eyes met hers.

"I believe the two of you have already met," Avery said, as Tyler continued to stare. "MI-5 has been kind enough to loan us Owen for the duration. I know you'll join me in welcoming him to the team."

Actually, she thought, swallowing a bubble of hysteria, she'd already done that, in spades.

CHAPTER 4

But I don't understand why we need outside help on this," Tyler said, working to pull her rioting thoughts in order.

"Well, to begin with," Owen said, looking absurdly calm, all things considered, "the detonators that were stolen belonged to Great Britain. Not to mention the fact that we helped fund the development of the devices. So I think it's completely understandable that we'd want a part in any effort to recover the stolen technology and unearth the culprits."

They'd all five moved to sit at the conference table, Avery at the head, with Nash and Hannah flanking him on either side. Tyler sat next to Nash with Owen directly across from her, next to Hannah.

"But, surely there's no need to be *here*," she protested, unable to stop the objection. "Can't you just work from London?" She knew she was being irrational, bordering on rude, but she couldn't keep the words from coming out. She'd allowed herself a moment of weakness and now here it was staring her in the face. So much for love 'em and leave 'em.

"Tyler, I realize you're a bit overwrought," Avery began, his voice gentle, his eyes concerned, "but—"

"I know," she held up her hand, cutting him off. "I'm sorry. It's been a long couple of days. I didn't mean that the way it sounded. I was just surprised. I didn't think I'd be seeing Owen again." Now there was an understatement. "I'm delighted that you'll be part of the team." She pasted on a smile, praying that she'd pulled it off.

"Great," Avery said, thankfully unaware of the undercurrents.

Nash, on the other hand, had the look of a man in the know. Or at least with a damn good guess. After shooting him her most indignant glare, she turned back to Avery. "So where are we? Nash said there weren't any new leads beyond identifying Petrov?"

"Petrov is the man who tried to kill you?" Owen asked, his expression hardening.

"Yes," Nash affirmed. "We've run into him before. In Colombia."

"He was part of the team hunting Drake Flynn, right?" Owen asked.

"How did you know that?" Tyler frowned. "It's not like it was common knowledge."

"I've been briefed on the unit's recent activities. And Petrov is on British watch lists, so I'm familiar with his work. Is Flynn going to be a part of this operation?"

"No." Avery shook his head. "He's on leave. In California. No need to drag him back for this. With you on board we've got more than enough help."

"Makes sense." Owen nodded. "So do we have any idea who Petrov was working for?"

"If only it were that easy," Hannah sighed. "I'm digging now. But so far he has managed to stay off the grid. So there's nothing linking him to anyone in particular."

"Part and parcel of the job," Nash said. "Hard to be an effective hit man if you can be traced back to your kills or your bosses."

"Yeah, well, at least now, thanks to you and Emmett, he's out of the game for good."

"But that doesn't mean they won't send someone else to finish the job," Hannah said, her eyes worried.

"True." Tyler nodded. "I'd be a fool not to consider the possibility. But if they do try it again, I'll be ready. It's not the first time someone has come after me. And I'm sure as hell not going to let them frighten me into hiding. I need to find out who did this. Which means I have to stay focused." She waited a beat, her gaze encompassing them all, and then continued. "So where do we stand?"

"General Fisher's forensics team is going over the site with a fine-tooth comb, and Hannah has been working overtime trying to sift through the chatter," Avery said. "So far, the only thing we know for sure is that no one is talking."

"Which could actually tell us something," Tyler said, leaning back in her chair as she considered the possibilities. "If no one is claiming responsibility, then surely that tells us about the people involved."

"Primarily that they're not interested in publicity," Nash agreed.

"Which rules out most of the major terrorist networks," Owen said. "Without visibility they've accomplished nothing."

"I'm not sure that that's completely true," Hannah said, opening the computer console in front of her. "The way I see it, there are four possible reasons someone would steal the detonators. The first, would be to embarrass the principals involved—in this case both of our governments. The project's political dynamite. And in the right hands…"

"It could be calamitous," Owen agreed.

"But we've already established there's been no claim of responsibility and no public demands," Tyler said. "Which would seem to rule out embarrassment."

"I agree." Hannah nodded. "Which brings us to the second reason. And probably the most obvious."

"Money," Nash said.

"Exactly. The detonators are prototypes. Which means they're worth a great deal of money on the black market. I'd think there'd be interest from all kinds of parties."

"For all kinds of reasons," Tyler sighed. "All of them potentially dangerous."

"So we're probably looking at someone trying to sell the technology." Nash said, steepling his fingers as he surreptitiously watched Owen across the table.

"I'd say it's a high probability," Hannah said.

"But you said there were four reasons to steal the detonators." Owen frowned. "What about the other two?"

"Because the technology is new," Hannah said, "there's always the chance that someone simply wants to steal the technology outright."

"A competitor or another country." Avery nodded. "Seems plausible. But if that's the case, then it'll be more difficult to pick up the trail. Following that train of thought, it's also possible that someone is trying to keep us from transferring the technology to the Brits."

"That doesn't really seem likely." Owen shook his head. "I mean, we still have the plans. So nothing's been accomplished, really, except maybe slowing the project."

"I agree," Hannah said. "I'm just trying to present all the options. It's actually the last one that worries me most."

"You mean that stealing the detonators is part of a larger scheme to build a bomb." Nash's words hung in the air for a moment.

"That wouldn't be all that easy." Tyler frowned. "I mean, the detonators are extremely sophisticated. And as Hannah said, they're prototypes. It's not like they come with instructions."

"Yes, but with the right training it would be possible to work out how to use them," Owen countered.

"Okay, say that somehow they do figure it out. There's still the problem of building the nuclear device to go along with it—suitcase bombs unlike anything the world has ever seen."

"I thought suitcase nukes were an urban myth perpetuated by the Cold War," Hannah said.

"Would that they were," Owen sighed. "But believe me, they were very real. Just not particularly practical. And by modern standards outdated. But with the advances in nanotechnology the possibilities are endless, the most likely scenario a super nuke small enough to fit in a backpack."

"But it's all theoretical," Tyler said. "The ban on nuclear proliferation extends to research as well."

"So why work on the detonators at all?" Nash asked.

"They have other applications," Owen responded. "Most of them industrial. For instance, they can be used underwater for precision blasting, allowing for more environmental protection in efforts to secure deep-water oil and natural gas."

"Anyway, the point here is that if the people who took the detonators did so with the idea of building some kind of miniature nuke," Tyler said, "they're going to find that it's not so easy to get their hands on the technology necessary to do that."

"Forty-eight hours ago I'd have said the same thing about the detonators." Owen shrugged.

"He has a point," Nash said, shooting Tyler an apologetic look. "And while I think it's more likely that the detonators are heading for the black market, I don't think we can ignore the possibility that the theft was just one step in a much larger operation."

"Okay, so ranking motivations in order based on what we know, we'd start with money." Hannah typed the word and it appeared on the large monitor behind Avery's head. "And then what?"

"I'd say stealing the technology." Owen studied the list as Hannah typed. "And then building a bomb."

"Discounting embarrassment, for the moment," Tyler agreed, "since we haven't heard anything. If someone is going to claim responsibility they usually do it within the first couple of days, right?" She looked over to Hannah for confirmation.

"Yeah." Hannah nodded. "Usually the first twenty-four hours."

"Okay, so we've got a list," Avery said, turning so that he could see the monitor. "Looking at each possible motivation, what kind of people are we looking for?"

"Well, with the first one," Owen frowned, "I'd think we'd principally be looking at arms dealers or cartels.

They're the only ones with the proper contacts for selling the goods."

"True," Tyler said, trying to work through her thoughts, "but it's easy enough to get someone like that to serve as middleman. Which leaves us open to any number of possibilities, from a terrorist or insurgency group trying to raise funds to an individual looking for a financial windfall. At the end of the day, everybody needs money."

"But not everyone would sell state secrets to get it." Nash shook his head. "And I think the key here—in any of the four scenarios—is that it's probably a combination of people working together. There's no way that this could have been pulled off without some kind of inside help."

"That's a given," Hannah said. "First off the detonator project was top secret. More specifically, only a handful of people knew exactly when and where the transport was to occur. So in order to pull off the heist, there would have had to be a security leak of some kind."

"So is it possible then," Owen asked, his attention centered on Tyler, "that the leak came from somewhere inside your organization? You've already admitted that there have been problems within the unit. And it's common knowledge within Intelligence that there were problems with the mission in Colombia. Someone helping the arms dealer."

"I don't think we can discount the possibility," Avery said. "But the present situation wasn't initiated by the Colombian cartel. For all practical purposes, Jorge di Silva's organization has been rendered impotent. They're no longer capable of mounting this kind of operation."

"But there are commonalities," Owen argued. "Insider knowledge and the involvement of Alexander

Petrov. Surely you're not saying that all of that is a coincidence?"

"I'm saying that the pieces of the puzzle don't fit," Avery clarified, his tone brooking no argument. "Which most likely means we're missing part of the picture. And I'm not going to make any assumptions until I'm in full possession of all the facts."

"Starting with why A-Tac was called into the mission in the first place?" Owen queried. "It's my understanding that the order didn't originate with General Fisher."

"Or maybe he's the one trying to cover his ass." Nash frowned.

"As I said before," Avery shrugged, "we have to consider all of the angles. Including the origin of the initial order for A-Tac's involvement. So far it seems to have come down through proper channels with valid authorizations. The only missing piece is the author of the original request. We're working now to trace it back to its source, and we should have something definitive soon. In the meantime, we need to start looking at everyone who had knowledge about when the shipment was leaving and where it was headed."

"Which includes both of you," Hannah said, looking first to Owen and then to Tyler, her smile negating any accusation. "Did either of you tell anyone else about the details of the transport?"

"No one." Tyler shook her head. "Except for Avery. He passed the info on to me."

"And although the entire team was briefed on the mission, I didn't share anything beyond generalities. The details, like time and location, were strictly need-to-know."

"Were there any records, Avery?" Tyler asked. "Anything someone here could have stumbled across?"

"No." Avery frowned. "Nothing in writing. Just a couple of conversations we had and a couple of phone calls from Langley. No physical trail. What about you, Owen?"

"Just my bosses in London."

Tyler wasn't certain, but he seemed to hesitate, as if there were something more. "Are you sure you didn't tell anyone?"

"Positive. There simply wasn't time. I wasn't brought up to speed until I arrived at the base about half an hour after you'd already left."

"Seems to put him in the clear," Hannah said, typing something into her computer. "Who else knew?"

"At higher levels I've no idea," Tyler said. "Except for General Fisher. And of course Gerardi and Mather."

"Well, I hate to speak ill of the dead," Nash grimaced, "but we probably should check into their backgrounds. Make sure everything was on the up and up. Fisher, too."

"Mather's wife was pregnant," Tyler said to no one in particular, the words making her stomach tighten with regret. "And Gerardi was just a kid. God, I feel so helpless."

"When I talked to you on the phone, you indicated that there was something more to tell us. Something that needed to be said in person."

"I know, but that was just me freaking out." No way was she going to trot out her theories about the scarf and her mother in front of a stranger. An intimate stranger, to be sure, but a stranger nonetheless. And besides, it was probably just her overworked imagination. It would keep until she and Avery had a moment alone. "I'd just been through the debrief with Fisher. And he'd insinuated that

I had some part in all of this. And I was feeling guilty about Mather and Gerardi's deaths. You said it yourself—I was overwrought. I didn't mean to make it sound like there was some big secret."

"So what did you mean?" Owen asked, his curiosity clearly roused.

"Just that the whole thing felt off. My involvement. The motorcycle. The serendipity that kept me alive—which seems even more amazing in light of what happened in the parking garage. Anyway, the truth is that I just didn't want to talk about all of it on the phone."

"Understandable," Avery said. "I'd have done the same in your position. I just wish there were something more. Something that would crack this thing wide open."

"I know," Tyler sighed. "And I'm sorry."

"Nothing to be sorry for," Avery's tone was brusque as he pushed her words aside. "What we need to do now is start at the beginning and dig until something shakes loose. Tyler, you and Owen will be in charge of the investigation. Pull whatever resources you need. Hannah will continue to provide support services."

"Actually," Owen said, his expression somewhere between a demand and an apology, "I'm bringing in someone of my own. A computer specialist. I think his skills will complement Hannah's."

"Why do you need to bring in someone else?" Tyler asked. "Don't you trust us?" There was a gauntlet in there somewhere, but she wasn't ready to examine it.

"Quite frankly, I don't know any of you. And I'm charged with making sure my country's best interests are served. I'd just feel better with someone I know on the team."

"So you're bringing in another Brit?" Hannah asked, her gaze appreciative as she looked over at Owen.

"I'm afraid not." He smiled, clearly following her train of thought. "He's an American. Harrison Blake. Former FBI. He's been working with a friend of mine on a specialized task force. Best of the best. Clandestine stuff. He'll fit right in. So I trust there won't be a problem?"

"Not as long as he respects the chain of command," Avery said.

"Absolutely."

"When do you expect him?" Hannah asked.

"Tomorrow sometime. I'm sure the two of you will get on famously. He's got quite a reputation for finding information where there seemingly is none. And he's great with computers."

"Sounds like a match made in heaven," Nash teased. "Not that you need any help, Hannah."

"It could be interesting," she said, still smiling. "Just don't tell Jason."

"Jason?" Owen repeated.

"He's our computer guru," Nash explained. "Although Hannah gives him a run for his money. Anyway, he's a little bit possessive when it comes to his domain."

"You think?" Hannah laughed. "Seriously, Owen, he'll be fine. And when the time comes, hopefully we'll be able to pull him into the project. With something this difficult the more hands on deck, the better."

"This has nothing to do with expertise, though, does it?" Tyler asked, the truth smacking her upside the head. "You're doing this because of the problems A-Tac's been having. You honestly believe one of us had a hand in all of this."

"I think it's better to be safe than sorry," Owen offered.

"That's a cop-out and you know it. You've already implied you think it could be me. Is that why you've been sent here?" Suspicion boiled hot and ugly.

"Tyler, I was sent here by my government to help find the detonators and bring the people that stole them to justice. I've been charged with doing whatever I think is best, and that includes providing any personnel that I think might be able to help us with the task at hand."

"Look, Owen's right," Nash said. "We need the best team possible. And whether we like it or not, there is a very real possibility that someone within A-Tac has been sabotaging our operations. I don't want to believe that the inside information about the transport came from our unit. But, until we can prove otherwise, I think Owen is well within his rights to want someone from the outside involved."

"Not to say that we're not going to be equally cautious," Avery added. "Hannah's running a check on both you and your associate—although I've every confidence that our findings will mirror what we already know. So to that end, I've arranged for you to officially be here as a visiting professor. We'll capitalize on your background in physics."

"My specialization was in nuclear physics. Although I did quite a bit of research in quantum physics as well."

"You lost me with the word physics," Nash said, with a grin, clearly already accepting Owen as a member of the team.

"Most people, I'm afraid." It was Owen's turn to smile.

"Well, we have graduate students who'd be delighted

to hear from a former Oxford fellow," Avery said. "So I've arranged a couple of lectures. It'll give you cover for being here."

"And Tyler's got a guesthouse," Nash said, still grinning. "Nobody ever uses it."

Owen's gaze shifted to Tyler, his expression questioning. "That'd be great, actually. Using a hotel would be somewhat of a security risk."

"I, um…" Tyler shot Nash a quelling look. "I don't think—"

"It's an excellent idea," Avery said, his tone brooking no argument. "Since the two of you will be working closely together it makes perfect sense."

"And there'll be room for Harrison," Nash added, his expression contrite now.

"Sounds like a plan, then. I'll just go to my hotel and collect my things." Owen pushed out of his chair, carefully avoiding her gaze.

"Why don't I come with you." Nash rose, too. "I can show you the way back to Tyler's. She lives next door to us." There was a warning in his words, and Tyler felt her frustration lessen. Nice to know he still had her back.

"Fine then. I guess it's all set," she said, wondering how she'd gotten herself into such a mess.

Somehow she'd gone from a one-night stand to Owen practically moving in. And to add insult to injury, he hadn't acted as if there were anything between them at all. A part of her was relieved, of course. She didn't want anyone at A-Tac to know just how careless she'd been. But another part of her, the feminine side, was pissed that their night together had clearly meant so little.

Then again, wasn't that exactly what she'd wanted?

CHAPTER 5

"So what have you got for me?" Logan Palmer asked, his voice reverberating a little with the connection.

"It hasn't even been twelve hours. They accepted my involvement without question, so I'm in. For now. But they are going to check on my credentials. So you'd better be certain your friend will hold up his end of the bargain."

"I told you, he was only too happy to acquiesce. What about Tyler Hanson? How'd she take your sudden arrival?"

Actually she'd done pretty well considering the situation, but he wasn't about to share that with his boss. "She was fine."

"I assume there's still nothing concrete to implicate her?"

"I'm working on it. In fact, I'm going to be staying in her guesthouse. Which ought to make nosing around that much easier. But I'm still not convinced she's the one we're looking for. Shortly after she arrived back in New York, someone tried to kill her. Man named Alexander Petrov. You've heard of him?"

"Yes. Gun for hire. Can't say that he'll be missed."

"So you know that he's dead."

"Word travels quickly in this business. You know that. Anyway, I don't think that we can use the attack as a reason to clear Tyler. It could have been a set-up. She didn't know that her associates would ride to the rescue."

"I don't know. I find it hard to believe that she wasn't telling the truth. To hear them talk about it, she damn near died."

"So maybe the attack wasn't tied to the detonators being stolen."

"We talked about that—and I think it's too big a stretch to believe that someone attacked her independently. The timing is just too suspect."

"I disagree. It doesn't make sense that she was spared in Colorado only to be hunted down a day or so later. I still think she's the one to watch. But as I said before, I wouldn't be surprised if there was more than one of them involved."

"Well, maybe when we figure out who was behind the original request for A-Tac's involvement it'll give us some direction. In the meantime, we're looking at the other people who knew about the transfer. Starting with General Fisher."

"That's a slippery slope. Fisher has friends in high places."

"And so do you. I'll be fine."

"Well, keep your eye on the prize. Finding the mole in A-Tac is job one."

"I hear you. And I'll keep my eyes open. Anything you can find out from your end would be appreciated as well."

"I'll see what I can do. When does Harrison arrive?"

"Tomorrow morning, if everything goes as scheduled."

"And Solomon was fine with his inclusion on the team?"

"Yes. Tyler was a bit more vocal in her disapproval, but I think it was more about my sudden appearance than anything to do with Harrison. They did make mention of another team member. Jason something."

"Jason Lawton. He's been with the team about six years. A whiz at all things IT. I'm sending you dossiers on the rest of the team. Figure it'll help if you know who's who."

"Good. I'll be glad to have additional information. One thing I've observed about A-Tac is that the team is intensely loyal. My guess is that they're not going to turn on each other easily. In fact, there's even a possibility that they'd cover for one another if push comes to shove."

"Well, then, you'll just have to convince them otherwise."

"Easier said than done, I'm afraid. I know the loyalty this kind of work can generate. Being on the front lines in stressful situations creates bonds that can't easily be broken."

"Perhaps," Palmer mused. "But you know better than most that friendships forged under fire can often be broken the same way. Look at what happened to you."

"It wasn't the same and you know it."

"Do I?" Palmer's voice was devoid of inflection, but Owen was clear on his meaning.

"I did what I had to do."

"Yes, but at what cost?" Silence stretched for a moment. "Look, all I'm saying is that under the right circumstances, with the right incentive, people will do what they perceive is in their own best interest, loyalty be damned."

"Now whose life are we talking about?" Owen forced himself to breathe. Logan Palmer had his own skeletons, but that didn't mean he wasn't right. "Anyway, if I had it to do over, I wouldn't do anything different. I thought you understood that."

"I do. But I just wanted to remind you that nothing is absolute. If someone at A-Tac is guilty, I'd make book on the fact that someone else knows about it. Or at least suspects. So all you've got to do is get them to talk."

"There's always the chance that you're wrong. That no one here was involved with the theft."

"Wishful thinking, my boy. They're involved all right. It's just a question of how many. And more specifically, who. And as much as you don't want to hear it, my money is still on Tyler Hanson."

"Well, if she's responsible, you can be certain I'll find out."

"That's exactly what I'm counting on."

The phone went dead as Palmer disconnected the call. Owen flipped his cell closed and stared out into the nighttime shadows, his mind turning to Tyler Hanson. She was definitely the kind of woman who inspired extreme loyalty. Independent. Tough. Drop-dead gorgeous. He closed his eyes, remembering the fire in the depths of her smoky green eyes, her soft cries of ecstasy as he'd plunged deep inside her. God, she was hot. The epitome of everything right with America. The girl next door, with a body to die for.

Quite literally.

He sobered, pulling his thoughts away from the memory of their night together. He stared out the window, across the lawn at the dark windows of her house. She still hadn't come home, which meant that he had an opportunity. A chance to dig for her secrets. And he knew she had them.

He'd recognized the look in her eyes.

Tyler climbed the steps of her front porch, grateful to be home. Although in truth she'd never really viewed it that way. Still, the cul-de-sac housed all of her friends; Nash and Annie next door, Drake just beyond them—although he'd been on leave for a couple of months now, ostensibly to recuperate from an operation in Colombia, but they all knew that he was really romancing Madeline. Interesting how things worked out.

She smiled, as she looked across the street. Emmett Walsh's house was dark. But that wasn't surprising. He was a creature of the night and usually worked late either in his office in the Social Sciences building or somewhere in the labyrinth of A-Tac HQ tinkering with the latest in communication technology. Lara and Jason's lights were on, spilling out over their meticulously groomed flowerbeds, the blue and pink hydrangeas undulating in the breeze.

Tyler had peonies. They reminded her of her mother, although she hadn't inherited her mother's green thumb. Fortunately, one of the perks of living on "professor cove," as the students had dubbed it, was a set of full-time gardeners.

The lights were on at Annie and Nash's, too. It was tempting to go over and share a glass of wine. But it was late, and she resisted the urge, moving across the porch to unlock the front door. The house was quiet, the ticking of the grandfather clock in the entryway the only sound. The clock had belonged to her grandmother, a tiny woman with a shock of white hair and a penchant for doing exactly as she pleased.

She'd died when Tyler was still a kid, but she'd left behind the clock and an indelible impression. She'd been the one to encourage Tyler to express herself in whatever way seemed best. Which, the summer Tyler turned nine, had included rerigging the family fireworks. The final result hadn't been pretty. The gnarly old oak in her grandmother's backyard had caught fire, and Methuselah, her grandmother's tabby, hadn't come out from under the bed for a week.

Still, her grandmother had laughed and said she had spirit. Her father, on the other hand, had grounded her for a month. Although she was certain she'd seen a flash of pride when he'd seen how high her enhanced bottle rockets had flown.

She closed the door, and reached for the foyer light, her hand stopping as she sensed something out of place. Straining into the darkness, she waited, listening. But there was nothing but the slow steady ticking of the clock.

Nerves.

No one could possibly get to her here.

Letting the dappled moonlight from the windows guide her, she walked down the hallway, stopping at the foot of the stairs to look out the French doors that led to the backyard. There was no light from the cottage. Either

Owen had retired already, or he was still with Nash. Either way it was probably for the best. She needed a little distance, some time to put everything that had happened into context. It wasn't as if she had married the man. She'd just slept with him. And since they were two consenting adults, it shouldn't be such a big deal.

But it was.

She sighed, shaking her head. That's what she got for sleeping with James Bond. She climbed the stairs, stopping on the landing. The hallway was shrouded in darkness, and she reached for the light, then hesitated, her senses going on red alert again.

Something was definitely off.

It wasn't anything she could put her finger on. Just a feeling. Still, the house remained silent, and so, pushing aside her jitters, she flipped the switch. Light flooded the hallway, the shadows retreating along with her fears. Everything looked exactly as it was supposed to. Clearly, the past few days had her on edge.

She walked into the bedroom and almost tripped on her suitcase. The airline had clearly found her luggage, and Avery or Nash had most likely accepted the delivery, which went a long way toward explaining her feelings of unease. Someone *had* been in the house. But the context was innocent. She sighed and sank down on the end of the bed, her ribs protesting the movement.

Across the room on the bureau sat a wooden box. It had been her grandmother's. She'd always referred to it as her secretary, a tabletop holder for envelopes and stationery. There was even an old compartment meant for an inkwell. All of it hidden behind the rich patina of burled walnut.

For a long time she'd kept everything just as her
grandmother had left it—embossed stationery, fountain
pens, sealing wax, and ancient stamps. But slowly, over
time, the box had become the keeper of memories, Tyler's
precious store of the things she held most dear. A letter
from her father, the only one he'd ever written her, his
words as sure and strong as he had once been. A string
of pearls, also her grandmother's. Tyler had never worn
them. She wasn't the type. But she loved them anyway.
There were family photographs, and even a poem some
boy had written for her in grade school.

Little pieces of a life.

And then, there was the secret compartment. When
she was little, her grandmother had showed it to her, and
she'd thought it better than anything in a Nancy Drew
novel. And when her grandmother died, and she'd inherited the secretary, she'd put the compartment to good use.
The perfect place for cherished memories of her mother.

She pushed off the bed, crossing over to open the box.
Everything inside was just where it should be. Old friends
treasured from the past. She ran her hand along the
smooth wood, and then with a flick of her finger released
the catch that held the bottom in place. Carefully lifting
the tray from the box, she braced herself. It was always
difficult to see her mother's things. Although there wasn't
much. After she died, her father had tried to exorcise her
from their lives. But Tyler had managed to save a few
things. A gold locket, a dog-eared photograph, and the
blue scarf.

Except that the scarf wasn't there.

Her heart lurched as she searched the box again.
There was no sign of the scarf. She frowned, trying to

remember when she'd last seen it. It had been months, perhaps even a year, but it had most definitely been there. And she never took it out. She didn't really like touching it. As though by association, it still reeked of death and desperation. But even so, she hadn't been able to let it go.

And now it was gone.

Her throat tightened as her mind's eye rolled out images of the Colorado roadside and the scarf floating on the breeze. It had been the last thing she'd seen before passing out. But some part of her had assumed that it was a trick of her mind, past and present merging together. No one else had mentioned seeing it.

But now, staring down into the empty compartment, she wasn't so sure.

A noise from downstairs penetrated her whirling thoughts, and she dropped the photo she was holding, reaching into a drawer for her gun. This time she was certain of what she'd heard. There was someone inside the house.

She stepped into the hallway, careful to keep her back to the wall, and began to move forward. At the top of the stairs, she stopped, flipping off the light, listening for something to give her an indication of where the intruder might be. But the house was quiet again, and for a moment, she doubted herself. Then somewhere out toward the kitchen, she heard another sound.

Gripping her gun, she carefully worked her way downstairs, moving through the foyer into the living room. Ahead of her, just beyond the open French doors, she heard footsteps against the tile. She swung out into the room, gun at the ready.

"One more step and I shoot."

"Only if you've got eyes in the back of your head." Owen's voice carried from behind her, the kitchen's fluorescent lighting flickering to life as he hit the switch.

"Son of bitch," she whispered, her heart hammering in her throat. "You scared the shit out of me."

"I'm sorry," he said. "I'm afraid I acted on instinct. And for the record, I wasn't breaking and entering. The door was open."

"So you decided to sneak inside?"

"I wasn't sneaking anywhere. I called your name. No one answered. So I thought I'd better check it out. I know things are more relaxed over here in America, but I didn't think that extended to leaving your back door wide open." He laid a lethal-looking Walther on the countertop. "I'm just glad you're all right."

"Yeah. Me, too." She fought to control her cascading emotions, crossing the room to shut the door. Beyond the glass, she could see the cottage, the porch light shining across the lawn. "I didn't see any lights when I got home. I assumed you'd gone to bed."

"Actually, Nash and I shared a pint. Good man. You're lucky to have people like him and Avery on your team."

"You don't suspect them of double-dealing?" The question just popped out and she immediately regretted it.

"I don't suspect anyone, Tyler. I'm just here to observe. And to help if possible."

"And I'm not usually such a shrew." She shook her head. "I'm just not used to finding strange men in my kitchen in the middle of the night."

"Not to put too fine a point on it, but it's not that late,

and I'm hardly a stranger." His appraising gaze slowly traveled the length of her body, and she felt her cheeks flame, more from memory than embarrassment. The man had a way of discombobulating her. "And I was honestly concerned."

"Well, I appreciate the thought. But as you can see," she laid her gun down next to his, "I'm fully capable of taking care of myself."

"So did you leave the door open?" he asked, leaning back against the counter.

"No. I didn't. In fact, I'm quite positive I locked it before leaving for Colorado. But Avery has a key, and so does Nash. And someone brought my bag in. Must have been one of them."

"So you think it was an accident?"

"Honestly, I don't know what to think." She sank down onto a kitchen chair, her mind turning to the missing scarf. "I had a feeling when I got home that something was off. But then when I saw the suitcase I figured I was just being jumpy. And then I heard you—"

"And you had second thoughts."

"More or less." She shrugged. "I guess I'm working on high alert. After all, someone did try to kill me earlier. I just figured it was better not to take chances."

"I guess I should be glad you didn't shoot me."

Her smile was less than convincing, and she exhaled slowly, trying for a calm she didn't feel.

Owen frowned, watching her, his gaze speculating. "There's something more, isn't there? Something you're not telling me."

She started to deny it—to create some kind of smoke screen, but the words died before they could form. After all, he was right, he wasn't a stranger. She'd trusted him in the dark of her bedroom. It couldn't possibly be harder here in the full light of the kitchen.

"You're right. There is something. I should probably have mentioned it earlier, but under the circumstances, General Fisher wasn't exactly a go-to guy. And by the time you and I met up in the hotel, I was beginning to have doubts."

"But not anymore."

"No." She shook her head, thinking of the empty writing box upstairs. "None at all. Look, I want to tell you. But I've got to tell Avery, too. And to be honest, I don't know that I can get through it more than once."

In truth, she didn't want to go through it at all. But there was no choice. Someone was using her past against her, and keeping quiet was only going to make things worse.

CHAPTER **6**

Thanks for coming," Tyler said, as Avery settled in the big wing chair by the fireplace. Owen was sitting across from him on the sofa, watching the two of them. There was a comfortableness between them he envied, a friendship of long standing.

"So now that you've gotten me out of bed," Avery began.

"Oh, please," Tyler protested with a smile. "I know you weren't sleeping. The Yankees are playing in California. Which means a late-night game here on the East Coast."

"Guilty as charged. But we're not here to discuss the Yankees."

All signs of frivolity vanished, her face tightening, as she considered her words. "As I told Owen, I probably should have said something sooner. It's just that I decided I was overreacting."

"To what?" Avery asked, showing no sign of the impatience Owen was feeling.

"On the road, when I went to the embankment to make sure there was no one down there, I saw something blue. And it triggered an emotional reaction. That's why I decided to check it out."

"As far as I know, no one found anything down there." Owen wondered if she was playing some kind of game. If maybe she'd decided to lead them on a wild goose chase of some kind. Keep them away from the real truth. It certainly fit with Palmer's belief that she had been involved in the theft somehow. But he, of all people, knew it was best to wait for all the facts rather than jumping to any kind of conclusion. "Certainly nothing blue," he finished.

"That's why I hesitated to say anything," she said. "I thought maybe I'd dreamed up the whole thing, especially the last bit. But none of this is going to make any sense if I don't explain why it mattered."

She paused for a moment, looking uncomfortable as she warily watched the two of them. Then with a sigh, she turned her attention to Owen. "I told you that my mother was dead," she said, lacing her fingers together over her knees, the gesture making her look like a kid. "What I didn't tell you was that she killed herself."

"Good Lord." The words came of their own volition, but he could feel her pain. Losing people one loved was never easy, but when there was violence involved, it made it all the worse.

"It doesn't hurt as much now." Tyler shook her head. "At least that's what I tell myself. The truth is my mother wasn't particularly stable. So in some awful way, it was a relief that she finally found peace. But, that's not the point. The reason I'm dredging this all up again is that it's beginning to look like it plays into what happened in Colorado. At the very least I think there was a calculated attempt to manipulate my actions."

She paused, reaching for her coffee, sipping the beverage and then carefully placing the cup back on the table. Her motions were slow and exact, and Owen recognized her actions as a struggle for control.

"My mother jumped off a bridge," she said, without preamble, her voice shaking ever so slightly as she spoke. "And when she went over, her scarf caught on the railing, hanging there like a banner, marking the spot." She sucked in a fortifying breath. "But despite the fact that there were both cars and pedestrians on the bridge, no one saw it. Or her. Or if they did, they didn't bother to stop. The police found her body six hours later, a few miles downstream." She paused, looking down at her hands. "If someone had just stopped. Or called 911. But they didn't."

"People see what they want to see," Owen said, his words meant as comfort. He wasn't sure why he wanted to ease her pain, but he did.

"I'm guessing the scarf was blue," Avery said, pulling them both back to the moment.

"Yes." She nodded, her gaze encompassing them both as everything fell into place. "I gave it to her when I was eight. For her birthday. It had little paisleys on it. She always said it was her favorite." Tears welled and she dashed them away.

"How old were you when she died?" Owen asked, careful to keep his tone neutral.

"Twelve. Well, actually eleven and three-quarters. My birthday was in two weeks. She'd said I could have a party." She paused for a moment, ducking her head, then lifted her chin, pushing away whatever demons still tormented her. "Anyway, at the side of the road, when the flashlight picked out something blue, I guess I went into overdrive. I wasn't going to make the same mistake people had made with my mother. If someone was hurt, I wanted to help."

"That's understandable," Avery said. "And it makes sense that you wouldn't have wanted to talk about it with General Fisher."

"I didn't want to talk about it with anyone. I just feel so guilty that I let someone lure me into reacting."

"But surely you're not saying that someone intentionally left something blue out there for you to find." Owen reached for his own coffee, taking a sip as he tried to sort through what she was telling them.

"That's exactly what I'm saying. And I know it sounds crazy. But I also know what I saw."

"But you couldn't have had that good a look. I mean, it was dark and you were in a hurry." Avery frowned. "You said the attack started before you had a chance to investigate."

"That's true, but there was time enough to pick it up. And it was definitely a scarf. But then, before I could examine it, everything exploded, shots firing from up above. And in my effort to get back up the slope to help my team, I lost it. I stumbled and the wind grabbed it."

"And that's when you were hit." It was a question, not a statement, and Owen could see a visible flash of memory as Tyler winced.

"Yeah." She nodded. "It all happened really fast. There were four gunmen, and I was too far away to take any of them out. Anthony was already dead. But Roger was alive. And I tried to provide cover while he scrambled to safety." She closed her eyes for a minute, still remembering. "He almost made it. But I was too late. Next thing I know I'm hit, the impact sending me back down the incline. I tried to hang on to consciousness. But I couldn't. And the last thing I saw was the scarf. It was snarled in the limbs of the tree hanging over me."

"I can see how that would spook you," Owen said, meaning every word, although he still wasn't entirely sure she was telling the whole truth.

"I remember thinking that it looked exactly like my mother's," she continued. "Only even in that moment, I didn't really believe what I was seeing. And then when I woke up—it was gone."

"And you questioned whether it was ever really there," Avery prompted.

"At the end, yes. I know it was there before. I held it in my hands. But like Owen said, no one else mentioned it. I even checked the preliminary forensics report. And there was nothing in it about a scarf. And General Fisher was already having a field day with my surviving. I just figured I'd let it go until I got back here."

"And finding the scarf is what you were alluding to when I called?" Avery asked.

She nodded. "I just didn't want to talk about it on the phone. I was either totally crazy, or I was on to something, and I had no idea if the phone was really secure."

"Sound thinking." Avery nodded.

"But you still didn't tell us," Owen said. "Even after you got back."

"Well, I was a little surprised to find that you were

here. And since I don't really know you," she winced
again on the last words, "I figured it was better to wait
until I could talk with Avery on my own."

"Only something changed your mind."

"I just realized that it was pointless trying to keep it
from you. You're part of this operation whether I like it or
not. And when I found you in my kitchen—"

"Hold on." Avery lifted a hand to interrupt. "What the
hell were you doing in her kitchen?"

It was a valid question, and one Owen had no intention
of answering honestly. So he stuck with the story he'd told
Tyler. "Her back door was open. I was worried. Figured
I'd check things out."

"And scare the hell out of me." Her smile was faint,
but there was genuine amusement there. "Although I
was already jumpy. I knew when I came through the
front door that something wasn't right. It was only when
I found my bag in my room that I realized you'd been
here." She looked to Avery for confirmation, but the big
man was frowning.

"It wasn't me." He shook his head.

"Well, someone must have deposited it," Owen said,
his gaze encompassing them both. "I assume you have
security?"

"There are surveillance cameras," Avery said. "Which
means someone is monitoring the cul-de-sac 24/7."

"Are there any cameras on the property?" He'd
checked, of course, and found nothing, but it was always
possible he'd missed something.

"Unfortunately, no." Avery shook his head. "But there
is an alarm system. We all have one."

"Only I rarely remember to turn it on." Tyler grimaced.

"Not that it really matters, I've got CIA operatives living on all sides of me. Anyway, it must have been Nash. I told you he had a key."

"But Nash was with you," Owen said, his instincts going on hyperdrive. "And subsequently with me. So there wasn't time."

"Well, then it was probably Annie."

"That should be easy enough to check," Owen said, reaching for the telephone.

"Not now," Tyler said, glancing down at her watch. "It's late. Adam will be asleep. We can check it out tomorrow."

"I agree." Avery nodded. "But if you haven't already, don't touch the suitcase. We need to be certain that it wasn't tampered with. And there's always a chance we can get a print."

"Fine. There's nothing in it I can't live without for a night. And besides, the suitcase isn't what spooked me into telling the two of you," she said on a sigh. "After the inquiry into my mother's death, the police returned her things. And my father promptly disposed of most of them. But I managed to sneak off with a couple of items, including the scarf. I know it's silly, but holding on to it made me feel closer to her somehow."

Owen thought of the boxes he still had, in London, in storage. It wasn't exactly the same, but he understood her motivation.

"Did you have the scarf here?" Avery's use of past tense said it all—and Owen waited, the pieces finally falling in place.

"I did. I kept it upstairs in a special place. A hidden compartment in an antique writing box. And tonight when I opened it to check on the scarf—it was gone."

There was a beat of silence, and then Avery whistled. "So you think someone stole it?"

"Yes, I do. I mean, there's no other reason for it to have gone missing. I never take it out of the box. Hell, I don't even look at it that often. I think someone took it and used it in Colorado to lure me into leaving Gerardi and Mather."

"They knew how you'd react to seeing the scarf." Owen frowned, trying to line it all up in his mind. "And combined with the motorcycle and the damaged guard rail, they gambled it would be enough to send you down the hill."

"So they stole the scarf to use it as bait," Avery summarized.

"If this is true," Owen said, "and I can't say that I'm completely convinced—then it would seem that someone involved with the detonators' theft knows the intimate details of your life. At least with regard to your mother's suicide."

"But why go to all this trouble?" Tyler asked. "I mean, surely they could have just outgunned us. I mean, why the elaborate effort to get me down the hill? And why use my mother's scarf? It's almost like it's personal."

"Maybe someone is trying to frame you," Avery said.

"By stealing my mother's scarf?" Tyler's eyebrows lifted, her expression incredulous. "That doesn't make any sense."

"The whole thing feels off to me," Owen said, taking a sip of his now-tepid coffee, his thoughts turning to his earlier conversation with Logan Palmer. "But for now, it's the best lead we've got. Who else knows what happened to your mother?"

"Besides Avery, only Nash. But I didn't share details. So he doesn't know about the scarf. And even if he did, he'd never betray me like that."

There was a first time for everything. Even betrayal. Owen had learned that the hard way.

"But the suicide was public, right?" Avery asked, his brow furrowed as he sought answers. "It was on the news and in the paper."

"Sure." Tyler nodded. "But that was a long time ago."

"Doesn't matter. It means that the information is out there." Avery leaned forward. "If the news of your mother's scarf was made public—or even if it was simply noted in a police report—that means it's accessible today. And with the internet, and a moderate degree of technical savvy, anyone would be able to find it."

"So we're right back where we started," Tyler sighed. "And even if they did access the information, I still don't see the payoff. So, again, what's the point of getting me involved?"

"Like you said, maybe it's personal," Avery said. "We've certainly made enemies over the years."

"But it still doesn't make any sense," Tyler protested. "Unless you're right and someone is trying to frame me. And even if that's the case, there are countless other things they could have done that would have been a hell of a lot more damning."

"So maybe this is just smoke and mirrors," Owen suggested. "A way to throw us off the scent." If Palmer was to be believed, Tyler was the one behind the smoke and mirrors. But even if Owen accepted that theory, Avery was right, the pieces still didn't fit.

"Maybe." Avery frowned, clearly considering the possibility. "Or maybe it's simply a way to make certain that A-Tac is involved."

"So what's the motive?" Tyler queried.

"If someone from A-Tac has been playing the other side," Owen said, phrasing his words carefully, "and if that person was a party to the theft, then the group responsible would have someone on the inside running interference with any investigation on our part."

"But it's not a foolproof plan. I mean, wouldn't they figure we'd eventually put it together and ferret out the guilty party?"

"There's a risk in any kind of inside operation," Avery said. "But there's also the possibility that we won't find the source. And that he—or she—will be successful at thwarting our efforts."

"Or maybe it isn't about stopping the investigation. Maybe it's about buying time," Owen suggested. "Keep us chasing our tails until they can accomplish whatever it is they've set out to do."

"The very thought of which makes my blood run cold," Tyler fumed. "What if Nash is right and they're planning to use the detonators?"

"Let's not get ahead of ourselves," Avery said. "One thing at a time. If someone is working against us— someone on the inside—then we have to consider the fact that they're getting better."

"I'm not following." Tyler shook her head.

"The original attempts to sabotage things were basic. Interfering with communications, weapons. Things that would jeopardize a mission, but not national security. But in Colombia, the damage increased exponentially.

The leaked information could have done serious damage to the unit's credibility, not to mention costing the lives of more than one of its operatives. Hell, you and Drake could easily have been casualties."

"You're talking about Ortiz and di Silva again," Owen said, thinking of the jagged scar beneath Tyler's breast. "Tyler mentioned she'd been shot."

"Exactly. But even more important, the failure of that mission could have put millions of lives at risk if Ortiz's weapons stash hadn't been destroyed."

"But from what I read, it sounds like A-Tac, particularly your man Drake, more than carried the day."

"An understatement," Avery acknowledged, "but the point here is that if the efforts to subvert us have been cumulative, then we need to be on our guard."

"And work together to find answers," Owen said. "No matter how uncomfortable you feel doing it."

"Well, the first thing to do is to check the tapes," Avery said. "If someone broke into Tyler's house, we ought to have a record of it, as well as footage of the person who brought your suitcase to the house."

"If we're right about my involvement being a decoy, it's even possible that the scarf was stolen after the fact," Tyler mused. "To scare me, maybe. Or just to confuse the situation further."

"Hopefully your surveillance will tell us more," Owen said, hoping it didn't expose him as well. Still, he had a reason for being on site, and Avery had said there were no cameras on Tyler's property.

"In addition, we need to check for prints and any other forensic evidence," Avery said, "as well as checking your bag. And at this point, I don't think we should wait until morning." He picked up the phone, walking over to the window as he talked.

"God, this is all so damn complicated," Tyler said, pushing off the hearth to settle restlessly on the arm of a chair.

"Maybe that's exactly how they want you to feel," Owen suggested.

"Well, if that's the objective, it's working." The look of anguish on her face was heart wrenching, which meant either she was one hell of an actress, or she was telling the truth.

"We'll get to the bottom of it," he said, reaching out to cover her hand with his. "I promise."

She stared down at his hand for a moment, and then pulled away, the distance emotional as well as physical.

"All right," Avery announced, cutting through the tension as he flipped his phone closed. "I called Hannah in to review the surveillance tapes. I'm heading over to the war room to brief her and see what I can do to help. And I've got people coming over here to take prints and check out the house."

"Sounds like a plan," Tyler said, her voice less than enthusiastic.

"Look, I know you're beat," Avery said, his eyes full of concern. "And there's no need for you to be here. We can bring you up to speed in the morning. Why don't you go over to my house and get some sleep?"

"No, way. I'm not leaving. I need to know what they find."

Avery opened his mouth to object, but Owen cut him off. "I'll stay here with her. That way, at least, she won't be on her own. And when they're gone, I'll see that she gets some sleep."

"Good luck with that," Avery murmured, his expression shifting to rueful. "But I will feel better if someone's with her."

"I'm standing right here," Tyler said, "and I don't need a fucking babysitter."

"I'm not suggesting that you do." Avery smiled. "But I am accepting Owen's offer. And it's not up for debate. You choose. My house and bed. Or here—with Owen."

"Fine. You win. It's not like I have a choice." She grabbed her coffee cup and stomped off to the kitchen.

Owen started to follow, but Avery reached out to stop him. "I don't know what's going on between you and Tyler. And frankly, it's none of my business. But a man would have to be blind not to see the sparks flying between the two of you. All I've got to say is that you'd better watch yourself. She means a lot to all of us here. And we're not likely to take kindly to anyone who hurts her."

CHAPTER 7

"You can turn on the light."

Owen's voice broke through the darkness, sending Tyler's heart skittering to her throat. She sucked in a fortifying breath and flipped the living room light switch, blinking in the bright light. "I couldn't sleep. So I came down here to get something to drink. I didn't mean to wake you."

"I wasn't sleeping either," he said, lifting his arms to stretch. She tried to ignore the ripple of muscle, but her body wasn't listening, every particle inside her responding to his presence.

She blew out a breath, quelling her tumbling emotions. This was exactly why she hadn't wanted him in the house. She needed her wits about her, and something about him continually unnerved her. She'd tried to fend him off. But he'd insisted on sleeping on the couch, even after she'd made it more than clear that she didn't need him to watch over her.

Damn the man.

"There's just too much going on, I guess," she sighed, leaning down to pick up a discarded piece of paper. The forensics team had been thorough if not particularly forthcoming. There'd been fingerprints all over the house, and until they were run through a database there was no way to know whose they were.

The suitcase hadn't been tampered with, but they'd taken it anyway, apparently to perform more tests. Tyler had offered to come along, but Avery had insisted she stay out of it, at least until the morning when they had some answers. But the morning was too damn slow in coming.

"What do you say I make us both a cup of tea." Owen pushed to his feet, his words pulling her from her thoughts. "You do have tea, I presume?"

"Somewhere," she said, following him into the kitchen. "Cooking isn't really my thing."

"Well, making tea isn't rocket science," he said, opening her cupboards to search for tea bags.

"I think maybe in here?" she suggested, pulling open the cabinet by the sink. Behind a jumble of half-empty containers and boxes she found a tin of Earl Grey. "Will this do?" She held out the canister. "My stepmother gave it to me last Christmas. There are no bags, so I wasn't really sure what to do with it."

Owen took the tea and pried off the lid, sniffing the contents appreciatively. "Your stepmother knows tea. This is the good stuff."

"Maybe she had a premonition I'd have a British houseguest. Anyway, I haven't got the right gizmo to steep it. I mean you can't just toss it in a cup, can you?"

"In a pinch, it'll work, but coffee filters work much better." He reached for the box next to the coffeemaker and extracted two. "I don't suppose you have a kettle?"

Tyler shook her head, watching as he filled the coffee pot with water and emptied it into the machine. "It won't be perfect," he said, smiling, "but it'll do."

The machine hissed as the water started to drip down into the pot. Owen measured out spoonfuls of the tea leaves into two cups topped with modified filters.

"It all seems very domestic," she said, perching on the opposite counter. "I'd have expected you to know how to make a martini, but not so much with the tea."

"I'm English," he shrugged, "it comes with the territory."

"Not all Englishmen drink tea," she protested. "If I remember correctly, James Bond didn't drink it."

"Quite right. He referred to it as a 'cup of mud,' actually. But he was a fictional character, Tyler. And at the risk of disappointing," he turned around, his velvety eyes turning to steel, "I'm afraid I'm not that kind of superspy, just a civil servant, making a living the best way I can."

"Somehow, I'm not sure that I buy that. But I'll accept the tea thing. And anyway, Della will be delighted I'm actually using the stuff. She doesn't quite know what to make of me, I'm afraid."

"Your stepmother, you mean?"

She nodded as he poured the now-boiling water over the tea leaves, letting the water level rise until they were covered.

"I expect she isn't used to women with a penchant for ordnance," he said.

"She isn't used to women who wear pants. She's amazingly old-fashioned. Every time we talk I can just feel the disapproval."

"Maybe she's intimidated," he said, going to the refrigerator and opening a carton of milk. He sniffed the milk and pulled a face. "Not exactly fresh."

"I've only been back for the better part of twelve hours. Give a girl a break."

"Fine. We'll make do with sugar. Anyway, I can see where you might be a bit off-putting."

"Thanks a lot."

"No offense meant. I'm just feeling fondly toward the woman who provided our tea. Without Della, I'd be drinking coffee."

"You had some earlier. And there were no complaints."

"I'm nothing if not flexible." He picked up the cups and walked over to the table. She followed carrying spoons and the sugar bowl. "In a pinch coffee will do. But it's not the same as a good cup of tea."

"All right, I'll cede the point. After all, you're the expert. I just think tea seems a bit domestic." She added a spoonful of sugar and took a deep whiff. "Although I have to admit, it smells pretty damn good."

"That's the bergamot. Makes Earl Grey, Earl Grey. Anyway, for me, it's a touch of home, if you want the truth. Don't get me wrong, I like your country, but there are moments when I long for the comfort of the familiar."

"You make it sound as if you've been away a long time."

"Time is relative. Anyway, we were talking about your stepmother."

"Actually, there's not much more to say." Tyler took a sip of her tea, her thoughts turning to the general and his wife. "To be honest, I've always gone out of my way to avoid her. Stepmothers aren't really my thing. And as I said earlier, she's not the first. But the truth is, she makes my father happy, which isn't an easy task. And now that he's sick, she's been there for him. In fact she's wonderful. Patient and loving."

"Sounds like you admire her." He sipped his tea, his dark eyes watching her over the rim of the cup, the whole idea of tea's being emasculating going right out the window with one swallow.

"I don't know that I'd go that far," she said. "But I've certainly come to appreciate everything she does for my father."

"You said he's sick?"

"Yes." She nodded, swallowing the sudden surge of pain. "He has Alzheimer's. But it's still in the early stages. Which means he has lucid days. But sometimes it's really bad. He doesn't even know me. And the doctors say it's only going to get worse."

"It's a difficult situation for all of you."

"Especially my father," she said, surprised at how easy it was to talk to Owen. "He's used to being in charge, to being the smartest man in the room. I can't imagine what it's like for him to know that it's all slipping away."

"All the more reason to cherish the time you have left." A shadow passed across his face, his jaw tightening with momentary emotion, but before she had time to form words to ask, it was gone. "So is that what was keeping you awake? Your father?"

"No. At least not directly. I just keep going over

everything in my mind, trying to put the pieces together in some way that makes sense."

"Any luck with that?"

"None at all." She shook her head ruefully. "How about you? You said you'd been awake, as well."

"I've been trying to figure out why they didn't kill you the first time they had the chance."

The words were like cold water, any intimacy she'd imagined evaporating in an instant. "What the hell do you mean by that?"

"Just what I said." His gaze was steady. "It doesn't make sense. They killed both of your colleagues. And by your own admission they had a clear shot at you when you passed out. But here you are, sitting in your kitchen drinking tea."

"Well, don't sound so happy about it." She frowned, taking a big gulp, almost choking on the hot beverage.

"Don't get me wrong, I'm delighted that you're here." His gaze traveled the curves of her body, her skittering nerves reacting as if he'd touched her.

Heat flushed her face and more nether regions, and reflexively she crossed her arms over her chest. "Don't go there," she warned, her words coming out on a raspy breath of air.

His lips lifted in a slow, crooked smile. "I don't know why not."

"Because you just accused me of lying about what happened."

"I most certainly did not." The lines of his face hardened as he dropped any further attempt at flirtation. "I merely said I was questioning why you were left alive."

"Maybe they thought I was dead," she suggested,

knowing that she sounded defensive. "I was at the bottom of the ravine and it was dark."

"But these men were professionals. I'd have thought they'd check to be certain."

"So what are you suggesting if not my complicity in what happened?" She tried to keep her voice calm, but she didn't like feeling cornered—especially by him.

"I don't know. The only other option I can think of is that there was some reason they wanted you alive."

"Then what about the shooter in the parking garage?" Her thoughts were tumbling end over end now, and she struggled to keep her anger from consuming her ability to think.

"Maybe it was unrelated. Or maybe they changed their minds. I don't know. That's why I was puzzling over it."

"What possible reason could there be for them to have wanted me alive?"

"Possibly to confuse. I mean, they had to know that anyone who found you would assume first off that you were involved. If nothing else that would slow things down a bit."

"Especially when you factor in my mother's scarf," she sighed, her anger dissipating as quickly as it had come. "And I suppose they could also have been counting on my getting A-Tac involved. If they knew me well enough to know that I'd react to seeing the blue scarf, they'd also know that I'd want to be the one to hunt them down."

"Agreed," he said, still watching her.

"But it still doesn't explain Petrov."

"As I said, maybe he was on a different mission. Revenge for Ortiz. Or maybe for some reason you became a liability."

"I don't know, it just seems more logical to assume they thought I was dead. I took like four rounds full-on. And they had no reason to believe I'd be wearing body armor."

"Because of the hit you took in Colombia."

"Let's just say I have a passable learning curve."

He nodded, frowning as he considered something.

"What? What are you thinking?" she prodded.

"Just that whoever stole the detonators clearly has a bigger agenda than just theft. It's the only way the other pieces can fit."

"Hopefully, Hannah and company will be able to identify the prints on the suitcase. That could help give us insight into who was in my house. And there's still the matter of where the order for my involvement originated and figuring out Petrov's connection to all of this. I just wish we knew something."

"It takes a while to gather facts," he said. "I bet they'll have found something by morning."

"If it ever comes," she sighed, pushing away from the table to walk to the window. The sky was still dark, although the stars had faded, and the edge of the horizon was lightening. "Anyway, you were right about one thing."

"And that would be?" he queried, his breath teasing her ears, as he moved to stand behind her.

"I do want revenge. And I'm not the type to give up easily when I want something."

"That I can believe," he said, his hands coming to rest on her shoulders, his fingers kneading gently. "But you can't let it take control, this need for vengeance. It'll just get in the way."

"You sound like you have firsthand experience," she said, turning to face him, tilting her head to look into his eyes.

"In our line of work it's an occupational hazard."

The words were a toss-off, an easy answer to a difficult question, but she knew there was something more. She could see it in his eyes. They stood for a moment watching each other, the distance between them measured in inches. She could see the rise and fall of his breathing, feel the warmth of his breath on her face.

And she could remember the feel of his arms and his lips. Without conscious thought she leaned forward, and he took the opening, pulling her to him, his lips slanting down over hers. There was nothing gentle in the kiss. It was desire personified. Raw and hungry. And she pushed against him, opening her mouth, wanting to feel him inside her.

He twined his hands in hers, lifting her arms over her head as he pressed her back against the cool glass of the window. She arched against him, reveling in his heat as it radiated through the thin cotton of her T-shirt, her nipples hardening as they rubbed against him.

His tongue dueled with hers, thrusting and parrying, an intricate game of giving and taking. She whimpered against her will, the sound pulled from somewhere deep inside her, her whole body aching with need. Sensory memory took over, heat pooling between her thighs. She tipped back her head, his kisses trailing down her neck, each soft lave of his tongue sending spirals of pleasure racing through her.

Still holding her captive, he bit her ear lobe, then thrust his tongue inside, and she bucked against him as he moved back to take possession of her mouth. Dropping her hands, he cupped her ass, lifting her so that she could feel his erection.

God, she wanted this man.

He pushed up her shirt and closed his lips around one breast, biting gently at first, and then harder, her head spinning now as waves of pleasure racked through her. He lifted his head, his smile sensual as he bent to kiss her once more, and she thrust her tongue deep into his mouth, her fingers lacing through his hair, as she pressed closer.

Then somewhere behind her a door slammed shut, a cold breeze rushing through the room, passion dying in an instant.

Moving almost in tandem, they both went for their guns, Owen's tucked into the back of his pants, Tyler's still lying on the kitchen counter. With a nod, she covered him as he moved in the direction of the slammed door. Staying just behind him, she kept her gun ready as they swung into the living room.

"Clear," Owen whispered, moving his gun arm in a semicircle as he continued to monitor the room. "Is that door usually closed?" He nodded across the foyer at the dining room.

"No." She shook her head. "That must be what we heard. I'll circle back through the kitchen. You go that way."

He nodded and she moved quickly back the way she'd come, leading with her gun as she swung out into the kitchen, relieved to find the room still empty. Walking silently across the floor, she counted to three and then pivoted through the back door of the dining room, just as Owen came through the front.

For an instant they stared at each other, guns raised,

then with a wash of relief, Tyler lowered her gun. "There's no one here."

"But the window is open." He nodded toward the curtains stirring in the breeze. "The screen's intact though, which means it was probably just the wind that slammed the door."

"Scaring the hell out of me."

"Seems to be a regular occurrence around here." He moved over to where she was standing, his eyes searching hers. "You're sure you're all right?"

"Yes." She nodded. "Except for the fact that my heart's pounding."

"It's possible that's not just because of the wind." He reached out to touch her face, but she caught his hand in hers before he could make contact.

"We can't do this. Not now."

"But just a few minutes ago—" he started, his eyes darkening as he frowned.

"We got carried away," she finished. "And then the door slammed and I came to my senses. You know as well as I do that it's not a good idea to mix business with pleasure."

"I think that ship has already sailed." The remark was caustic, but there was something vulnerable in his eyes.

"When I…when we…" she stumbled trying to find the words.

"Made love," he prompted, still scowling.

"Slept together," she corrected, determined now to make her point. "When we slept together, I didn't think I was going to see you again."

"So it was fine to screw me when I was a stranger, but not now that we actually know one another?"

"Damn it, Owen, you know as well as I do that this is a bad idea." She waited, watching as he fought against his own demons.

"Maybe you're right." He ran a hand through his hair. "I don't know. I just don't like the idea of being used."

"I didn't use you. Or if I did, the using was mutual." It was her turn to frown as an unwelcome idea planted itself front and center. "You didn't already know, did you? That you were coming here, I mean?"

"No. I swear I had no idea. I didn't find out until the next morning. I believe I told you I had a meeting. That's when I found out I'd be coming here. I would have said something, but you'd already left the hotel."

She nodded, not completely convinced, but satisfied for the moment with his answer. "I don't mean to sound so suspicious. It's just that I haven't got a lot of experience with this kind of thing."

"One-night stands showing up for more?" There was a hint of laughter in his voice, and despite herself, she relaxed a little.

"Something like that. Anyway, I've always made it a point not to play where I work. I've been down that road before and it doesn't end well."

"I see. So you're punishing me for something somebody else did to you?"

"Of course not," she sighed. "It's just simpler this way. I'm no good at relationships."

"Who said anything about a relationship?" he asked.

The words hurt more than she would have expected. "Look, Owen," she said, careful to keep any emotion out of her voice, "I don't do one-night stands either. I just don't like being entangled."

"So what? You made an exception for the Brit?"

"No. I needed you. It's as simple as that. And for once I let myself take what I wanted. And I loved every minute of it. But that was then..."

"I get it," he lifted up a hand. "And I'm sorry I messed with your perfect little love-him-and-leave-him plan." It sounded even worse somehow with the accent.

"You make it sound so crass. And besides, you were right there with me."

"Yes, but I was also in the kitchen with you. I can still feel the aftereffects. And I'm thinking you weren't as opposed to a second act then. If the door hadn't slammed—"

"But it did. And I'm glad. And we're not going to do this again." She crossed her arms, daring him to contradict her. A part of her wishing he'd ignore all the rhetoric and carry her away. But this wasn't the movies. And he wasn't the caveman type.

"Fine. If that's the way you want it." This time he lifted both hands. "You're probably right. Any continued involvement would just invite problems. And God knows we've already got more than enough of those."

"Owen, I..." she trailed off, not sure exactly what she wanted to say, but in the end it didn't matter because he was already gone.

CHAPTER 8

"Come say hello to the new recruit," Hannah called as Tyler walked into the war room.

Today Hannah's hair had bright orange streaks, her glasses a mottled blue on black. Next to her at her computer console sat a man with tousled brown hair and eyes that were neither green nor brown but maybe both. His boy-next-door good looks combined with the studious bent of a professor to make him oddly compelling. But she also recognized the computer geek. It was there in his eyes. And in his smile.

"Harrison Blake," he said, swiveling his chair to hold out his hand. "You must be Tyler. Hannah described you perfectly."

Tyler shot a look at her friend, eyebrows raised, but Hannah just shrugged.

"Harrison's been filling me in on some of the latest computer technologies. The outfit he works for has unlimited funding. Can you imagine?" Hannah sighed.

"You've got some pretty sophisticated stuff here, as well," Harrison said, his words of concession clearly sincere. "This is going to be fun."

It had been a long time since anyone had described their work as fun. And despite herself, Tyler smiled. "When did you get here?"

"Crack of dawn. I went to the address Owen gave me, but no one seemed to be home."

"We had a late night," she said, immediately regretting her words. "I mean, there was an intruder, so we spent most of the night with forensics."

"I know. Hannah told me. I figured something was up when no one answered. So I figured I'd explore a little, and I ran into Hannah."

"How did you know it was him?" Tyler frowned, suddenly suspicious.

"She'd checked me out." Harrison grinned.

"He looks just like his pictures. And he's got an amazing background," Hannah said. "Started with the FBI, right?"

"For a couple of years." He nodded, still smiling. "And then I'd kind of had enough. So I went to work for a private company. Phoenix."

"I've heard of it," Emmett Walsh said, striding into the room. "Out of Austin, right? They do some pretty amazing stuff. You must be Harrison. Avery's been singing your praises."

"Considering I've only just met the man, I appreciate the endorsement. And yes, Phoenix is in Austin."

"Phoenix is a computer forensics company," Hannah added by way of explanation. "One of the best in the country."

"I met the owner once," Emmett said, taking a seat at the table. "Really bright guy. I would love to work with him someday. Why'd you leave?"

"Got called into something else. Through a friend."

"The top-secret task force, right?" Tyler said, grateful to finally be on the same page with everyone else. "Under order of the president."

"Exactly." Harrison beamed as if she were a prize pupil.

"And that's how you know Owen?" Emmett questioned.

"More or less. He's friends with a friend of mine. And we've worked together a couple of times. Anyway, sounded like you all could use some help, so here I am. Although I'm not sure Hannah really needed me." He centered his smile on Hannah, and Tyler could have sworn she actually blushed.

"I haven't seen you since the parking garage," Tyler said, turning to Emmett. "Where've you been?"

"Trying to run down information on Petrov."

"Any luck?"

"Nothing substantial. He arrived in the country a couple of days ago under an assumed name."

"Before I went to Colorado?" she asked.

"Yes, as a matter of fact. Which means he could be connected to all of this. But according to my sources he's still on di Silva's payroll. So I can't definitively say how it fits together. Anyway, Avery called me back in. All hands on deck, I guess. Jason and Lara are here, too. I saw them in the computer room."

"I think it's pretty cool that you all get to teach," Harrison said, swiveling around on his chair to face them. "I've always thought I'd be good at it."

"Too bad we don't need another professor in IT," Jason Lawton said, his eyes speculative as he strolled into the room. Lara followed behind him, deep in conversation with Owen. Despite herself, Tyler shivered, just seeing him sending her nerves into overdrive.

"There's always room for someone new," Lara Prescott said, laying her hand on Jason's arm. The two of them were almost inseparable. The CIA's rules about fraternization were overlooked here at Sunderland. Given the nature of their work, it was easier to form liaisons with people who got it, although Tyler had always thought it a bit risky. After all, if things went south, it'd be really difficult to conduct business as usual.

Still, she couldn't deny the fact that with the right two people it seemed to work.

As if to emphasize the point, Annie and Nash walked in, the two of them as always seeming to exist in a separate world when they were together. There were times Tyler actually envied their relationship. But only occasionally and never with any lasting conviction. She was happier on her own. It was as simple as that.

Not that she hadn't had opportunities. She and Emmett had come close to starting something once. But she'd stopped it before it had gotten out of hand. And now, years later, she was glad they'd just stayed friends. It was easier.

She moved around the table to sit beside Annie, trying not to watch as Owen crossed the room to shake hands with Harrison.

"He's hot," Annie whispered, her hazel eyes appreciative. "I always did have a weakness for British men."

"Watch it, Red," Nash said. "I'll have to challenge him to a duel or something."

"God, I hope not." Owen laughed as he sat down across from Tyler. "I was abysmal at fencing. A total laughingstock at school."

"Somehow I doubt that," Tyler said, smiling despite herself. It was hard to imagine that Owen ever failed at anything.

"No one's perfect, Tyler," Jason groused, clearly still annoyed at Harrison's presence.

"Good to see everyone's here," Avery said, striding into the room. "And I can see you've already met Harrison. We're lucky to have someone of his caliber joining us."

Harrison ducked his head in embarrassment as Jason coughed surreptitiously. Nash looked amused, and Emmett irritated, but neither of them said anything.

"I think it's going to be great," Hannah said, sounding more enthusiastic than she'd sounded in years.

"Good, that's just want I wanted to hear," Avery said, as he walked to the front of the room. As usual he was perfectly groomed, his khakis creased, his white button-down crisp. Years in the military had a way of making a man compulsive about neatness. Her dad had always insisted that his civvies be kept up to military standards. It had been the bane of his many wives' existence, but Tyler had always thought it made him look more powerful. Of course, now all that was gone. These days, according to Della, he sometimes forgot to get dressed at all.

She swallowed, her eyes tightening with tears. Fortunately, they knew better than to drop. Tyler didn't cry.

"So," Avery said, "I assume everyone's read the briefing papers and we're all up to speed. Which means we'll be able to hit the ground running. Hannah, why don't you tell us what you've got so far?"

"Where do you want to start? There's the scene in Colorado, the parking garage, and the forensics in Tyler's house." She crossed over to join them at the table, flipping up a concealed computer screen. Harrison dropped down next to her, propping his laptop on his knees.

"Let's start with the forensics. Harrison, I assume Hannah filled you in?"

"She did." He nodded, looking up from his computer. "But isn't there someone missing? Drake Flynn?"

"He's on leave," Lara said. "He had a rough go of it recently, and he's taking some time."

"To romance Madeline," Jason offered, quirking his eyebrows.

"Well, if he hadn't, I might have." Emmett grinned.

"They're not always this bad," Tyler said, "but Drake kind of took us by surprise on this one."

"Not the type to risk involvement?" Owen asked, his gaze meant for her alone.

Tyler frowned, shaking her head in warning, but thankfully no one was paying attention. "He's just more cautious than most," she gritted out. "Which isn't a bad way to go, if you ask me."

"I don't know," Annie said, smiling up at her husband, "sometimes it's better just to give in. I mean, we tried to stay apart, and look where it got us."

"Married." Avery smiled. "But this isn't getting us anywhere. Hannah?"

"Right," she said, pushing her glasses up onto her nose. "As you know, I spent most of the evening going over the surveillance tapes. And despite the fact that

Tyler's bag made its way from her office to her house, there's nothing on the tapes to indicate how it got there. The suitcase seems to have just appeared."

"Which we know is impossible," Tyler said. "I assume you've checked with Nash and Annie?" She looked over at Nash, who shrugged.

"Hannah called first thing this morning. It wasn't us."

"And we didn't see anyone either," Annie said. "And I was home most of the afternoon, at least until Adam and I headed out to soccer practice."

"So someone must have doctored the tapes," Jason said. "Did you check to see if there were signs of tampering?" It was clear he was still annoyed at being left out of the loop.

"I ran the diagnostics programs and couldn't find anything." She shot him an apologetic look and then turned back to Avery. "But I've asked Harrison to go over it again. Maybe he'll find something I missed."

"Or maybe I should take a look?" Jason suggested.

"Too many chiefs," Avery said, shaking his head. "Besides, I need you monitoring day-to-day activities. This operation is important, but it isn't the only thing we're working on."

"Got it." Jason raised a hand and sat back in his chair, clearly accepting the inevitable.

"Anyway," Hannah continued, "for the moment at least, we've got nada on the surveillance."

"Except that someone managed to spirit my suitcase into the house." Tyler frowned, the news doing nothing to ease the worry that had been gnawing at her since last night. "What about fingerprints?"

"Nothing solid. Yours, of course. And Nash's and Annie's. Jason's turned up in a couple of places."

"We're over at Tyler's a lot," Lara said, tilting her head to one side as she watched everyone, her expression hard to read. Lara tended to keep to herself, so much so that it was impossible sometimes to guess what she was thinking. An asset in the field, but a definite liability in a friend.

"We all are," Nash said, opening his hands as he shrugged.

"What about the suitcase?" Avery asked.

"There was one interesting result, actually," Hannah said, turning to look at Owen, her eyes blinking owlishly behind her glasses. "Your print was found on the suitcase. On the side. We had a hell of a time pulling a match. It's not in any of our systems. But you had a glass of water when we met in Avery's office."

"And you pulled the print from there," Owen said, clearly unperturbed by the looks of accusation coming from Emmett and Jason.

"So how did your print get on Tyler's suitcase?" Emmett asked, his tone protective.

"He helped at the hotel," she said, shooting him a look for verification. "I know I mentioned we ran into each other."

"You did," Avery said, his dark eyes meeting hers. "Which obviously explains the fingerprint. Anything else?"

"There are a couple of partials we haven't been able to identify—either because there isn't enough to make a match or because they're not in the system. We're checking against airline security to clear anyone who moved the bag in the airport. And we're also working to enhance the others so that we can confirm identity. Unfortunately, it just takes time."

Avery nodded, crossing his arms over his chest. "What about the doorknob? The one in the kitchen?"

"Just Owen's prints. Anything else was either wiped clean or his fingers obscured anything else that was there."

"I'm sorry," Owen said, raising a hand. "I should have thought to be more careful. I'm afraid my first thought was to get to Tyler."

"Definitely the right reaction." Nash nodded approvingly.

"Yes, but now we don't have any clue who was trying to get in," Jason said, as he studied Owen.

"I said, sorry," he repeated.

"For all we know, the door's been open since before I left," Tyler said, surprised at her need to protect Owen. "Or maybe the wind blew it open. It slammed a door last night. Scared the hell out of us, actually."

"Us?" Emmett queried.

"Owen was kind enough to stay with Tyler last night. On my orders." Avery's tone brooked no argument.

Emmett shrugged. "Just trying to keep an eye out for Tyler."

"Thanks." She smiled over at her friend. "It's nice to know you've got my back."

"We all do," he said, his answering smile including the entire company. "Sorry if I came on a bit strong, Owen."

"No worries." Owen shrugged. "If you were invading my team I'd be just as suspicious. It only speaks well of all of you. You're a close-knit unit, and that makes outsiders all the more difficult to suss out. Anyway, Harrison and I are only here to help. For whatever that's worth."

"Sounds like we've covered all the bases," Avery said.

"But I'd definitely like you to continue with your assessment of the tapes, Harrison. The way I see it someone's got to have tampered with them to cover up bringing in the suitcase, and quite possibly earlier when they broke in to steal Tyler's scarf."

"Unless it was taken at the same time?" Lara suggested.

"A definite possibility," Avery agreed. "This whole thing has the ring of someone who wants to play with Tyler's head."

"Or fuck with us all," Nash said.

"Also a possibility. Emmett, why don't you coordinate another search of Tyler's house. Property included. I want to make sure there isn't another way in, some way that would avoid being caught on camera."

"Ever since we had trouble with Annie," Jason said, "we've made certain that the perimeter behind the houses is secure."

"But the fact remains that I got around it," she added sheepishly. "And if I could do it—"

"Exactly," Avery said. "Which is why we need to check every possibility."

"Don't worry, I'll handle it," Emmett said.

"So what about Petrov?" Avery asked. "Did you find anything new?"

The group listened as Emmett related what he'd already told Tyler.

"So we can't conclusively say that the attack was predicated by the heist." Nash frowned.

"Not with the connection to di Silva. His operations have been crippled of late, but that only gives him motive for revenge."

"But why me?" Tyler asked.

"It was you who blew the stash," Emmett said. "Hell, maybe he was after all of you."

"Well let's keep digging. Jason, you can help Emmett with that."

Jason nodded, popping up another computer screen.

"All right, then," Avery said, his gaze encompassing them all, "where are we with forensics at the scene in Colorado?"

"As expected, there weren't any fingerprints," Hannah said. "And the Army techs went over everything twice, including the motorcycle."

"Was it registered?"

"Yes, to a Walker Mason." Hannah nodded, consulting her notes. "He reported it stolen five days ago. According to the police report, it was taken from his garage. It's separated from the house and at night basically open to anyone who wants access."

"What do we know about Mason?" Nash asked.

"He's local to the area. No warrants or arrests. No record. Nothing to indicate that he's telling anything but the truth. He's had the bike for about five years. Kept the license up to date. It's just too easy to track him down for him to be involved."

"Unless it's a smoke screen," Jason offered.

"We certainly can't eliminate that possibility," Hannah began, "but—"

"Actually, we can," Harrison interrupted. "I just checked and Mason's alibi is good. Unbreakable actually. His wife was delivering a baby. He was at a hospital in Colorado Springs all night."

Tyler's thoughts flew to Roger Mather and his unborn

child, her heart constricting. Across the table, Owen's eyes met hers, his gaze full of sympathy as he followed the train of her thoughts. "There wasn't anything you could do," he mouthed.

She nodded, not sure that the words helped, but soothed somehow nevertheless.

"How about the transport truck?" Nash asked. "Has there been any sign of it?"

"Yes, as a matter of fact," Hannah said. "They found it early this morning. Abandoned on a logging road about twenty-five miles from the scene. Nothing to indicate whether the detonators were transported inside. General Fisher's men are going over it with a fine-tooth comb. But so far, it's totally clean."

"So we're obviously dealing with professionals," Avery said to no one in particular.

"What about the scarf?" Owen asked. "Did it turn up?"

"No." Hannah shook her head apologetically in Tyler's direction. "And I asked them to search again. There was no sign of it."

"So we're saying it wasn't there?" Lara questioned, her guileless blue eyes trained on Tyler.

"We're saying nothing of the sort." Avery shook his head. "Anyone could have taken it. Either before they discovered the heist, or even afterward. Tyler, you said you had it at one point, right?"

"Yeah. I did. But the wind blew it away. So maybe that's what happened. It just got caught on the breeze."

"Or maybe it's just another way to play with your head," Emmett suggested.

"I'd say it's a definite possibility." Avery turned to

Harrison. "Any chance you can find out if anyone has been asking questions about Tyler's mother's death? Maybe the police? Or the newspapers that covered it at the time?"

"Not a problem," Harrison said. "I should be able to have some answers within the hour."

"One other thing," Hannah reported, her face scrunched up as she considered her words. "The damage to the railing was definitely fresh. But it couldn't have come from the motorcycle. The indentations were too high. More consistent with a larger vehicle."

"Like a car?" Annie queried.

"Or small truck," Hannah agreed with a nod. "And the skid marks were all wrong, too. Not the same size as the motorcycle tires. And from the photographs, while it matches the railing damage, it doesn't work with the way the motorcycle was positioned. And the tire tread doesn't match either."

"I should have seen that." Tyler clenched her fists, angry at herself for missing so obvious a clue.

"Blinding glimpse of the obvious," Emmett offered. "We see what we want to see."

His words echoed Owen's, and without volition she turned to him, seeking some kind of absolution.

"Emmett's right." Owen nodded, his dark eyes gentle. "In the heat of the moment, it's hard to see everything."

She could tell that he'd meant what he said, but somehow it still wasn't enough to make the knot in her gut go away.

"There's no point in rehashing the past," Avery admonished. "Those detonators are on the move, and our only hope of finding them is to dig deep and move quickly. What about the chatter? Anything new there?"

"The boards are lighting up," Jason said. "But nothing definitive. Just talk about the heist. No hint at all as to who might be behind it."

Hannah nodded her agreement. "And the investigation into General Fisher and the men with Tyler are no-gos as well. They've all got clean records, with no skeletons to hide."

"Everyone has skeletons," Lara put in.

"Well, if they do, they're got them buried pretty deeply. I checked phone records, bank accounts, police files. All the usual sources. There was nothing to sound an alarm."

"Somewhere out there, there's got to be a clue," Tyler said, her frustration crescendoing. "We've just got to find it."

"And we will. It just takes time," Hannah assured her.

"Time, we don't have," Annie said, her words echoing all of their thoughts as a cell phone on the table next to Hannah began to ring.

"Excuse me," Hannah mouthed, as she headed to the corner.

"One good thing," Avery interjected, pulling their attention away from the phone call. "The protocols for the detonators weren't on the truck, which will make it damn difficult for anyone to use them."

"Yes, but from what I can tell," Jason added, looking up from his computer, "there weren't any fail-safes to protect them either. Someone with the right clearance could easily have lifted them off a computer—secure or otherwise."

"So you're saying anyone could have access. With the right connections, I mean." Harrison sighed, typing something into his computer.

"Obviously, the defense lab's security has been tightened since the theft, but there was definitely a window of opportunity," Jason said. "Both before and immediately after the detonators were taken."

"I've got news," Hannah said with a frown, as she rejoined the group, "That was Langley. They've managed to track down the source of the original order for A-Tac's involvement."

"And…" Avery prompted.

"It isn't good." Hannah's gaze moved to Tyler's. "It seems that the original request came from your father."

CHAPTER 9

McLean, Virginia

Still nothing?" Owen asked as they drove down a street in her father's neighborhood. "No." Tyler shook her head, disconnecting her cell phone. "And it's odd. I told her I'd call when the plane landed."

Tyler had contacted her stepmother as soon as Hannah's pronouncement had sunk in. She'd explained that she needed to talk to her father and that she'd be on the next plane. Della tried to dissuade her, arguing that her father was having a particularly bad spell, rambling on about debts of honor and how this wasn't a good time. But Tyler had insisted. And Della had acquiesced, saying that her father had been asking for her anyway.

In short order, Hannah and Jason had everything arranged. At Avery's insistence, Owen was accompanying her. And although she'd protested Owen's coming at first—partly because she hadn't wanted company and partly because it was Owen—now that they were almost there, she had to admit she was glad to have him along for moral support.

"Maybe they've gone out and just aren't getting reception," Owen said, pulling her from her tumbling thoughts. "Or maybe they're out in the garden."

The idea of her father doing yard work was laughable, but it was just easier to agree. "I suppose it's possible," she replied, looking out the window, unable to shake her worry. "It's just that this is all sort of overwhelming. You know? And I told her to stay put. She knows this is important—even if she doesn't know why."

"But she'd also have known it would be hours before we could get here. Maybe there was a doctor's appointment or something."

"I suppose you're right. And I'm sure there's a perfectly logical explanation for my father's involvement. But at the moment, I've haven't got a clue what it could be. Turn left here," she said, nodding toward the upcoming intersection.

Twenty minutes outside of D.C., McLean was a gentrified area for Washington insiders. The homes were both large and elegant with immaculate lawns, and all the other accoutrements of wealth. Tyler'd been surprised when her father had decided to retire here. But she figured it had been Della who'd pressed him into it. She'd always had a penchant for living high off the hog.

Her father's house was one of the smallest on the block, but it was as lovely as any of its neighbors—Federal style with green shutters and double doors. Stately trees studded the front yard, their leaves shimmying in the wind. They pulled up at the curb, and Tyler frowned. "That's my father's car in the driveway."

"Maybe I was right about the garden. Or maybe they took the other car. I assume Della has one?"

"Of course." She smiled, despite her unease. "This is America. We're crazy about our cars."

"And conspicuous consumption." He nodded toward the house as he turned off the engine.

"Well, that's more Della than my father. She has certain ideas when it comes to their public persona. But like I said," Tyler shrugged, "she makes him happy."

"Are you an only child?" he asked as they stepped out of the rental car.

"No," she said with a shake of her head. "Quite the opposite actually. I have an assortment of stepsiblings, most of whom I've never even met. My father didn't exactly inspire familial loyalty. And then there's my half-brother, Mark. Della's his mom. He's in grad school at Johns Hopkins and he's a good guy. I'm probably as close to him as anyone in the family. I guess we bonded over our dysfunction."

"Do you see him often?"

"Unfortunately, no. Between my work with the unit and his studies, it's hard to get together—but we talk when we can. And being apart doesn't change the way I feel about him."

"Does he know what you do?"

"Not specifically, no. Neither does Della. They know I work for the government, but that's all. It's just easier that way. But my dad knows." She could just imagine Della telling everyone at her bridge parties about her stepdaughter the spy.

"I'm surprised you got permission to tell your dad. My father hasn't a clue."

"Well, it was kind of hard to keep it from him. At one point, his clearance was higher than mine."

"I can see where that would make it a necessity."

"Actually, it didn't go down well. My father is old school. Little woman in the home and all that. Makes me a bit of a black sheep. But somewhere in that hard head of his, I know he's proud of me. Still, it makes it all that much more odd that he'd request my involvement in the transport."

"We don't know that he requested you. Just that he requested A-Tac."

"Except that the logical person to be involved is the munitions expert. Which would be me. And my father knew that. I told you he's a very smart man. At least when his mind is all there."

As they approached the front steps, Owen stopped and pointed, nodding toward the front doors. "Do they usually leave them open?"

"No." She shook her head, keeping her voice low, as she reached for her gun. "Della's something of a security freak. She has locks for her locks."

Owen produced his weapon and the two of them moved cautiously up onto the porch. Two large pots of chrysanthemums flanked the open doors, their gaiety a stark contrast to the splintered casing of the door.

Tyler's heart jumped to her throat as her eyes met Owen's. He signaled that he'd go first, and she nodded, lifting her gun to cover him. As they swung into the foyer, she forced herself to focus on the moment. She wouldn't be of any use to anyone if she let her imagination get the better of her.

The foyer ran the length of the front of the house, with the living room opening off to the right, and the dining room to left. The doors to the dining room were closed, but the living room was open. With their backs to the wall, they moved toward the doorway, swinging together through the opening into the room. It was empty.

"Clear," Tyler whispered, her heart thudding against her chest. There was no other entrance to the room, so they backtracked, this time flanking the door to the dining room.

"On three," Owen mouthed.

Tyler nodded, hand on the doorknob, waiting as he silently counted down. Then with a turn of her wrist, she pushed the door open, using it as a shield as she moved into the room. The large dining room table sat in the middle, its polished veneer reflecting the empty room.

"There's no one here," Tyler said, releasing a breath she hadn't realized she'd been holding. "The kitchen's through there." She nodded to a swinging door in the rear wall. They walked forward, moving in tandem, and again, on the count of three pushed through the door into the sunny yellow kitchen.

Della's favorite color.

At first Tyler thought it was empty. But there were signs of a struggle—a broken plate on the floor and a half-empty cup of coffee teetering dangerously on the edge of the counter.

"Tyler."

Owen's tone froze her blood, and she turned slowly, her heart twisting. Della lay in the breakfast room where she'd fallen, a second plate still clutched in her hand, her favorite pearls glowing white against her blood-splattered skin. Her eyes were wide with surprise and fear.

"Is she..."

Owen nodded, reaching down to gently close her eyes.

"Oh, God." Tyler's stomach threatened revolt. She took a step toward Della, and then froze, her thoughts turning to her father. "He's probably upstairs," she whispered, still staring at her stepmother. "In his office."

She turned to Owen, and he nodded at her unspoken question, urgency suddenly pushing her back into the foyer. She took the stairs two at a time, heedless now of making noise, Owen right behind her. When she reached the landing she strained for some sign that someone was here, but the hallway was silent, the only sound the plaintive call of a blue jay outside the hallway's open window.

She raced past the bedrooms, skidding to a stop outside her father's office door. He was stretched out across the desk, one arm hanging over the edge, the other reaching below it, most probably for his gun. The papers beneath him were soaked with his blood.

"Daddy," she screamed as she sprinted across the room, her only thought to get to him, to pull him back to life. She leaned down, reaching for a pulse, as Owen entered the room. "I can't find it." She forced herself to breathe, using her fingers against his wrist. His skin was cold. "Oh, God, Owen, help me."

He pushed her away, his fingers against the artery in her father's throat. "It's here. It's thready, but it's here," he said, his jaw tight with anger. "Call 911."

She nodded, whipping the phone from her pocket, fumbling as she tried to dial the numbers, her fingers shaking uncontrollably.

Owen released her father and grabbed the phone. Tyler sucked in a breath, ignoring the blood as she carefully turned her father over. His face was ashen, his lips going blue. She'd seen enough gunshot wounds to know that they were battling against time. Grabbing a sweater from the back of his chair, she wadded it into a ball, pressing it against the wound, trying to stanch the flow of blood.

"The police are on their way. And they're sending an ambulance," Owen said, his tone wonderfully calm. "Where does your father keep the medical supplies?"

Tyler sucked in a breath, forcing herself to find the words. "In the bathroom. Last door on the right, just before the stairs." She turned back to her father, the sweater now soaked with his blood. "Dad, can you hear me?"

His eyes remained closed, but she could feel his breathing now. Shallow and fast. His hands were white, the blue veins gnarled with time. The liver spots on his hands seemed so familiar, the progression of old age unnoticed as the years had gone by. But now she realized just how fragile he'd become. "Come on, Dad," she urged. "Fight. Come back to me."

Owen arrived carrying towels and bandages. "I wasn't sure what you'd need exactly. The medicine cabinet didn't run to sutures." The wail of sirens echoed through the air.

"Just the towels, I think. I need to keep pressure on the wound until the EMTs get here."

Owen handed her a neatly folded towel, and she replaced the sweater, pressing down with every ounce of strength she could find.

"Tyler," her father moaned, his voice barely more than a strangled whisper. "Is that you?"

"It's me, Daddy. I'm here. You just hang on. We're going to get you to the hospital."

Her father's hand closed around hers, his fingers tightening as he struggled to say something.

"Just stay quiet," she said, leaning down so that he could see her. "You need to save your strength."

He shook his head, his breath coming in rasps. "Need to tell you…"

"It can wait until we get you to the hospital. I'm not going anywhere."

"No." The word was forceful this time, his faded blue eyes meeting hers. "Can't wait." He opened his mouth, but closed it again, confusion and pain taking over.

"It's all right. Just rest," she said, grateful to hear the sound of footsteps on the stairs. "They'll be here any second."

His fingers fluttered against hers, and then with obvious effort he pulled her closer. "Winter…" he whispered, the effort clearly costing him. "India…winter."

"There's been no further word." Owen spoke into his cell, as he walked through the sliding glass doors. "I'm just at hospital now. The general is still in surgery. I'm on my way to find Tyler."

"So what did the police say?" Logan Palmer asked. Owen had already been through everything with Avery, but he knew that he had to tell it all again. The attack on the general would be major news. Which was just exactly what they didn't need. Still, there was time for damage control.

"They basically confirmed what I'd already surmised. Someone broke into the house and tried to kill the general, taking his wife out in the process. It's possible that our arrival is what kept the general alive, although I don't have any evidence to back that up."

"So what? You're thinking a robbery?"

"I wish I could say so, sir. It would make it all that much easier. But there was nothing missing. At least nothing that we could find. I'll need Tyler to confirm it."

"Maybe you did interrupt things."

"I don't think so. At least not a robbery. This has all the markings of an orchestrated killing. Someone wanted the general dead. Which, considering that he seems to have been at the epicenter of all of this, makes total sense. And it dovetails nicely with the attack on Tyler at the garage."

"Except that there's at least some evidence supporting the idea that Petrov's attack stemmed from the Colombian affair."

"At this point I can't say."

"Which is exactly the problem," Logan sighed. "How did Tyler react?"

"Pretty much as you'd expect. She was devastated." He clenched his hand, still seeing the horror on her face.

"I thought you said she wasn't close with her father."

"She wasn't particularly. But that doesn't mean she doesn't care. Whatever her degree of involvement, she definitely wasn't expecting to find her father dead. And judging from her reaction when we found out, I don't think she knew anything about his involvement with the request for A-Tac to be a part of the detonator transfer either."

"Or maybe," Logan was saying, "she's playing you."

"And the rest of her team? I suppose it's possible, but it doesn't seem in character."

"What the hell would you know about her character? You've only known the woman a few days. Is there something you're not telling me?"

Owen swallowed, the question catching him by surprise. "Of course not. You know as well as I do that we're trained in this business to make a quick study of character. I'm just giving you my initial impressions. That's what you pay me for, right?"

"I pay you to find answers. Someone at A-Tac is guilty—and considering the general's involvement, the most likely suspect is still Tyler. And I don't need to remind you how important it is that we succeed in this investigation. If we can identify the traitors within A-Tac it's going to go a hell of a long way toward legitimizing our department. Congress gave us the power to investigate whomever we please, but respect has to be earned. And I want that respect. So no one is exempt from suspicion until we've got solid evidence proving them innocent. And that doesn't leave room for sentiment. Am I making myself clear?"

"Crystal," Owen snapped, not certain exactly why he was angry.

"So, did the general say anything?" Logan asked, shifting the conversation.

"Nothing that made any sense," Owen said, shaking his head as he forced himself to focus. "I think maybe he was trying to tell Tyler something, but if he was, he didn't succeed."

"How do you know for certain?" Logan asked. "Maybe she's just not telling you."

He'd considered the possibility, but dismissed it. She'd been too shaken to lie. And she'd also desperately wanted to make sense of his words. Unfortunately, there was no rhyme or reason.

"She's telling me the truth. But I'll ask her more about it later. And maybe when her father's out of surgery, he can explain it himself."

"Among other things," Logan's voice was devoid of emotion, but Owen knew him well enough to decipher his frustration. "What are the old man's chances?"

"I'm not sure. I do know it's touch and go. He's lost a lot of blood. And as you said, he's old. Not a great combination. But Tyler says he's a fighter."

"Just seems odd to me that he'd still pull enough weight to get the CIA to fall into line with an unauthorized request. The man's retired, after all."

"Yes, but he's a decorated veteran of three wars. Not to mention several high-ranking positions with the Pentagon. That's got to translate to some serious political capital after all these years. And it's my understanding that Avery Solomon served under the man twice."

"And what did he have to say about the revelation of General Hanson's involvement?"

"Just that he must have had a good reason to pull rank." Owen smiled, thinking of Avery's stern reaction. It was clear that he admired Tyler's father.

"Or maybe he's in this up to his neck as well. Wouldn't that just be the icing on the cake."

"You make this sound like it's personal."

"I don't like the man—I'll admit it. But for now that's all you need to know. Anyway, what did the rest of the team have to say when you told them about the attack on the general?"

"They were concerned about Tyler. I told you they're a tight-knit group. Tyler is one of their own, and so, by extension, is the general. They're looking to tie the attack into what happened to the detonators, especially given the fact that her father seems to have instigated A-Tac's involvement. But they've got the same number of leads

we do. Which for the moment doesn't add up to much."
He stopped outside the elevator bank.

"So what are your impressions of the other team members?" Logan asked. "Anyone else besides Avery or Tyler stick out as a possible suspect?"

"I've only really had the chance to interact with Nash and Hannah. And for my money they're not the double-dealing type. And despite your obvious history with the man, Avery Solomon doesn't strike me as the turn-on-his-country type. More important, he'd never put Tyler in harm's way."

"So maybe they're in it together. We said it could be more than one of them. So what about the rest of the team?"

"It's too early for me to tell. But Harrison's in place, and he'll have a chance for more direct observation."

"Not to mention a little technical eavesdropping. It's amazing how much you can learn about people if you can access their computers."

"Speaking of which," Owen said, "I have the general's computer. I told the locals it was crucial to our operation. Figured if there was anything on it, we'd want first crack."

"Good work," his boss said.

"I don't have to tell you, Logan, that this whole thing is leaving a bad taste in my mouth."

"Nature of the beast, I'm afraid. But you knew what you were signing on to when you came to work for me. So you just swallow your discomfort and do your job. If they know what you're really up to, they'll clam up. Shut you out. Even if they're innocent. There's no love lost between the NSA and the CIA, believe me."

Particularly not when it came to divisions that spied on

spies. But Owen held his tongue. The best way to get to the bottom of everything was for him to keep his eye on the ball. He needed this job. It had been his last chance. And Logan was right, Owen couldn't afford to let sentiment get in the way of his finding the truth. Especially when it came to Tyler.

"Look, Logan, I've got to go now. The elevator's here and they don't allow cell phones on the upper floors." As if to underscore the fact, an exiting nurse pointed to the cell and shook her head.

"Fine. But keep in touch."

"I will." Owen disconnected and slipped the phone back into his pocket as he hit the number for the floor where Tyler was waiting. The elevator jerked to life, and Owen stared up at the changing floor numbers, his mind spinning as he tried to assemble the puzzle pieces, hating the idea that everything still seemed to point to Tyler—or, at the very least, her father.

The doors slid open and he stepped out into the corridor, following the signs pointing to the waiting room. He loathed hospitals. The smell, the sterile environment—it all reminded him of death. He prayed that Tyler's father was in good hands and that there was still a chance. The man had clearly been close to dying. Owen had seen death enough times to recognize the signs.

He closed his eyes, summoning inner strength, banishing his memories of that awful morning in London—the high-pitched wail of the sirens, the haggard attempts to resuscitate what was already gone.

It was all in the past.

And Tyler needed him now.

The thought surprised him. Not so much for the

logic—which he'd certainly entertained before—but for the power of the emotion accompanying the desire. He blew out a breath, clearing his mind. This wasn't the time for contemplation.

"Owen."

Following the sound of his name, he turned into the waiting room. She was sitting on the edge of a rickety chair, her hands gripping the arms so tightly he thought she might break them.

"Is there any news?" he asked, crossing to her, resisting the desire to pull her into his arms. She was holding on by a thread, and she wouldn't appreciate the show of emotion. He knew because he'd been there.

"Nothing yet. It's been almost two hours."

"These things can take time. You know that yourself. You've been through it."

"Yes, but when you're the patient you don't remember any of it, really. At least until after the fact." She rubbed her hand across her shirt and the scar it concealed. "I'm just so afraid."

"I know. But there's nothing you can do except wait."

"And try to figure out who did this," she said, pushing to her feet, her arms crossed as she walked over to the window. "Did you find anything new?"

"No. Pretty much just what I told you on the phone. Does he have any enemies?"

"Thousands probably, if you count all the people he fought against. But that's not the kind of thing that promotes revenge. And he was—is—an honorable man. I can't imagine someone wanting to kill him."

"Unless he's mixed up in all this somehow. Maybe they were afraid he was going to talk."

"I've told you my dad doesn't have the mental acuity to have been a part of it. At least anything substantial."

"Well he was definitely the one who made the request for A-Tac's involvement. Hannah has proof."

"It could have been someone using his name. Or maybe somehow, someone he knew pulled him into it. And even then it still could be totally innocent. If he did do it, maybe he had a sound reason for wanting my involvement—something that has nothing whatsoever to do with the theft."

"Or maybe he wasn't in his right mind. I know it's an awful suggestion but…"

"I've thought about that." She nodded. "But I've no idea where to begin looking."

"Have you had a chance to think about what he was trying to say?"

"I've thought of pretty much nothing else," she said, turning around to face him. "But it just doesn't make sense. India winter? Is he talking about the Himalayas? Abnormal weather? Hell, for all we know it was just gibberish. Sometimes stress triggers the Alzheimer's."

"And there's nothing more stressful than being shot," Owen said, sitting down on one of the chairs. "Still, your father was a methodical man, right? By the books, one step at a time."

"How would you know that?"

"Because you said as much. Besides, given his military background, it follows. So, am I right?"

"Yes." She frowned, but came over to sit beside him. "But I'm not sure what you're getting at."

"Well, just that maybe even when his mind fritzes out he's still trying to be logical. So maybe the words make more sense than we realize. Maybe they're associated with something."

"If they are, I've got absolutely no idea. Did you talk to Avery?"

"Yes. And Hannah. She said to tell you that they're all thinking of you and your father."

She nodded, the ghost of a smile crossing her face.

"They'd have called themselves," he assured her, "but you're not allowed to use a cell up here. Anyway, as far as the attack, they're on it, trying for damage control and to dig up something associated with winter in India that actually makes sense."

"If anyone can get to the bottom of it, I'd put money on Hannah and Harrison. Especially if you throw Jason into the mix. They all know their way around a computer."

"Which reminds me, I have your father's computer. I thought maybe we'd get more use from it than the police."

"Where is it?"

"At the hotel. I figured you'd need a place to crash. So I booked rooms at the Marriot. It's not far from here."

"You think of everything." Her smile was faint, but still full of gratitude. "What about Della?" she asked, choking on her stepmother's name.

"They brought her here. They're going to do an autopsy. Standard operation in this kind of situation."

"Oh, God," she gasped, misery reflected in her eyes. "I haven't called Mark."

"No worries. I gave the police the information. I figured it'd be more than you could handle. They're going to track him down and fill him in—in person. I'm sure he'll come as soon as he can."

"God, I don't know what I'd do if you weren't here."

She ran a hand through her hair, her face lined with anxiety. "I know I should be more clearheaded. I've been trained to handle this kind of thing, after all."

"Tyler," he said, reaching over to cover her hand with his, "there's nothing that can prepare you for this. You love your father. And despite your protestations to the contrary, I suspect you cared about your stepmother, too. No one is ready to deal with losing people they love. Not even us. So right now, you just need to concentrate on your father, on his pulling through this. You said he was a fighter."

"He is. It's just that, well, he's old. I don't think I really saw it before. And, to be honest, I just don't know if his body is up to the battle. You know?"

"Well, then you'll just have to have faith."

"Did they find fingerprints?" she asked, shifting the topic. "Anything that can give us a leg up on who might have done this?"

"Nothing so far. The place was clean, surgical, almost. Like the garage and the roadside in Colorado. The only odd thing was forcing the door. But that could be explained by any number of things. Your stepmother was obviously caught by surprise. My guess is that she didn't even have time to call out."

"And then whoever it was went upstairs and shot my father. He must have recognized the danger. He was reaching for his gun." She stumbled over the words, sucking in an audible breath. "I guess he didn't have enough time."

"But it does show that he was clearheaded enough to know what to do. Which goes a long way toward supporting his ramblings as something with real meaning."

"Except that we have no idea what it is." She sighed as a man in scrubs came through the door.

"Ms. Hanson?" he asked, wearing the stoic expression of people who deal with death every day.

"That's me," she said, her fingers tightening around Owen's.

"I'm Dr. White," the man said, but Tyler cut him off, clearly uninterested in the social niceties.

"My father?"

"He came through the surgery just fine. He's in recovery now."

"Can I see him?"

"Not until he's moved to ICU," the doctor said. "One of the nurses will come and get you when he's situated."

"ICU?" Her grip on Owen's hand increased. "I thought you said he was fine."

"I said he came through the surgery. As for recovery, we'll have to wait and see. The next twenty-four hours will be crucial. If you have any further questions, the ICU nurses can help." It was clear the man was ready to move on to the next person in crisis.

Tyler seemed to have the same thought, letting the man go without further questions. "So what do we do now?" she asked, her eyes suspiciously bright.

He squeezed her hand, wishing there were something he could say to take away the pain—make everything all right. But there was nothing. So he settled for the obvious. "We wait."

CHAPTER **10**

They were standing outside the ICU, Tyler pacing as she waited for the all-clear to see her father. It seemed she'd been in the hospital forever. And despite the fact that she wanted to be with her father, there was another part of her that wanted to be out there working to find the people responsible for killing Della and putting his life in danger.

She knew intellectually that there was every possibility that the attack on her father was unrelated to the theft of the detonators, but every particle of her being was screaming that there was a connection. And she trusted her instincts.

"How much longer?" she asked a passing nurse, trying not to sound as frustrated as she felt. The staff had been more than generous with her, answering questions and offering reassurance. There was nothing they could do to make her father come around any faster.

He'd been moved from recovery almost an hour ago,

but was still unconscious. The doctor had assured her that it was not at all unusual, considering the severity of her father's injury, for him to still be out. The bullet had torn a ventricle, and the general had required open-heart surgery to repair the damage.

"He's still not awake," the nurse said, her smile kind. "But the doctor says you can go in if you'd like. Just for a few minutes."

Relief flooded through Tyler as she looked across the hall to where Owen was standing. For a man she hadn't known a week ago, he was being amazingly supportive. And she was grateful for it. In truth, she wasn't sure what she'd have done if she'd been here on her own.

He nodded with a gentle smile, and taking a deep breath for fortification, Tyler pushed through the ICU doors. There were six units arrayed in a semicircle, with the nurses' station in the center. The cubicles were all equipped with sliding glass walls, offering at least a modicum of privacy. The nurse at the desk pointed to the far cubicle, and Tyler made her way past the beeping monitors of the other patients to look through the glass door at her father.

"He hasn't been awake at all, right?" she turned back to ask the nurse.

"No." The woman shook her head.

"So he doesn't know about my stepmother?"

The woman shook her head. "And the doctor has asked that we not tell him. At least not until he's a little stronger."

They obviously had no idea of the strength of will of the man lying in the hospital bed, but Tyler didn't see any sense in arguing the fact. They'd find out soon enough.

She nodded and turned back to the cubicle, pushing aside the sliding door.

Her father lay on the bed, eyes closed, his large frame seemingly dwarfed by all the machines working to keep him alive. His hair, now snowy white, curled wildly against the pillow. He'd always been proud of the fact that he'd not lost his hair, but it had only been with retirement, and a little coaxing by Della, that he'd let it grow longer than his customary buzz cut.

One of the machines clicked rhythmically as she pulled the single chair close to the bed, her hand closing around her father's. "Dad?" The words came out on a strangled whisper as she fought against the rising lump in her throat. "It's Tyler. You're in ICU. You've had surgery, but the doctor says you're going to be fine."

She waited, hoping against hope that he'd open his eyes and tell her everything was going to be all right. He'd always been a strict disciplinarian, but he was also the first to offer praise when it was called for. And he'd saved her from her childhood torments on more than one occasion. Her very own knight in shining armor.

Things had changed when she'd gotten older and more capable of taking care of herself. She'd longed to be like her father, desperate to prove she wasn't weak like her mother. But the stronger she'd become, the greater the distance between them. By following in his footsteps, she'd effectively pushed him away.

And while she wouldn't have changed the decisions she made, she wasn't above wishing that the cost hadn't been losing her relationship with her father.

"Who's there?" Her father's voice was weak, but there was still command in it.

"It's me, Daddy," she said, squeezing his hand. "Welcome back."

"Where'd I go?" he asked, clearly confused, his eyes searching wildly for something familiar.

"You're in the hospital," she repeated. "You were shot. But you're going to be fine."

"And my unit?" he barked. "How many casualties?"

"It wasn't a battle, Dad." She closed her eyes, praying to find the right words. "It happened at home."

"Oh." He blinked, seeming to let her words settle in. "Tyler?" he said.

"Yes. It's me," she repeated. The nurse had said that he'd be confused. The sedatives combined with his dementia would act together to impair his ability to reason.

"Good. Need to talk," he rasped, one of the monitors protesting the action.

"Dad, you need to rest. We can talk later."

"No," he said, his voice gaining strength. "Now. Might not be a later." His eyes cleared for an instant and she was certain that he really saw her. "You have to forgive me."

"For what?" She'd expected more cryptic talk. Not an apology.

"My duty. No choice."

"I don't understand," she said, leaning over so that she could hear him better.

"Didn't mean for anyone to get hurt," he mumbled. "Should have known better." His eyes closed, and for a moment she thought he'd fallen back asleep. But then he opened his eyes, his fingers gripping her wrist. He struggled for words, the confusion back again. Clarity fading.

"Winter," he murmured, repeating the word he'd said

in his study. "Debt. Indian. I shouldn't have…" The last words faded out to less than a whisper.

"Dad, can you hear me?" she asked, her mind scrambling to find sense in his words. "Dad?"

"It's the medication," a nurse said, as she bustled into the room, adjusting the beeping monitor. "He's not going to make a lot of sense. And I understand he's early-stage Alzheimer's. That's only going to complicate matters. Best we let him sleep now. Maybe he'll be clearer tomorrow."

Tyler nodded, still fighting her emotions, and leaned down to kiss her father's forehead. His skin was clammy and pale. The nurse cleared her throat, and Tyler forced herself to walk away. The woman was right—her father needed his rest, but she hated to leave.

She'd made it past the nurses' station when the monitors erupted in furious cacophony. She turned around, frozen, as two nurses pushed their way into her father's room, a third calling a code over the intercom, and a fourth going for a crash cart in the corner.

"What's happening?" she asked, as she rushed forward, frantic to reach her father.

"His heart's stopped," one of the nurses answered, pushing past her and then sliding the door shut, effectively sealing her out.

Tyler stood rooted to the spot, watching with horror as they tried to bring her father back, but she knew just from looking at him that he'd stopped fighting. Hands shaking, she tried to open the door herself, certain that if she could get inside she could somehow will him to live. But the door wouldn't move. And she watched one of the nurses look up at the clock—mouthing the words "time of death."

"No." Someone shouted, and Tyler looked to see who it

was, only to realize the voice was her own. She pounded on the glass, unable to manage the door, and then hands pulled her away, hands she recognized.

"He's gone," Owen's words forced themselves through her beleaguered brain.

"But he was just talking to me," she whispered, her chest constricting so tightly she wasn't certain she could breathe.

"You have to let him go." Owen's arms slid around her. "There's nothing else you can do."

"There wasn't time to tell him I loved him," she said, turning to bury her face in his chest—needing to draw on his strength.

"He knew. I promise you, he knew."

She nodded against his chest, the monitors finally silent, the nurses going back to their normal activities. In the ICU, death was an everyday occurrence.

For her, it was anything but ordinary.

Her father was dead.

Tyler steeled herself, pushing away from Owen, embarrassed at her lapse. There was one thing she could still do for her father—she could avenge his death. But she couldn't do it if she fell apart. She had to be strong.

"We've got to find the people who did this," she said, fists clenched, as she stood staring at her father's lifeless body.

"We will," Owen promised, his hands closing around her shoulders. "And I swear we'll make them pay."

Owen hung up the phone, turning back to Tyler, who was sitting in a waiting room chair. "That was Avery. He said for you to take whatever time you need."

"I'm not sure what to do." She shook her head, her gaze still locked on the doors leading to the ICU. "I know I should stay here and make arrangements. They've both got to be buried. But I also need to figure out why all this is happening. And to stop the bastards that did this."

"I know," Owen soothed. "But you've hardly had time for it all to sink in. You need time to grieve, Tyler."

"I need to do something," she said, pushing away from him, pacing restlessly in the corridor. "Don't you understand? It's the only thing that's going to keep me sane."

"Well, there's nothing more you can do tonight. So at least let me take you back to the hotel. We can regroup and figure out our next move."

"I'm sorry I dragged you into all of this," she said, reaching up to loosen her ponytail and then tighten it again.

"We're working together on this, remember? There's no place else I want to be."

The elevator doors slid open and a young man with dark windswept hair stepped into the corridor.

"Mark," Tyler said, the name sounding like the answer to a prayer. And for just a moment Owen felt the pull of jealousy. Ridiculous notion. He pushed it aside, waiting while the half-siblings embraced. "Did they tell you?" she murmured, pulling back to look her brother in the face.

"Yeah," he said, sucking in a breath. "But I can't believe it. I kept telling myself all the way over here that it had to be some kind of mistake." He reached for her hand, his eyes full of tears. "But it's true, isn't it?"

She nodded. "I'm so sorry. I tried to get there, but I was too late."

"You couldn't have known this was going to happen. And if you'd been there, I'd have lost you, too."

"I should have been there. I should have stopped it."

"Tyler, don't be crazy. There's nothing you could have done."

Owen waited, wondering how much she'd tell her brother, but she only shook her head.

"I was on my way. He knew I was coming. If I'd just gotten to the house sooner."

"Stop it," Mark said, leaning back, his gaze locked with hers. "This isn't your fault. You'd have done anything for them. And they knew it."

She studied his face for a moment, then sighed, pulling free, seeming to accept his words, at least for the moment. Owen knew better than to believe her guilt, however unfounded, could so easily be assuaged.

"This is my friend, Owen Wakefield. We've been working together. And he was with me when we found them."

Mark offered his hand, and Owen shook it. "I'm so sorry for your loss." The words were totally insufficient. He'd heard the same a thousand times. And never once had they brought comfort.

"I'm just glad my sister wasn't alone," Mark said, his eyes filled with gratitude. "She always tries cover it up, but she's not as strong as she'd have everyone believe. No matter what she says. Family is everything. And now we're all we've got." He choked out the last words and Tyler reached for his hands again.

"Have you seen your mom?"

"Yeah. I went there first. I didn't know about Dad. I thought I had time. And now...now..." he trailed off, his own grief reflected in his eyes.

"He wasn't lucid. I'm not even sure he knew who I was," Tyler said, her voice low and soothing. "It all happened so fast."

"Oh, God, Tyler, I can't imagine life without him in it. I mean, we hardly ever saw eye to eye and sometimes he could be a real son of a bitch, but I loved him."

"I know." She reached up to wipe away her brother's tears. "I loved him, too. And he knew that. He did. And he was so proud of you, Mark. He was always talking about how well you were doing in school and how you were going to change the world."

"Is he still in there?" He nodded toward the ICU.

"Yeah, I asked them to wait. I knew you'd want to see him."

"I can't believe any of this. I keep expecting to wake up and find out this is all a nightmare. How can they both be gone? I just talked to Mom this morning."

"Did she sound worried about anything?" Tyler asked.

"You mean something that would explain what happened? No. She was fine. Worried about Dad as usual. He'd been having a particularly bad spell, I think. I promised I'd come home for the weekend. It all seemed so normal at the time. If only I'd known..."

"There wasn't anything you could have done," she said, struggling to reassure her brother. The two of them protecting each other, coming together in their grief. It touched Owen's heart in a way he'd not thought possible.

Mark nodded, squaring his shoulders. "I'm sorry. I didn't mean to fall apart on you. It's just so hard to contemplate losing them both."

"I know."

"So do they have any idea who did this?" He stepped back, studying them both.

"No. I haven't heard anything. I swear. I'm just as confused as you are."

"So why were you here? I mean you said you were on the way to the house." He looked confused now, as if reality was just now sinking in.

"I was just hoping Dad could help me with something I've been working on. You know how good he—he was with a puzzle," she said tripping over the past tense. "Anyway, if I knew anything definitive, I'd tell you." Owen admired the way she handled her brother, clearly caring enough to shield him from the worst of it. Not to mention protecting the operation.

Mark searched her face for a moment more, and then nodded. "Okay. I guess I'll go and see him now. You'll be here when I get back?"

"I'm not leaving you," Tyler said, reaching up to touch his face. "We'll handle it all together. Okay?"

He nodded and pushed through the ICU doors.

"He seems like a good guy," Owen said.

"He is. And he's handling this better than I'd have expected. I think he's trying to be strong for me."

"Well, that's what brothers are for."

"Big brothers maybe. But it's my job to take care of him now. He's all I've got left. You know?"

They waited in silence, the minutes seeming to stretch on endlessly, and then Mark was back, his cheeks streaked with tears. "He was so still. Like he was asleep. I kept wanting to reach out and try to wake him. But maybe this is for the best, right? I mean he was just going to get sicker. And he'd have hated that."

"But he'd have been alive," Tyler whispered, her hands clenched again into fists.

"Anyway," Mark said, taking a deep breath, "tomorrow I'll make arrangements."

"I'll be there with you."

"No," he shook his head, "you won't."

She looked up at him, startled, then shot a questioning glance in Owen's direction.

"Look, Tyler," Mark said, "I don't know what happened here. I'm not even sure I want to know. But I do know that you're in a position to do something about it."

"I don't..." She shook her head, but her brother put his finger to her lips.

"Don't deny it. Dad told me what you do. At least some of it."

"Then why didn't you say something?"

He shrugged. "I just figured if you wanted me to know you'd tell me. Anyway, the point is that someone murdered our parents. And I need to know that the people who did it are going to be brought to justice. So while I take care of things here, I want you out there working to find out who did this. I need you to do that for me, okay?"

"Mark's right," Owen said. "We're the only ones who are truly motivated to find answers. But to find them, you're going to have to leave this hospital."

"I can't just leave my father here on his own."

"He's got me, Tyler. So it'll be all right." Mark looked to Owen for support, and for a moment he remembered what it was like to be a part of a family. But he pushed the thought away. He was only a passing stranger in their lives. A lying one at that.

"What do you say I take you back to the hotel?" Owen said, ending the conversation where it had begun. "Mark can keep you updated. And we'll do the same for him. Sound like a plan?"

"I don't know," Tyler said, looking first at Owen and then at her brother. "I think I should stay. We should do this together. You need me."

"What I need is for you to figure out who did this," Mark said. "It's the only way we're ever truly going to be able to lay this to rest."

CHAPTER 11

How are you holding up?" Owen asked as they stepped off the hotel elevator and headed for their rooms.

"I'm okay. I'm just concentrating on going one minute to the next," Tyler said, knowing the words were a lie. She was far from okay, but giving in to her grief wasn't going to help anyone. There'd be time to mourn her father. Just not now. "I'm still not sure I should have left Mark on his own. It just seems like I'm deserting him."

"You're not. Think of it as a two-pronged attack. He's handling things on the logistics end so that you can deal with finding the culprits."

"On an intellectual level, I know you're right, but my heart is screaming that I should be with my father."

"Yes, but given a choice you know he'd want you to fight." Owen stopped in front of a set of doors.

"I know he would. I do. It's just hard." She sighed. "Which one's mine?"

"I put your things in 202," he said, holding out a key-card. "I'm here, in 204. The rooms connect. I figure that way I can watch over you without being in your face."

"That wasn't necessary," she said, thinking that the last thing she needed was proximity to Owen Wakefield. She'd already leaned on him far too much. Caring was dangerous. And for the first time since Justin she felt as if she were teetering on the brink. "I can take care of myself."

"I don't doubt that for an instant, but your friends at Sunderland would never forgive me if I let something happen to you."

"I suppose that's a point," she conceded, taking the key.

"Do you want me to come in with you?" he asked, his eyes telegraphing his concern.

"No. I think I'd like some time on my own, if you don't mind. I know there's a lot to discuss, but we can talk later. And don't worry, I'll unlock my side of the connecting door." She gave him the ghost of a smile. "To give you piece of mind. I mean you're right about Avery and Nash, you don't want to get on their bad side."

Tyler slid the key through the lock, and the light glowed green. She pushed open the door, a whoosh of refrigerated air smacking her in the face even though it was early October. Letting the door close behind her, she walked inside, the effort just to take the next step almost more than she could bear. So instead, she stood in the room's cool darkness, eyes closed, wishing that she'd wake up and find all of this a bad dream.

Instead, she heard a tiny noise. An infinitesimal click.

But it was a sound she recognized. Adrenaline surged as she hit the floor, drawing her gun and firing as bullets strafed the door behind her. Her assailant fired once more

and moved to the window. The curtains billowed, his profile highlighted for a moment, but before she could get off
a second shot, he jumped.

Tyler screamed for Owen as she pulled to her feet and
ran for the window. Outside, the night was still, the parking lot below filled with cars and shadows, but no sign of
the intruder. She waited, gun ready, not daring to breathe,
but nothing moved. The man was gone.

Behind her, Owen was pounding on the adjoining
door, the adjacent wall shaking with each contact. She
thought about going out the window and giving chase, but
there was nothing to give her an idea of which direction
he'd gone. So, with a sigh, she turned and walked back
to the connecting door, freeing the lock and stepping
back as it burst open, Owen's face black with anger as he
brandished his gun.

"Are you all right?"

"I'm fine," she said, slipping her gun back into its holster.
"I'm not so sure about the door, though." Pinpricks of light
showed through it like some macabre Lite-Brite pattern.

"Bloody hell." He stood for a moment staring at the
bullet holes, then turned to face her. "Where the fuck did
the bugger go?"

"Out the window." She held back a smile as she watched
him cross over to have a look, his shirt untucked, his hair
going every which way. She'd never seen him so flustered,
and despite the seriousness of what had just happened, his
disarray amused her. "Whoever he was, he's long gone.
I was behind him by only a few seconds and there was
already nothing to see. It's just too dark out there."

"Did you at least get a look at him?"

"Only his profile. So all I can be sure of is that it *was*

a 'him.' It was darker in here than it was outside." She reached over to flip the light switch, blinking as the lamps flickered to life. Other than the holes in the door, the room looked unharmed, her suitcase sitting benignly at the end of the bed. "There's nothing out of place."

"Mine's untouched, too," Owen said. "I was just reaching for my bag when the shots rang out. I've got to tell you those were the longest couple of minutes of my life."

"Seemed pretty fast on this side of the door. Sort of duck or die. I'm not even sure how I knew he was in the room. Thought I heard a click. Maybe the safety. I don't know." She sank down on the end of the bed, her energy sapping as quickly as it had come.

"Any chance you hit him?" he asked, dropping into the chair across from the bed.

"I don't think so. I only got off one round and I was shooting wild. He certainly didn't act like he was injured. But it all happened really fast..." She trailed off, reality hitting like an IED, shrapnel hurtling through her, threatening to tear her apart.

"You all right?" Owen asked, his face tightening with concern.

"Yeah." She nodded, shaking off her thoughts. "I just realized what a close call that was. The whole time I was thinking that the shooter was after my father's computer. But it wasn't in here. And the room was dark. He was just waiting—waiting for me. Owen, the man wasn't here to steal anything—he was here to kill me."

"Feel better?" Owen asked as Tyler stepped out of the bathroom, towel in hand, her hair slicked back in a ponytail, her face still flushed from her shower. She was

wearing a pair of sweats and the same camisole she'd
worn when they'd…He shook his head, clearing his
thoughts. Best to keep his mind off the soft curves of her
breasts and focus instead on the situation at hand.

They'd moved hotels, opting to share a room in light
of the need for security. And just to be certain, two local
CIA officers were stationed outside. Another group from
Langley had also run interference with the first hotel,
scouring the scene for evidence as well as signs of the
intruder. So far, not unexpectedly, there'd been nothing.

"The shower helped." She nodded, tossing the towel
into the corner. "But I won't feel better until we nail the
bastard behind all of this."

"Well, I'm afraid we've got our work cut out for us,"
Owen said, frowning down at the notes he'd made. He'd
called Logan and filled him in, then suffered through
his boss's continued pontification on the importance of
weeding out bad seeds. Logan's sights were still centered
on Tyler. And despite everything that had happened,
Owen found that he couldn't dismiss the idea either.
Which left him feeling conflicted on more levels than
he could count. None of which he wanted to examine in
any detail.

While he'd been on the phone with Logan, Tyler
had talked with Avery, and then while she was being
debriefed, Owen had talked with Harrison. So far they
hadn't found anything that might help identify the man
who'd attacked Tyler. Whoever he was, he'd been a professional. No fingerprints. No fibers. "Nothing."

"Come again?" Tyler said, eyebrows raised in confusion.

"I'm sorry. I didn't realize I'd spoken out loud. I was

just thinking that we still don't have anything to go on. These people always seem to be one step ahead."

"Have you tried my dad's computer?" she asked, sitting cross-legged on the bed opposite the one he was lying on.

Clearly she had absolutely no idea the effect she had on a man. The men in A-Tac had to be either saints or eunuchs. And since he was pretty sure they were neither, he wondered, with another insane surge of jealousy, if she'd had relationships with any of them. She'd mentioned something about going down that road before.

Still, his reaction was completely unfounded. For God's sake, she was under investigation. *His* investigation. Best case she'd hate him for lying. Worst case he'd slept with a traitor.

"Owen?" Tyler prompted, and once again he found himself shaking his head to clear his mind.

"Sorry," he said. "I was off on another tangent." A particularly lascivious one. "I haven't turned the computer on yet. I thought I'd wait for you."

"Well, no time like the present," she said, springing off the bed to retrieve the computer. Returning to the bed, she pressed the power button and for a moment the computer hummed approvingly, but then she frowned. "Something's wrong. It's not booting properly."

He came over to sit beside her, squinting down at the black screen, a cursor flashing angrily at the top. "This isn't good." He reached over her shoulders to restart and try to boot in "safe" mode, but the computer refused, presenting the blinking cursor instead.

"Damn," Tyler said, frowning as she watched him work.

He tried the procedure again, this time accessing a Help screen that offered to "fix" the problem. He hit ENTER, and waited. The computer whirred to life and then presented him with a blue screen, this one with a simple message. There was nothing to access.

The computer's data had been destroyed.

"Son of a bitch," he mumbled, blowing out a frustrated breath. "There's nothing here. Someone got to it first."

"But not in the hotel room?"

"No. The computer wasn't disturbed. I had it hidden in a drawer beneath the extra blankets. Besides, we've already established that he wasn't after the computer." His gaze met hers and for a moment there was just the two of them—and the fragile bond they'd been building. Then a shadow crossed Tyler's face and she broke away, frowning down at the computer.

"So you think they did it after they shot him? Surely there wasn't time. Did you have it checked for prints?"

"Yes." He nodded. "They found your father's prints. Which would indicate it hadn't been wiped down. But I'm guessing whoever's behind this erased it by remote. It's easy enough to implement something like that through an email or a virus. All your father would have had to do was open it, and everything's gone."

"So the damn thing's useless."

"Maybe to us," he acknowledged, "but I've seen people like Harrison do miraculous things with hardware more complicated than this. And you've already said that Jason is a whiz at this kind of stuff. We can get the guys outside to take it to Langley."

"No." She shook her head. "That's my father's private computer. There's no telling what's on there. So if we can open it, I'd rather it be someone I trust. Like Jason or even Harrison. Please? We can overnight it to Sunderland in the morning."

He hesitated for a moment. Logan would probably prefer it be sent to Langley. But Harrison was there to make sure nothing was tampered with. And he could understand wanting to protect a loved one's privacy. Even in death. "All right. We'll do it your way."

She nodded her thanks, then frowned. "So in the meantime all we've got are my father's ramblings. Fat lot of good that does us."

"I still think there's logic in there," he insisted. "We've just got to figure out the key."

"Winter in India?" she asked, her frustration evident. "I don't see what that could possibly have to do with anything we're dealing with."

"Well, first off, he never actually said it that way, did he?"

She thought about it a moment. "No. In the study it sounded like he said 'winter...India winter.' But in the hospital it didn't sound the same." She scrunched up her nose, trying to remember. "My mind wasn't exactly on what he was saying. Wait. In ICU, I think he said Indian, not India." She rubbed her temples, clearly willing herself to pull forth the memory. "Yes. I'm certain. It was Indian."

"Tell me exactly what he said," Owen urged.

She opened her eyes, her expression determined. "He was really confused. Even the nurse said so."

"It doesn't matter. Just try to remember the words."

She nodded. "He asked me to forgive him. But he never really said why."

"What else?"

"I don't know, everything was happening so fast. And I can't believe it's important. The man had Alzheimer's."

"Tyler, we can't know if it's important until we've gotten a look at the whole puzzle."

She started to argue, then apparently thought better of it. "Okay, um, he said something about duty and not having a choice. And then he started to fade. After that it was just words. He said 'winter' again. And then 'debt.'" She closed her eyes, concentrating. "And I'm pretty sure the last word was 'Indian.'"

"Ending with an *n* as opposed to an *a*."

"Yes, I think so. And then he started to say something else but I couldn't make it out. Then the nurse came in and asked me to leave and after that—" She cut herself off, her fingers curling into fists.

He reached out to cover her hands with his, waiting until she regained control. "All right," he said, letting her go, knowing that she needed to fight through this on her own, "we've just got to make sense of the message."

"If it is a message." Tyler frowned.

"Keep thinking about the words. What do you think he meant by 'debt.' Something monetary?"

"No." She shook her head. "When I talked to Della about our coming to see them she said Dad had been rambling on about a debt of honor. That's got to be it."

"Does that mean anything to you?"

"Nothing tangible. I mean, my father's a soldier. Honor is everything. But how that ties into regrets, and Indians, and winter, I've no idea at all." She pushed off the bed, walking over to the window, the line of her shoulders telegraphing her frustration. "This is like trying to find a firing pin in the middle of a fucking jungle."

Owen laughed and she whirled around, confusion warring with anger. He held up a hand, shaking his head in apology. "I'm sorry. I'm not trying to make light. It's just that your version of 'needle in a haystack' is so— well, I don't know, *you*. It's all about ordnance."

She ducked her head, but not before he saw the trace of a smile. God, he wanted to hold her. To promise that he'd make things all right. But he wasn't any more capable of righting her world than he was his own. Hell, considering his mission, he was more likely to blow it to bits.

"So what do we know?" she asked, coming back to sit on the bed again. "My father regretted something. Something that may or may not have been connected to the detonators disappearance. And whatever it was, it was related to a debt of honor. *His*, one would presume. And all that is possibly related somehow to the words 'Indian' and 'winter.'"

"Did he say anything else? Something that might tie this all together?"

"No." She shook her head. "At least I don't think so. Although he did say that he should have known better. Oh," she stopped, wheels turning. "I just remembered. He also said that he didn't mean for anyone to get hurt. But again that could mean almost anything."

"Or it could be referring directly to the men who died on that road in Colorado." It was his turn to try to make sense of the old man's ramblings. "You haven't talked to your father since before Colorado. Right?"

"Yeah. The first time I called home was when I called Della."

"Did you tell Della any of it? Anything she could have told your father?"

"No. I just said I needed to talk to Dad."

"Did you tell anyone else who could have told him?"

"I don't think so, but I don't see…wait a minute… I did talk to a friend of my father's. His best friend, actually. Mike Hollingsworth. He's a bigwig in the Pentagon. Worked his way up through the Army, like my father. He's like family, really. Oh, God," she sighed, "I need to tell him about Dad's death. He should hear it from me."

"If he's as connected as you say, he already knows. Word of this kind of thing travels quickly. Especially in military circles. He wouldn't expect you to drop everything to call."

"I suppose you're right. There's just so much to think about. You know?"

"Which is why we have to stay on topic." He tried to keep the words gentle, without rebuke.

"You're right. I'm sorry."

"So what made you call him?"

"General Fisher spooked me. He was so certain that I'd been part of the theft somehow." Owen felt a wash of guilt. General Fisher wasn't the only one. "I just wanted to be sure someone had my back. Someone in the military. And I trust Mike. So I called him. I kept the information need-to-know. But, technically, it was a military operation, so he already knew most of it. Anyway, he promised to see what he could do about General Fisher. It was a quick call, really. And I haven't talked to him since."

"But he probably talked to your father."

"And told him what happened," Tyler finished for him.

"But that doesn't prove that my father's remorse was directed at Mather and Gerardi's deaths."

"No." He shook his head. "But maybe Hollingsworth can help clear things up. Maybe he knows why your father wanted you to be part of the transport team. Or maybe he can tell us what your father's last words meant. It's certainly worth a try."

"You're right. If anyone knew what Dad was up to, it'd be Uncle Mike. I should have thought of it myself. It's just that…" she trailed off, looking down at her hands.

"I know it's tough," he said, sliding an arm around her. "But for what it's worth, I think your father would be really proud of you. And whatever this is, we're going to figure it out. And when we do, I promise, we'll blow this thing right out of the water."

She nodded, giving him a watery smile. "Now who's all about ordnance?"

Tyler was standing in the ICU. There was blood everywhere. Pooling on the floor, spattering the walls and ceilings. In front of her a nurse screamed and fell, clutching her side, a chrysanthemum of red bursting through her scrubs. She tilted her head, her eyes pleading, and then she slid to the floor. Dead. Dead. *They were all dead.*

Tyler spun around, trying to find the shooter. Trying to make sense of the situation. And then from somewhere behind her she heard Della calling. She turned again and Della was standing there, arms outstretched. "Tyler," she whispered. *"Help me." Blood dripped from her head, her perfectly manicured nails ragged, as if she'd tried to claw her way out of something. "Help me, Tyler."*

Tyler reached out, but something blocked her way.

Glass. It was the glass door of a cubicle. She fumbled against the smooth exterior, trying to find a handle, to pull the door open, but there was nothing. Inside, Della's cries had become more frantic. "Tyler. Please. Help me." She heard the staccato sound of gunfire. And Della fell to her knees, her arms still outstretched. "Tyler..." she whispered as the life faded from her eyes.

Another voice called across the room. Her father.

She spun around again and there he was in full military regalia.

"Tyler, what have you done?" he asked, his voice tight with anger. "What have you done?"

"Daddy, it isn't my fault," she said, holding up her hands to ward off his wrath.

"Of course it is." His face hardened, his expression condemning. "You've killed us. This is all on you."

"It wasn't me," Tyler protested, slipping in the blood as she tried to scramble backward, falling to her knees in the process. "It wasn't me."

"You have to take responsibility for your actions. It's the only way you'll ever measure up. Am I making myself clear?" He seemed to tower above her, his face mottled with rage. She shrank back, tears streaming down her face.

"It wasn't me. It wasn't me," she kept repeating the words, a mantra to hold him at bay.

Then suddenly the scene shifted, and it was her father behind the glass, his face worn and haggard. "Help me, Tyler. I don't know where I am." He stretched out a hand and she reached for him, slamming her knuckles into the glass. "You have to help me."

"I don't know how," she cried, again struggling to find a way through the door. "I can't get in."

"Yes you can," her father said. *"Use the Indian. He knows the way. It's all in the details, Tyler. The details."*

Finally she found the edge of the door, her fingers cramping as she worked to slide it open, her father's hands pressed against the glass as he called her name. "Help me, Tyler. Help me."

Suddenly the door slid open, the motion sending her flying to the ground. From behind her someone opened fire, the bullets making her father's body jerk like a puppet on a string.

"No," she screamed, *her heart shattering as he fell, the blood so thick now it almost obscured the glass. "NO."*

"Tyler, sweetheart, wake up."

Someone else was calling. Someone who could help her. Help her father. But she couldn't reach him. Couldn't find him.

"Owen? I'm here," she screamed, *clawing at the doors to ICU, unable to make them open, the blood sticky between her fingers. "I'm here. I'm here."*

"Darling, it's only a dream," his voice said. "Open your eyes."

"Tyler," her father's voice called. *"Don't leave me."*

She slid to the ground, torn between her father and Owen. Knowing that one would lead her to safety, the other...

With a jerk, she opened her eyes, Owen's worried face spinning into view. "Oh, God," she whispered, the horror still real. "Oh, God, it was awful. There was blood, and my father, and Della, and I could hear you, but I couldn't get out and—"

"Hush, now," he said, his arms pulling her close against

him. "I've got you. It was just a dream. Nothing is going to hurt you."

"But he said it was my fault," she whimpered, still caught in the clutches of the nightmare.

"None of this is your fault," he said. "You just had a bad dream. But it's over. And you're here with me. Safe."

She nodded, burying her face in his shirt, the spicy, crisp smell of him comforting in its normalcy. She had the oddest feeling that she belonged here. That together they were better somehow. It was a silly notion. She knew it. But it made all the bad things seem less frightening.

She knew she ought to shake it off. To push away the nightmare and his comfort. To face all of this on her own terms as she did everything else in her life. She didn't need anyone. She was perfectly capable of standing on her own. But right now, all she wanted was to feel Owen's arms around her. To feel the beat of his heart against hers. To know that, for the moment at least, she wasn't alone. Surely she was allowed one moment of weakness?

And somewhere in her mind's eye, as she drifted back to sleep, she saw her father smile.

CHAPTER **12**

Owen and Tyler followed a secretary down the hall as she led them through the Pentagon's maze of passageways. Lieutenant General Hollingsworth had agreed to see them without fanfare, which, considering he was an undersecretary for the U.S. Department of Defense, was impressive. Although Owen supposed that considering who Tyler's father was, he shouldn't have been surprised.

Tyler had slept through what was left of the night, waking with a renewed sense of purpose. She hadn't mentioned the dream. Nor had she mentioned the fact that she'd woken in his arms. And Owen was wise enough not to make something out of nothing. She'd been hurting and he'd been there. It wasn't personal. He felt certain that she would have accepted any warm body.

The connection between them was based on the situation—nothing more.

Although, if he were being honest, there was a part of him that wished it could have been different. But life wasn't a bloody romance novel. He'd be wise to remember that.

"The general's office is right through here," the woman said, waving them through a set of double doors.

A young man sat at a desk, typing something into his computer. He looked up with an obligatory smile, his face clouding when he recognized Tyler. "I'm so sorry," he said, standing to hold out his hands. "I only heard this morning. You must be devastated."

Tyler nodded, her face tight with the effort to hold back her emotion as she gave the man's hands a squeeze. "Thank you, Randy. I know my father thought the world of you."

"I worked for the general," Randy said to Owen, his shoulders straightening with pride. "For almost ten years. Until he retired."

"And now you work with me," a booming voice said, the man attached to it standing well over six feet, his gray eyes warm as he shot a warning look in Randy's direction. "Which means there's work to do."

"Yes, sir." Randy gave a little salute. "I'm truly sorry, Tyler. If there's anything I can do?"

"Just remember him fondly," she said.

Randy nodded, then settled back in front of the computer.

"Come in," Hollingsworth said. "Both of you." They moved into his office, and the big man shut the door. "Tyler, honey, there just aren't words." He pulled her into a bear hug, the gesture softening the man. Tyler rested her head against his shoulder for a moment, then pushed back.

"It's been hard. But I'm doing okay."

"Well, I've been having all kinds of trouble accepting it," the lieutenant general shook his head. "Barbara and I just had dinner with them last week. Your father was having a good day. We talked about old times. And the idea that someone broke into their home and shot them—well, it's just unfathomable."

"I know." She nodded. "For me, too. Have you talked to Mark?"

"Yes, last night, as soon as I heard. I tried to call you, too. But there was no answer on your cell. And Mark wasn't sure how to find you."

"I'm sorry. I turned the phone off. Things were a little crazy. And then we had to change hotels."

Hollingsworth frowned. "Did something happen?"

"Nothing I couldn't handle. I promise." There was truth in there somewhere, and Owen respected Tyler's decision to keep the details of last night's attack to herself. But it was clear that Hollingsworth was still concerned.

"This thing with your father," he said, as they settled into three artfully arranged armchairs, "it's got something to do with the detonators going missing, doesn't it?"

"I think it's possible. But before we get into that, let me introduce Owen Wakefield. He's MI-5."

"You're a long way from home, son," Hollingsworth said, his eyes narrowing as they studied him.

"He's been working with me, Uncle Mike. Trying to sort through what happened out there."

"So this has been kicked up to the CIA?"

"Under the circumstances, my bosses fought for it, yes."

"I see." He shot another look in Owen's direction, and Owen wondered suddenly how much the man really knew. "And you've been helping her?"

"I've been doing my best, sir." He wasn't sure why

he was showing the man deference except that clearly he cared about Tyler. So at least in that respect they had common ground.

"Just be sure you know which side you're playing on," he warned.

"Uncle Mike," Tyler chastised. "Owen's been great. I wouldn't have gotten this far without him."

"I'm sorry." The lieutenant general bowed his head. "I just know that international cooperation can only go so far. Sometimes even friendly governments have different objectives. Anyway, if I offended you, it wasn't my intention."

No, the man had been issuing a warning. Hurt Tyler, and there'd be hell to pay.

"Uncle Mike can be a little overwhelming," she said, signaling her own rebuke.

To Owen's surprise Hollingsworth smiled, the gesture softening his face. Honest emotion reflected in his eyes. "I'm going to miss your father. We go back a long way. But I've still got you. And that's something pretty special. But all this blubbering isn't getting us anywhere." His expression steeled. "So how do you think your father's death fits into all this?"

"I honestly don't know. It's just an educated guess at this point. What I need to do is connect the dots. And that's where I'm hoping you can help us."

"Of course." Hollingsworth's frown spoke volumes of his respect for Tyler's father. "But if you're implying that your father..."

Tyler held up a hand. "I'm not suggesting that he was part of the plan to steal the detonators. But maybe he inadvertently played a role. It turns out he was behind the request for A-Tac's involvement in the detonators' transfer. But so far we haven't been able to find out why. We were on our way to ask him about it when we—" she paused, then squared her shoulders. "Did Dad say anything to you about it?"

"No, nothing. I'm afraid this is the first I've heard anything about it."

"Well, I suppose it was too much to hope he'd have said something. Anyway, I can't understand why he'd have been involved at all. Not to mention why someone would have agreed to it under the circumstances."

"Well, first of all," Hollingsworth said, "not that many people know about the Alzheimer's. Your father'd been pretty successful at keeping it under wraps. And second, he still had a fair amount of political clout. It's possible he called in a favor. Or maybe he simply pulled rank. I wouldn't have wanted to stand against him, and I suspect there are a hell of a lot of people, even at Langley, who felt the same way. And it wasn't as if the request was off the wall. The detonators' transport was critical, and your team—you in particular—were more than equipped to handle it."

"Except that the detonators were stolen on my watch," Tyler said, regret flickering in her eyes.

"Things happen. And no matter what you're hearing, I know that you didn't have anything to do with their being stolen. It's just standard ops to question everyone. And General Fisher, in particular, has reason to want to shift the blame elsewhere."

"Thank you for that. But it can't change the fact that because of my decisions, two men are dead. And now, the only thing I can do to atone is to try to sort through this mess and find answers. Starting with Dad. You're sure he didn't say anything?"

"No. When we were together we mainly talked about happier times. A lot of it about you. I know he'd never have said anything. It wouldn't fit his image as a ballbreaker. But I know for a fact that he was extremely proud of you."

Her shoulders tensed, and Owen resisted the urge to reach for her hand—partly because he was fairly certain the lieutenant general would feel compelled to break it. And although Owen figured he could hold his own, he had no doubt that, push come to shove, Hollingsworth would win the day.

"Thank you, Uncle Mike," Tyler said, forcing a smile. "That means a lot. And no matter what his role in this, I know he would have wanted me to get to the bottom of what's happened. And to do that I've got to put all the pieces together, starting with my father's involvement."

"I meant what I said." Hollingsworth nodded. "Anything I can do. Just tell me."

"At the end, at the hospital, he said some things. But none of it really made any sense. So I'm hoping maybe, because you knew him so well, you'll be able to shed some light."

"What specifically did he say?"

"Well, a lot of it was rambling. And some of it I couldn't really understand. But at the hospital, he kept saying he was sorry. And that he should have known better. But more important, he kept repeating the words 'winter' and 'Indian.'"

"In that order?" Hollingsworth asked.

"At the hospital, the words were 'winter' then 'debt' and then 'Indian.' All of it very disjointed. But he also said the same thing at the house. Only the order was different. Indian winter. Although at the time I thought he said India. Anyway, whether it's India or Indian, whatever the order of the words, it still doesn't make any sense. At least not to me."

"Well, maybe there is a reason to the rhyme, so to speak." Hollingsworth tilted his head, his expression thoughtful. "I told you that your father and I had been discussing old times. And for us that means talking war stories. We fought in three of them and helped orchestrate a couple more. Anyway, suffice it to say that the military has been the main focus of both of our lives."

"And Indian winter has something to do with your past?"

"Maybe," he said. "In Vietnam, in '69, there was a major offensive in the A Shau Valley. The North Vietnamese were using the valley as a major supply corridor. A way to get troops and munitions into South Vietnam. We'd tried to stop them before without success. But the big brass thought that it was important enough to try again."

"You're talking about Hamburger Hill," Tyler said. "I remember Dad talking about it."

"Hill 937." Hollingsworth nodded.

"Were you there?" Owen asked, impressed even though his country hadn't approved of the war.

"In 'Nam, yes. But not Hamburger Hill. But Zachary was."

"Tyler's father," Owen clarified. It was the first time anyone had used the man's given name.

"Right. He was smack dab in the middle of it. Hell of a fight. And all of it for nothing."

"But I thought the Americans took the hill?" Owen queried.

"They did," Tyler said. "But they abandoned it two weeks later."

"I don't understand." Owen shook his head.

"It was a turning point of sorts," Hollingsworth said. "Americans were tired of the fighting. And the battle had moved to Congress. Hamburger Hill became a symbol for everything wrong with the war. Most of it misinformation, mind you, but it didn't matter, the tide had changed. Anyway, we lost a hell of a lot of good men on that hill, but the powers that be suddenly lost interest in holding it."

"And your father was part of the fighting," Owen said, bringing the conversation back to the matter at hand.

"Yes. He was." Tyler nodded. "He almost died, actually. He was shot. But they managed to get him out of there. Others weren't so lucky. But I don't see the tie-in to Dad's ramblings."

"Well, I could be wrong," the lieutenant general said, "but the battle was definitely on his mind. He's the one who brought it up. Said it was important never to forget. That there were still debts to be paid."

"Debts of honor?" Tyler asked, repeating her father's words.

"He didn't use those exact words, no," Hollingsworth said. "But I can see how it might fit. I mean, if someone pulled me off that hill, I'd have owed him more than a debt of honor."

"So do you have any idea who it was that rescued him?" Tyler frowned, clearly trying to make the pieces fit. "Maybe that's the connection."

Hollingsworth shook his head. "He never mentioned anyone specifically. I always assumed it was just a routine evac. But you know your father, he wouldn't have liked talking about what he considered to be his failure. I take it he never mentioned it to you?"

"No," she said. "He never liked talking about it with people who weren't there. Said there was no way for us to understand."

"Well, he has a point, but you were Army."

"Yes, but I was also his daughter. And no matter who saved him, I still don't see how his surviving Hamburger Hill has anything to do with Indian winter."

"I don't know, maybe I'm way off, but you have to understand that even though your father's mind was failing, there was still a certain kind of logic, even on the worst of days. It was as if some part of his mind was still working, but the connection between meaning and words had been severed. Like he knew what he wanted to say, he just couldn't find the right words. It all came out jumbled."

"So you do think he was trying to tell me something?"

"Yes, I do. And I think it had to have been something about what happened at the house. Something that would help you find the shooter. Or at least point you in the right direction."

"He just had trouble communicating his thoughts," Owen said. "But I'm with Tyler, I still don't see the connection to 'Indian winter.'"

"As I said, maybe it's a stretch, but if I'm right, there's an odd kind of symmetry."

"So what do you think he meant?" Tyler asked, leaning forward with a frown.

"I think he *was* referring to Hamburger Hill. And maybe the person who rescued him. His debt of honor."

"And you think this because?" Owen prompted.

"Simple." Hollingsworth shrugged. "The operation that launched the offensive into the A Shau Valley was called Apache Snow."

CHAPTER 13

"I'm not finding anything," Tyler said, looking across her father's desk at Owen.

After Uncle Mike's revelations they'd decided to tackle her father's study in hopes of finding some kind of clue that might give them insight into who had saved her father on Hamburger Hill and whether or not he was somehow linked with the stolen detonators. It seemed a long shot, but for the moment it was all they had.

She'd talked with Hannah as soon as they'd left the Pentagon, filling her in on the latest developments. They'd shipped off her dad's computer first thing this morning. And she'd also asked her friend to download the general's LUDs in the hope they'd get lucky with his phone records.

In addition, Hannah had promised to see what she could dig up about her father's unit. He'd been part of the Third Battalion, 187th Infantry. And by narrowing it to the time frame for Operation Apache Snow, she was hopeful that between her father's papers and Hannah's expertise, they'd dig up a name. But she was quickly becoming disillusioned about the chances of their finding something here in McLean.

The room and its contents had already been examined by the tech team from Langley. And as part of their efforts, the room had been cleaned up, some semblance of normalcy returned. But Tyler could still see her father lying on the desk, his blood dripping to the floor. She shook her head, forcing her thoughts back to the contents of the desk.

"None of this makes any sense," she said, staring down at a pile of unpaid bills, some of them months old. "I know they weren't having financial problems. And my father was always a stickler for paying bills on time." She picked up an envelope. "This credit card is six months overdue. And the interest is more than the balance."

"His files are a mess, too," Owen said, looking up from the filing cabinet he was sorting through. "It's like two different people were working in here, one of them organized almost to the extreme and the other one without any seeming logic at all. Did your stepmother help with their business affairs?"

"No." Tyler shook her head, pushing the bills away. "She was more into spending money than managing it. Although I don't mean to speak ill of the dead." She shuddered, her mind clamping down before grief could gain control. "Besides, even if she'd had an interest in helping, my father wouldn't have let her. He was a complete control freak."

Owen sighed. "Then I'm afraid we've got a major problem. Up until about seven months ago, things seem to be in pretty good order, but after that they're chaotic. And unfortunately at least two-thirds of the files in here fall into the latter category."

"Well, the timeline follows the progression of the Alzheimer's. He'd been exhibiting symptoms for the past couple of years. But none of them were debilitating enough to set off alarms, although, in hindsight, they were things we probably should have recognized."

She closed her eyes for a second, remembering the momentary bouts of confusion. Repeated stories. Lapses in memory. Words slipping away. The truth was, she just hadn't wanted to see it.

"Anyway," she sighed, "last winter, everything came to a head. The symptoms suddenly magnified. They were still coming in isolated bursts, but they were happening more frequently and when they came, it was really bad. Della started having difficulty taking care of him. He'd just wander off. And she'd be worried sick. So we took him to the doctor—against his will, I might add. And we got the diagnosis."

"It must have been hard," Owen said, his eyes telegraphing his sympathy, her heart twisting with emotion, butterflies fluttering in her stomach.

She hadn't had the courage to talk to him about last night. About the nightmare. About his holding her while she'd slept. She wasn't sure that she was ready to put her feelings into words, but she was self-aware enough to know that something had shifted. Something had changed between the two of them. They'd crossed a line last night. Or at least she had. It wasn't about James Bond anymore. It was about Owen. And it mattered. A hell of lot more than she was ready to admit.

She frowned, angry at herself for letting her emotions get the best of her. After what had happened with Justin, she should know better than to let herself care. The cost was too damn high. She shot Owen a tight smile. "It was difficult. But mostly for Della. Mark and I were both out of the house. She's the one who had to deal with it day to day. But there were medications, and they helped to calm him, if nothing else. And I think knowing what he was facing helped, too. There's always something more frightening about the unknown. You know?"

"I do." Owen nodded. "But I can't imagine trying to cope with knowing that you're slowing losing yourself—bit by bit—a little more every day. It must have been terrifying."

"And my father doesn't do fear," she said, still unable to use the past tense. "And I honestly believed he was coping. But now, looking at all of this," she glanced down at the papers jammed into the desk's drawers, "I'm not so sure." She pulled out a dog-eared file, flipping through the contents. "He hadn't paid their insurance premium in months. Or their house payment." She dropped the file on the desk, tipping back her head, closing her eyes.

"Why don't you let me deal with all of this? Go back to the hotel. Or go find Mark. I can handle this."

"No. I need to be here," she said, opening her eyes on a sigh. "The work is good. It's distracting. And I need to feel like I'm accomplishing something. So is there a file for correspondence? Maybe he wrote to this mystery man of ours."

"Nothing like that. Although there are letters scattered among all the other stuff." Owen frowned, reaching down into the back of the file cabinet to pull out a small box. "Did your father always keep his medals in the filing cabinet?" He held out the little velvet box. Inside, nestled in satin, was a Bronze Star.

Tyler frowned. "His medals are all on his uniform.

And best I know, he was never awarded a Bronze Star. He used to tell me what each of the medals meant. How they originated. Even why they were designed the way they were. He was proud of his. So I can't imagine why he'd have hidden one away."

A sound from the doorway had them both spinning around, Tyler reaching for her gun. "Shit," Mark said, stepping into the room, hand clasped to his chest. "Way to scare the life out of a guy. I live here, remember?" He held up a shaking hand, a key dangling from his finger.

"Oh, God, Mark, I'm sorry," Tyler said, dropping her gun on the desk and reaching for her brother's hand. "I didn't mean to scare you, it's just that—"

"I know…under the circumstances you can't take chances. I should have called. But I didn't think about you being here."

"No. You're right. This is still your house. I should have called you and let you know we were going to be here."

"No harm, no foul," Mark said, the color returning to his face. "I hadn't realized the son of a bitch had gone through dad's office." His eyes moved around the room, taking in the obvious disarray.

"He didn't," Tyler said. "This is all Dad's handiwork. It seems Alzheimer's drives organization out the window. Did you have any idea that he'd stopped paying bills?"

"Of course not." Mark frowned, picking up the file of unpaid bills. "If I had I would done something about it. Mom just kept telling me that everything was all right and that I should stay at school. I should have done more."

"You did what you could," Tyler said, reaching out to squeeze her brother's hand. "Besides, if anyone should have been more involved, it's me. I should have known that Della needed help."

"She'd have just kept it from you, too. She could be stubborn like that. All she really wanted to do was protect him. Anyway—woulda, shoulda, coulda. Best to look forward, not backward. Mom always used to say that. So what are you looking for?"

"It's probably a long shot, but I'm trying to find the name of the man who saved Dad during the battle of Hamburger Hill."

"Say what?" Mark shook his head, his expression indicating he thought she'd totally lost it.

"Your father said some things to Tyler before he died," Owen said. "And we think maybe they were connected somehow with whoever it was that did this."

"You think the guy who saved him in Vietnam killed him?"

"No," Tyler said, holding up a hand. "We think that he's the link that got Dad all mixed up in this—whatever the hell *this* is." They filled Mark in on the details of what their father had said and what they'd learned from Uncle Mike. "So have you got any idea who this guy might have been?"

"Not a clue. Dad wasn't big on talking about that kind of thing."

"No, he wasn't," Tyler said with a sigh.

"What about this Bronze Star?" Owen asked. "Does it mean anything to you?" He passed the box across the desk, and Mark reached for it, just missing. The box rolled off the desk and bounced on the floor, landing under a chair.

"Dad didn't have a Bronze Star," Mark said as he bent to the box. "Hang on." He frowned. "What's this?" He straightened, the box in one hand, a folded slip of paper in the other. "I think it fell out of the box."

"Let me see," Tyler said, leaning over her brother's shoulder for a better look.

"It must have been knocked free when I dropped it." He unfolded the paper as the three of them huddled together to have a look.

It had been folded in quarters so that it would fit, and when opened presented itself as a black-and-white photo, the edges curling and turning yellow. In it, two soldiers sat on a cot in what was clearly a makeshift medical facility. One of the men, her father, had an IV drip running into his arm as he reclined with a jovial grin on the bed. The other man sat next to him, in fatigues, his face grimy, but his grin as big as her father's. The two of them were making victory signs.

"Is that your dad?" Owen asked.

She and Mark nodded in tandem.

"He looks so young," Mark said.

"I'd say not much older than you," she agreed, staring down at the photo, the two of them lost in shared memories.

"Is there anything on the back?" Owen asked impatiently, pulling them both back to the present. "Something to tell us where they are or who's in the photo with your father?"

Mark flipped it over. "It's stamped June 1969."

"Hamburger Hill," Tyler said, her gaze locking triumphantly with Owen's.

"Is there anything else?" he asked.

"It says Kodak," Mark offered unhelpfully. "Wait, there's something else written here, in the corner, but it's really faded." He held the photograph up to the light, squinting as he tried to make out the words. "I think it says 'Smitty and Ace.'"

"Not a lot of help." Owen frowned.

"Well, we know 'Ace' is Dad," Mark said.

"We do?" Tyler asked, eyebrows raised.

"Yeah, everyone called him that. He kinda knew his way around a deck of cards. Won a lot of money. His unit liked to set him up against other units that didn't have a clue. Apparently, he was pretty proficient at coming up with aces."

"Meaning he cheated."

Mark grinned. "Well, he never admitted it to me. But let's just say he didn't ever seem to square off against the same opponents twice. Anyway, if Ace is Dad, then this guy must be Smitty."

"And given the date and the surroundings of the photograph, not to mention the Bronze Star, which we know isn't Dad's," Tyler said, "I'd say we're on to something."

"Except we've got no idea who Smitty is," Owen said, "or how to find him. And we still have no idea how your father came to be in possession of Smitty's medal."

Mark and Tyler sighed in unison. "Killjoy," she said, but she knew he was right. All they'd done was deepen the mystery.

Tyler's phone vibrated against her thigh, and she slipped it from her pocket, flipping it open, checking the caller ID. "Hannah," she said, "perfect timing. I was just about to call you. I've got some more information on the Hamburger Hill angle. A guy named Smitty. May have been awarded a Bronze Star."

"Actually," Hannah said, a thread of excitement in her voice, "he was."

"Come again?" Tyler asked, her heart starting to pound.

"I just ran him down myself. Working backward through your dad's unit. You said you were looking for the guy who rescued your dad. And Hamburger Hill was a big deal. So I figured I'd start with men who'd won medals. From there, I got lucky. Came across an anniversary tribute on the web. Turns out the guy who saved your dad was one of the men interviewed for the article. Anyway, his name is Jefferson Smithwick. Saved three others in the unit as well. He was awarded the Bronze Star for his valor. And it gets more interesting from there. Want to know why?"

"Do tell," Tyler prompted, barely containing her excitement.

"It seems that Mr. Smithwick went to college after he was discharged. Studied nuclear physics. MIT."

"And..." Tyler held her breath, certain that Hannah's pronouncement was going to fill in a lot of blanks.

"*And*," Tyler could almost hear Hannah's smile of triumph, "your Smitty went on to work for DOD. And from there moved into the private sector. But he kept his government connections, and because of that—" she paused, dramatically, "he wound up the chief designer on the detonator project."

"Oh, my God." Tyler blew out a breath, her heart still racing.

"I know," Hannah said. "But there's more. Seems Smithwick called his old friend several times, the first occurring three days before your dad requested your presence on the transport team and the last the morning of the day he died. How's that for connecting the dots?"

CHAPTER **14**

Boulder, Colorado

"So what have you got?" Owen asked, juggling his cell phone as Tyler signaled she was going inside the minimart to pay.

They'd flown from D.C. almost as soon as Hannah had given them Smithwick's location. It had been everything they could do to convince Mark to stay put. The man was almost as single-minded as his sister. But he'd finally agreed to stay behind and help make final arrangements for Della and the general. And he'd also be available if they needed something else from Tyler's father's house.

So now all that was left was tracking down Smithwick and making him talk—with a little help from Harrison, they hoped.

"Quite a bit, actually," Harrison said, after an aside to Hannah. "I hope you know we're working our asses off up here."

"At least no one's shooting at you," Owen countered.

"Well, I guess there is that." Harrison chuckled. "Anyway, I'm afraid Mr. Smithwick has some serious problems."

"The kind that might tempt one to sell state secrets."

"Unfortunately so," Harrison acknowledged. "His wife has stage-four colon cancer."

"That's not good." Owen frowned, waving away Tyler's attempt to interrupt. "But I'm not seeing the temptation to turn traitor."

"Well, apparently, none of the traditional approaches were working for Mrs. Smithwick. So her doctor prescribed a controversial new chemical cocktail instead. The drugs individually have all been approved but this particular mix is too new to have made it past the FDA."

"Let me guess," Owen said. "It's illegal."

"No, just off the books. Which makes it expensive. Close to a hundred grand a treatment."

"That's absurd. No drug should cost that much."

"Yes, well, I don't suppose you can put a price on a life. Anyway, the point is that she's been receiving the new treatments on and off for just over a year now."

"So Smithwick's budget is stretched really thin," Owen said, anticipating Harrison's next words.

"Actually, more like tapped out. He stopped making payments to the hospital four months ago. So, as you can imagine, the money owed has been climbing, to the point where the hospital refused to continue treatment."

"Let me guess," Owen said, "suddenly the payments resumed?"

"About two weeks ago."

"Just before the detonators disappeared. Have you been able to identify the source of his windfall?"

"Not specifically, but Hannah managed to get hold of his bank records, and starting about the time the payments resumed there were three cash deposits made, totaling close to a million dollars."

"Nice payday. And a pretty solid motive. Sounds like we've found a key piece of the puzzle. Anything else I should know?"

"Only that Smithwick hasn't been in to work for the better part of the week. They figured he was taking care of his wife. Anyway, we've done our part, now it's up to you and Tyler."

"We're in Boulder now. We just got petrol. So assuming our directions are accurate, we ought to be there shortly."

"Hannah's insisting that I ask you about Tyler. How's she holding up? They're all really worried about her here."

Owen could see her through the store's windows, discussing something with the clerk as she paid. "Tell them she's fine. She's a strong woman. And right now she's focused on finding the people responsible for killing her father. It's keeping her going—for now."

"And have you had the chance to check in with your boss?" Harrison said, leaving no doubt who he was referring to.

"Not since last night, but between the two of us, I think he's having a little trouble seeing the forest for the trees. He's so bent on taking down A-Tac, I'm not sure he's really getting the bigger picture."

"But you are?" It was clear that Harrison had his doubts about Logan, and now he was feeling his way with Owen.

"Seeing the whole thing? I'm doing the best I can. Unfortunately, until we have more answers there's no way to prove Logan right or wrong. So anything we've got is just supposition, although I'll admit Tyler's father seems to have been in it up to his neck."

"And if he is, then it follows that Tyler is as well?" It was a question, not a statement, and for some reason Owen found that he was pleased that Harrison hadn't jumped onto Logan's bandwagon. "I don't know. The circumstantial evidence is certainly there. But, Harrison, she's really been shaken up by all of this. And I was there last night when someone took a shot at her. Hell, the more we dig the murkier it seems to get. So keep your eyes open, my friend. And watch your back."

"Will do. You be careful, too."

"Count on it. I'll check in as soon as we know anything more." He snapped the phone closed, watching as Tyler walked back across the parking lot.

She moved with the ease of a woman comfortable in her own skin. There were circles under her eyes, part and parcel of her grief, but her eyes were clear, her stance determined. There was a fire there he recognized. A zeal to separate the wheat from the chaff. To separate good from evil. A noble pursuit. One he'd believed in once upon a time.

That is, until he'd figured out that sometimes it was damn near impossible to tell the difference between the two.

"Mr. Smithwick?" Tyler asked, stepping back as a man opened the front door.

The years hadn't been kind to her father's friend. His skin was pallid, his face bloated from too little sleep and probably one too many stiff drinks, although, considering the situation with his wife, perhaps his looking haggard was understandable. Not to mention the fact that he was most probably guilty of treason. That kind of thing had a way of wearing on one's soul.

"Can I help you?" he asked, his gaze shooting from Tyler to Owen and then back to her again, a flicker of alarm cresting in his eyes.

"We're here to talk to you about my father," she said, careful to keep her tone friendly. They'd agreed in the car to try for a low-key approach. "Zachary Hanson."

The man visibly paled. "I heard about his death. It's tragic. But why would you want to talk with me? It was a robbery, right?" Thanks to timely intervention by the powers that be, the press had been convinced that the murders were the result of a robbery gone bad.

"That's what the papers say," Owen said, "but we're not as sure. And we're hoping that you can help us. We believe you were one of the last people to talk with the general."

"I'm afraid now isn't really a good time." He edged back from the door and would have managed to close it except that Owen managed to get a foot inside.

"We're really not prepared to take no for an answer," he said, lifting his jacket to expose his gun.

Smithwick blanched but released his hold on the door.

"You're the only one who can help us find the people who did this to my father," Tyler said, holding out the photograph of the two of them. "You saved his life once. And I don't for a minute believe that you meant for this to happen. We just need your help."

Smithwick opened his mouth to refuse them, but then his eyes fell to the snapshot in her hand. With a sigh, his shoulders sagged, and he stepped back from the door, gesturing them inside.

The house was dark, draperies drawn, newspapers and half-eaten takeout littering almost every available surface. It was clear that Smithwick's life didn't consist of much more than subsisting. Despite the circumstances, Tyler felt a wave of sympathy for the man. No matter what he'd done, his wife's illness wasn't an invention.

"You look like your father," Smithwick said, as he cleared away the clutter to make room for them to sit at the dining room table. "I can see it in your eyes and your smile. Your dad was a good friend." A wave of sadness washed across his face. "Sometimes I wish we could go back to those times, when we were young and anything was possible."

"You were in the middle of a war," Owen reminded him, his mouth drawn into a disapproving line.

"Yeah, well." Smithwick shrugged, his gaze falling to an abandoned pizza box on the floor. "It's all relative, isn't it?"

"Look, Mr. Smithwick," Tyler began.

"Call me Smitty, that's what your dad called me." His tone was almost hopeful, as if somehow by using that name he could wash away all the horrible truths.

"Okay," she said, struggling for the right approach. "But before we go any further, you should know that we're not just here for my father."

"I know," he nodded. "You're here on behalf of the CIA. I know what you do, Ms. Hanson."

"Tyler," she offered. "And if you know that, then you won't be surprised to find out that we know about your wife's illness, and the financial problems resulting from the cost of her treatment. We also have bank records that prove that almost a million dollars was recently deposited into three separate bank accounts. All of them yours. And all of the money was deposited in cash."

He shook his head in protest, but she raised her hand, Owen shifting so that he could easily reach his gun.

"We also have phone records showing that you called my father at least three times. Once two weeks before the detonators you designed were stolen, and then again just a few days before my father asked that I be part of the transport. And as Owen mentioned at the door, we know you called him the morning he died."

"I didn't—"

"Don't bother denying it, I have the records right here." Tyler pulled the copy of the LUDs Hannah had faxed her and dropped them on the table.

"I wasn't going to deny it. I was going to say that I didn't know that I was putting him in danger."

"But you knew you were putting me in harm's way, which is almost the same thing, isn't it?"

"They promised me they wouldn't hurt you," he rushed to assure her, then stopped as he realized what he'd done.

"So, we were right, you were the one who leaked the information about the time and location of the transport."

"You don't understand. I had to do it."

"To save your wife," Owen said. "We get that."

"They offered me money, yes. And I was tempted to take it. The hospital was refusing treatment, and it was our only hope. But Vivianne wouldn't let me. She said it was wrong. That it was blood money. So against my better judgment, I turned them down."

"But clearly you changed your mind," Tyler suggested. "We saw the deposits."

"It wasn't me. It was them. They threatened to kill Vivianne if I didn't do what they wanted. You have to believe me; I didn't have a choice."

"That's exactly what my father said. That he had to help. Because it was a debt of honor. That's why you sent him the Bronze Star, wasn't it? To remind him what he owed you."

Smitty looked down at his hands, his face tightening with emotion. "I asked him first. On the phone. But he refused to help me. He acted as if he didn't know who I was."

"That's because he was sick, Smitty," Tyler said, fighting a surge of anger. "He had Alzheimer's. If your call came on a bad day, there was no way he could remember you."

"Oh, God." Smitty shook his head, his face crumpling as he considered the fact. "I didn't know. Look, you have to understand, I was desperate, and I knew that the medal would remind him that he owed me. It never occurred to me that something was wrong. I just needed him to agree to arrange for you to be part of the transport team."

"Why?" Tyler asked, still fighting against her anger. Whatever the reason, this man had cost her so much. "Why me?"

"I don't know," he said, his eyes brimming with tears. "I swear to you, I don't. They just told me to find a way to get you on the team. And if I didn't they…they'd kill Vivianne. You have to understand, she was my whole world."

"Was?" Tyler asked, her anger vanishing in the wake of his obvious anguish.

"Yes," he said. "Vivianne died yesterday. We waited too long. The cancer had taken hold again. The doctors said there was nothing to be done. And now, she's gone. And everything I did—I did for nothing."

"Then help us stop the people who did this, Smitty," she begged. "Tell us what you know."

"I only wish I could. But there's nothing to tell. I never talked to anyone in person. Everything was dead drops and email. A blind account. I tried to trace it once, but it just doubled back to me."

"But you said they threatened your wife," Owen probed. "Surely there had to have been something more direct than just email."

"Yes. There was." He nodded, chewing on his bottom lip. "When we resumed the treatments, Vivianne had to be admitted to the hospital. And whoever these people are, they managed to gain access to her room and tamper with her medications. They could have killed her. But they used it as a warning instead. A way to prove they could get to us, even in the security of the hospital. Don't you see, there was nowhere for us to hide." He laced his fingers together, his thumbs moving nervously. "So I did what they asked. I gave them the information about the transport. And I used the medal to get your father to help me pull you into it."

"And everything was done by email?"

"Yes. Or instant message. With the occasional dead drop. You know—things taped under a park bench, or with a key to a locker at the bus station. That's how I got the money."

"In three installments."

"Yes."

"Do you have the bags the money was in?"

"No." He shook his head, regret coloring his expression. "I burned them. Just as they told me to."

"What about your computer? Do you still have a record of the emails?" Owen asked, his frustration evident as he gripped the edge of the table.

Smitty shook his head. "I had them. But two days ago when I turned on my computer it wouldn't boot. There was power, but nothing else. The hard drive had been wiped clean. I tried everything I could think of, but it was all gone. All of the emails. All my data. All my research." It was evident that the latter upset him the most, the importance of tracking down the culprits clearly not registering.

"There were three payments," Tyler mused. "Were they specific for work done?"

"Yes." Smitty nodded. "The first was for giving them the timetable and the second was for getting you on board."

"And the third payment?" Owen asked.

"That was for giving them my schematics. The blueprint for using the detonators in conjunction with a suitcase nuke."

"But I thought all work on nuclear weapons had been banned?" Tyler frowned.

"It was," Smitty sighed. "At least in theory. But scientific curiosity isn't as easily eliminated. And as the work in nanotechnology became more advanced I became interested in the possibility of designing something new. Something better. All of it theoretical, mind you. Until the government got wind of my work. That's when I was invited to join the team here in Boulder."

"The U.S. government sanctioned your work on a miniature nuclear weapon?" Tyler asked.

"Not politically, no. That would be international suicide. But, if you're asking if they played a part in what I was doing, the answer is yes. They funded it—discreetly. Along with the British." He cut a look in Owen's direction. "The project for the detonators was meant as a smoke screen. The real research was the weapon itself."

"But there were no nuclear weapons on the transport," Tyler said. "I checked them myself."

"I told you, the work was theoretical. We weren't building the bomb, just designing it. The detonators came out of that research."

"And because there was a practical use for them without political consequence, you actually manufactured prototypes."

"Right. And that's what you were transporting."

"But the people who stole them wanted more than just the detonators?"

"Yes. They wanted the plan and schematics I'd developed for the bomb. The detonators were just icing on the cake. I held on to the plans until they paid me for everything else. Anyway, the reality is that now, thanks to me, they have everything they need to build and detonate a suitcase nuke."

"And you believe this was their overall goal?" Tyler asked.

"I have nothing to substantiate the idea except what they told me, but yes, I believe they're planning to build a bomb."

"Jesus, man," Owen said with a scowl, "what were you thinking?"

"I wasn't." The older man shook his head. "I was just trying to save my wife."

"It doesn't matter," Tyler said, holding up a hand. "There are more important things to worry about than what you've done. If there is a bomb, that raises the stakes exponentially. Whoever these people are, they're playing hardball. They've already killed my father. And they've tried to kill me." She waited for the significance to sink in.

"You think they'll try to take me out, as well," Smitty said.

"They've already managed to wipe out your computer," Owen agreed. "Tyler's right, they're eliminating loose ends. And you're a liability."

"It isn't safe for you here."

"But this is my home," he said, waving his arm at the dilapidated room.

"It won't do you much good if you're dead," Owen said. "Besides, there's still the matter of your giving up government secrets. I'm afraid we can't just leave you here."

Smitty sighed with a resigned nod, pushing away from the table. "I suppose not. I knew that sooner or later this would all catch up to me. It's not like it's something that can be whitewashed away. And now that Vivianne's gone, it doesn't even matter. The truth is that there's nothing left for me here, anyway. I just wish I had something more to give you."

"We'll need your computer," Owen said.

"But I told you, there's nothing there," he protested, with a frown.

"You never know." Owen shrugged. "Might as well let our people look at it."

"Fine. It's over there. On the desk." He nodded toward a rolltop in the corner. "Can I pack a few things?"

"No." Tyler shook her head, the conviction growing that they were on borrowed time. "We'll get you whatever you need when we get you to safety."

Owen picked up the computer and they started for the door.

"Wait," Smitty said, his brow furrowed as he focused on something. "There's a flash drive. I use it to transfer data from my computer at the center to the computer here. Easier than lugging around a laptop."

"Do you back everything up?" Tyler asked.

"Just the important things. Like I said, files from work."

"What about the emails? Did you back them up?"

"Not purposely, no, but the program does everything for me, and to be honest I don't know exactly what all that includes. I just access whatever I need and ignore the rest. But it's certainly in better shape than the computer. So it might be worth a look." He eyed them both hopefully, and Tyler realized that he genuinely wanted to help.

"Sure. Why not? It can't hurt. Where is it?" she asked.

"In the bedroom, I think. I usually leave it on the bureau. But I haven't been following a normal routine. I haven't been in to work in a while. I wanted to be here with Vivianne."

"Well, why don't we see if we can find it," Tyler said, wondering if maybe they'd finally been handed a break.

"I'll be outside," Owen called. "I want to check in with Sunderland and let them know what's happening. They should be able to make arrangements for Smitty from their end."

Tyler nodded and followed her father's friend down the hall.

Unlike the rest of the house, the bedroom was neat as a pin. An empty hospital bed sat next to the window, flanked by a table covered with medicine bottles. A vase of dying flowers sat on the windowsill, the browning petals drooped and forlorn.

"She loved tulips," Smitty said, following Tyler's line of sight. "I bought her fresh ones every day. I just couldn't bring myself to throw the last of them out."

"I can understand that. It's hard to let go. Is there a picture or something you want to take with you?" she asked, not sure why she was trying to be kind. "Something to remind you of Vivianne?"

"Yes, over here." He pointed to a group of photographs, reaching down to pick one up. "This is from our wedding." Tyler obediently came over for a look, but stopped when she recognized a picture of Smitty and her father. The two of them stood at the opening of a tent, arms thrown around each other in that casual way of men who are fast friends. So much had changed. Her eyes filled with tears, and she angrily pushed them away.

"I loved your father," Smitty said, his eyes on the photo, his voice hoarse with regret. "He was one of the best men I ever knew. I was proud to have called him friend. If I'd known...if I'd had a choice..."

"What's done is done," she said, shaking her head, determined to maintain control. There was nothing to be gained in losing it now. "Just get the flash drive. We need to keep moving."

He nodded, his face tight with anguish as he scooped up the device along with his wallet and keys. "Here," he said. "You take it."

She nodded, and they made their way back to the front of the house. On the porch, Smitty paused, his face twisting into a wry attempt at a smile. "It's stupid, I know, but can you hang on a minute? I need to lock up."

"Fine," she said, heading down the steps toward Owen, who was standing in the yard, talking on the phone. He started to smile, and then his face shuttered with alarm.

"Move," he shouted, diving forward, tackling her hard enough to drive her down into the grass, his body covering hers as the house exploded, the ground shaking with the force of the blast, a fiery ball of smoke and debris shooting high into the evening sky.

The sound of the explosion reverberated down the street and for a moment, they lay still, her heart pounding against his. Then he rolled off her, his face concerned. "Are you all right?" he asked as she pushed up to a sitting position.

"I think so," she said, releasing a slow breath. "It all happened so fast. How did you know?"

"Instinct." He shook his head. "Or maybe I heard something, I have no idea really."

"Well, I didn't hear anything. I was just walking down the steps and whoosh, the whole house went up."

"But I was there," he interjected, reaching over to pull a piece of debris from her hair. "I just wish I'd been able to do something more."

"Something for Smitty, you mean." She trailed off, staring at what was left of the house. The front porch was completely gone, a gaping hole where there used to be a front door. There was no sign of her father's friend. "I don't think there's anything we could have done. The bomb must have been triggered off the lock on the front door. If he hadn't sequestered himself over his wife's death, it probably would have blown sooner. Then we'd never have had the chance to question him."

"Serendipity in the worst kind of way," Owen said, reaching down to help her up. "At least he's with his wife now," Owen said, his eyes on the house, a trace of grief etched across his face. "Maybe that's the silver lining in all of this."

"You believe in an afterlife?" Tyler asked, surprised at the severity of Owen's reaction.

"Not really, no. But there's a part of me that would like for it to be true." He shook his head. "Sorry for the mumbo jumbo, but it's just such a bloody waste. You know?"

"Man's inhumanity to man," Tyler agreed. "There's a reason it's a global theme."

"Well, I, for one, get pretty damn tired of being a firsthand witness."

"You and me both." She lifted her eyes to the burning rubble, the sound of sirens filling the air. "But maybe it's not a complete loss." She opened her hand to reveal the flash drive. "Thanks to this little guy, at least we're still in the game."

CHAPTER **15**

W ell, I can't get anything off the damn thing,"
Tyler said, pulling the flash drive out of her
computer. "It's either got some kind of crazy encryp-
tion or there was never anything on it to begin with. My
laptop recognizes that there's something in the UBS slot
but it isn't reading the drive." She tossed the device onto
the table, leaning back in the hotel chair. "Maybe Smitty
lied."

"Or maybe it's just something with your machine,"
Owen offered. "We'll be at Sunderland tomorrow, we can
turn it over to Harrison then."

"Or Jason," she said automatically, her objection to
Owen and Harrison being on the team more rote now
than anything. "Although you'd think I could work out
how to access the thing. What time is our flight?"

"Crack of dawn," Owen said, looking out the window.
"Assuming the weather holds."

Tyler followed his gaze. The clouds were still

threatening, although the rain seemed to have ended
for now. The storm had started just as the emergency
vehicles had arrived at Smitty's, the wind and lightning
making securing the scene even more difficult. They'd
stayed until well past dark, huddled beneath umbrellas
and makeshift canopies, determined to make sure the
rain didn't wash away evidence. Unfortunately, as she'd
expected, there was very little left.

There was nothing at all of Smitty, except a few
charred bones and his wedding ring. She'd found a bit of
the trigger lodged in a piece of the door lock, which confirmed her suspicion about point of origin. Beyond that,
however, there was nothing substantial.

She'd probably have stayed on, but Owen had insisted
that there was nothing more to be done. So they'd
checked into a hotel and she'd worked on the flash drive
while he arranged for a flight to New York and ordered
dinner—such as it was.

Her hamburger had left something to be desired, and
judging from the remains of Owen's omelet, it hadn't
been much better. Although in truth, she wasn't really
hungry. She'd seen what bombs could do, so that wasn't
anything new. But she'd never seen someone blown to bits
right in front of her.

It wasn't that she couldn't stomach it. It was just unset-
tling, one more horror in a growing list of atrocities. She
shook her head and pushed out of her chair, walking over
to the window. The lights in the parking lot bounced off
the low-hanging clouds, giving the rain-wet pavement an
eerie glow. Just beyond the hotel, the highway presented a
ribbon of light, the weather playing havoc with the traffic,
the sound of angry car horns diluted by the mist.

"Maybe I'll have a go at it," Owen said, moving to sit down in front of the laptop. "Could be it just needs a man's touch."

"Have at it," she shrugged, turning from the window. "I've never been good with computers. It's like they see me coming."

"Oh, surely it can't be that bad?" Owen teased, the computer whirring to life as it tried to access the flash drive. "Hey, I've got something."

"Told you," she said, as she moved to stand behind him. The screen blinked once then presented a box requesting a password. "At least you got farther than I did."

"Yes, but a fat lot of good it did. Any thoughts about what Smitty's password might be?"

"Well, Jason always insists it's the obvious." She picked up the file that Hannah had faxed, extracting a sheet of paper with basic information. "Try his birth date or his phone number."

Owen consulted the sheet and then typed. The machine beeped denial and re-presented the password screen. He typed again with the same results.

"Okay, maybe it's his driver's license number."

"You actually know the number on your driver's license?" Owen asked, tilting his head to look up at her.

"No. But I'm betting other people do. Or wait, how about his Social Security number?"

"Too risky." Owen shook his head. "Besides, Jason's right, people tend to go for the obvious. What was important to Smitty?"

"His wife. Try 'Vivianne.'"

He entered the name but the computer beeped again, refusing entry.

"Wait a minute," Tyler said, staring down at the laptop. "Type it again."

Raising an eyebrow, Owen repeated the action without argument.

"There," Tyler said, pointing at the screen. "It's beeping before you finish typing. It's only accepting five characters."

"Great," he sighed. "That narrows the possibilities to like a trillion."

"No." Tyler shook her head. "We've just got to think. It's going to be something obvious."

"Like what? Smitty's favorite food. His favorite sports team. Or maybe we're totally off track and it's related to Smitty's work. A word that was on his mind. You know, like 'nukes.'" Owen typed in the word just for effect. The computer beeped twice.

"Be careful." Tyler laughed, forgetting for a moment the seriousness of their situation. "You're pissing it off."

"Well, at least I got it to engage," he said. "You couldn't even get it to pay attention."

"We're never going to find the password," she said, dropping into the chair beside him. "You're right. There are just too many possibilities."

"Well, I still think you were on to something with his wife." He typed the word "wife" in just for the hell of it.

"What about 'cancer'?" she suggested. "It's a macabre choice, but sometimes an illness consumes you." Her thoughts flickered to her father, but she pushed them away.

"No." Owen shook his head, typing, the effort followed by the stupid beep. "That's not it. Besides, I'd think it would be something positive. Something he thought about routinely, but also a word that meant something to him. For instance, my password is usually a shortened version of the town where we had a summer cottage. It's good memories."

"Well, I haven't the foggiest notion where Smitty vacationed. You could try Vietnam. He said those were great times."

"Seven letters," Owen chastised. "Besides, in his case I think it would be something closer to home. And I'm still betting it has something to do with Vivianne."

"Her maiden name?" Tyler suggested.

Owen looked down at the fact sheet. "Oldermeyer." Definitely more than five letters. "What else?"

"I don't know." Tyler closed her eyes, trying to remember Smitty's house. Maybe there was something she'd seen. Her mind's eye trotted forth the messy living room, the hallway, and finally the bedroom. There'd been the photographs, the medicine bottles, the hospital bed, the dead flowers... "Hang on. Try 'tulips.'"

"Too long." Owen frowned. "That's six characters."

"Okay," she said, opening her eyes to focus on the computer again. "Try 'tulip,' singular. Smitty said it was Vivianne's favorite flower. He bought them for her almost every day. There were still some in the bedroom. Good memories. And a word that would have been on his mind."

Owen shrugged, and typed. The computer was silent for a moment and then happily hummed to life, opening a new screen, this one with a directory. "Well, bugger that," Owen stared at the directory page, "we're in."

"Maybe I'm better than I thought," Tyler said, bending closer to peer at the list. "So what have we got?"

"A lot of technical stuff," Owen said, opening one of the documents. "This must be the schematic he was talking about."

"For the detonators." Tyler nodded, studying the screen. "Pretty damn impressive. I can see why people would want to steal it. It's the perfect combination of simplicity and sophistication. I had no idea it was so advanced."

"I'd thought you'd have seen the detonators when you packed up the transport."

"I did. But only from the outside. And the casing isn't anything to write home about. But this..." she tapped the screen, "this is truly amazing."

"And of absolutely no help in finding the people who stole it."

"Okay, so what else is on there?"

Owen paged through a long list of documents, including the blueprint for the nuclear weapon the detonators had been designed for. They paused for a moment staring at the deadly intricacies of the diagramed nuke. "Something like this could change the face of war as we know it." Owen whistled.

"The face of the world, more like it," Tyler said, shaking her head. "Again, I can see why we'd want to keep this out of enemy hands."

"Which should have been more of a concern when they designed security for the project."

"I'm sure they thought they had. But Smitty was on the inside. And security is designed against outsiders coming in—not insiders ferrying information out. He had clearance, so it would have been easy enough for him to transfer the data. It's all about variables, isn't it? I mean, this project is over a decade old. Vivianne probably wasn't even sick when it began. So there'd be no reason for anyone to have thought that Smitty presented a risk. And yet, in the end, he was the weak link. Bottom line, there are always going to be weaknesses that simply can't be predicted."

"And someone who wants something badly enough can figure out how to trade on those variables."

"Unfortunately, yes," Tyler shrugged.

"So how the hell are we going to stop these people from using the information they've gained?"

"We've got to come at it from both sides," she said, frowning, as she sorted through her thoughts. "Inside and out. First off we have to do everything in our power to figure out who's pulling strings and what exactly they're planning. And second, we have to find out who else has been selling secrets."

"Beyond Smitty, you mean."

"Yeah. I know that you and Avery believe someone from A-Tac is involved in this. In fact, originally you probably thought it was me."

"Not Avery," Owen said, shaking his head. "He never believed it."

"But you weren't sure." She sat back, waiting, not sure that she wanted the whole truth.

"The evidence wasn't on your side," he admitted with a shrug. "You have to admit there were things that made you look guilty."

"Like the fact that I was still alive?"

"That, and the discovery that your father was the one who initially got A-Tac involved. But I think Smitty has sufficiently thrown cold water on that notion. We know

now that you had nothing to do with arranging to be part of the transport team."

"I knew it all along, Owen. You're the one who had doubts."

"Well, suffice it to say, I wasn't alone," he said. "Anyway, the point is that no one can possibly buy that anymore. As I said, Smitty's confession made that perfectly clear."

"But just because you've accepted that it isn't me doesn't mean there's not still someone working on the inside—through A-Tac. It's the only reason I can think of for the people behind the heist to want me involved in the transport."

"My thoughts exactly. If there is an insider at A-Tac, what better way to monitor the investigation into the stolen detonators than to have the team assigned to the case? And once that was accomplished, they'd be able to use the inside information to throw off the investigation. They must have been ecstatic when they learned that Smitty had a previous relationship with your father."

"Or they chose him in part because of that relationship. Anyway, the point is all they had to do was get my dad to call in a favor, and voilà, A-Tac's involved and I'm on the team."

"And they've got access to any number of ways to screw with our progress," Owen said.

"Like breaking into my home. Stealing my mother's scarf."

"Leaving it at the scene." He frowned. "They obviously knew enough about you to predict the way you'd react upon finding the scarf. And more than that, they were counting on how A-Tac would respond when one of its own came under threat."

"And we played right into their hands." She shook her head.

"Yes, but we're gaining ground. And you're right about the two-pronged attack. We've got to go on the offensive—as well as ferreting out the traitor. It's the only way we'll ever be able to stop them."

"So what about the emails Smitty said he got?" she asked, pulling them back to the disk drive. "Any sign that he backed them up on the disk?"

"Not in this directory. But I wouldn't have expected them to be here. They'd be stored separately." He hit a button and the screen changed, this time broadening to show them a listing of the contents for the entire disk. He scrolled through the list, opening an occasional file they couldn't recognize from its extension.

"They're not here."

"Wait," Owen said, "there's another file here. And the extensions are .pst. That's the extension Microsoft uses for Outlook, I think."

"For emails?"

He nodded, attempting to open the file, but nothing happened.

"I don't use Outlook." She sighed. "I switched to a Mac ages ago. Jason swears by them. But there's got to be a way to convert the files, right?"

"Definitely. We could probably Google it, but I don't want to take the chance. I'd be too afraid we'd lose something important in the process."

"So you were right in the first place. We need the people at Sunderland—Harrison or Jason or someone who understands the intricacies of retrieving and tracing emails."

"Yes." He nodded. "But the good news is that we've got something. And I'm betting they'll be able to turn it into something tangible. Something to help us stop these people before something even more hideous happens."

"Like the detonation of a suitcase nuke," she said. "If the prototype in these schematics is actually produced, they'd be able to transport the bomb almost anywhere. With these specifics the damn thing could fit into something as small as a backpack."

"With catastrophic results."

"I bet you wish you hadn't walked into all of this," she said, rubbing her temples as she leaned back in her chair.

"It's what we do." He shrugged.

"But don't you ever wish for something normal?" she asked. "You know, two and a half kids and a picket fence?"

"This is normal—at least for people like you and me. We made a choice, Tyler. And the one thing I've learned in this life is that there are costs for every decision we make. And most of the time, once the choice has been made, there's no going back."

"You make it sound so fatalistic."

"Hey, you're the one who said people like us weren't cut out for relationships."

"So maybe I was wrong." She leaned forward, her gaze locked with his. "Maybe I do want something more."

"With me?" He frowned, studying her face.

"No, with the guy who delivered our room service."

"He was a little old," Owen said, "but I guess I could see him behind that white picket fence."

"You're being purposely dense." She stood up, walking over to the window.

"I suppose I am," he said, moving to stand behind her. "It's just that things are complicated. You said it yourself."

"*Life* is complicated. And like I said, maybe I was wrong." She turned to face him, their bodies separated by inches.

"I thought you were opposed to playing where you worked?" he taunted.

"It was a stupid choice of words," she countered, her eyes on his mouth.

"But you told me you didn't want entanglements. No relationships, remember?"

"God, what are you, a fucking tape recorder?" She lifted a hand to touch his face.

"At the risk of ruining this charming interlude, I need to know what you meant when you said you'd been down this road before."

She stilled, her heart pounding. But there could be nothing gained without honesty. "I was in love once. When I first joined the Army. I did a tour in Iraq and I met Justin there. He was special ops. It was one of those instant connections. I don't know, in hindsight, maybe it was the situation. Danger magnifies emotion and all that. All I know is that I thought it was the real thing. He even asked me to marry him."

"I see."

"No, actually, you don't." Her fingers were still pressed against his skin, and she looked up at him, her heart twisting. "I said yes. And then he informed me that he couldn't wait for me to get the hell out of Iraq. He'd arranged for a discharge. He didn't want his wife in the line of fire. He thought I'd be overjoyed."

"But you weren't."

"No, I wasn't. This was the man I thought I was going to spend my life with and he didn't even know who I was. If he had he'd never have asked me to give up my career. Hell, Owen, it's who I am. And when I refused to go home, he just stood there completely silent, staring at me as if I'd grown two heads. I don't know, maybe as far as he was concerned I had. Anyway, that was the last time I ever saw him. Just as simple as that: He turned his back and walked away."

"And you?"

"I signed up for two more tours and then joined A-Tac. I'm nothing if not predictable. And I swore I'd never risk my heart again."

"Not all men are afraid of strong women, Tyler."

"I want to believe that. I do. It's just that I'm afraid. I wouldn't be standing here at all except that finally after all this time I think I know what it is that I need."

"And that would be?" His eyebrow quirked upward, his hands closing over hers.

"You," she whispered, shivering in anticipation. "I need you."

"If we do this, if we open those doors, there are bound to be repercussions."

There was a warning there, but she ignored it, her desire for him overpowering common sense. "I don't care," she said, her breathing coming in little gasps, the fire inside her building to a fever pitch.

"Well, I do." He sighed, releasing her hands, a shadow crossing his face. "And there are things we should talk about, things I need to—"

"Later." She grabbed his shoulders, forcing him to look at her. "We'll talk later. Right now, I just want to feel

you inside me." She paused, searching his eyes, relieved
to see that she wasn't alone in her desire. "*Please*."

She reached for his hands again, capturing his fingers.
With a soft, slow movement, she kissed his palm. Desire,
hot and insistent, spread through her belly, reaching
lower, quivering, waiting. She raised her hand and ran
it along the curve of his jaw, feeling the rough begin-
nings of his beard, then trailed her fingers across his lips,
pleased when she felt his body tremble at her touch.

With a moan of pleasure, he pulled her into his arms,
crushing her to him, nuzzling the soft skin of her neck,
and her heart threatened to break through her chest. With
soft, dry kisses, he traced the line of her neck and shoulder, stopping along the way to explore with his tongue.
She closed her eyes, allowing sensation to wash over
her, his hands massaging the small of her back, her skin
prickling with need.

She arched against him, his lips at her ear now, his
tongue licking, exploring. Shivers of ecstasy ran up her
spine and something deep inside her began to pulse
in response to his ministrations. His hands found her
breasts, his strong fingers cupping them, thumbs circling
and squeezing, heat pooling deep inside her until she was
rubbing against him like a crazed cat, her body begging
for more.

He bent his head, circling her nipple with his tongue,
and she gasped, pushing against him. God, she wanted
this man, wanted him on a level far beyond the physical.
The thought should have frightened her, but it didn't. It
was almost as if he were a part of her. As if without him,
she would never be whole again.

Clearly, she'd lost her mind—but what a wonderful way to go.

With a playful smile, she stepped back, pulling the shirt over her head. Then, closing her eyes, moving to the rhythm of unheard music, she let her hands slide across the curves of her breasts and stomach. And then she slipped her hand into the waistband of her jeans, inching the zipper down, still moving, caressing, dancing—only for him.

She stepped free of her jeans and panties, licking her lips as she undulated slowly, offering herself to him. His eyes devoured her, and she danced closer, still touching herself, each stroke slow and sensuous.

"Ah, Tyler," he breathed, closing the distance between them, his hands hot against her skin, his lips crushed against hers. Their tongues intertwined—a duel of senses—both of them taking and giving, their need a living, breathing thing.

Swinging her up into his arms, he carried her to the bed, laying her against the cool cotton of the sheets, leaving her only long enough to remove his clothes. And then his hard, muscled body covered hers.

Her mouth found his and her tongue playfully traced the line of his teeth. He gently slid a finger between the soft folds of her skin, and she writhed against him, biting down on his lip, as he lightly flicked the tiny nub. Fire licked through her, threatening to send her over the edge. Here and now. But it was too soon. Too soon.

She shifted, the motion taking his finger deeper, her body tensing and then releasing as she pulled free. And then together, gazes still locked, they rolled over, her legs straddling the hard length of his body. She looked down into his eyes and smiled as she settled against him, then leaned down, her hair dropping around them like a curtain. With a half-moan, she pressed against him, rubbing her nipples against the scarred skin of his chest.

Owen shuddered as Tyler wrapped a hand around him. It had been so long since he'd felt like this. As if anything were possible as long as she was here, as long as she was part of him. Her fingers were moving now, stroking, squeezing. Up, down, up, down. Oh, God, she was amazing.

He found her lips and kissed her deeply, sucking and stroking with his tongue, mimicking the actions of her hand, longing to bury himself in her throbbing warmth. Finally, he pulled free, his breathing coming in rasps, and she raised her arms to twine them in his hair, her breasts pressed against his chest.

They gyrated together, following the moves of a spontaneous dance, the feeling of their bodies rubbing together almost more than he could bear. He tried to maintain rational thought, but his heart was beating in tandem with hers and he knew that, at least for this moment, she belonged to him.

And he would give her all that he had to give.

With a groan, he bent and took a nipple into his mouth, circling it with his tongue, feeling it tighten with his touch. Then he trailed his fingers down her belly in slow, sensuous circles, moving lower and lower, until he slid a finger inside her again, her muscles tightening around him in welcome, her heat surrounding him. She cried out as he found her soft center, and he smiled, nipping at one taut nipple with his teeth.

Pleasure combined with pain as his fingers moved deeper, stroking and pulling, ecstasy coiling inside, waiting, wanting. Tyler's body sang with each stroke, each tug of his mouth at her breast, the heat building inside her, until she literally throbbed with desire, wanting him so badly it hurt. She moaned his name, throwing her head back, as he drove her higher.

Then he lifted her, shifting so that his lips replaced his fingers, his tongue and mouth making her writhe, her breathing coming in shallow gasps, his tongue darting in and out, in and out, the glorious tension ratcheting within her. Sensation surrounded her, driving her higher and higher, until there was nothing but the feel of his mouth and her deep, desperate need.

He changed the rhythm, moving higher and circling her clitoris with featherlike strokes, pressing, releasing, pressing again, her body tightening like a spring until suddenly she split apart, shaking as spasms of pleasure racked through her. Breathing his name, she fell against him, boneless, his warmth enveloping her as his arms closed around her.

For a moment he held her, and then his mouth found hers again. His tongue ravaged her, sliding into her mouth and thrusting with a rhythm that matched her own. She felt the fire building again and marveled at the power of her need.

"I want you."

She hadn't realized she'd spoken the words until she saw the answering desire flash in his eyes. Circling her waist with his hands, he lifted her up, and with a moan, she twined her legs around him, as he lowered her, impaling her with his heat. They sat for a moment, coupled together, one soul, one heart.

And then they began to move.

She closed her eyes and allowed the sensations to surround her as he thrust, pleasure building as they moved—in and out, up and down. Passion surging, she urged him on, begging for more. She wrapped her arms around him, holding tightly as he held her pinned above the world, her entire being concentrated on the exquisite feel of him pounding deeper and harder.

She bent and kissed him then, her breasts dancing against his chest, and together they found a rhythm that carried them beyond passion, beyond anything Tyler could possibly have imagined. And she called his name as fragments of light and color twirled around them like a kaleidoscope gone wild. She locked her arms around him, feeling his body spasming inside hers as she, too, found her release.

And suddenly she knew that, in this moment, with this man, everything was perfect. Absolutely perfect.

But if she'd listened to her head instead of her heart, she'd have remembered a lesson hard learned—some things were simply too good to be true.

CHAPTER **16**

The sun was shining through the overhanging trees, the dappled light painting the campus in a sheen of gold. Everything was still a mess. Tyler knew that. Her father was dead. Somebody out there was quite probably planning to detonate a nuclear bomb. Those same people were trying to kill her. And she had a stack of papers on her desk that weren't going to grade themselves.

But somehow, none of it had the power to affect her mood. She'd been up since early morning, flown halfway across the country, been inundated by texts from Emmett and Avery. And yet all she could think about was last night.

She hadn't any idea how it would all turn out. She wasn't even certain that she and Owen had a real future. But there was a chance. And that alone seemed a small miracle. She'd even told him about Justin. Admitted her worst fears.

God, she had it bad.

And, she hoped, so did he.

The thought sobered her and she slowed her pace, the sun slipping behind a cloud. They hadn't actually discussed anything. Owen had said he wanted to talk. And Tyler knew that they should. But the morning had been hectic. Their flight had literally left before sunup and then there'd been the hassles of travel combined with the urgency to get the flash drive to Harrison.

The only reason she wasn't with them now was that she had a class. And Avery was a stickler about maintaining balance between their so-called normal lives and operations. It wasn't always easy, but Tyler prided herself on being able to simultaneously deal with both worlds. After all, without the Aaron Thomas Center and the cover it provided, there'd be no A-Tac.

She shook her head, pulling her thoughts away from Owen. There'd be time for talking later. Right now, she had work to do.

"Tyler," Emmett called from across the paved courtyard fronting the library. "There you are. I've been trying to reach you."

"I'm sorry," she said, immediately feeling guilty. "I got your texts, I just didn't have a chance to answer. It's been really hectic. A lot going on. I just figured I'd find you once I got back."

"I'm sorry about your dad," he said, falling in step beside her. "I know it must be hard."

"You know, the funny thing is," she shook her head, "I feel more numb than anything. I guess it's going to take time to sink in. And in the meantime, I'm just concentrating on finding the people who killed them."

"I heard you guys managed to secure a flash disk."

"Yeah, we're hoping there's something there that will lead to Smithwick's contact. Although it's a long shot. Owen and Harrison are working on it now. Jason's supposed to be helping. So what was so urgent?" she asked.

"I'd rather wait for Avery. He's in your office, actually." Emmett shot her a sheepish look.

"Well, that sounds ominous. Am I in trouble?"

"No. Of course not. I just stumbled on something a little disconcerting and Avery and I thought you should know."

"Something about the detonators?"

"Indirectly." He waved his hand, dismissively. "Just hang on. We'll be there in a minute."

"Did Avery send you to find me?" This was becoming a regular occurrence. First Nash and now Emmett. "I don't need babysitting, you know."

"Of course not." Emmett smiled. "We're just all worried about you. It's been a rough couple of days."

"And then some," she sighed, suddenly grateful for her friends, even if they were a bit on the pushy side.

They walked up the steps of the humanities building and down the hall to her office. She stepped through the door, followed by Emmett. Avery stood in front of the bookshelf leafing through a treatise on Shakespeare's use of comedy in drama. The book had been written by a friend considered an expert on the topic.

"I see Emmett found you," Avery said, closing the book and returning it to the shelf.

"Yes, and he's been very cloak and dagger about why you felt it necessary to send a search party."

"You haven't been answering your phone."

Tyler sighed. "So what's this all about?"

"Sit down," Avery said, as Emmett perched himself on the windowsill. Behind him the scarlet leaves of a sugar maple undulated in the wind, a group of students spread out on the ground beneath it, the perfect picture of academia.

Tyler walked behind the desk, dropping down into the chair, waiting as Avery sat down across from her. "Okay, I'm a captive audience." She frowned. "Spill."

The big man exchanged a glance with Emmett and then crossed his arms, his dark gaze meeting Tyler's. "I know that you've been working closely with Owen Wakefield."

This was not the topic she'd been expecting. She'd assumed they were going to talk about her being too involved to deal with the investigation professionally. "Yes," she said, her frown deepening. She wasn't about to tell them just how intimate the two of them had become. And she prayed that they weren't going to ask. Some things were meant to be kept private. Even from close friends. "I mean, isn't that what you wanted?"

"Absolutely." Avery nodded. "It's just that Emmett has discovered some things that may make that more difficult. And I wanted you to find out before we confront Owen."

"Confront him?" Now she was confused. "What the hell did you find out?"

"Well, for starters," Emmett said, "his name isn't Owen Wakefield."

Tyler felt as if someone had just nailed her with a sucker punch. "I beg your pardon?"

"His real name is Owen Cantor," Avery said. "And he's not working for MI-5. He's working for Logan Palmer."

"IA."

The internal affairs division of the NSA was universally hated by everyone in the Intelligence community. Created in the wake of new government "transparency," it was especially loathed by the CIA. There had never been any love lost between NSA and the Central Intelligence Agency. But the post-9/11 era had only increased the rift. And the creation of Palmer's IA team had sealed the deal, the National Security Administration using its newly minted powers to hamstring the CIA's black ops divisions. Basically, Palmer was a major thorn in their side.

"You're telling me that Owen is actually working for IA?" She shook her head, willing there to be some alternative explanation.

"Yes." Avery nodded, his expression grim.

"And you're sure?" she asked, the idea not sitting well at all.

"Positive," Emmett sighed. "I ran a check on his cell phone calls. And it was right there in black and white. He's been talking back and forth with Palmer this whole time."

"But I thought you checked his credentials when he showed up at Sunderland." She shook her head, her stomach churning at the thought that Owen had lied.

"We did," Avery said. "And he checked out. But we didn't really dig that deeply. And it turns out it was all a scam. I talked with the director of MI-5 this morning. Took a little browbeating but he finally admitted that the confirmation had been at Logan's behest. A little NSA arm twisting. Fortunately, the CIA still trumps NSA when it comes to foreign operatives."

"So he was never with MI-5?"

"Oh, he was with them," Emmett said, disgust chasing across his face. "But they ran him off the reservation.

Issued a burn notice. Apparently he went rogue and inter-
fered with an operation. Two MI-6 operatives were killed
in the process. He's lucky he wasn't tried for treason."

"When did all this happen?" she asked.

"About six years ago," Avery said. "We don't have all
the details, they're classified. I've started the ball rolling
to get them released, but it has to go through diplomatic
channels. Anyway, the bottom line is that Owen Wakefield is actually Owen Cantor. And as far as the Brits are
concerned, he's a liability, not an asset."

"Have you talked to Palmer?" Tyler asked, her hands
turning clammy.

"No." Avery shook his head. "We wanted to confront
Owen first. But Emmett's digging did produce another
piece of information you should know; Owen was tasked
with proving that someone in A-Tac had a hand in the
detonators' disappearance."

"And the primary suspect was me. Actually, he admitted that he thought I was guilty. But he said he didn't
believe it anymore. I guess he was just playing me."

She'd thought Owen was different. That he was one
of the good guys. Someone she could trust. She thought
about all the things she'd told him. She'd been so fucking gullible. She'd opened her heart, and yet, when she
thought about it, he'd told her practically nothing. And
the hard, cold truth was that anything he had said had
probably been a lie.

"I'm sorry," Avery said, his eyes conveying more than
just perfunctory sympathy. He knew how much she'd
started to care. The idea made her physically sick. She'd
let down her defenses—and it had all been a trap.

"I'm fine," she lied. "I just can't believe any of this. What about Harrison? Does he work for Logan, too?"

"No," Emmett said. "He seems to be exactly who he says he is. But clearly, he knows who Owen is working for. And what their objectives are."

"To nail me for something I didn't do."

"I think that might be putting it a bit too strongly," Avery said, his eyes kind. "I think the truth is that Owen was sent here to try to figure out if we had anything to do with what happened. And you of all people have to recognize that on the surface there were good reasons to assume you might be involved somehow."

"Agreed." She nodded once, her fingers curling into fists. "But that doesn't excuse his pretending to be something he's not. We offered him carte blanche because we believed he was part of the Intelligence community of an allied nation. And that that nation had been our partner in the detonator project. If we'd known he was from IA—"

"We'd have shown him the door in short order. Which explains why he had to lie to gain our trust."

"It might be an explanation, but it doesn't do a damn thing to excuse the transgression," she said, anger surging to replace the initial wash of despair. "The man's been lying to us about everything. And you know as well as I do that Logan Palmer would like nothing better than to bring down A-Tac. He hates everything we stand for."

Logan Palmer had worked for the CIA long before Tyler had opted in. He'd been a rising star, to hear some people tell it. But he'd also had a single-minded need for power, and he didn't much care what he had to do to get it. He'd pushed the limits and placed his people at risk.

Avery had been among the people to call him on it,

succeeding in tarnishing the star and pushing him back down the ranks. But Palmer wasn't about to let anyone stand in his way. So the minute public sentiment turned against covert ops, Palmer had seen his opportunity, outing Intelligence operatives and operations that never should have seen the light of day.

Heads had rolled, people's careers had been ruined. And worse, public exposure had meant the death of several key undercover operatives, the other side only too delighted to have their adversaries unveiled.

And as a result of his handiwork, Palmer had moved to NSA as head of the newly established Internal Affairs division.

"I'll handle Logan," Avery said.

"So what do we do about Owen?" Emmett asked.

"Nothing we can do. I've talked with Langley, and to avoid a public spectacle they want us to work with NSA on this. And if it's not Owen, it'll be someone else. Or worse, they'll send in someone else to work behind our backs, which will just make a mess of everything."

"But it seems to me that Owen is dangerous," Emmett said. "He's gotten operatives in England killed. What if he goes rogue again?"

"There's nothing to indicate that'll happen." Avery shook his head. "So far, I believe he's been totally forthcoming."

"Except for lying about everything," Tyler said, bitterness coloring her tone.

"I know this is going to be difficult." Avery's gaze was probing. "Especially for you."

"It's no worse for me than any of you," she snapped.

"He was investigating you," Emmett said. "And you

have to work closely with him. That'd be hard for anyone."

Tyler nodded, knowing that protesting too much would be the same as confessing she'd fallen for the man. *Past tense.*

Turned out there hadn't really been anyone to fall for.

"So it's just business as usual?" she asked.

"I think we'll need a little more oversight. I'm going to pull the full team in on this now. And as I said, if you want out—"

"No fucking way."

"All right then. I'll tell him we know. Which ought to at least even the playing field."

"I'm not so sure," Emmett began. "Logan is a dangerous adversary. And Owen Wakefield, or Cantor, or whatever the hell his name really is, seems to be cut from the same cloth."

"I can understand your concern," Avery acknowledged. "And I'm grateful that you uncovered it. But I think we're better off staying in the mix."

She didn't like it one little bit, but Avery was right. "What's the old saying?" she asked with forced brightness. "'Keep your friends close and your enemies closer?'" Little had she known she'd been doing exactly that.

So much for happily ever after.

CHAPTER 17

've managed to isolate a server," Jason said, frowning down at his computer. "It's out of Washington, but there's no ID, and it's definitely not the end user."

Owen swiveled his chair so that he could see as well. "Can you tell how close to the source we are?" They'd been working on an email extracted from Smitty's flash disk. There'd been a whole series, actually. But so far none of them had been traceable.

"No. But we've got to be closing in," Jason said. "Harrison, I'm sending it to you. Maybe you'll have more luck." For the moment at least, Jason seemed to have dropped his animosity. He'd been quite useful as they'd worked to try to isolate the source of the communications.

"I'll give it a shot," Harrison said. "And I'll go over the original protocols again. Maybe there's something we've missed."

Owen stifled a yawn. It was slow and painstaking work, reminding him of why he preferred the field. Give him a gun and a good lead any day. Computers were the wonder of the modern age, but computer forensics was slow and ploddingly dull stuff.

Of course, there was another reason he was having trouble concentrating. Tyler. The woman had worked her way under his skin. In a good way, to be sure, but there were so many complications. Not the least of them being that he hadn't found the courage to come clean with her. He'd tried, but she'd been focused on other things, and to be honest, he'd been relieved.

There was nothing to say she wouldn't run for the hills as soon as she learned the truth. Not only because he was working for Logan and had originally suspected her, but also because of what he'd done six years ago. There had been good reasons, of course. And at the time it had seemed his only option. His only way to avenge. But there were costs involved. And now, for the first time in a long time, he wondered if he'd made the right choice.

"Hang on a minute," Harrison said, looking across at Jason. "I think I've found a link between the server in Washington and one in New York. And this one isn't just a relay. Which means it's possible the emails originated from this network. But so far I'm not finding access to IPs for individual computers."

"What about a physical location?" Owen asked, forcing himself back to the present.

"Nothing that helps." Harrison shook his head. "At the moment all I've got is Manhattan."

"Great, that narrows it down to a few billion computers."

"I said it wasn't much." Harrison shrugged, still studying the display.

"Hey, it's a start," Jason said, rolling over to Harrison's station, squinting at the computer screen. "It might not be as difficult as it seems to narrow it down. It just takes perseverance." He grinned at Harrison, whose answering smile was like a secret handshake. They were clearly lost in their own little world. And even though neither completely trusted the other, they still spoke the same language.

"Tell me we're making some progress," Avery said, striding into the room, his stature, as always, imposing.

Emmett stood in the doorway behind Avery, arms crossed, watching Owen. There was something in his expression—a warning maybe—that set off Owen's internal alarm.

"Everything's fine," he said. "Harrison and Jason think maybe they've got a lead." His gaze shifted from Emmett back to Avery. "What's going on?"

"We need to talk." Avery hadn't moved since he'd walked into the room, his expression carefully guarded. "Jason, why don't you go with Emmett."

"But I..." Jason began, his frown mirroring Owen's confusion.

"Emmett will explain everything," Avery said. "Harrison, I'll ask you to go as well."

Harrison shot a questioning look toward Owen, but he shook his head, thankful for the support, but equally certain that it was better to deal with Avery one on one. "Just keep looking for answers. I'll check in when I'm finished here."

"Jason," Avery called as Harrison gathered his laptop, "I want you to work with Harrison. Make sure you mirror everything he's doing. I want to be sure we're all working on the same page."

Owen's stomach twisted. Avery knew. The question was how much.

Jason shot another quizzical look in Avery's direction.

"No problem," Harrison said. "We're all after the same thing. Finding the nuke and stopping it." There was an undercurrent in his words, but his face remained affable. And Owen wondered, not for the first time, if anything ever rattled Harrison Blake.

Avery waited until everyone had left the room, then indicated a chair at the table. Owen sat down, and Avery followed suit. For a moment there was silence, the older man studying him intently. "I'm guessing you know what this is about," he began.

"I have an idea," Owen said, settling back, determined to keep his cool. "But why don't you tell me anyway."

"Emmett ran a check on your phone records."

"My phone is secure."

"And I make my living end-running that sort of thing. NSA's technology isn't good enough to stop us from gaining access, although to be honest, I'm not so sure you were as protected as you'd like to think."

"So what? You're saying Logan wanted you to find out who I was?"

"I wouldn't put it past him. Sort of a way of thumbing his nose. As you probably are aware, the two of us have a history."

"I didn't know specifically, but it doesn't surprise me. Alpha dogs seldom agree to play nice."

"Yes, well, we're cut from slightly different cloth, Logan and I. And to be frank, I'm surprised you're willing to play on his team. I wouldn't have pegged you for a whistleblower."

"Desperate times and all that. Have you ever been burned?"

"Can't say that I have," Avery said, "but I can imagine it's not a pleasant situation. It's not designed to be."

"It's like being erased. As if you never existed at all. No records. No bank account. Nothing. One minute you're a contributing part of society and the next— everything that made you 'you' is gone."

"Sanctions like that exist for a reason, Owen."

"Perhaps." He shrugged. "But it's possible the reason isn't what you think it is. There are two sides to every story."

"I don't doubt that. But your past isn't my concern. What I care about is the viability of my organization. And the well-being of my people. And just at the moment, you are a threat to both."

"All due respect, I think you have a hell of a lot more to worry about than my involvement with A-Tac. We may not be on the same team, Avery, but we're playing with the same goal in mind."

"You understand if I'm a bit skeptical about that. Logan Palmer is out for one thing and one thing only. To work his way up the political ladder any way he can."

"I take it you're not going to keep this under wraps?"

"I don't lie to my team. I find it undermines authority. And besides, Emmett made the discovery and he's not the strong and silent type."

"So what happens now?" Owen asked.

"If I had my way, you'd be out on your ass. But we're in a strange new world politically and Langley wants us to take the higher ground. Meaning you're still part of the team. But I warn you, if I see anything that makes me think you're acting outside my authorization, I don't give a damn if the president himself wants you to stay—you're gone. Am I making myself clear?"

"Perfectly. And just for the record I don't give a damn if I stay or go."

"Somehow, I'm not buying that. I'm not blind, Owen. I've seen you and Tyler together."

His heart leaped into his throat, an awful possibility presenting itself. "Does she know?"

"Yes." Avery's gaze was steady. "I thought she had a right to hear about it before everyone else found out."

"Bloody hell." The words came of their own accord. "I wish you'd waited."

"For what? For you to twine her around your finger and then blow her to bits?"

"It's not like that."

"Prove to me it isn't. Walk away. Walk away now."

"I can't do that. For any number of reasons. But most principally because of Tyler. She's become very— important to me." The words sounded lame but he wasn't going to delve into his private life with Avery. Hell, he hadn't really even dealt with it himself.

"Then I'd say you have your work cut out for you," Avery said. "As you can imagine, my news didn't go down well."

"You say you don't want to hurt her," Owen growled, coming to his feet. "What the hell did you think was going to happen when you told her?"

"I didn't lie to her, Mr. *Cantor*. You did." Avery stood up, hands on the table as he leaned forward, his anger palpable. "And I can promise you that if you so much as lift a finger to upset her, you'll have to deal with me, and believe me, I have the power to make your burn notice seem like a walk in the fucking park. Am I making myself clear?"

"Crystal," Owen said, his fists clenched as he fought for control. "But you also need to know that I've been to hell and back again and I've survived, partly because I'm not big on cut and run. I stay to see things through. And that's exactly what I intend to do now. So you can either work with me or against me. But I'm not walking away. Not from this operation. And not from Tyler. Got it?"

Surprisingly, the big man smiled. "I have to admire your determination. But I'm not sure that it'll be enough. I've known Tyler a really long time. And she isn't exactly the type to forgive and forget."

"All right, so who can tell me the difference between the poem's first two stanzas and the third?" Tyler looked out across her class, trying to keep her focus.

Everything in her life seemed to be imploding. She'd always prided herself on being able to deal with anything. And now it was almost as if fate were pushing back. Trying to see just how much it would take before she fell completely apart.

She should have known better. Known that Owen was too good to be true. So much so that he didn't even exist. His interest in her had only been a means to an end. And Tyler had opened her heart like a star-struck adolescent.

With a sigh she pulled her mind back to the present and their discussion of Emily Dickinson's poem 341. How utterly fitting.

"Brian," she said, nodding at a student in the front row, waving his arm with an enthusiasm worthy of Harry Potter's Hermione.

"The last stanza is a summary of sorts," the boy began earnestly. "A clarification of the first two, really."

"Well put," Tyler said, forcing a smile. "Anyone else?" Of all the days to cover Dickinson's poem about grief and the mind-numbing pain that comes along with it.

"Well, literally it's about dying in the snow, isn't it?" a girl in the corner shrugged. "I mean, first you think it's all beautiful and then the next thing you know you're colder than hell, and then you sort of just drift away, forgetting the very thing that's killing you."

"I think that's a bit too literal. But you're on the right track," Tyler said. "Dickinson is using the snow to symbolize the journey we take in dealing with grief. At first it stuns us, and then we're numbed completely, but eventually, the pain wins through and we face it and then finally we can let go. And while the obvious parallel is death. I think we grieve over all kinds of things."

Like love lost and lying men.

As if conjured by her thoughts, Owen appeared in the doorway, and even though she was angry, she couldn't help but notice how her heart lifted at the sight of his face.

Damn the man.

And damn Dickinson and her poetry. Snow, chill, stupor—her ass. Grief might be something one could let go, but betrayal was an entirely different thing.

"Anyway," she continued, "though the degree of grief can vary, the process is always the same. What Dickinson has done is put it into universal terms. And that's the essence of good poetry, isn't it? Finding the right words? A truth that resonates with everyone." She smiled at the class, careful to keep her eyes away from the door—and

Owen. "Okay, that's it for today. Next class we'll continue with Dickinson's poem 254."

Great—from "grief" to "hope" in one fell swoop. God, life would be simpler if only she were a poet. She gathered her notes, avoiding her students as she made her way to the back exit, intent on avoiding a public confrontation.

But Owen clearly had other ideas, intercepting her before she could make it safely out the door. "I wanted to tell you myself," he said without preamble, as several students gave them curious looks.

"Not here," she said, grabbing his elbow and pulling him out of the lecture hall. They walked in silence to her office, and only when they were safely inside with the door closed did she dare to look at him, her heart pounding as both anger and disappointment swirled inside her.

"Tyler, I'm sorry." He lifted his hands palms up in supplication, but she shook her head.

"I don't want to hear it. In fact, I don't want to hear *you*."

"I can understand that," he said, his dark eyes clouded with regret, "but you've got to give me a chance to explain."

"Why? You've been lying to me from the moment I met you. I trusted you, Owen, and you made a fool out of me. Why should I listen to anything you have to say?"

"Because I care about you. And because you know that there's something going on between the two of us."

"Believe me, anything between us died the minute I found out who you really worked for. And besides, how can I possibly believe anything you've said, when clearly you were just working an angle to get what you needed."

"I wasn't working anyone. I told you I didn't know I'd be asked to come here when we spent the night together."

"Yes, but you were already lying. You told me you were MI-5."

"Actually, you told me, if I remember correctly. I just didn't bother to deny it."

"That's just semantics," she said, waving her hand. "It's still the same thing. And besides, it's not just that you didn't work for them anymore, they'd issued a burn notice. For God's sake, Owen, you got your own people killed."

"I promise you, there's more to the story than that."

"Well, I'm not interested in hearing it. I actually believed you were someone special. Someone I could believe in. Someone I could trust. And instead, you're... you're a figment of my imagination. Or yours. Was anything you told me the truth? Is your father really a fisherman in Cornwall? And is his name Cantor or Wakefield?"

"Cantor," Owen said, a muscle in his jaw ticking. "And I didn't expect any of this to happen. I was just doing my job."

"Spying on us."

"Tyler, you admitted yourself that there's a problem within A-Tac."

"Yes, but it's our problem. We don't need some has-been from NSA snooping around. We can take care of our own."

"I'm not really seeing a lot of evidence of that."

"Yeah, well, you haven't exactly changed the status quo, either. You've been too busy seducing the enemy. Too bad I didn't roll over and give you everything you needed to convict me of something I didn't do."

"I wasn't trying to railroad you. I was just following leads. And the reality is that you looked guilty as sin."

"So you bedded me," she said with a tight little smile. "Makes perfect sense."

"I didn't *bed* you. I made love to you. And I might add, you were the one who did the original seducing."

"Because I thought you were someone else."

"Yes, a one-off. Not exactly sterling behavior on your part either."

"I didn't think I'd ever see you again. And I certainly didn't think we'd be working together."

"I'm just saying that maybe you ought to be a little more introspective before you start throwing around accusations."

"Don't put this off on me. I didn't lie to you. I didn't pretend to be someone I'm not. In fact, if anything, I opened up to you. Told you things I've never told anyone. Damn you, Owen, I believed in you."

"I'm still here. I'm still the same man."

"How the hell am I supposed to believe that?"

"You look in my eyes, and you see the truth."

"I look in your eyes and I see a low-life slimeball who's been digging for dirt using any means necessary. And even if I did see something else there, I wouldn't be able to trust it. Don't you see, you've ruined everything."

"It doesn't have to be like that. All you have to do is give me a chance."

"I gave you a chance. I went against all my better instincts and I let myself care about you. And then I find out that everything about you is a lie. Put yourself in my shoes. Would you give yourself a second chance?"

"Probably not," he sighed. "But you're a better person than I am."

"Clearly," she said, wishing to hell that she'd never laid eyes on him. "I tell the truth."

"So do I."

"Yeah, right." They were standing nose to nose, and Tyler could feel the heat of his breath against her face. Emotion threatened to swamp her, but she wasn't Zachary Hanson's daughter for nothing. "That explains the false name and fake background."

"I mean when it counts. And don't tell me you haven't used aliases for an operation before."

"Not in order to seduce someone. I don't use people like that."

"Neither do I." The words came out staccato, his anger almost palpable. "What happened between us was real."

"What happened between us is over."

"So what do you propose we do? We can't exactly ignore each other. We still have to work together."

"You could crawl back under the NSA rock and let A-Tac handle things."

"Not going to happen. I finish what I start."

"Well, so do I. And we're talking about finding the people who murdered my father. I'm sure as hell not walking away from that."

"Understood. So we'll just have to find a way to get along." His eyes met hers, his words meant as a challenge.

"I'm a professional. I can handle that. But you have to understand that there can never be anything else between us."

"Are you so certain that's what you want?" He reached

out to stroke her face and she shivered, desire surging up to mix with her anger.

"Yes." She jerked away, covering her cheek with her hand. "I'm positive." Except of course that she wasn't. A part of her yearned for him. For the joy she'd felt just this morning. But it had all been a lie. And she'd do well to remember that fact. "We're over, Owen. Hell, the truth is that we never really were."

"I beg to differ," he said, his gaze still locked with hers. "But I won't press the point. And for the record, I wanted to tell you everything. I tried last night."

"But I stopped you? So what? Now it's my fault?"

"Of course it isn't your fault. I'm the one who didn't disclose everything."

"Owen, you told me you were something you're not. And to top it off you were tasked with finding evidence to prove I was part of the plans to steal the detonators."

"I was doing my job."

"Maybe so, but you were also making me fall in love with you," she whispered, the words coming of their own accord. "And under the circumstances, that's about as reprehensible as it comes." She turned away, staring out the window, wishing the floor would open up and swallow her whole.

"Tyler," he said, her name like a plea. "If I could go back and do things differently I would. The last thing on earth I wanted was to hurt you."

"Well, you did." They stood for a moment in silence, Owen standing just behind her, his physical presence surrounding her—tempting her to throw caution to the wind. Despite everything that had happened, she still wanted him. Once a fool always a fool and all that.

"Tyler?" The door behind them squeaked as it opened, and she turned to find Jason standing in the doorway. "I'm sorry to interrupt. Avery told me you might be here." Her friend shot an angry glare in Owen's direction. "I wasn't expecting *him*."

"You and me both," Tyler said, forcing a smile. "But we don't always get what we want. So what did you need?"

"Oh, right," he said, still frowning in Owen's direction. "I've got good news. We've got a solid ID on the origin of Smitty's emails. They came from a computer that belongs to the German consulate in Manhattan. According to the logs, it's assigned to a low-level bureaucrat there. Marta Waller."

"Is she still in New York?" Tyler asked, her mind turning instantly away from her problems.

"Best we can tell, yes. We secured her home address. Figured it'd be easier to confront her there than at the consulate. Either way it's going to be tricky. Diplomatic immunity and all that. Anyway, there's a helicopter waiting and I've got all the info you need right here."

"Sounds great," Tyler said, reaching for the folder Jason held out, but Owen was faster.

"Excellent work," he said, tucking the file under his arm.

"What the hell do you think you're doing?" she asked, her voice terse.

"I'm going with you," Owen said, his eyes sparking a challenge. "We're a team, remember? And besides, I told you, I always finish what I start."

CHAPTER **18**

The Manhattan apartment building was a relic from an earlier time when tenement flophouses were the norm. Entire families crowded into a single room in a five-story walk-up. Now blocks like these were being razed for newer skyscrapers, so-called luxury apartments with exorbitant price tags and little or no curb appeal. Still, as far as old buildings went, this one had seen better days.

A row of buzzers outside the front door indicated that there were six tenants, the rest of the building empty, as witnessed by boarded-up windows and occasional broken glass. Marta Waller lived in 4B.

They'd made good time flying in from Sunderland, but the afternoon was waning, the sun sinking low on the horizon. Shadows stretched across the tree-lined street, the West Side quiet as the day faded into dusk.

"Not exactly the lap of luxury," Owen said, nodding up at the battered old building. "I guess maybe this explains why she'd find the dark side enticing. Anything for a step up from this dump."

"Hey, this is a good neighborhood. And in the city, that counts more than the physical apartment. And besides, we don't know for certain that she's actually involved in any of this. The only thing that we can be sure of is that her computer sent emails to Smitty. It's possible for someone to use a computer remotely."

"Yes, but Harrison didn't find any evidence of that. Anyway, the only way to find the truth is to find Marta Waller."

"Well then, let's hope we catch her at home, or at least find something incriminating, because once she realizes we're interested in her, she'll head for the sanctuary of the consulate. And then nobody will be talking to her."

"Maybe the Germans will surprise us."

"And admit they have a potential terrorist working for them? I find that highly unlikely. In my experience, governments, including mine, are far more likely to cover up that kind of thing than admit they allowed a mistake of that magnitude to be made."

"There's truth to that, I suppose," he acknowledged as they walked up to the apartment building door. "So do we ring the bell?"

"It's a buzzer. And no, I'd rather not announce ourselves."

So far they'd managed to keep everything on a purely professional level. The ride in the helicopter had precluded talking and they'd limited conversation on the way over to reviewing background info on Marta Waller. But despite all the effort, there was still an undercurrent of tension, both physical and emotional. And it only made their current situation more difficult.

"Right, then," he said. "So I'll see what I can do about picking the lock."

"Might be better to just wait for someone to come in?" She nodded toward an approaching couple. They were totally into each other. Eyes for no one else. Tyler shook off a wave of jealousy.

She grabbed Owen's arm and nuzzled his ear, giggling as if he'd said something charming. "Just play along," she whispered, as his eyes widened in surprise. With a nod, he framed her face with his hands, making a play of kissing her.

Her stomach swooped all the way to her feet, the stupid organ clearly not having gotten the memo about play-acting. Fortunately, she could see the other couple over his shoulder, the girl digging in her purse for keys.

"Almost there," she whispered against his lips, trying not to think about the feel of his hands warm against her back.

Damn the man.

"Hang on," Tyler said, laughing breathlessly, as the other woman opened the apartment door.

She and Owen moved forward, holding hands, as the man held the door.

"Have a good one," she called over her shoulder, as the other two followed them into the foyer. The door clicked closed behind them, and the other couple turned into the first-floor hallway. Tyler dropped Owen's hand and headed up the stairs.

"Quick thinking," Owen said. "Except that now they'll have seen us."

"It's not as if we're here to commit a crime."

"Maybe. But I'd have preferred that we be a little more circumspect."

"I didn't notice you complaining outside when you were kissing me." She clenched her fists as they rounded the second-floor landing.

He stopped her, his hand closing around her arm, his fingers burning through the thin cotton of her blouse. "I'm not the one who has a problem with our relationship. Kissing you for business or pleasure is one and the same as far as I'm concerned."

"Oh, please. There isn't a relationship. You made sure of that when you pretended to be something you weren't."

"I'm not the one who brought up kissing," he said, with a crooked smile.

She clenched her fists, giving him what she hoped was her most indignant stare. "Can we please just get on with it?"

"Fine," he said, heading up the second flight of stairs. She followed behind him, fingering her gun, imagining all kinds of lovely comeuppances. Most of them ending with Owen groveling at her feet.

The third set of stairs was narrower than the first two, the risers worn and uncarpeted. The paint on the walls was peeling to reveal old wallpaper beneath. In its heyday the building had been loved. Not so much now.

They reached the top of the stairs and moved cautiously into the hallway. There were three apartments, Marta's the second one from the landing. They stood for a minute, waiting, listening, but everything was quiet, a fluorescent light bulb in the ceiling buzzing as it flickered off and on again.

"So how do you want to handle this?" Owen asked.

"Well, I hate to go in with guns blazing, but I don't

think we can take a chance. So why don't you knock on the door, and I'll stay off to one side, gun drawn. Just in case Ms. Waller is expecting us."

"Sounds like a plan." He waited as she moved into place to the left of the door, back to the wall. "Ready?" he mouthed.

She nodded and as he lifted his hand Tyler's gaze moved to the doorframe, her heart skipping a beat as her mind registered what it was that she was seeing.

"Stop," she ordered, her hand whipping out to pull his back. "The door's booby-trapped. There's a bomb."

They stood frozen for a moment, her fingers still wrapped around his wrist, the light fixture buzzing, the sound of laughter floating up from somewhere downstairs.

Normalcy surrounded by insanity.

"Are you sure?" he asked, both of them starting to breathe again.

"Yes." She nodded at two strands of filament running the length of the doorframe's header. "It's really rudimentary. But that doesn't mean it can't do a lot of damage."

"So what do you want to do?" he asked, backing away from the wires.

"Shouldn't be that difficult to dismantle," she said, producing a tiny tool kit.

"Girl Scout?" he quipped, watching as she assessed the situation.

"Nope." She shook her head. "Military father." For a moment she hesitated, grief threatening, but she shook it off, forcing herself to concentrate on the task at hand. She took a step closer to the doorway, careful not to set off any vibration. "I'm guessing the contact is made when the door is opened. The fatter wire should be the ground, the thinner one responsible for ignition." She studied the wires and then selected a pair of clippers. "Shouldn't take but a second."

"Should I take cover?" Owen asked, his tone more mocking than worried.

"Not necessary," she said, snapping the thinner wire. Again they froze for a moment, but just as she expected, nothing happened.

"Well done," Owen noted, as he moved toward the door.

"Hang on," she said, still eyeing the filament. "Let me make sure there isn't a secondary charge." She ran her fingers along the edge of the doorframe, moving from the center of the header down each of the sides. Then she bent to check the threshold. "All clear." With a quick twist of a pick, she jimmied the lock, and they carefully opened the door.

Inside, above the door, two sticks of dynamite were taped to the wall, the cut piece of wire dangling in the open doorway.

"Close call," Owen said. "Looks like someone wants Ms. Waller out of the picture."

"Or she knew we were coming." Tyler moved into the room, gun drawn. Despite the run-down appearance of the building itself, the inside of the apartment verged on elegant, the upholstered furniture high-end, the rugs Persian, and the art, at least some of it, real. "Talk about not judging a book…"

"She's definitely got good taste," Owen said, picking up a crystal vase. "Steuben."

"So why the riches among the rags?"

"Could be any number of reasons, but I'm betting none of them are on the up and up."

"I think we can rule Ms. Waller out as the source of the bomb." Tyler flipped through a copy of Alistair MacLean's *Guns of Navarone*. "This is a first edition. No way would she want to blow this place."

"Actually, I think she's past caring one way or the other." Owen was standing in the doorway to a bedroom. Tyler's skin pricked with alarm as she rushed to his side. A woman was sprawled across the floor, her head leaning unnaturally against the bedpost. A trickle of blood trailed from the side of her mouth.

"Is she dead?"

"Looks to be," Owen said, squatting to check her pulse. "Someone broke her neck."

"Someone who knew what they were doing." Tyler frowned. "Based on the picture we've got, I'd have to say that this is Marta Waller."

Owen nodded. "There's no sign of a struggle. Maybe she knew her attacker."

"Or they simply caught her by surprise. Either way, she's not going to be much use to us."

"Well, if it matters, she hasn't been dead very long. The blood is clotting, but it's not dried. And she's still warm."

"But if she was already dead—why the booby trap?"

"For us," Owen said, pushing back to his feet. "Someone knew we were coming."

"And wanted to take us out." Tyler nodded, her mind turning over the possibilities. "But if they know as much about me as we think they do, then they'd have to have known that I'd see the bomb and dismantle it. Anyone with a modicum of experience could have figured it out."

"It was worth a try, I suppose. If we'd triggered the thing it would have accomplished two goals. Evidence of Ms. Waller's death would be covered up. And we'd have been taken out of the equation permanently."

"Or maybe someone knew exactly how we'd behave and wanted to buy themselves some time."

"To what? Set a trap?"

"It's possible." She moved back into the main room, letting her eyes scan the room, looking for some secondary source of danger. "Otherwise, why not use something more sophisticated to blow the place? Like the explosives at Smitty's?"

"Maybe they didn't have time. Or maybe you're right, and they just wanted to keep us off-balance. It fits with everything else we've encountered. Any sign of her computer?" Owen asked. "Not that I'm expecting it to be here, mind you. If they were smart enough to get rid of her, they'll definitely have taken care of anything that might tip us off to their identity."

"Well, one thing is for certain," Tyler said, frowning at the overdecorated apartment as she searched for the computer. "This is a hell of a lot bigger than just stealing some high-tech detonators. We've got six dead if you count Petrov."

"Let's not forget they've tried to take you out as well," Owen said, disappearing back into the bedroom. "At least twice that we can be certain of."

"Three, if you want to count the explosives at the door. Find anything?" she asked, following him.

"It was here," he said, pointing to some loose cables lying across a small table in the corner. "I'm guessing the killer took it."

"Any sign of backup devices? A zip drive or an extra hard drive?"

"Not that I can see." He pulled open a couple of drawers. "There's nothing here."

"How about a case somewhere? Maybe she never got a chance to unpack it?" Tyler moved back into the living room and then on into the kitchen. There was no sign of a purse or any kind of briefcase or laptop. "Someone's been through the apartment. And it definitely wasn't with an eye toward robbery."

"So we've got nothing."

"Well, slightly more than that," she said. "We've got the body and her apartment. I'll call it in and have Avery arrange for someone from the New York office to come and handle forensics. Maybe they'll see something we're missing."

"Worth a try." He nodded, sorting through a stack of unopened mail.

Tyler flipped open her phone and waited for a signal, but the little phone stubbornly refused. "I'm not getting any bars," she said, shaking her head. "I'll try in the bedroom closer to the window."

Owen nodded again, still engrossed in Marta Waller's correspondence.

In the other room, Tyler turned her back on the body and punched in Avery's number. The phone rang on the other end, and she waited, her mind trying to make sense of the latest developments.

She heard Avery's deep voice on the other end of the line just as the front door splintered open and gunfire rang staccato through the living room. "Incoming," she called into the phone, jamming it into her pocket as she pulled her gun. Dashing forward, she fired into the main room, using the door for cover.

Owen was down, but not hit, two men alternating fire from the door. She could hear a third in the hallway outside, which meant they were well and truly penned. Motioning to Owen, she popped out from behind the door firing as he crawled toward the relative safety of the bedroom.

Once he was safely inside, Tyler dropped back behind the door. "You okay?" she asked, as she reloaded her gun.

"I'm fine," he said, taking a shot as one of the men moved into the room. "That your last clip?"

"Yes. What about you?"

"This is all I've got. Didn't realize we'd be dropping into a war zone. Any chance Ms. Waller's hiding a weapon somewhere in here?"

"It's possible, but I don't think we've got the time to search. We need to get the hell out of here before they're all in from the hall. If I counted right, there's three of them. Which means we're outgunned."

"Four, actually. At least that's the count I got." He dove out, shot twice, and then retreated again behind the door. "Well, there's three now. But I'm almost out of ammo."

"All right then, it's time to sound retreat. There's a fire escape outside the window. If we're lucky they're not watching the street."

"And if they are?"

"We'll need to move quickly." She reached out and squeezed his shoulder. "We can do this. Worst case we'll head for the roof. I got Avery just before they came through the door. He'll call for help. And the lovers downstairs are bound to call 911, which means this can't go on forever."

"If they're still alive," Owen said.

"Not much of an optimist, are you?" She smiled. "Cover me while I get the window open. Then be ready to run."

Owen nodded, shifting so that he could more easily shoot around the door. "We could always use Ms. Waller as body armor."

"Don't put it past me," Tyler said, casting a glance in the direction of the dead woman. "But she'd just weigh us down. I'm going now." She scrambled across the floor, careful to keep low and out of the line of fire, but the men in the living room clearly saw her, shots ringing out from both their direction and Owen's.

Moving on a burst of adrenaline, she pushed to her feet and tugged at the window. It groaned once and then moved upward. Above her a bullet shattered the upper pane, but she kept pushing the sash. "We're clear. Get ready to move. I'll cover you," she called behind her as she swiveled and began to fire.

Owen dove across the open space between the door and window and then rolled to his feet. "You go first," he said, turning to shoot as the men in the living room rushed forward. "I'm right behind you."

Tyler threw a leg over the sill and pushed herself out the window, moving to the right toward what should have been the ladder leading down to the third floor. Only there was nothing there. The ladder was missing.

"Score one for the bad guys," she called over her shoulder. "There's no way down, and it's too far to jump. We'll have to go up."

Owen nodded, fired another volley through the window, and then reached up to pull down the ladder leading to the roof. "Ladies first," he said, pointing upward with his gun.

Tyler jumped onto the ladder and began to climb. Below her, from the street or possibly a building across the way, someone fired, the bullet breaking brick beside the ladder. "We've got a sniper," she called, as Owen pulled himself up onto the ladder below her.

"Company from inside as well," he said. "Just keep moving."

She covered the last few rungs as quickly as possible, swinging over the edge of the masonry onto the roof. The two-foot ledge gave her a modicum of protection, and she used it as a momentary advantage to locate the shooter. He was on the fire escape of the building across the street, a floor below them.

She risked a shot, and the man ducked for cover, the seconds bought allowing Owen to pull himself up onto the roof.

"Now what?" she asked. "We've got at least one shooter across the way. And three below us. My guess is that at least one of them will double back and use the stairway to the roof."

"Not if we can jam the door first."

She nodded and they ran across the roof toward the open door leading to the stairwell. It was tempting to risk trying to muscle their way down the stairs, but with limited ammo, she knew it would be foolhardy to try.

"We're going to have to find our way off the roof another way," Owen said, echoing her thoughts. "Do you see anything we can block the door with?"

She scanned the roof as a volley of bullets bit into the tarpapered roof a few feet behind her. "I think we're too late. They're almost here."

A head appeared at the top of the ladder, and Tyler got off a shot, sending him scurrying down again for cover.

"We've got to go now." Owen nodded toward a second rooftop adjacent to theirs, and they sprinted across the open roof just as a gunman emerged from the stairwell. Owen fired behind him, hitting the man in the shoulder, but not bringing him down.

Running full-out now, Tyler and Owen crossed the second rooftop, the men behind them in full pursuit. Using chimney stacks and other protrusions for cover, they made their way forward, until suddenly, the building ended, a huge gap separating it from its neighbor.

"Shit," Tyler said, flailing as she pulled herself to a stop, pieces of roofing raining down into the courtyard below them. "Now what?" She shot a look behind her. The men were closing fast, their gunfire getting closer to the mark.

"We'll have to jump." Owen backed up, his muscles tensing in preparation. "It's our only chance."

"Are you sure you're not just trying to get rid of me?"

"Darling, you're the one who wanted to end things. Not me. I'm fully prepared to spend my dotage with you. But that isn't going to happen unless we jump. *Now*."

He sprinted forward and leaped into the air, sailing over the gap and landing with a roll on the far side. "Come on, Tyler," he said, as a bullet hit the roof next to her foot.

"Dotage, my ass," she murmured as she followed his lead and raced for the edge, using her legs to launch herself into space.

For a moment she felt as if she were flying, and then she realized that she wasn't going to make it. Stretching forward in panic, her fingers closed on the stone rain gutter edging the rooftop. Her arms snapped with the tension, her body slamming into the wall, but she held tight.

"Hang on," Owen called. "I've got you." His hands closed around her wrists, and she forced herself to breathe.

"They're going to kill us," she said.

"They're still a little way off," he replied, his voice soothing. "Which means we've got a couple of seconds."

"I'm all ears," she said, her grip on the bricks weakening.

"Good." She felt his hands tighten in reassurance. "I'm going to count to three. And when I do, you're going to push off the wall with your feet. I'll pull at the same time and the combined momentum should propel you up onto the roof."

She nodded, her arms feeling as if they were going to break out of their sockets.

"One…" he started, a shot ringing out but going wide. She pressed her feet against the wall, bending her knees slightly. "Two." A second shot followed, this time much closer. She sucked in a deep breath, her muscles tightening as she prepared to push. "Three."

She shoved herself off the wall, as Owen jerked her upward, and she felt herself vault up and over the edge, her skin scraping against the masonry, the bricks below her exploding with the impact of a round of bullets.

"Perfect timing," he said. "Now I suggest we get the hell out of here."

"I'm right behind you," she called, already running across the open roof, the sound of sirens wailing in the distance. "Sounds like the cavalry's on the way."

She turned to look behind her, but with a last shot, the men were already withdrawing, intent now on making their escape.

At the far side of the building, Owen and Tyler stopped, the Hudson River visible on the horizon, the last rays of the sun turning the water a glittering gold.

"Looks like we're home free," he said, his dark eyes meeting hers as he bent to give her a quick hard kiss. "Glad to see you're still in one piece."

"Yeah, well don't get any ideas." She shook her head, sucking in a breath. "You may have saved my life, but that doesn't mean I'm ready to forgive you."

CHAPTER 19

ey, I heard what happened," Nash said, joining Tyler in the elevator leading down to A-Tac operations. "How are you feeling?"

"Pretty banged up," she said, ruefully indicating a scrape across her cheek. "Turns out buildings are hard. But whatever aches and pains I have, it's a hell of a lot better than what I'd have been if Owen hadn't been there."

"So you're not angry about his lying to us?" Nash asked, as the elevator doors slid shut and the box lurched downward.

"I'm furious. But that doesn't change the fact that he saved my life." She paused, trying to find the right words. "Sometimes I guess it isn't always easy to characterize the good guys. I mean, he's working for the king of slime, but that doesn't necessarily mean he's cut from the same cloth?" The last bit came out sounding like a question, which of course symbolized perfectly Tyler's screwed-up emotions when it came to Owen Wakefield.

"Hey, I'm the go-to guy on making wrong assumptions." He held up his hands with a grin. "I thought Annie was a traitor, and she's the love of my life. Talk about conflicts. Sometimes it's just hard to sort out the facts. In all honesty, none of us are above reproach. And even the most reprehensible people have saving graces. Basically, people aren't perfect."

"But how do you figure out the real truth then?"

"Maybe there isn't such an animal. Best I can tell you is that if your gut says you can trust someone, you probably can, no matter what the facts are telling you."

"You make it all sound so easy."

"Look, Owen lied to all of us about his background—in part because that's his job. We've all been in similar situations. But as far as his work here, he seems to have been on the up and up. And he's certainly come through for you on more than one occasion. So, if nothing else, I think that warrants giving the man the benefit of the doubt. The main thing I learned from the situation with Annie was that there are two sides to every story."

Tyler nodded, her mind spinning with her conflicting thoughts and emotions.

"And hey," Nash smiled, reaching out to squeeze her shoulder, "for what it's worth, I know you'll make the right decision. Whatever it turns out to be."

"Thanks," she said, as the door slid open, the phone in her pocket vibrating. She pulled it out as Nash swiped the back of Aaron Thomas's head, the panel in the opposite wall sliding open. Following Nash, she flipped the phone open, reading the text displayed. "It's from Jason," she said. "Says he needs to talk to me."

"Well, it'll have to wait," Nash said, nodding toward the war room. "Duty calls."

"You're right." She nodded, closing the phone. "I'll track him down after the debrief."

They walked into the war room to find Hannah and Harrison already ensconced at the front of the room, as usual hard at work behind their computers, Harrison looking particularly preoccupied. Avery was talking to Owen, the two of them animated in their discussion.

Tyler's stomach flipped as Owen lifted his head and smiled. There was just something about the man that called to her, no matter how many times he lied. She shook her head, forcing her thoughts away from Owen. There were more important things to deal with. Like who the hell had attacked them in Ms. Waller's apartment.

"So what have we got?" she asked, taking a seat next to Nash as Avery and Owen settled into chairs on the other side of the table.

"The dead man is an international mercenary," Hannah said, her pale blue glasses cat-eyed with decorative crystals. "Vincent Delano. He's not in the same league as Petrov but he's definitely in the same game. Gun for hire."

"I've heard of him," Nash said. "He was involved in the assassination of the vice chancellor in Belgium, right?"

"He's wanted for questioning. As to his guilt, there's nothing solid to pin it on him." Hannah clicked a button and the man's face filled the screen on the wall. "He seems to have no particular allegiances. He pretty much just follows the money. He's worked all over the world. And of course, as you'd expect, there's very little to link him to specific employers."

"Anyone at Interpol been tracking him?"

"Always. And we've got eyes on him as well. But he's good at staying out of sight. And nothing he's been seen doing recently would indicate who he might be working for."

"What about immigration? Any idea when he came into the country?"

"Yes," Hannah said, flipping to another photograph. "He came in across the Canadian border. Used the passport you see there. Obviously, it's an alias. The only reason we managed to track it down is that the border crossing he used into New York has been trying out new equipment. They're photographing documentation. Kind of like running surveillance. Anyway, we know he came in just under two weeks ago, which lines up perfectly with everything that's been happening around here."

"What about the scene?" Owen asked. "Did the forensics team find anything?"

"No fingerprints," Hannah reported. "Which isn't surprising. Ms. Waller's neck was broken. She died instantaneously. There was no struggle. And no sign of forced entry. They're running a tox screen just to be sure there isn't something we're missing. But basically, it looks like she knew her killer, let him into the house, and turned her back long enough for him to take her out. Again, the signs point to someone who has a specific set of skills."

"A professional," Nash said. "Anything in Delano's bio that would point to him as the killer?"

"It's possible," Harrison nodded, pulling himself away from the computer screen he'd been absorbed in, "but his MO is using guns. Sniper rifles mostly. He doesn't seem to be that keen on up close and personal."

"Which doesn't mean he wasn't the one," Avery pointed out.

"I agree," Hannah said. "Originally he was a commando in Portugal. Which means he had all the requisite training. He'd know how to break someone's neck. So even if it wasn't his preferred methodology, he'd have been more than up to the task."

"Besides, there were at least four other men involved in the attack on Owen and me." Tyler frowned. "It could have been one of them. Was there anything to give us insight into who they might have been? Ballistics, maybe?"

"Nothing popped when we ran it through the various registries, and the ballistics tests were inconclusive. Ammo was definitely not local. Possibly Russian. They're doing additional analysis at Langley."

"Whoever these people are they know what they're doing," Tyler said.

"Harrison, have you got anything to add?" Avery asked.

He jerked his head up, blinking owlishly, and shook his head, clearly trying to focus. "No. But I wasn't expecting we would. These guys knew enough not to use traceable weapons."

"What about Ms. Waller?" Owen asked. "Anything in her past that might give us a clue as to who she was working with?"

Hannah changed the photo again, this time projecting a picture of Marta Waller. "Ms. Waller had been working in the United States about eighteen months. Before that she worked for the German Foreign Service in the Berlin office. Low-level stuff, secretarial, for the most part. The move to the consulate in Manhattan was a big promotion, but not enough to have subsidized the things that were found in her apartment. According to immigration documentation, only a few of the things came over with her. The rest were acquired while she was here."

"But you're saying her salary here doesn't support those kinds of purchases." Nash leaned back in his chair, studying the photo on the screen.

"Exactly," Hannah said. "And her bank accounts both in Germany and here back that up. There's a combined balance of a couple thousand dollars and nothing to indicate that she's withdrawn more than the usual amounts needed for daily living."

"So where did the money come from?" Tyler asked.

"Well," Hannah smiled, red highlights gleaming, "thanks to Owen's quick thinking, I think I might just have the answer."

Tyler shot a questioning look at Owen.

"I stuffed the pile of mail in my pocket," he said. "Figured it might come in useful."

"And it did," Hannah said. "Most of it was local. But one envelope made reference to an offshore account. Of course, that sort of thing is highly protected. But they weren't counting on Harrison and his magic fingers." She smiled across the table at Harrison, who was still totally engrossed in what he was doing. Silence stretched for a minute and then he looked up.

"I'm sorry," he apologized, with a shake of his head. "I'm afraid I missed out on what was said."

"Must be something really interesting on that screen," Nash observed.

"You have no idea," he said, "but I didn't mean to lose track of the conversation." He looked askance at Hannah, who smiled and repeated what she'd said. "Right, the off-shore accounts. There are certain numbers that are used to identify international accounts for U.S. tax purposes. So I could tell from Ms. Waller's correspondence that the account was somewhere in the Cayman Islands. From there it just took a bit of digging."

"And calling in a couple of favors," Hannah added. "Anyway, the bottom line is that we managed to gain access to the account. The money situation was similar to Jefferson Smithwick's. Large cash deposits, in Ms. Waller's case going back for the past three or four years."

"So she was getting the money while she was still working in Germany?" Owen asked.

"Correct." Hannah nodded. "The payments were slightly less at that point. Right at twenty-five thousand. When she arrived here, the deposits jumped to just over forty thousand."

"That's a hell of a lot of money," Nash said.

"It is. But the really interesting thing is that the payments stopped last month."

"So maybe Ms. Waller had been paid in full."

"Or maybe her usefulness had simply come to an end," Owen suggested. "It certainly fits with her being killed."

"They definitely seem to be trying to tie up loose ends," Avery said.

"Or destroying them," Tyler said. "The question is why now?"

"Maybe because they know we're on to them?" Nash offered.

"But we're not." Tyler shook her head. "So it must be more than that. Maybe they're nearing endgame.

Whatever the hell that might be. Any way to tell where the money came from?"

"Not specifically. No," Harrison said. "As we mentioned earlier, the deposits were all made in cash. So the paper trail isn't as transparent. But it does look like the deposits were made from somewhere in Europe."

"We're working now to try to narrow it down," Hannah added.

"Did we get anything from Ms. Waller's employers at the German consulate?" Owen asked.

"Just that she was a good worker. Apparently quiet and kept to herself. They professed surprise when I explained that she was dead. And although they made all the right noises about helping, I got the general sense that they weren't actually planning to step up to the plate. They weren't even willing to accept the idea that this was something beyond a robbery." Harrison shrugged and returned his focus to his computer.

"Plausible deniability," Avery said. "I can't really say that I'm surprised. What have we got on Ms. Waller's background? Anything that might point to where the mystery money came from?"

"Nothing that jumps out at me," Hannah said. "She has no record. And no indication that she has strong political leanings one way or another. She's voted across the board in German elections. Mostly middle of the road with an occasional foray into supporting a conservative candidate."

"The perfect person to co-opt for this kind of thing. Run-of-the-mill, ordinary. The kind who floats under the radar. Any reason she'd need money?" Owen asked.

"Beyond her taste for the finer things, there's nothing."

Hannah shook her head. "She had a brief flirtation in her university days with a group with neo-Nazi leanings, but it's also possible she was just friendly with members. There's no record of her attending rallies or meetings. And the group broke up over eleven years ago. So it's not really anything that rings alarm bells."

"Well, see if you can track down someone who was a member," Avery said. "Then find out what they remember about Ms. Waller."

"Already on it." Hannah smiled, the light making her glasses sparkle.

"And let's also keep digging into Delano and Petrov. Maybe we'll stumble on something from that end of things. These people, whoever they are, have got to have made a mistake. We just have to find it and then turn it to our advantage."

"I assume we found nothing on my father's or Smitty's computer?"

"Nothing," Harrison said without looking up from his monitor. "It was a professional job in both cases, the computers wiped clean."

"What about chatter?" Nash asked. "Anyone claiming responsibility for any of this?"

"Not anything viable," Hannah said. "And I've been monitoring 24/7. I've even started to pull together a list of suspicious activities. Anything that might hint at obtaining the various parts needed to make the nuclear device in Mr. Smithwick's files. Particularly the sale or theft of weapons-grade plutonium. Getting information from the West is fairly straightforward. But it gets trickier when it comes to Russia and China. They're not as forthcoming. But sooner or later I'll get what I need."

"Let's hope it's sooner," Nash said. "If Tyler's right and they're nearing endgame, then that means the nuke will be ready for detonation. They've got to know that the more we dig, the narrower their window of opportunity becomes."

"Which means the clock's ticking," Tyler sighed.

"Well, one thing we know for sure," Avery said, his expression grim. "The only way they could possibly have set up an ambush at Ms. Waller's is if someone tipped them off that we were coming."

"So we've been right all along about someone working from the inside," Tyler said.

"Someone from A-Tac." Owen's words hung in the room, as everyone considered the full ramifications. They'd been talking about it for weeks. Had suspected it for even longer. But no one had really wanted to believe it. Now the idea was hard to deny.

"What about Logan Palmer?" Nash asked, his eyes probing as he turned to Owen. "Maybe we've been looking in the wrong place for the mole."

"I understand that you have issues with Logan," Owen said. "But he's not a traitor. And besides, he didn't know we were going. Unless you told him, Harrison."

"Not me," Harrison said, holding up his hands. "I barely know the guy. And to be honest, I've heard some things that would make me think twice about spilling my guts to him. But despite all that, I have to agree with Owen, he's not the turncoat type."

"Logan Palmer is all about Logan Palmer," Avery said. "And he'd sell out his mother if he thought it would get him ahead in the game. But the game, for him anyway, is rising to the top of U.S. Intelligence. Which, I agree, precludes turning traitor. Anyway, if he didn't know you were going to New York, he can't be the leak. And none of you told anyone else, right?"

Everyone shook their heads.

"Then I'm afraid it's got to be one of us."

"And for better or worse," Harrison said, looking up from the computer, his expression a curious mixture of triumph and regret, "I think I know who it is."

CHAPTER **20**

A ll right," Avery said, perching on the side of the table next to Harrison and his computer, "I've cleared the room. What have you got?"

Harrison had wanted only Owen present when he shared his discovery, but Avery had insisted on his and Tyler's staying as well, complying at least partially by ordering Nash and Hannah from the room. He'd made it clear, however, that once he had Harrison's information, he'd be the one to decide which team members would be privy to the news.

Owen was beyond worrying about who knew what. The A-Tac team was tight, and from what he'd observed, it wouldn't be long before this latest piece of the puzzle was common knowledge.

"So basically the whole thing started when I was helping Hannah with a glitch in her laptop," Harrison began. "Programs were bugging out. So I started digging around in her operating system, and I stumbled across something I wasn't meant to find. A key logger."

"I'm not sure what that is," Tyler said, shaking her head as she and Avery exchanged glances. Whatever Harrison had found, it wasn't going to be easy for either of them—Tyler because she was intensely loyal and Avery because he'd hate the idea that someone had played him. Someone they all believed they could trust.

"It's a way to follow the keystrokes on a remote computer. It allows access to information, passwords, documents, everything. Anything the person enters into the computer, there's a record of it. With a key logger, you can control email, add files, manipulate data—you name it."

"All without the other person being any the wiser," Owen said.

"Exactly. And this one was pretty sophisticated. Kernel-based. Part of the rootkit. I'd have never found it if she hadn't had the problem."

"Did the key logger cause the glitch?" Avery asked.

"No. It was totally unrelated. A lucky break, really."

"So are you saying that Hannah is the mole?" Tyler asked, her expression mutinous.

"Absolutely not," Harrison said, shaking his head vehemently. "In fact she has no idea. I wanted to be doubly certain before I went public. So first I searched her terminal here. And sure enough, I found the same program. But I figured I still needed more information, so I just left the key loggers in place and fixed the problem with her laptop."

"So you haven't told her," Avery said.

"No. It just seemed wiser to wait until I knew for certain what we were dealing with. Plus, I didn't want to alert whoever was behind the key logger that I was on to them."

"How long have you known?"

"Just since this morning. I'd have come clean sooner if I thought it would help. But I figured it was better for me to make sure it was tied in to all of this. There are valid reasons for using key loggers. So first off I had to eliminate those."

"And I assume that's what you were doing while we were discussing the attack at Ms. Waller's," Avery prompted, his expression thoughtful.

"Yes," Harrison nodded, looking chagrined. "I'm sorry to have been so distracted. But I had to concentrate and be careful what I was doing so that there was no way I'd be noticed."

"I'm not following," Tyler said.

"I was hacking into a computer. The person I thought might be responsible for installing the key logger. When Hannah told me Jason had set up her system—both her laptop and her terminal here—I figured he was the most likely candidate to have inserted the program."

"He had the knowledge and the means," Owen agreed.

"And unfortunately for him, the proof was on his computer. I found hard evidence that he'd been accessing the information from the key logger. Apparently for quite some time."

"That would explain how the arms dealer in Colombia knew our every move. If Jason was tracking Hannah's work, he'd have known everything we were going to do. And there'd have been plenty of time to funnel that information to Ortiz."

"I don't know." Tyler shook her head. "I find it hard to believe that the mole is Jason. He's been with the team almost as long as I have. And we've been through some pretty serious shit together. The idea that he'd turn on us is really hard to swallow."

"I can't pretend to understand his motivation," Harrison said. "I can just tell you what I found. And to be honest, I was really disappointed. I like the guy. He's really good with computers. But that's kind of the point. I mean, the key loggers he used are really sophisticated. Almost impossible to detect. Like I said, I stumbled on the first one by accident. And to be honest, if I hadn't known what I was looking at, I'd never have suspected it was anything worth worrying over. But I've had a lot of experience with this kind of thing."

"On both ends, I'd imagine," Avery said, his tone friendly.

"Pretty much." He grinned, then sobered. "Anyway, there's more."

"It gets worse?" Tyler asked, crossing her arms over her chest, a sure sign she was fighting her emotions.

"Yeah." Harrison nodded. "A lot worse. I found evidence that Jason tapped into the security footage of the area in front of your house."

"From the night we found the suitcase?" Owen asked.

"Yes. He edited it so that a segment showing him with the suitcase, letting himself into Tyler's front door, was cut."

"But the time stamps matched."

"He fixed that, too. It's not that hard if you know what to do, and Hannah mentioned Jason walked her through the process when you guys were in Colombia. Anyway, I made a copy of the unedited version. He still had it on his computer. I guess he hasn't had time to clean it up."

"Or maybe he's just secure in the fact that no one is on to him." Owen sat back, watching Avery and Tyler. For them, Harrison's revelations were personal.

"This all just seems so unreal," Tyler said, her face showing her frustration. "Jason is my friend. It seems crazy to think that he was the one who broke into my house."

"Actually, he used the key in the flowerpot by the door," Harrison corrected.

"Great," Tyler's voice was tight. "I helped him break in."

"You had no reason to believe you couldn't trust him, Tyler. We were all fooled." Avery sighed, his expression resigned. "So you're absolutely certain about all of this?"

"Unfortunately, yes." Harrison nodded. "I'm positive. And there's one more thing. Jason planted a bug in Tyler's bedroom." He paused, looking decidedly uncomfortable. "Video and audio."

"In my bedroom," she repeated, her gaze shooting over to Owen, who was suddenly seeing red.

Harrison nodded again, clearly embarrassed. "I'm sorry. I had to look at some of it. To be certain it was what I thought it was. I mean, Jason intruding, not the—" He broke off, looking down at his computer.

"It's okay," Tyler said, releasing a slow breath, putting her hands on the table. "There's nothing there I'm ashamed of."

"I swear I didn't watch but a couple of seconds. Long enough to verify the angle and probable location of the bug. I promise." Harrison held up his hands to underscore his words. "And I'm sure there's no need for anyone else to see it?" He shot a questioning look in Avery's direction.

"No," the big man said. "Not as long as we've got other proof. I assume you left it all in place."

"Of course," Harrison was quick to assure. "I didn't want to tip my hand. As far as I can tell, Jason had no idea I'd hacked into his computer. But he's smart. Which means it's possible he'll figure it out. I did my best to cover my tracks. But you never know. Anyway, I thought it would be safer if I left everything the way I found it."

"Including the bug?" Tyler asked, looking as if she'd like to crawl into the floor. Unable to stop himself, Owen reached across the table and covered her hand with his, surprised when she didn't pull away.

"I verified it was there." Again Harrison looked embarrassed. "It's in the ceiling. A small hole, drilled just to the right of the light fixture."

"Over the bed," she whispered, then lifted her head, pulling her hand free from Owen's. "The truth is that Jason's invading my privacy is the least of our problems. Were there other bugs?"

"I didn't search for them. I figured you guys could do that. I felt weird about being in your house in the first place. I just wanted to be certain I'd documented my findings before I presented them. So I took pictures of the bug." He hit a key and the device filled the screen above their heads.

"It's one of ours," Avery observed, his jaw tightening with anger. "And of course it would be easy enough for Jason to get his hands on it."

"Wait a minute," Owen interrupted, frowning at Harrison as a new thought moved front and center. "If Jason's bug was recording video, won't he know you figured it out? I mean, won't you be on tape?"

"If he was watching when I went in, then maybe. But I was monitoring the whole time and I'm almost a hundred percent certain that he wasn't on the computer while I was in there. And then, after the fact, I went back in and did some editing of my own."

"A little taste of his own medicine," Owen said, still seething that Jason had recorded Tyler's intimate moments.

"Yeah." Harrison tilted his head with a crooked smile. "Figured what was good for the goose and all that. Anyway, he won't be able to tell that anyone was there."

"What about Lara?" Avery asked. "Is there any sign that she was in on it?"

"They're together?" Owen asked, frowning. The dossier hadn't mentioned that they were a couple.

"Yes." Avery nodded. "They live together. Have for quite a while now."

"But I thought there were rules against that kind of thing."

"We tend to turn a blind eye. It hasn't affected their work."

"Which could be a problem," Tyler said. "Do you think Lara knows what Jason's been up to?"

"There's nothing I've seen to indicate she's complicit," Harrison said. "But if there's a relationship..."

"I don't know." Tyler shook her head. "I can't imagine Jason involving Lara in anything that would put her in danger. He loves her too much."

"Maybe that's all been a lie, too," Avery said.

"Well, either way Lara wouldn't be involved."

"But we can't know that for certain," Owen said.

"So we'll have to tread carefully." Tyler shrugged.

"But it doesn't change the fact that we've got to confront Jason. I mean, otherwise we'll just be sitting ducks for whatever he decides to do next. Not to mention the fact that I'm not going to feel safe in my own home."

"I suppose there is an argument for trailing him and letting him lead us to whoever he's working for." Owen didn't like the idea, but the option had to be considered.

"Was there anything on his computer that might help us figure out who's calling the shots?" Avery asked.

"No." Harrison shook his head. "And I had a pretty thorough look around. The truth is, for all we know, his part in this is purely reactionary."

"So we could plant a false lead and see what happens," Owen suggested.

"*Or* we could just ask him what the hell is going on." Tyler's fists were clenched, her earlier embarrassment turning to rage. "Actually," she said, pulling her phone from her pocket, "he texted me. Just before our meeting. He said something about needing to see me. Maybe he was going to come clean."

"Seems pretty unlikely. But it's at least worth finding out what he wanted," Avery said. "Did he say where he was?"

She consulted the phone. "Yeah. He's at home."

"Are you sure you want to do this?" Avery asked.

"Yes. I'm fine. If my talking to him can help us nail his ass to the wall, then it's no problem."

"Well, she can't go alone." Owen worked to quash his own fury. He'd learned the hard way that actions taken in anger seldom paid off in the long run.

"I agree," Avery said, his expression speculative as he watched the two of them. "Owen, you go with her. Jason won't be surprised, since the two of you have been working together."

Tyler's gaze was steady as she squared her shoulders and pushed away from the table. "No time like the present, I guess."

"He may not give anything away," Avery warned. "And if he doesn't, don't push. Just try to pull whatever you can out of him. And see if you can gauge his mood. Confident, worried—you know the drill. And then, based on what you get, coupled with Harrison's evidence, we'll figure out what our next move should be."

"We'll be careful." Owen stood up, his gaze meeting Tyler's. "But I think we've got to push at least a little. We haven't got the luxury of time. And there's the small matter of what he's done to Tyler."

She placed a hand on his arm. "He hasn't done anything to me. At least not the way you mean it. Avery's right, we have to be careful. There'll be time for confrontation. It just might not be now."

"You ready?" Owen asked as they walked up the steps that led to Jason's front door. She hadn't said much of anything on their way over, and he hadn't wanted to push, but he knew this couldn't be easy for her.

"Yeah." Tyler nodded, her eyes dark with emotion. "He asked to talk to me. I can't imagine that he's going to confess, but he's clearly got something on his mind. Maybe it's something we can use."

"Or maybe he just wants to try to figure out how much you know."

"The thought crossed my mind. But if he's trying to play mind games, I've got the upper hand. And there's no way he can possibly know that." She lifted her hand to ring the doorbell, but the door opened before she had the chance.

"Tyler," Lara said, a broad smile creasing her face. "I'm so glad you're okay. I heard it was a really close call out there."

"We're fine. But I wouldn't be here if it weren't for Owen." Tyler's voice was a little too bright, but Lara didn't seem to notice. Instead, she turned her smile to him.

"Then we owe you a debt of gratitude. We're all really fond of Tyler."

"I can understand why." Owen nodded, his smile for Tyler.

"So what can I do for you?" Lara asked.

"Actually, I got a text from Jason. He wanted to see me. Only I've been stuck in a meeting. Is he here?"

"As far as I know. I've only just walked in myself. I had a late class. But when I left, he was in his study. You know the way." She moved aside, motioning them into the hallway. "I really am glad you're okay," Lara said, squeezing Tyler's arm as she walked by. She certainly sounded genuine. But then what the hell did he know?

"Thanks." Tyler smiled. "We'll catch up later? Maybe grab coffee or something when everything dies down."

"That'd be nice," Lara said. "I was really sorry to hear about your father."

Tyler nodded. "I just want to figure out who did it."

"I know," Lara said, her smile fading. "Which is my cue to leave you to it. I know Jason's been working hard trying to find out who's behind all of this. Maybe that's why he wanted to see you." The hallway split and Lara headed for the kitchen as they moved the opposite direction toward Jason's study.

"You're right. She doesn't seem the type to betray her country," Owen said as they walked down the hall.

"It just seems impossible to me that she would be in on this. But then it seems just as impossible that the traitor is Jason. So what do I know? Anyway, the important thing is that she didn't seem suspicious."

"One step at a time, eh?" He reached out to squeeze her hand as they slowed in front of a closed door. "Is this it?"

Tyler nodded and reached for the door, turning the knob and pushing it open. At first Owen thought the room was empty. It was only when they walked all the way inside that they saw him—swinging from a rope looped through the rafters.

Clearly, there'd be no confrontation.

Jason Lawton was dead.

CHAPTER 21

I thought you'd still be up," Owen said, standing in the doorway to Tyler's bedroom holding a tray. "I know it's just me being English, but I thought maybe some toast and tea would help."

Tyler sighed, leaning back against the wing chair. Nothing was going to help. Her father was dead. Della and Smitty, too. And now Jason.

Jason.

She still couldn't wrap her head around the idea that he'd been a traitor. But there really wasn't any other choice. Between Harrison's evidence and the note Jason had left it was all pretty clear. He'd said he wanted something more. Something bigger and better than A-Tac, and that the group behind all of this had offered that. Or at least they seemed to. Jason had written that he'd lost faith. That their goals and his no longer were the same. That too many people had died.

He'd apologized. To Tyler. To A-Tac. And to Lara. Then he'd written that dying was the only noble way out.

In truth, it seemed a cowardly excuse. But she hadn't been in his shoes. So who the hell was she to judge? Nothing was what it seemed. And suddenly, sitting here, staring up at Owen, she knew one thing for certain. Life was short. And there weren't that many chances to get it right.

"I think it's a lovely idea," she said, pushing aside the afghan she'd been huddled under. "Besides, I could use the company. I just keep going over everything in my head. Trying to make it come out differently."

It was late, dawn not that far away. Tyler had spent the better part of the night at Jason's, first supporting Lara, and then, after she'd finally fallen asleep, thanks to heavy sedation, Tyler had stayed to help the forensics team. Nash had been there, too. And Emmett. The three of them pulling together, along with Avery and Hannah. But then there had been nothing left to do. The body gone. The study cordoned off. Yellow tape like a beacon announcing something horrible had happened there.

So she'd come home, relieved to find that Owen and Harrison had cleared the house of bugs, Jason's death removing the need to play along. So with mumbled excuses she'd gone to bed. But sleep had eluded her. And so she sat, her mind spinning as she tried to find answers where there were none.

"There's nothing more you can do," Owen said. "At least not tonight."

"Somewhere inside, I know that," she replied, accepting the steaming cup of tea. "But I can't turn it off. I just keep seeing Jason hanging there. And Lara's screams are echoing in my ears. And then it's my father. Oh, God, Owen, it's like everything's been turned inside out. Like I've fallen down the rabbit hole and lost my way."

"I understand," he said, putting the tray on the table and then sitting on the edge of the bed across from the chair. "Honestly, I do. Too much happening, too fast. It's impossible to process. We're simply not built that way. But I promise we will find answers. It's just going to take time."

"And what if we don't have time? What if there is a bomb? And they're already setting the plan in motion to use it? Owen, we don't even know who *they* are. Jason said a group. And he implied they had big plans. Smitty thought they were going to build his bomb. But that's not enough for us to find them—to stop them." Her voice rose with every sentence, until she knew she was teetering on the brink of hysteria.

She took a sip of tea, closing her eyes, letting the liquid warmth soothe her.

"I'm sorry." She shook her head, her gaze lifting to meet his. "I'm all right. I promise. It's just harder than I would have thought."

"You've lost a friend." He reached over to cover her hand with his. "And not only that, he betrayed you. That's a lot to deal with. And I haven't been helping matters."

"What do you mean? You saved my life. You were there with me when I found my father. You stayed with me at the hospital. And you were there tonight when we found Jason. All you've been doing is helping me."

"But I lied to you."

"Yes, you did. And I won't pretend that it didn't hurt. But Nash reminded me that there were two sides to every story. And I didn't give you the chance to tell yours. I was too angry to listen. And I said some horrible things." She shook her head, tears pricking the back of her eyes. "Anyway, if it matters at all, I'm ready to listen now."

He bent his head, and silence stretched between them, Tyler holding her breath, wondering if she'd waited too long. Pushed things too far.

"I had a wife," he said finally, his eyes dark with pain. "Angela. We met at university. I really did study nuclear physics. That much at least was true. And I was recruited by MI-5. Angela thought it was exotic. She urged me to take the offer. And so I did. A year later we were married."

Tyler hadn't thought she could hurt any more than she already did. But the idea that Owen had loved someone, someone besides her, was as painful as it was irrational.

"We were happy, Tyler. I won't pretend otherwise. I loved her with every part of me. And when she told me she was pregnant, I thought the world couldn't possibly get any better."

He paused, and she waited, not trusting herself with words. She'd been so wrapped up in her own problems she hadn't even stopped to think about Owen. About the story she'd heard from Emmett. If Owen had truly betrayed MI-5, then that meant that he'd acted counter to everything she knew about him. Which meant there had to be something more to the story.

Something awful. She could see it in his eyes.

"Jacob was the light of my life. He was so full of energy and curiosity and joy." He smiled, memories clearly playing in his head. "Everything was perfect. Except of course that there is no such thing. Or if there is then the fates will see to it that it doesn't last." There was a trace of bitterness in his voice, but also a wistfulness that made Tyler want to cry.

"I was working an operation to stop an alleged attack

by a terrorist cell centered in London." His voice became softer as he faded back into his past. "It was fairly routine. Or so we thought. We needed to infiltrate the cell, and to do it we used a friend of mine. From university. Bashir Hadad. He fit the profile. And he'd had experience with MI-5 working on a couple of special projects with me. So he agreed to help, and in short order had worked his way up the ranks."

He stopped to take a sip of his tea, and then continued. "He managed to get information that not only thwarted their plan to bomb the London Underground, but gave us hard evidence against the leadership in the cell. We planned a raid. And everything went swimmingly. The threat was averted, the cell taken down. Score one for the good guys."

"But something happened," Tyler said, almost afraid to ask.

"Yes." Owen nodded, anger flashing across his face as he remembered. "The cell had been a splinter of a larger organization. One based out of Pakistan. The leaders there wanted revenge. And somehow they got word that my friend, Bashir, was the traitor. It wouldn't have been a problem, except that there was political strife in London at the time. And my bosses, who'd promised Bashir protection if necessary, went back on their word. Bashir was kidnapped and tortured. Ultimately, they killed him."

"Oh, my God, that's horrible."

"Yes, well, it was my fault. I'd gotten him involved in the first place."

"But you had no part in pulling his protection."

"Maybe I could have fought harder, I don't know. It all

happened so fast. Anyway, I raised holy hell, told anyone
who'd listen. And quite clearly, that didn't sit at all well
with my superiors. They couldn't get rid of me, but they
made life as difficult as possible."

"Why didn't you just quit?"

"I thought about it. And Angela certainly wanted me
to. But before I could make a decision, something else
happened. The terrorist group discovered that I'd been
behind Bashir's infiltration. That I was, in fact, MI-5.
And as a result, they threatened me. So I went back to
my bosses, apologized for my insubordination, and asked
for their help."

"But they considered you a liability."

"Exactly so. They assured me they'd look into the
threat, of course. But they did nothing. I don't know if
they didn't believe me or if they truly thought they'd be
better off if I were dead. But the bottom line is that there
was no one there the day the terrorists planted a bomb
in my car. And no one there when my family headed out
for the day.

"Angela was buckling Jacob into his car seat when I
realized I'd forgotten my wallet. I was on my way back
into the house when she started the car." He blew out a
breath, his eyes glazed with pain. "It was over in seconds.
Angela died instantly—but Jacob was still alive. He was
so little, Tyler. And there was nothing I could do. He'd
just turned three, and he died in my arms."

"Owen," Tyler said, reaching out to take his hands. "I
don't know what to say. It must have been so awful—to
be there and to...to—"

"—have lived?" he finished for her, his fingers tightening around hers. "It was beyond anything I could have

ever imagined. Even now, it eats at me. But at the time all I wanted was revenge. Revenge against the people who killed them."

"So you went after the leaders of the group in Pakistan."

"Yes." He nodded. "And in the process, I managed to upend a long-term operation. MI-6. Two operatives were killed. But I got the bastards who did it. And at the time that's all I cared about."

"And MI-5 used the information to run you out of the organization. They issued a burn notice. And played it all up to make it look as if you'd gone rogue."

"For all practical purposes they were right. Anyway, I didn't give a damn. I just wanted the pain to go away. So I changed my name—my mother's, by the way, she's American—and came to the States. At first I just went underground, but then money started to run out, and I needed to find a job. Unfortunately, thanks to her majesty's government, I was persona non grata in both Intelligence and academic circles. I couldn't find legitimate work. So I turned mercenary. And that's how I met Logan Palmer."

"And joined IA."

"Actually, I'm not officially on their rolls. I'm more of a contract player. Someone Logan calls in when he has special projects. You have to understand he was the first person to treat me as if I weren't a pariah. No matter what else he's done, I'll always be grateful for that."

"Well, I don't like the man," Tyler said, still holding Owen's hands. "But I suppose I'm grateful that he gave you a chance. If he hadn't, I wouldn't have met you."

"And I wouldn't have started to feel alive again."

"Working can do that." She stood up, moving to the window. There was a light on in the guesthouse. Clearly Harrison wasn't sleeping either.

"Tyler," he said, coming to stand behind her, his hands on her shoulders, "you're misunderstanding. It wasn't work that brought me back. It was you. Being with you. But then I screwed it all up by not telling you the whole truth when I had the chance. And now, I don't know if you can ever forgive me."

She turned around, placing a finger against his lips. "Stop. It's me who should be begging forgiveness. I never should have listened to Emmett and Avery."

"They were just trying to protect you. And they weren't wrong."

"No, but Nash was right, I should have trusted my gut. I should have given you the chance to tell me. I should have known that there was an explanation."

"Could have, would have, should have. Isn't that what your stepmother used to say? If I've learned anything over the past six years it's that the only way forward is to let go of the past. I have no idea what the future holds, but I do know that I care about you. And I want you in my life. That is, if you still want me."

"I do," she whispered, marveling at the power of those two little words. "I do," she repeated as she felt the familiar sensation beginning to build. Her breath caught in her throat at the fire in his eyes. There was desire there, and something more.

She swallowed, touched by the raw emotion reflected in his gaze. She was hesitant to put a name to it, but hope flashed inside her. Sparks flew between them and she pushed against him, wanting the contact, amazed at the intensity of her need. He smiled and pulled her closer, a tiny smile curling the corners of his lips.

Then he lowered his mouth to hers, teasing her with his tongue, their bodies fitting together like pieces of an intricate jigsaw puzzle. Shivers streaked through her as he deepened the kiss, his spirit calling to hers, pulling her deeper and deeper, until she wondered if she would drown in the pure sensation of him—a prospect that, she had to admit, sounded rather appealing.

He slid the strap of her nightshirt off one shoulder, his fingers curving around her smooth skin, massaging lower and lower until he held her breast in his hand, her nipple going tight at his touch. She arched against his hand, driven by her need, and she felt his body harden against hers, desire surging as a tidal wave of emotion threatened to swamp her.

With fumbling hands, they removed their clothes, touching, exploring—the need to be skin to skin driving them both to a frenzy.

Finally, when they were both naked, he kissed her, his tongue leaving trails of hot fire as it traced the contours of her mouth. Their gazes locked, his eyes dark pools, blue on black, deep as the ocean. Eyes a girl could lose herself in. And Tyler knew she was already lost.

With a groan, he picked her up and carried her to the bed, positioning himself on top of her as he looked down into her eyes. "I want you, Tyler," he whispered, his words full of promise.

And suddenly she knew that this time was different. That this time they would be joining more than just their bodies. She opened her legs, welcoming the feel of him against her skin. Her need burned strong, but this time it was laced with something more—an overriding feeling that this was right; that somehow, here, now, with him, it was meant to be.

Bracing himself above her, he thrust into her and she welcomed him, cradling him deep inside. They rocked together, the rhythm coming naturally, as if it had been specially choreographed just for them. She clung to him, sensation splintering through her, realizing, for the first time in her life, what it meant to be in love.

Nothing had changed. Danger and grief still surrounded them. Her father was dead. Jason had killed himself. And somewhere out there a bomb was waiting. A threat building. But here, in the warmth of her bed, locked in Owen's arms, Tyler let herself go. Let herself dream. Let herself believe, for the moment at least, that anything was possible.

CHAPTER 22

The war room was completely quiet. Almost eerily so. Everyone was there—except Lara. Tyler sat next to Nash, with Annie on his other side, and Emmett across from her. Hannah was next to Emmett and Avery sat in his customary place at the head of the table. And new to the scenario, at least for Owen, was the man they called Drake. The one who'd battled his way back from the jungles of Colombia. He'd apparently arrived late last night. A show of solidarity, no doubt.

Harrison sat in the back with Owen, the two of them feeling like the outsiders that they were. A-Tac had closed ranks. And Owen knew that if it hadn't been for Tyler, they probably wouldn't have been allowed in the meeting. But Tyler had insisted, going toe to toe with Avery, who'd finally relented.

"So by now, I assume everyone knows what's happened," Avery said, without further preamble. "Drake, it's good to have you back. I'm just sorry it had to be under these circumstances."

"I'm still having a hard time buying the idea of Jason playing mole," the man said, his expression fierce.

These were warriors, and even though Jason had caused his own demise, they were ready for battle. Ready to find the people who'd brought them to this place. Owen had to admit he admired them. In point of fact, he'd been like them—once. Maybe he could be again. The very fact that he was even entertaining the notion was telling.

"I think we're all coming from the same place," Hannah said, her usually over-the-top glasses a subdued brown today. "None of us could have predicted this."

"Has anyone checked on Lara?" Emmett asked.

"I went over there this morning," Annie said. "She was still sleeping."

"They gave her some pretty powerful drugs," Nash nodded. "I imagine she'll be out for a while."

"There's a nurse with her." Annie reached out to touch her husband's hand. "So at least she's got someone watching over her."

"Where's the body?" Tyler asked, looking up from the stack of papers she'd been studying. She'd been up since dawn, going over everything—reports, photos, the note—trying to find answers. To make sense out of the seemingly senseless.

"It's with the county medical examiner," Hannah said. "Because it was a suicide, there has to be a cursory investigation and there's all kinds of paperwork to be filed. Someone at Langley is friendly with the local ME and he's going to walk it through for us. Make sure Jason is all right."

"Jason is dead," Emmett said, his tone bleak. "And

while it's nice that we have strings to pull, I've no idea why we're protecting the son of a bitch. He betrayed every one of us. Hell, some of his stunts could have gotten us all killed."

"I know you're right," Tyler said, with a sigh. "But it's hard for me to reconcile the Jason I knew with the man you're describing."

"Look, this is hard on all of us," Avery said. "But we need to stay focused. We need to concentrate on what we know and work from there."

"Any idea why us? I mean why target A-Tac, specifically?" Nash asked.

"With Jason dead, there's no way to know for certain," Avery replied. "It could be that our operations coincided with their needs. Or maybe we're not the only organization to be infiltrated. If we're really talking about detonating a nuclear bomb, then that's going to take all kinds of coordination."

"And that would be a hell of a lot easier with inside help at every step of the way," Drake frowned.

"But we're talking a massive undertaking," Tyler said. "We haven't seen that kind of recruitment since the Cold War."

"Look, we're jumping to conclusions. The reason they used Jason could be as simple as his offering his help. They'd have been foolish not to take advantage of the opportunity. And once he was on board, we've seen how easy it was for them to manipulate the situation so that A-Tac, and therefore their eyes and ears, was involved."

"So what about the note?" Drake asked. "I haven't had a chance to look at it. Was there anything there that could give us a lead to who these people might be?"

"Nothing substantial," Tyler said, rummaging through her pile of papers. "Here's a copy." She passed it across the table to Drake. "He talks about being disillusioned. And losing faith. Then says he's taking the only way out."

"Didn't he say something about the end being near?" Annie asked.

"Yes," Avery said, "but he doesn't clarify what that end might be. It's possible it's just a reference to his suicide."

"Or, if there really is a bomb," Annie mused, "then it could mean that they're planning to detonate soon."

"But wouldn't we have heard rumblings?" Drake asked, tipping his chair back to lean against the wall. The man was almost as big as Avery, his icy gaze ruthless. "Something in chatter that would hint at an impending attack somewhere?"

"There's always talk like that. The key is to try to figure out what's credible and what's not," Hannah said.

"So what *are* we hearing?" Nash asked.

"Nothing that out of the ordinary," Hannah said, as she scrolled through pages on her computer. "A couple of implausible threats against groups in Israel. A vague reference to London—that everyone agrees is nothing to worry about. And then the usual cluster of threats against the United States. Most of them in or around New York City."

"Anything there that fits with our scenario?"

"Some of the chatter seems to indicate that there might be something big going down in Manhattan," Hannah said. "But we always get a flood of that kind of thing this time of year because of 9/11." She frowned down at the screen. "I've been over the intel a couple of times, and I spoke with some of the research people at Langley. And while we agree that some of the language could be interpreted to mean a nuclear strike, there's nothing that points to it being a legitimate threat. Ninety-nine percent of the time this stuff is just empty talk."

"Yes, well, it's the other one percent that comes back to bite us in the ass," Drake said.

"So is this chatter attributed to anyone?" Emmett asked.

"Not specifically, no." Hannah shook her head. "Although there is some indication that it's originating locally. Which probably narrows it down a bit. There aren't that many active cells in the Northeast. And we're not seeing any kind of movement from the people we normally track. Both Homeland Security and NSA sources have marked the chatter as low threat, meaning they don't believe anything will come of it. Of course, that doesn't mean they're right."

"Yes, but even if it was a credible threat," Tyler said, her frustration evident, "there's no way to verify that it's related to our situation. I mean, other than what Smitty said, we really don't even have evidence that there is a bomb."

"But we do know that they have the means to make one," Avery said. "And in light of everything that's been happening here, I'd say things are escalating. So if detonation is the endgame, then my guess is that it's going to be soon. So while we don't have anything to specifically confirm our suspicions, I think we're better off covering our bases. And that means working from worst-case scenario."

"A suitcase nuke detonated on U.S. soil," Annie said, putting their fears into words.

"If that's the plan, they're certainly setting their standards high. It won't be easy getting a nuclear weapon into the country."

"Who says they have to get it in?" Emmett said. "It's possible they're building it right here under our noses."

"Hannah, you've been working on compiling information on possible theft or black market sale of parts needed to build the thing," Avery said. "Have you got anything?"

"I've started, but I haven't really—" She broke off with a sigh. "It's just that..."

"Actually," Harrison said, speaking up for the first time since the meeting began, "I worked on it last night. I had all the stuff Hannah and I'd been culling." He shrugged, looking a little bit sheepish. "I didn't mean to overstep bounds. But Owen and I figured you guys had other things on your mind."

"At this point we can use all the help we can get." Avery smiled, his gaze including Owen as well. "So tell us what you've got."

"Well, first off," Harrison said, "it's important to understand that even for a device as sophisticated as the one Smitty designed, most of the working parts are easily obtained on the open market, no questions asked."

"But I thought this thing was state of the art," Drake said.

"It is," Owen agreed, as Harrison hit a key and the blueprint for the bomb filled the overhead screen. "But sometimes the most sophisticated weaponry is also the simplest. For instance, the early suitcase nukes designed by the Russians were simply a series of three aluminum canisters, each about the size of a coffee can. To work, they simply had to be connected together and then detonated. A battery was used in the meantime to keep the thing powered while in transit or storage.

"This bomb," he continued, looking up at the diagram, "works off the same principle. It's just been refined to make everything even more efficient and compact. The whole thing is about half the size of the ones originally designed in Russia. And the lithium battery used today is more reliable and certainly smaller than the ones used during the Cold War."

"One of the major problems with those old suitcase nukes was a lack of stability. The core material was prone to deterioration. And the components, crude by today's standards, were prone to misfiring," Harrison said. "All of which goes to explain why they existed but were never actually used."

"But if it's really that easy to get the components," Annie asked, "why haven't we seen more portable nuclear devices in terrorist hands?"

"Access and money," Tyler answered. "Obtaining the subsidiary parts of a nuclear weapon may be easy. But not so much with obtaining and securing fissionable material. Especially in a post–9/11 world. And even if you do have the infrastructure to pull it off, you're still going to need a lot of cash, for production as well as for obtaining the needed parts."

"Eight pounds of plutonium was offered recently on the black market for ten million dollars," Owen said. "The culprits were arrested before a sale could be made, but that gives you an idea of the going rate."

"Isn't there a possibility that they could produce their own uranium at a significantly reduced cost?" Hannah asked.

"Not in this case." Owen shook his head. "Uranium is much heavier than plutonium. You'd have to use around 130 pounds of uranium to get the same yield as about twenty-two pounds of plutonium. So while uranium is easier to obtain, it's more difficult to transport, and virtually impossible to use efficiently in a miniaturized nuke like the one Smitty designed."

"But the very fact that plutonium is so much harder to obtain," Harrison added, "makes it that much more valuable on the black market. Hence the prohibitive price."

"Well there's no question these people have money," Tyler said. "I mean, look at the amounts they paid Smitty and Ms. Waller."

"So it's possible they bought the stuff," Avery said.

"Or maybe they stole it," Nash suggested. "They've certainly proven themselves adept at that. Either way I think we're in agreement that they have the means to have obtained weapons-grade plutonium."

"Yeah, but it would be a lot harder than you're making it sound," Tyler said. "Plutonium isn't just lying around waiting for someone to steal it."

"Isn't the stuff transported from nuclear plants to storage facilities?" Drake asked. "Seems to me all you'd have to do is figure out when the stuff is being moved and intercept it. Kind of like with the detonators."

Tyler nodded. "It's possible. Last year nuclear inspectors discovered that a plant outside Tokyo couldn't account for some of its plutonium—enough to make at least twenty-five bombs."

"But it's more likely that the 'lost' plutonium was actually discarded in small increments after being reprocessed," Owen said. "The stuff sticks to pretty much anything it comes in contact with. But the amounts are so minute there's no way to reconstitute it into something that could be used to make a nuclear bomb, suitcase or otherwise."

"So, you're the expert," Nash said. "What do you think the most likely scenario is for obtaining plutonium with a minimal chance at discovery?"

"In a word, Russia." Owen nodded to Harrison, who exchanged the blueprint on the screen for a map. "This is a map of nuclear weapons storage facilities in the country. As you can see, there are over a dozen documented sites, and these are just the ones we know about."

"Our people have been working with their government to help safely dispose of as much of this material as possible," Avery said. "But as it stands now, it would be easy enough to get into any of these facilities. Most of them are in poor repair and understaffed."

"Yeah, but I'd think you'd still have to have access," Tyler said, studying the map, her brow furrowed in thought. "I mean, surely if there was an overt attack on one of the facilities we'd have heard something."

"Not necessarily," Harrison said. "Especially considering the current political climate. Russia is being more guarded than ever these days, and if someone did steal plutonium, the Russian government is far more likely to cover up it up than to take it public. That said, I've done a little digging and I've got two possibilities. A facility southwest of Voronezh. Golovchino. Near the Ukrainian border. Here." He used a pointer to indicate it on the map. "And a second facility, Borisoglebsk, just south of there, also near the Ukranian border."

"I assume there's significance to the location?"

"Yes," Harrison nodded. "There's no love lost between the Russians and the Ukrainians, and it's well documented that there is a huge black market in the Ukraine for stolen Russian goods, particularly weapons."

"Makes sense," Nash said. "But is there anything specific to make you think that plutonium has been liberated from either facility?"

"Actually, they've both come up short on recent inspections. But Golovchino had a significant amount go missing. More than enough to fuel the weapon we've been discussing. The Russians claim the material was moved, but there's nothing to verify that. And the timeline works. If the plutonium was stolen—it would have been within the last six months, because it was noted as present in the previous inspection, which took place in March."

"It's still a shot in the dark," Annie said, frowning up at the map.

"But at least it's something we can follow up on," Avery said. "Hannah, let's go back over the chatter for the past six months with an eye to substantiating the possibility of a heist or possibly a black market sale out of the Ukraine."

"Emmett, you and Drake work on sorting through the list of terrorist groups with the kind of infrastructure and financial backing to be able to pull something like this off—particularly ones with cells or connections in the Northeast, since most of the threats made in America center on New York City. And include outliers as well. Anyone that potentially could have the wherewithal to orchestrate this kind of operation."

"But what if this is someone new? Someone off the radar?" Tyler asked.

"By eliminating known possibilities we'll be able to narrow our focus and quite possibly turn up evidence that will lead us to the real culprits. But I'm guessing it isn't someone new. They've been too organized, and it takes time to build up the kind of infrastructure necessary not only to build and deploy a nuclear weapon, but also to infiltrate an organization like ours. I'm thinking it's someone we already know, but who may be wearing a new face. Or realigning in a new way. Maybe that's what Jason meant when he mentioned their changing focus."

"What do you want us to do?" Tyler asked, looking over at Owen.

"I want you to go through Jason's things. See if there's anything there that can give you a lead as to what he was involved with. Nash and Annie can help." Avery pushed back from the table. "I don't have to tell you all how critical it is that we move quickly. They've got to know that eventually we'll be able to track them down, especially now that their conduit to knowing our every move is gone. Which means, whatever it is they're planning, they're going to need to execute quickly, before the opportunity is lost."

Jason's study was filled with mementos of a life lived well. As Tyler went through the contents of his desk drawers, she found it hard to justify the smiling man in the photographs with the one she'd found hanging from the rafters. It just didn't fit. And no matter how many times she went over it, she still couldn't make herself believe that Jason had turned on them.

He'd pulled her ass out of the fire so many times she couldn't even put a number to it. How could someone so intent on saving her life have decided suddenly to play for the other team?

"I feel awful. Like we're invading his privacy," Annie said as she leafed through the books in the bookshelf. Jason had been a huge fan of comics—*Batman* in particular. His collection had been his pride and joy.

"He didn't leave us a choice," Owen shrugged. "If there's a chance that something here could lead us to finding the bomb, then it's worth whatever discomfort we might feel."

"Yes, but he wasn't your friend," Annie said, the words not meant unkindly.

The three of them had been at it for more than an hour. Nash had begged off—Adam had soccer practice. Tyler wished she'd had an excuse, particularly one so incredibly removed from the reality of their everyday lives. Here, surrounded by Jason's things, Tyler wondered if all the sacrifices they made for king and country were worth it.

On the one hand, Annie and Nash had triumphed, created a niche of normalcy in the middle of the chaos that seemed to always surround A-Tac. But they'd come close to losing it all. And then there was Jason—funny, tech-headed Jason—he'd had his chance at real life, too. With Lara. But he'd thrown it all away for reasons she couldn't understand, and somehow, somewhere deep inside her, knew she didn't believe.

"Let's just keep digging," she said, with forced brightness. "The sooner we get through this stuff, the sooner we can get out of here."

Lara had let them in, looking like a ghost, her face pale, dark circles under her eyes. She hadn't even asked them why they were there, just let them in and waved them back to the study. Though Tyler couldn't imagine her pain, she could come close. She knew what it would cost her to lose Owen. And they'd only just begun their journey together, wherever the hell it would lead.

"I think he's got every *Batman* comic ever made," Annie said, taking one out and carefully shaking it to be sure that nothing had been hidden inside.

"There are more in the basement, if you can imagine."

"I loved comic books when I was a kid," Owen said to no one in particular. "Although I was more into *Superman*."

"Personally, I preferred *Betty and Veronica*." Annie laughed, the mood lightening a little. "Although I gave up on *Archie* when I was about ten."

"I think that's the wonderful thing about Jason," Tyler said, her throat tight with emotion. "For all his sophistication with computers, he'd never really grown up. I mean, look at how he related to Adam." Jason had been one of the first ones to reach the boy after his kidnapping, the two of them playing computer games for hours on end, whooping and hollering like there was no tomorrow.

"Case in point," Owen said, lifting a baseball glove from the bottom drawer of the filing cabinet. "The great American pastime."

Tyler held her hands out and he tossed her the glove, the smell of worn leather bringing back hot Saturday afternoons spent at the baseball field. To her father's dismay, she'd shown an early aptitude and played with the boys instead of the girls.

She opened her fingers to slide her hand into the glove, then froze, everything falling neatly into place. "I think I know what it is that's been bothering me. About Jason's death, I mean." Her gaze encompassed both Annie and Owen as she lifted the glove for them to see. "Jason was left-handed."

"All right," Owen said, frowning at the glove in her hand. "You want to tell me why that matters?"

"It's in the photographs." Tyler dropped the glove on the desk and reached over to pull out the file she'd been carrying with her since the night before. "From the scene. When Jason was—"

"Hanging," Annie finished for her, her eyes lighting with comprehension. "The knot was wrong."

"Exactly." Tyler nodded. "I knew something wasn't right, but my mind wouldn't let me see it. And then I picked up the glove and everything suddenly made sense." She pulled a photograph from the file, laying it on the desk. "Look, here," she said pointing at the knotted rope. "It's a standard slipknot, but it's on the right side. If Jason had tied it himself, it would have been on the left." She moved so that Owen could see as well. "And it's more than just the knot. Look at the placement of the rope." She tapped the picture impatiently, her heart pounding.

"It's under his chin," Annie said, staring up at the rafters, reinvisioning the incident. "If he'd hung himself it should have been lower. Caught on the Adam's apple."

"This is more like somebody lifted him up there," Owen mused. "Bloody hell, this means that Jason didn't kill himself."

"No," Tyler said, her heart leaping to her throat. "He was murdered."

CHAPTER 23

So if Jason didn't kill himself," Avery said, "who did?"
He was sitting across from Tyler and Annie at a picnic table in Tyler's backyard. The smell of fall filled the air, but it was a warm day, and it seemed safer to hide in plain sight, out in the open away from prying eyes and listening ears. If someone had been able to get to Jason, there was every possibility that person had access to other parts of campus as well.

Owen was pacing along the fence line, talking on the phone, updating Logan Palmer, his hand cutting through the air as he attempted to explain the newest developments. Inside the guesthouse, Harrison, who'd also been apprised of the situation, worked feverishly to re-examine the evidence against Jason.

"Well, the most obvious answer," Annie said, "is that the people behind all of this murdered him just like everyone else that had some kind of link to their operation. Maybe Jason simply outlived his usefulness."

"Maybe, but if this was simply about getting rid of a loose end, then there'd be no reason to disguise it," Avery mused. "We still don't have anything to give us a lead to the identity of this phantom group. And thanks to Jason, they probably know that. Besides, they've been offing people right and left without seeming to care that we know. So I'm thinking there's got to be more to it."

"Okay, what about this?" Tyler flattened her palms on the table, the wood still warm from the now-fading sun. "What if we got it wrong? What if Jason wasn't the mole? Instead, what if he'd figured out who the real traitor was? He said in his text that he had something to tell me. Maybe the *something* was that he knew who'd been betraying us. Lara said he'd been working really hard to try to find answers. Maybe he found some."

"And somehow the real culprit figured out that Jason knew the truth." Annie frowned as she considered the possibilities. "So then to keep Jason from spilling the beans, he or she silenced him. But why the cover-up?"

"It's the perfect way to safeguard identity," Tyler said. "I mean, if we believed Jason was the traitor, then we'd stop looking over our shoulders, leaving Jason's killer free to continue his work with none of us the wiser."

"But you said there's a possibility of forensic evidence." After their discovery about Jason's death, Tyler had called the ME and requested additional tests to verify their suppositions.

"There is. But if I hadn't asked for it, no one would have bothered to look. Initially the ME was only there to help cut through the bureaucratic red tape. I'm sure the killer didn't expect anyone to figure out Jason was murdered. The truth is that if I hadn't seen Jason's baseball glove, I might not have realized what had been bugging me. Or if I had, it would have been too late to prove anything."

"But what about the evidence Harrison found on Jason's computer? The key logger and the surveillance video?" Avery asked, playing devil's advocate.

"Evidence can be planted," Tyler said.

"Yes, but your house had been bugged. And Jason had the live feed on his computer. Harrison verified it was the real deal."

"I'll admit the stuff Harrison found was pretty damning. But I remember when the evidence said Annie was guilty of murder," Tyler said, shooting her friend an apologetic look. "Only she wasn't. It was a set-up. And this smells like one, too. Which is why Harrison is in there going over all the evidence again, this time with an eye toward proving Jason was framed."

"Well, if you're right and Jason *was* framed, then we've still got a traitor in our midst. The question is who?"

"My money's on Lara," Annie said. "She lived with Jason. Which means she'd have access to his files and all of his computers."

"Yeah, but she wouldn't have had the expertise to pull it off." Tyler shook her head. "She's a doctor, not a computer tech."

"Jason could have showed her," Annie said, "maybe in conjunction with another operation. Or maybe Jason was in on it with her. Maybe he really did get cold feet. If he was going to come clean to Tyler, then Lara would have had reason to take him out."

"But she can't be more than five foot five," Avery scoffed. "How the hell do you think she managed to get an incapacitated Jason into a noose hanging from a twelve-foot ceiling?"

"Where there's a will, there's a way," Annie said. "She could have put the noose on him first, and then, using it like a pulley, hauled him up into the air."

"I suppose it's possible," Tyler admitted. "But you can't discount her reaction on finding out Jason was dead. I was there. And she totally lost it."

"Or maybe she's just a good actress," Annie said.

"Come on," Tyler argued, "this is Lara we're talking about."

"I'm not trying to point fingers, but it does make sense. She's the logical conclusion. She had access. She had the means. And if I'm right about Jason threatening exposure, she had the motive as well."

"But she loved him," Tyler protested, having trouble wrapping her mind around the idea that Lara had killed Jason.

"Sometimes love isn't enough," Annie said. "Reality gets in the way. You cared about Jason. He was your friend. But when the evidence pointed his direction, you bought into it."

"And look where that got me."

"The bottom line here, ladies," Avery said, "is that this is all speculation. We don't have anything to connect Lara to Jason's death. And nothing that would make us believe that she had reason to sign on as a turncoat."

"Actually, I might have something," Owen said, flipping his phone closed as he dropped down on the bench next to Tyler.

"I'm assuming you brought Logan up to speed?" Avery asked.

"I did. And I'm sorry to report he's not all that keen on A-Tac continuing to take the lead in this investigation."

"Well, it's not his call."

"True," Owen said, "but he can make a lot of noise when he puts his mind to it."

"That's the God's honest truth," Avery sighed. "And at least in this case, I can't say that I blame him. If I were in his position, I'd probably want us out, too. Maybe he's right. Maybe it's time to turn this over to someone else."

"No," Tyler said, pushing to her feet. "I won't step back. This all started on my watch. And these people killed my father. I'm not going let the NSA waltz in here and take over. We're getting close to a breakthrough, I can feel it."

"While I admire your passion, Tyler," Avery said. "I don't know that we're going to have a choice. Once word about Jason's murder spreads, it may be a fait acompli."

"Well, it hasn't happened yet. So we've still got time," she insisted. "And Owen said he had something on Lara."

"It's not anything that would hold up in court. Just something Logan dug up. As you know, he's been investigating everyone on the A-Tac team. And according to him, Lara's made two trips to the USSR in the last six months."

"That's not all that surprising," Avery said, shaking his head. "Lara's been working closely with the Russians. They're in the process of building a new state-of-the-art storage and disposal facility for both chemical and nuclear weapons. As part of the nuclear proliferation agreement, the United States has been providing funds and technical advice for the project. Lara's been part of the American team advising them on the chemical weapons component."

"Yes, but the new facility is located in eastern Russia. And on both of these trips, she started there, but ended up in the west. The first one was in May and she went to Golovchino."

"The facility where the plutonium went missing?" Annie asked, her eyes widening at the implication.

"Exactly." Owen's expression was grim. "And there are no chemical weapons stored at Golovchino. So why would Lara be there?"

"Did you know she was taking side trips?" Tyler asked, turning to Avery.

"No. But then I had no reason to question her itinerary. Arrangements were made by the State Department, since this is a joint effort crossing agency lines. But she wasn't alone. At least on one of the trips, I know that Emmett went with her. He speaks fluent Russian and was going to help her with some translations. Is there any record of his being at Golovchino?"

"No." Owen shook his head. "According to the intel Logan's got she was traveling on her own. He made no mention of Emmett at all."

"What about the second trip?" Tyler asked.

"There's a record of her visiting the Golovchino facility again in June, and from there crossing the border into the Ukraine. NSA claims she was going there to meet with a prominent member of the Ukrainian mob. An arms dealer by the name of Yuri Strevski."

"And how the hell would Logan have access to information like that?" Avery asked, his expression thunderous.

"I told you, it's all circumstantial," Owen said, holding up a hand in defense. "They've got a tape of Yuri talking to an unidentified woman about delivery of a package. Very cloak and dagger. Nothing to prove definitively that it was Lara in the meeting or that the package was the plutonium."

"So why do they think it was her?"

"Because immigration records show that she was in the country at the time the conversation was recorded. And to make matters worse, she was registered at the same hotel where the alleged meeting took place."

"So just to be clear on what you're saying," Avery said, "the NSA believes that Lara used the cover of her work with the Russians to make two unauthorized visits to a nuclear weapons depot from which a large amount of plutonium was believed to have been stolen. And that after the second visit, she went to the Ukraine, where she allegedly met with a known arms dealer and discussed delivery of a package that may or may not have been the missing plutonium."

"That's pretty much the sum of it." Owen nodded. "As I said, they were investigating all of you. It was only when we uncovered the information about the missing plutonium that Lara's file was red-flagged."

"Well, as much as I hate to say it, it seems pretty damning," Annie said.

"And it does kind of give credence to the idea that Lara might have been working with Jason," Tyler frowned. "I remember her arguing in a meeting about wanting Jason to go with her to Russia. I just assumed it was because they wanted to be together. But maybe it was something more."

"Was it one of the two trips we've been talking about?" Owen asked.

"No." She shook her head. "This would have been earlier. When we were planning the mission into Colombia. But it was the same task force. So if they really were involved in stealing the plutonium, they could already have been making plans."

"I don't think Jason was in on it," Harrison said, coming down the guesthouse steps, the screen door slamming behind him. "But he may have been on to it. I did some more digging in his computer files and I've come up with a couple of things." He settled into a lawn chair across from the picnic table. "First off, I'm fairly certain that the image of Jason walking into your house was digitally added to the footage."

"Someone just wanted us to believe he'd been in there?"

"Yes. I had no reason to doubt the footage when I found it. But I ran some tests on it once we started having concerns, and there are differences in the quality of the background image and Jason's figure. The image of Jason isn't consistent with the kind of film used in your surveillance cameras. It's higher quality. More like the kind you'd find in a digital camera. And if you magnify the image, you can actually see that he's not lined up properly with the shot. Bottom line, the footage was created and planted to sucker us into believing Jason was guilty."

"What about the video feed to my bedroom?" Tyler asked. "Did you find something there?"

"Nothing to find." Harrison shook his head. "We know the feed existed. We've got the camera. But it would have been simple for someone to plant the feed on the computer, especially in light of the fact that someone went to all the effort to make it look as if Jason had doctored the surveillance video."

"What about the key loggers?"

"They could have been a plant as well," Harrison said. "I mentioned that they were deeply buried in both Hannah's system and Jason's. Obviously, since someone was trying to hide them from Hannah, that makes sense. But not as much for Jason's. But if someone was trying to hide them from Jason, then it fits. Of course that's just speculation on my part."

"Any evidence that might link Lara to the key loggers or the altered surveillance?"

"No. I can't find evidence to link it to anyone. I'm just fairly certain Jason didn't put it there."

"Do you have something besides the altered surveillance footage?"

"Not from the computer. But I did call a friend of mine at Quantico. She's an expert in handwriting. So I faxed a copy of the suicide note along with a second sample of Jason's handwriting Avery provided. To the naked eye the handwriting appears to be a match, but when she subjected it to more in-depth analysis it became clear that it was a forgery. And if Jason didn't write the note, I'm guessing he wasn't thinking about suicide."

"You said something about Jason being on to it," Tyler prompted. "I assume you mean he had information about the real culprit?"

"It looks like he at least had an inkling. I found a file hidden deep in the root structure of his computer. Just basic text. But he had all kinds of security protecting it.

Fortunately, I can usually find a way to end-run that sort of thing, and so I managed to access the files."

"So what was in it?" Owen asked.

"Nothing that really made a lot of sense. Primarily the document contained intel about some group called the Consortium. Ever heard of it?"

"Not with a capital 'C,' no." Avery shook his head. "Did Jason identify them beyond the name?"

"No," Harrison said, "only that it was a multinational group with a high degree of infiltration into various government entities. No information on who they might be or what their overriding goals are. But there's enough here to make me think that he'd linked them to our situation."

"How so?"

"Well, according to his notes, he'd been checking intel reports regularly, earmarking chatter that he thought might be attributed to the Consortium—including the threat to New York City, the one Hannah mentioned. He implies that the threat may have originally come from the group. And there's also a notation about Golovchino. He implies that this Consortium may have been responsible for taking the missing plutonium. And there's a list of dates." He held out a sheet of paper.

Avery took the sheet and scanned the contents. "I don't recognize all of them, but Lara's trips are noted here. And I'm thinking some of the others also coincide with other trips she made to Russia."

"So what are we saying?" Annie asked. "That Jason knew Lara was the mole? And that she killed him to keep him from exposing her actions?"

"It's frightening, but it seems plausible," Tyler admitted, hating the thought. "Maybe we should talk to

Emmett. See what he remembers about the trips. You said he was there for at least one of them, right?" She looked to Avery for confirmation.

"Yeah, definitely. And maybe both. I've got records somewhere."

"That's okay," she said, "he can tell me."

"What about Lara?" Owen asked Avery. "Are we going to confront her with any of this?"

"Normally, I'd want to verify Logan's information," Avery said, "but under the circumstances, I think we need to move as quickly as possible. So I'll talk to her. Why don't you come with me, Owen. Independent verification and all that."

"I'm glad you didn't ask me to go," Annie said, shaking her head. "I know what it feels like to be ambushed with something like this."

"I don't see that we have a choice." Avery pushed away from the table, his eyes full of resignation. "We need to know the truth. If we're wrong, it's still better that we asked. And if we're right, then we've got to force her to tell us everything she knows about this Consortium and the possibility that they're planning to detonate a nuclear bomb somewhere in Manhattan."

CHAPTER 24

T hanks for agreeing to see us," Avery said, as Lara ushered them into the living room. "I know things have been tough."

"I'm not sure that that's the word," Lara said, perching on the edge of a wing chair, "but I appreciate the sentiment. The doctor wanted me to take more sedatives. But I refused. Jason wouldn't want me wallowing in my pain."

"Sometimes you have to wallow a little bit just to survive," Owen said, thinking back on the first few days after Angela and Jacob died. Before the anger had come. He'd wanted nothing more than to crawl into a hole and die.

"You sound like you know." She frowned, tilting her head to study him.

"I do. I lost my wife and child. A car bomb."

"Oh, God, that must have been awful."

"It was," he agreed, his brain clamping down on the memories trying to surface. "*It is*. I don't think it ever really goes away. But it gets better."

"I'm not sure that I believe you, but it's nice to know that maybe there's hope." She gave him a tiny smile and then turned her attention back to Avery. "So what was it you wanted to see me about?"

Avery looked nervous and out of place for the first time since Owen had met him, fidgeting on the sofa like a schoolboy called into the headmaster's office.

"I'm not going to break, Avery," Lara said, obviously having the same thoughts as Owen. "You know me. So whatever it is, just spit it out."

"Look, Lara, this isn't going to be easy," he began. "We've reason to believe that Jason didn't kill himself."

"What are you saying?" Her eyes widened, her fingers twisting together.

"I'm saying there's no way he committed suicide."

She froze for a moment, letting the words sink in. And then she smiled—a real smile—leaving Owen feeling as if the sun had just emerged from behind a bank of clouds. "I never really believed it. Jason would never leave me like that. Never. But, if he didn't kill himself...then... then..." Her smiled faded as the truth hit home. "Oh, my God—are you saying he was murdered?"

"Yes." Avery nodded, his face tight with emotion as he repeated everything they'd learned, from Tyler's initial realization to the discoveries Harrison had made. When he finished, Lara sat for a moment absorbing it all, and then with a little frown, she sat back, her gaze encompassing them both.

"You think I did it, don't you? That's why you've come. And why you're so nervous." She nodded at Avery, who was still fidgeting. "You think I killed Jason."

"There are facts that seem to point that way. Yes,"

Avery said. "But understand, we're not here to accuse you, Lara. Just to try to understand what it all means. We want to hear your side of things."

"Well, first off, I didn't kill Jason. Period. He was my life. And if my brain wasn't still numbed by grief and pharmacology I'd probably be screaming mad. As it is I'm just dumbfounded. What in heaven's name could have made you think that I'd kill Jason?"

Avery sighed, his dark gaze holding Lara's. "Evidence from Logan Palmer."

"Logan Palmer is a self-absorbed son of a bitch," she said, shooting a glance in Owen's direction. "What could he possibly have on me?"

Tyler hurried down the lighted pathway, pulling her jacket closer. The wind had turned cold, and the leaves scurried across the ground, swirling in coppery eddies as she passed. The social sciences building was on the far side of the campus, and even though it wasn't really late, the area was deserted, students heading to the cafeteria for dinner or to the library to study, both buildings on the other side of the campus nearer the dorms.

She passed the administration building, the ivy-covered walls a deep russet now, the color blending in with the bricks. Sunderland had been around a long time, and this quadrangle was the oldest part of campus, the pathways made of cobblestones, the iron lampposts reminiscent of their gaslit predecessors.

Usually she loved the quaint feel and the dim lighting, but tonight all she could think about was Jason dangling from the ceiling beam. Killing Jason had made a mockery of everything A-Tac stood for. They were supposed to be the good guys. And yet one of them, maybe Lara, had taken Jason's life.

She shook her head, clearing her thoughts. Her brother had called earlier to check on progress and to let her know that he'd scheduled services for his mother and their father. Della would be laid to rest in a family plot, her father in Arlington Cemetery. It seemed sort of symbolic, the separation of the two. As if their lives had never fully been intertwined.

Tyler wondered if it would be that way for her. If she could really truly commit to someone. Someone like Owen. For the first time in her life, she knew she wanted to try. But in the wake of everything that had happened, she couldn't help but wonder if that kind of happiness was an impossible dream.

The social sciences building loomed out of the shadows and trees, its grand steps curving upward to the long portico that fronted the building. Emmett had a late class, which meant that he'd be coming to his office afterward. She'd called and left a message that she'd be waiting for him there.

With any luck at all, he'd be able to shed some light on the accusations Logan Palmer had made. Something that would clear Lara. Although, if Avery and Owen were successful, they'd be able to clear things up on their own.

Of course, the alternative was that Lara had actually been involved with the Consortium. That she'd helped them acquire the fissionable material they needed to make their bomb. But Tyler wasn't going to believe it until they were certain it was true. Either from Lara's own mouth, or because of something Emmett might know.

She walked up the stairs, her mind running over the

day's revelations again. It had been a whirlwind, that's for certain. And yet there was still so much they didn't know. She rounded the corner and walked to the end of the hallway. Emmett's office was at the very end, right next to the back stairs. It was actually more straightforward to come up that way, but Tyler liked using the old grand staircase.

She stopped in front of Emmett's door, reaching up over the transom for the key. Then she opened the door, slid the key back into place, and flipped on the lights. Emmett was a neat freak, everything in its place. But the office still had a homey feel. The desk was an antique, a partner's desk with sturdy Duncan Phyfe legs and the rich honeyed glow of old wood. The rolling chair behind it was covered in green leather, and it always reminded Tyler of a banker's chair.

Which suited Emmett somehow, considering he spent his academic life talking about interest rates, inflation, multipliers, and other fiduciary topics. She'd never trade literature for economics, but she'd enjoyed the classes she'd taken long ago, which at least gave her a healthy respect for Emmett's passion.

Of course their real point of common interest was poetry. Emmett's collection, some of which adorned the shelves behind his desk, was absolutely fabulous. She'd been known from time to time to borrow books for her classes and even on occasion had picked his brain for ideas on how to best present some new verse she'd uncovered.

It had been the latter that had cemented their friendship and might possibly have led to something more. But she'd been right to end things. At the time she'd done it to preserve their friendship, but now, considering her feelings for Owen, she realized she hadn't felt anything remotely similar with Emmett. At least they'd had the wisdom to realize it and not let things progress too far.

She walked over to the bookshelf and pulled out a favorite volume. Dylan Thomas. *Do not go gentle into that good night.* She'd always loved the poem, but it held even more meaning now. Thinking of her father, and Jason. Even Smitty. Life was so damn fragile. And there was only one. Thomas was right, you had to keep fighting. No matter the obstacles. No matter the fears.

She closed the book, her heart feeling lighter. There was something wonderful about words and the way they could be strung together to evoke memories and emotions, to paint pictures in your mind. To carry you away to a faroff place.

God, she was feeling fanciful. It was Emmett's fault. Him and his poetry. She reached up to slide the book back into its place on the shelf, but something caught her eye, her hand freezing as her brain registered what it was she was seeing stuffed back behind the books on the shelf above her head.

Hand shaking, she laid the book on the desk and, standing on tiptoes, reached back into the depths of the shelf, her hand closing on silk.

Blue silk.

She'd found her mother's scarf.

Heart pounding, Tyler swung around, the world moving in slow motion as the door opened, and Emmett stood there, looking almost comical in his surprise. But almost before she could finish the thought, he changed, his features tightening, anger mixing with regret as his eyes grew cold and he pulled the gun from his pocket.

"Ah, Tyler," he said, his eyes falling to the scarf in her hand. "I wish to hell you hadn't found that."

"Well, first off, I should tell you that I'm a total freak when it comes to anything electronic. Phones, computers, iPods, you name it, I can break it," Lara said. "Sometimes without even turning it on."

Her fingers were still laced together, the whites of her knuckles showing the effort it cost her to hold it together. But so far nothing they'd told her had garnered more than a mumbled curse directed at Logan Palmer. Owen had spent most of his adult life reading people, and although Lara was upset, she wasn't acting like someone with dark secrets to conceal.

"I actually remember Jason saying something to that effect once," Avery said, a smile lifting the corners of his lips.

"Yeah, probably wondering how he could possibly have fallen in love with a woman who can't program her DVR. Anyway, all of that to say that there's no way I could have manipulated programs on Jason's computer. And even if I could I couldn't possibly have gotten around his security systems."

"Harrison managed without any problems," Owen said. "Maybe things weren't as secure as you think they were."

"No, believe me, he's got security systems for his security systems. Harrison only got in because he's got game. Jason said he was the most talented person he'd ever worked with. And Jason isn't—wasn't—" she corrected, her voice cracking a little as she sucked in a breath, "he wasn't an easy sell."

"But even if we accept that you haven't tampered with Jason's computer, there are still some very serious allegations coming out of Logan's office."

"The trips," she sighed. "Actually, there's a sound explanation for most of it. And it's got nothing to do with plutonium. The second trip you mentioned, the one in June. I was in Golovchino. But only for a few minutes. I'd scheduled a trip to the Ukraine after the task force meetings, and I mentioned it in passing to a couple of the other members. Anyway, the day we adjourned, one of the Russians on the committee, Beral Kirov, asked me if I'd mind dropping some paperwork off for him in Golovchino. They were official reports of some kind, all in Russian. And since it was on my way, I agreed. I signed in, handed over the papers, and in like five minutes I was on my way again."

"To the Ukraine."

"Yes. To meet with Yuri Strevski. Logan was right about that. I suspect I was the woman they heard in the conversation. But the package wasn't plutonium." She closed her eyes for a moment, gathering her thoughts, then with a conscious exhalation of breath she opened them again with a soft smile. "A couple of years ago, I had a bit of a medical scare. I was pregnant. But it turned out that the baby was ectopic."

"I'm sorry," Owen said, understanding in a way Avery couldn't what it was like to want a child and then to lose it.

"It was tough. I made it through the first trimester before they found out what was what. And by the time they did find it, there'd been a lot of damage. Anyway, the long and short of it is that I can't have children." She stopped for a moment, her eyes misting over. "Jason wanted kids really badly. And I wanted to have them with him. So we looked into adoption."

"But you weren't even married," Avery said.

"We didn't think a piece of paper was that important," she shrugged. "Commitment comes from the heart. Anyway, we tried every legal channel we could think of, all with absolutely no success. Either they were appalled that we weren't married or they didn't think people in our line of work should be raising kids. So for a while we sort of shelved the idea. Then Annie and Adam came into our lives, and I saw Jason with Adam and just knew it was time."

"So you went to the black market," Owen said, everything suddenly making sense. "The package you were discussing with Yuri, it was a baby."

She nodded. "It was just a preliminary discussion. I found him through the same colleague I delivered the papers for. It was expensive. But we were considering it. I knew Yuri had other interests, but sometimes you have to look the other way. Anyway, my friend will confirm that he gave me the name as long as anything he says stays private. He's a government official so he can't be linked to someone like Yuri."

"What about the other visit?" Avery asked. "The earlier one to Golovchino?"

"That wasn't me." She shook her head. "I was in Russia. But I never left the conference. In fact, I never left the bed. I had food poisoning. A really heinous bout. Bad fish, we think. Anyway, the hotel doctors can confirm it.

They're required to keep records when foreigners get ill. And I was really, really sick."

"So there's no way you could have gone to the western facility?"

"Absolutely none. I could barely make it to the bathroom. Emmett can back me up. He was there. At least part of the time."

"What do you mean part of the time?"

"Well, like I said, I was really ill. So I had to stay on a couple of days past the end of our meetings and Emmett had somewhere else he had to be. So I sent him on his way. There was nothing he could do for me. And I figured it was probably some operation for you."

Avery pulled out his phone and keyed in a number, a frown creasing his brow. "Hannah?" he said into the phone. "Can you pull up the duty roster for May of last year?"

They waited while Hannah presumably logged on to her computer.

"Great," Avery said. "I need to know the dates for the conference they attended. And can you tell me when Lara and Emmett left for Russia?" He nodded. "And then when did they get back? I see. You're sure?" There was another pause and then Avery nodded once and disconnected.

"So what did you find?" Owen asked, ignoring the pulse of worry settling in his gut.

"Emmett didn't come back here for assignment. In fact, he didn't come back until the day before Lara. The conference ended on the twenty-third. And Lara was back on the twenty-seventh. The log at Golovchino has her there on the twenty-fourth."

"Which is impossible. Unless I have a clone," Lara said.

"Or someone used your credentials to get in."

"But that would have to have been a woman. I thought we were talking about Emmett."

"We are." Avery said, his jaw tightening as the full implication sank in. "Hannah got a call from Logan. He wanted to let us know that he'd talked to the people in Golovchino. Apparently, the first Lara Prescott was accompanied by a man. So Logan faxed them photos of everyone in A-Tac. The woman they saw wasn't you. But there was no question about the man. It was definitely Emmett."

"Bloody hell." Owen grimaced, his hand curling into a fist, the worry turning to full-fledged fear. "Tyler's with Emmett now. She was going to tell him everything. God, if he thinks we're on to him, she could be walking into a trap."

CHAPTER 25

I don't understand," Tyler said, holding the scarf in her hand as she stared down the barrel of Emmett's gun. "Why did you do this?" It was the only thing she could think of to say. Emmett was—or at least had been—her friend.

"Cutting right to the chase, as usual. One of the things I've always liked about you. Are you specifically asking about the scarf or my long list of other sins?"

"All of it, I suppose." She scrambled to clear her head, to keep him talking so that she could figure a way out. It was hard to believe that Emmett would kill her, but he'd clearly had no problem dispatching Jason, so she knew better than to let her distorted perceptions rule the day.

"Well, explaining the scarf is easy," he shrugged, a smile playing at the corners of his mouth. "I used it in part because it amused me, and in part because it suited my purposes. I needed to keep you off-balance. And you have to admit it worked like a charm."

"But how did you even know? I never talk about my mother."

"Tyler, you should know by now that there are no secrets in A-Tac. Everyone talks about everything."

"No one else knew, Emmett," she ground out, her fingers tightening around the soft silk, wishing it were a weapon of some kind. "At least not the details."

"Well, that sort of thing just takes a little digging. Isn't that what we do best? A copy of the police report, and a quick look into your personnel file. I even talked to Della. The woman was quite forthcoming, especially when she thought I was the love of your life."

"So that's how you knew about my father's connection to Smitty. And you used him to get to me." She inched forward, thinking there might be something in the desk drawer, or at least that she could use the desk for cover.

"Well, in truth," Emmett said, "I just stirred the pot a little so things would work out the way they were supposed to. I needed you to be on that road in Colorado. It was the easiest way to make certain A-Tac was involved. I knew they'd all bend over backward for you."

"What the hell do you mean by that?"

"Everyone knows you're the favorite child. Nash and Avery would sell their souls for you."

"And I'd do the same thing for them. Hell, I would have done it for you," she said, her fingers closing around the desk drawer handle, the scarf blocking Emmett's view. "But what I don't understand is why having A-Tac involved was so important."

"Because if A-Tac was in charge of the investigation, I could manipulate things. Keep you all confused. Allow the real agenda to progress without interruption."

"Building and detonating a bomb." She pulled the drawer open, sliding her fingers inside.

"For the greater good, yes," he said.

"You really believe that killing millions of innocent people is a greater good?"

"We're fighting a war, Tyler. And it's us against—well, *you* and others like you. Sometimes there is going to be subsidiary loss."

"Like my father?"

"I didn't actually pull the trigger," he said, his expression thoughtful. "Although I suppose I would have had I been asked. But you're missing an important point here. Your father was losing his mind, and with it his dignity and self-respect. He wouldn't have wanted to live like that."

"He'd have wanted to make a choice," she said, fighting down a surge of emotion. "You took that away from him."

"Half-empty, half-full." He shrugged. "I see it my way, you see it yours. Anyway what's done is done." His eyes narrowed, his gaze dropping to the scarf. "I want you to move away from the desk." He waved her toward the corner with his gun.

She held her position, her fingers closing around a letter opener.

"Move," he said, lifting the gun. "Now."

With a nod, she pulled the scarf into her other hand, holding both of them up as she stepped back into the corner, the letter opener safely concealed in her sleeve.

"Now I just have to figure out what to do with you," he said, tilting his head to one side as he studied her.

"I'm not the only one who knows," she said, praying the bluff would buy her time.

"Don't be silly." He laughed, the sound without humor. "I saw your face. If you hadn't found that scarf you wouldn't have had a clue. You'd have still thought it was Jason."

"No." She shook her head. "I knew it wasn't Jason when I proved that he didn't kill himself." She was satisfied to see that her words had at least penetrated his seeming indifference.

"You can't have done that."

"Oh, but I did. You see, you made a fatal mistake. Jason was left-handed. You used your right," she said, nodding at the hand holding the gun. "The knots were wrong. And the placement of the rope. From there we just needed to do a little digging, as you so gracefully put it, to prove that Jason was set up."

"Stupid prick was prying into my business. Fortunately for me, he hadn't told any of you."

"But he kept files. On the Consortium."

"Guess I missed them." He looked annoyed, but not overly concerned. "Not that it matters. He didn't know enough to be of any value to you or a danger to the organization. And I'm betting that when you worked out that Jason was innocent, you moved on to the next-most-likely suspect—Lara."

She tightened her fists, wishing she could knock the smug expression off his face, but he had the gun. "As a matter of fact, we were in possession of facts that seemed to point in that direction. I'm assuming you had a hand in that as well?"

"Circumstantially. A friend of mine borrowed her name to get me into Golovchino."

"To steal the plutonium."

"I prefer to think of it as a liberation. The Soviets would have happily given it to us had history turned out differently. But yes, if you want to use those words."

"So, what, you're a communist supporter now?"

"No, I'm a dyed-in-the-wool pragmatist. I'm in it for me. Money. Power. Recognition. The usual suspects. And I sure as hell wasn't going to get it from A-Tac."

"But we were your friends."

"Actually, you weren't. I was always the outsider. And nothing I ever did was good enough for Avery Solomon. He always gave me the worst assignments. Stay with the boat. Man the communications. He treated me like I was an imbecile. And the rest of you weren't much better."

"But you and I—" she started, then stopped, unable to finish the sentence.

"Were what?" Emmett asked, his handsome face almost a caricature. "In love? I thought maybe once upon a time. But you rejected me."

"We agreed to stop seeing each other. I thought it was mutual." How could she have not recognized his anger? His contempt? It was there now, boiling just under the surface.

"Well, you thought wrong," he said, his hand tightening on the trigger. "I loved you. And I had to watch while you screwed around with that traitor from IA. And don't forget, if it hadn't been for me, you'd never have known about his lies."

"Owen is a good man." She straightened her arm, the blade of the letter opener sliding against her palm.

"Owen was using you to get information for Logan Palmer."

"It's his job. And no matter what you think of him, or

me, you had no right to spy on me like that. How did that help the Consortium?"

"It didn't. I bugged your house long before I started working with them. I just liked knowing what you were doing." He smiled, his lips pulled tight, almost a grimace. "Did you find the one in the bathroom?"

She shuddered, bile rising in her throat, words impossible.

"I thought not. Nice to know I still have a few secrets. You look really hot in the shower, by the way."

"You bastard." Anger sent her flying forward with the letter opener raised like a dagger. She swung downward, but he was faster, catching her right hand in his left and twisting until she dropped the weapon.

Still enraged, she swung with her left hand, and he hit her hard with the butt of the gun. For a moment the world spun, and she stumbled backward, hitting her head against the wall. Then, by sheer force of will, she pulled herself upright, glaring at him angrily.

"Careful, Tyler," he said, his voice deceptively gentle as he screwed a silencer onto his gun. "I'd hate to have to shoot you. Although I suppose ultimately I won't have a choice."

She covered her cheek with her hand, her fingers growing sticky with blood. She'd known he meant to kill her, but his saying it out loud made it reality. "Why didn't you just let them kill me on the side of the road?"

"I told you, because you were useful to us. But once A-Tac was assigned to find the culprits, your usefulness was at an end. Although I'll admit, I was secretly pleased you avoided their attempts to take you out."

"But that didn't stop you from sabotaging our missions."

Her cheek was still hurting, but her head had cleared and she knew that she had to keep him talking and pray that either help arrived or she found some opportunity for escape. "You're the one who tampered with my explosives. Your mischief almost cost all of us our lives."

"That was actually the point—although I'll admit I was mainly trying to prove to the powers that be that I was capable of playing havoc with A-Tac missions without being detected."

"So all of it was you? The rope, the communications glitches—the intel leaks in Colombia?"

"Drake Flynn's a damn fool. He made it easy. He was so interested in getting into Madeline's pants, he couldn't see the jungle for the palm trees."

"You really hate us all, don't you?"

"I'd never waste time on hate. It takes too much energy. Suffice it to say that I'm indifferent."

"Think whatever you want. But I don't believe a word of it."

"And I don't give a fuck what you believe," he said, his brows drawn together in anger. "I have the upper hand here, Tyler. And you'd do well to remember that."

"I wouldn't be so certain," she taunted. "Everyone we've unearthed who was involved with the Consortium has been eliminated. My father, Smitty, Marta Weller. They're all dead. What's to stop the Consortium from sending someone after you, now that you've been outed?"

"You're overplaying your hand," he said, waving the gun at her. "You're the only one who knows. And I don't anticipate your getting the chance to tell anyone anything."

"I don't have to tell them. Avery and Owen are talking to Lara right now. It's only a matter of time before they figure it all out. And when they do, you'll become a liability. Your life won't be worth a damn."

"You have no idea what you're talking about. I'm far too valuable for them to take me out. They need people like me, insiders willing to do their dirty work."

"But once you've been exposed, you won't be an insider anymore," she goaded. "And believe me when I tell you that there are countless other toadies waiting in line to take your place. People who can be bought. People whose greed drives them to act stupidly."

His eyes flashed with rage and he fired the gun. Tyler hit the floor, the bullet smashing into the wall next to the bookcase. Pushing off with her hands, she rolled forward, slamming into Emmett's knees, his legs buckling as she jumped to her feet and ran for the door. But he grabbed her hair, throwing her onto the floor.

"Get the fuck up," he said, the barrel of the gun pushed tight against her head. "I'd shoot you right now, but you might still prove useful. If you're right, and Avery and company have figured it out, they'll be coming after me. But as long as I have you, I'll have the upper hand." He twisted her arm behind her, lowering the gun so that it was pressed against her side. "One wrong move and I'll splatter that beautiful body of yours all over the social sciences building. Am I making myself clear?" He yanked her arm, pain shooting down her side, and she nodded.

He pushed her in front of him, out the doorway and down the hall toward the back stairs. "Just keep your mouth shut and keep moving," he said, shoving her arm into the small of her back as he pushed her forward. "This would have been a happy ending if only you'd wanted me instead of that damn Brit."

As if on cue, said Brit, looking as if he wanted to spit nails, stepped into the hallway from the landing of the back stairs, his gun leveled at the two of them.

"Drop the gun," Emmett said. "Or I'll kill her."

Owen's gaze met hers, and she shook her head. But Owen dropped the gun anyway, his eyes moving back to Emmett. "Let her go."

"Fat chance. She's all mine now," Emmett said, his tone back to smug.

Tyler struggled against him, but his hold was too strong, and she couldn't get any leverage.

"Get on your knees, Owen," Emmett called. "Hands behind your head."

Owen's expression turned thunderous, but he did as he was told. Tyler felt tears of rage breaking from the corners of her eyes. Then she saw Owen's gaze shift to something behind her.

"This is for Jason."

Emmett pivoted, but it was too late, the report of Lara's gun exploding into the hallway. Tyler hit the floor as Emmett lifted his gun, and Lara fired again, the bullet slamming him back, a smear of blood staining the wall as he slid to the floor.

His gun fell from spasming fingers and Tyler knocked it away. Avery appeared from behind Lara and Tyler started to push to her feet, but Emmett's fingers closed around her wrist. "Wait," he whispered.

Owen raised his gun, but Tyler shook her head. "Tell me where the bomb is," she said, staring down into his fading eyes. "Emmett, please tell me how to stop it."

"It's too late," he said, his breath coming on a rasp. "The game is in motion. But you know me." He tried to smile, but only one corner of his mouth moved. "I always have contingency plans. And since I'm dying, I'll let you in on my secret." His fingers tightened and he pulled her closer, his words so low they were almost inaudible.

"We're all hollow men, Tyler. Shadows. Living in a world of gray. Thomas Stearns was right about that. But he was wrong about the world. It doesn't end on a whimper. At least not tomorrow—tomorrow it ends with a bang." He paused, struggling for breath. "Unless, of course, you can solve the riddle. Ask Eliot, he knows."

He held her gaze for a second more, and then his fingers went slack, his body going limp, life passing away without even a whimper.

CHAPTER 26

A re you okay?" Owen asked, kneeling beside Tyler as she tried to work through what Emmett had told her. "Your face." He reached out to caress her bruised cheek. "You're bleeding."

"It's just a scratch," she said, as Avery and Lara joined them.

"Is he dead?" Lara asked, her voice still filled with anger. "The bastard killed Jason."

"I know." Tyler nodded, reaching over to close Emmett's eyes. "He confessed to everything. I still can't believe it. I thought he was our friend."

"I did, too," Lara said, reaching down to touch Tyler's shoulder. "I'm glad you're all right."

Tyler smiled up at her friend. "Thanks to you."

"Look, I know how difficult this is for everyone," Avery said, "but right now we need to get Emmett's body out of here before any of the students figure out what's going on. It's going to be hard enough to explain Jason and Emmett's deaths without coeds witnessing the violence firsthand."

"I can call for help," Lara said, pulling out her cell phone. "But I'll need to go outside to get service. These old walls play hell with reception."

"I'll go with you," Avery said. "You guys will be all right?"

"We're fine," Tyler said, lifting her hand to wave them on.

"All right," he called, already moving down the hall after Lara. "I'll be back for the body and then we'll regroup in the war room."

Owen reached down to help Tyler up, using the sleeve of his shirt to wipe off some of the blood. "When I saw you with Emmett," he said, his dark gaze holding hers, "I was so afraid I was going to lose you."

"I know," she nodded, reaching up to caress his face, "I had the same thought. But we're here. And we're together. But this isn't over. Emmett was trying to tell me something when he died. Something about a riddle. I think in his own perverse way, he was trying to give me a shot at finding the bomb."

"What exactly did he say?" Owen asked, a frown creasing his forehead.

"He said that we were too late. That the game was on."

"That much we already knew."

She nodded, holding up her hand. "There was more." She closed her eyes, trying to pull up the words. "He said that there was a contingency plan. *His*. Anyway, we used to play this game where one of us would quote a bit of poetry, sometimes completely out of context, and the other one would have to identify it."

"I thought he was an economist," Owen said.

"He was. As well as an expert in game theory. But he loved poetry. He has a huge collection. Anyway, it doesn't matter. What's important is that he started rambling about hollow men and shadows and T. S. Eliot being right. I think he was talking about his life."

"I don't see how that's supposed to help us."

"It doesn't directly, but then he said that *he was wrong about the world. It doesn't end on a whimper. At least not tomorrow—tomorrow it ends with a bang.*"

"It's a play on Eliot's 'Hollow Men,' right?" Owen frowned, clearly trying to make sense of it.

"Right. And I think he was talking about the bomb. *Tomorrow it ends with a bang.*"

"But we still don't know where, or specifically when." Frustration colored his voice.

"I'm sorry, I'm not telling this well, I'm still a little shaken and I'm not thinking clearly. But he made it clear that the outcome he was talking about—the bang—could potentially be stopped. If I could solve a riddle."

"What riddle?"

"I don't know. All he said was *ask Eliot.* And he can't have meant it literally; Eliot died in 1965."

"Maybe there's something in the poem itself," Owen suggested.

"Doesn't seem likely." She shook her head. "But I suppose it's worth a try. I've got a copy in my office."

"You said Emmett had a poetry collection. Would he have a copy?"

"I'm sure he must. Eliot is an essential."

"It just seems like if there is anything to find, it'll be in his copy."

"That makes total sense. I should have thought of it myself." They walked together down the hall toward Emmett's office.

"You've been through a lot," he said, his eyes worried. "I'm sorry I wasn't here with you. I should have been."

"We had no way to know that it was Emmett we should be hunting." She shook her head, laying her hand on his arm as they came to a stop in the doorway. "And really it's my fault he went ballistic. I got to the office before he did, and I was flipping through one of his books, and when I went to put it away, I found my mother's scarf. It was stuffed behind the books on the top shelf. And before I had a chance to react, he walked in."

"And saw you with the scarf."

She nodded, as the memory replayed in her mind. "He hated us all so much, Owen. And I had no idea."

"Clearly he wasn't in his right mind. He can't have been. Did he say why he betrayed A-Tac?"

"Yeah. For money. And power. Pretty damn basic when you get right down to it."

"And predictable. Did he tell you anything more about the Consortium?"

"No. He kept it vague. He did confirm that Jason was on to them. Which means his information is probably right." She squared her shoulders and, ignoring her churning stomach, walked back into the office, leaning down to pick up her mother's scarf.

Owen moved past her, stopping in front of the back wall, lifting his hand to touch the shattered plasterboard where the bullet had slammed into the wall. "My God, Tyler, he could have killed you."

"But he didn't," she said, reaching out to squeeze his shoulder. "I'm fine. And he can't hurt us anymore."

He pulled her into his arms, tipping her head up to kiss her, his lips cherishing hers—celebrating the fact that they were both alive. Then with a wry grin, he pushed away. "T. S. Eliot is waiting."

She smiled back, her heart lighter, and after folding the scarf and putting it in her pocket, she started to search the bookshelf. There were probably a hundred titles, about half of them poetry. She followed the shelves from left to right, reading spines, looking for the right book. Finally, on the second-highest shelf, she found it.

"*The Collected Works of T. S. Eliot,*" she said, opening the book to scan the table of contents. "It's here." She flipped through the book to the proper page, the book falling open to reveal an envelope.

"Son of a bitch," Owen whispered.

She held the envelope up to the light, and then sniffed the back, nothing seeming out of place. "In for the penny?" she asked, looking to Owen for his approval.

"Go for it." He nodded

Carefully, she slit the top of the envelope and pulled out the single sheet inside. "It's a poem, I think. Or a riddle."

She held it out for him to read, her mind already spinning as she tried to find the logic in Emmett's words.

The second act always follows the first,
The time and the setting the same.

Though the mighty have fallen, the Divine still stands
And the righteous shall take the blame.

*   *   *

"Oh, my God, Tyler, I just heard," Madeline Reynard gasped, crossing the reception area of the underground A-Tac complex to give her a hug. "Are you all right?"

"I'm fine," Tyler said with a smile, genuinely happy to see Drake's fiancée. Although the two of them had gotten off on the wrong foot initially in Colombia, Madeline had more than proved her loyalty to Drake and to A-Tac, and Tyler was delighted for the two of them. "I didn't know you were back."

"I just flew in this morning," she said, tucking a way-ward curl behind her ear. "I would have come earlier, but Tucker's still dealing with the fallout from Ortiz's betrayal, so I wanted to make sure he'd be okay on his own." Tucker was Drake's brother, and the years he'd spent in a Colombian prison had taken a toll. He'd been through a lot, and both Drake and Madeline had been in California helping him with his recovery. "Anyway, I'm here now. And I'm so sorry about Jason, and your father—all of it."

"It's a lot to deal with," Tyler said. "But I'm not the only one affected. Emmett's duplicity has an impact on all of us."

Owen cleared his throat quietly and Madeline held out her hand. "Hi. We haven't been introduced. I'm Madeline. And you must be Owen."

"I'm sorry," Tyler said, shaking her head. "I forgot you wouldn't know each other. In some ways I feel like Owen has been here forever. I assume Drake's filled you in?"

"Yes." Madeline nodded, her gaze guarded. "Every-thing. But nevertheless, it seems that we're all in your debt. From what Drake tells me you've been there for

Tyler on more than one occasion. She means the world to all of us."

"A sentiment I share," Owen said, his fingers twining with Tyler's. "Believe me."

Madeline smiled at them both, her expression softening. "Sometimes it's in moments of crisis that we see things the most clearly. That's how I found Drake. But anyway, I know you need to get in there. Everyone's waiting. I just wanted to let you know that I'm here if you need me."

"Thanks," Tyler said. "That means a lot. I'm glad you're back. And congratulations on the engagement. Drake's a lucky man."

"Nah," Madeline said with a wave of her hand. "I'm the lucky one. Now get to work." She headed to the elevator, and Tyler walked through the sliding panel, Owen beside her.

"She's nice," Owen said, as they headed for the war room.

"Yeah, she is. And more important, she's good for Drake. Helps balance him, if that makes any sense."

"Glad to see you're still in one piece," Nash said as she and Owen walked into the war room. "Avery told us what happened."

"To be honest, it's getting to be old hat. I seem to run into someone who wants to kill me every other day." She tried for a smile, but settled for a crooked grin. Her body was aching, and her mind was still reeling, but there was work to be done, so after a quick shower and a change of clothes she was ready.

And apparently so was the rest of the team. Hannah and Harrison were ensconced in front of their computers, their heads bent together as they studied something. Annie and Nash sat on the right side of the table with Drake on the other side, his chair, as usual, tipped back against the wall. Lara was present, too, sitting on the edge of the table, talking with Avery, her face pale, but her expression resolute. If Jason had been there—and Emmett—it would have seemed almost normal.

But they were both gone and nothing would ever be the same.

Except that there was a national threat, and A-Tac was charged with stopping it.

Tyler slid into the seat next to Drake, and Owen dropped into one next to her. Hannah hit a key to project an image of Emmett's riddle up on the screen. Lara settled in a seat and Avery moved to the front of the room.

Behind them, the door to the war room opened and Logan Palmer walked in, his arrogant smirk reminding Tyler of Emmett.

"Sorry to burst into a closed meeting," he said, sounding anything but apologetic. "But I thought maybe it was time I took an active role in this investigation. Seems you've been having more than your fair share of trouble."

"You're welcome to have a seat," Avery said, waving toward a chair in the back. "We're always happy to welcome observers from our sister agencies."

"I wouldn't exactly call myself an observer," Logan said, moving to sit at the front of the room next to Lara. "Think of me more as a watchful eye."

Tyler turned to Owen, but he frowned and shook his head, clearly as surprised to see his boss as they were.

"All right, people," Avery said, ignoring Logan. "You've

all had a chance to be brought up to speed. And you've also had some time with Emmett's parting riddle. What we need to do is decipher it and then hopefully intercept the suitcase nuke before it can be detonated."

"What we need to do," Logan interrupted, "is figure out who or what the Consortium is. Have you found anything new?"

"We've been a little busy trying to stop a killer," Nash said, his eyes narrowed as he studied the older man. "We're not that keen on losing one of our own."

"Technically, you've lost two. Although one of them was admittedly a traitor."

"And though there's no question that it reflects on the unit, it has nothing to do with the integrity of the individuals still sitting here." Avery's expression was guarded, but Tyler could see the muscle ticking in his jaw.

"There's nothing to find, anyway," Hannah said. "Even with a name, there's not anything out there. Some innuendo. And some veiled references. Harrison and I located everything that Jason did, but there just isn't anything else. Whoever these people are, they're experts at staying under the radar."

"From what I can tell," Harrison said, still typing something on his computer, "they work in tiers. The lowest group, like the mercenaries assigned to take out Tyler, her father, and the others doing most of the dirty work, with a secondary level—with players like Emmett, Smitty, and Marta—allowed limited access and assigned specific tasks. And it's more than clear that these two tiers are completely expendable."

"What we don't know," Hannah continued, "is how many more layers or tiers there are. And right now, with all due respect, Mr. Palmer, I think the more important consideration has to be finding the bomb."

"Of course." Logan nodded, making a note of some kind on the pad of paper he'd brought with him. "Continue." He waved his hand like a king granting a favor, and Tyler almost laughed at the look of disgust on Drake's face.

"Okay, so let's start with what we already know," Avery said. "Hannah, can you make a list on the other screen?"

She nodded and hit a key, a second screen popping up next to where Emmett's riddle was displayed. "The first thing should be location. We've got a valid threat against New York and solid indications of cell activity in the area. It makes it a likely target, but not necessarily a certainty."

"Except that I've got further proof," Harrison said, tapping his computer. "You know I've been digging through Jason's files again. Trying to find something I'd missed the first time through. And I found a second hidden file. And there's a reference to the bomb. Along with a cyber trail of the evidence he'd been following. Evidence that seems to definitively link the bomb to Manhattan."

"You're sure about this?" Avery asked.

"I verified everything Jason did. And it seems to be accurate. And I had Hannah look at it, too," he said as he reached for a file folder and handed it to Avery. "I made a hard copy for you."

"Hannah?" Avery asked, scanning the pages inside the folder.

"I think it's the real thing," she said.

"So was there a specific location?" Logan asked, his tone skeptical.

"No. Just the city," Harrison admitted, "but at least it narrows our focus."

"Right," Avery said, nodding at Hannah. "New York." She wrote something on her ThinkPad and the words "New York" appeared on the screen. "What else?"

"Emmett implied that it was happening tomorrow," Tyler said, and Hannah added that to the list.

"We also know that the bomb is a suitcase nuke," Nash said. "Probably small enough to fit into a duffel bag or backpack."

"And they'll be using some jury-rigged version of Jefferson Smithwick's plans. Including the detonators they stole. Which means that there will probably be an electronic ignition and timing system." Owen frowned, his eyes on the screen. "That's pretty much all we've got. Unless we can figure out what the hell Emmett's trying to tell us."

"I don't see how any of you can possibly give any credence to the scribblings of a traitor," Logan said, shaking his head as his gaze encompassed them all. "He's either totally crazy and the poem doesn't mean a thing, or he's purposely leading you down the proverbial garden path. A final parting shot."

"You didn't know Emmett," Tyler said, shaking her head. "He was a master at games theory. He even taught a class. And the one thing he believed above everything else was the importance of winning. He used to say there was a strategy for everything. The key was to be prepared. So you have to understand that playing the game had no meaning at all unless he came out on top."

"What she's trying to say," Drake said, leaning forward, his chair legs dropping back to the floor, "is that when he knew he was dying, he still wanted to have the last word. Which means he wanted us to have a shot at finding the bomb."

"But he'd already written the poem," Logan insisted. "So it can't be about his dying."

"It can be if it was a contingency plan. I told you Emmett was all about being prepared for any eventuality. And it's not a poem," Tyler said. "It's a riddle. That's the whole point. We solve the riddle, we'll have the answers. The only question is can we do it in time?"

"So let's break it down," Avery said.

"No idea what specifically he means by first and second act," Annie mused, "but I'm guessing the bombing tomorrow is the second act."

"Which means the place and the time from the first act are going to be repeated in the second."

"Well, that clears things right up," Logan groused, shaking his head.

"It's a process, Mr. Palmer," Hannah said. "You have to be patient."

"Patience, I've got," the man said. "Time not so much so. Tomorrow is almost here." He held out his wrist, tapping his watch for effect.

"We know that the bomb is destined for New York, right?" Harrison said. "And we know that the act is being perpetrated by a group of terrorists known as the Consortium. So if their attack is a second act, what's the most obvious first act?"

"Another terrorist attack?" Lara asked. "No question, it's 9/11."

"Wait a minute," Tyler said, squinting up at the riddle. "That makes sense actually. *The mighty have fallen* could apply to America as a whole—but more specifically, wouldn't it apply to the Twin Towers?"

"Yeah." Harrison nodded. "I've seen those words used before somewhere. Maybe in the media. Or in the chatter and rhetoric following the attack. And if we're talking second act, it seems pretty damn fitting that tomorrow is October 11. Anyway, if we're right, then the riddle is telling us that the attack tomorrow is going to be at ground zero. And the time would be—" He typed something into the computer, waited for it to respond, and then continued "—eight-forty-six in the morning. When the plane hit the first tower."

"But that area is huge," Hannah said. "How are we supposed to narrow it down?"

"There's more to the riddle," Owen said, nodding up at the screen. "Maybe it helps clarify the location. *The divine still stands.* We need to figure out how that fits with the towers being destroyed."

"Well, churches are divine," Annie said, "but there are too many of them in the area for it to be a specific location."

"And besides," Nash said, "the sentence is singular."

"Plus the way it's worded, it seems as if he means the towers themselves," Logan offered, apparently having decided to go with the flow. "Or at least the site where they used to stand."

"What about the cross?" Lara asked. "The one that came from the wreckage. Wasn't it made of fused girders?"

"Yeah, I remember seeing it on television," Drake said. "It was pretty fucking inspiring."

"And it definitely qualifies as divinity," Owen said. "Some people have even implied that it was a sign from God."

"Wrong God, if you're on the other side."

"Yeah, but we've got no reason to believe that this is an Islamic extremist group. In fact, the members we've uncovered so far would indicate that it isn't."

"Maybe that's the point of the last statement," Tyler said, nodding up at the screen. "*And the righteous shall take the blame.* Righteous is sometimes used to refer to religious extremists."

"But didn't you just say that this Consortium doesn't play as an extremist group?" Logan asked.

"Read the statement again," Avery suggested.

Logan rolled his eyes, but obeyed, frowned, then nodded. "He's telling us that the plan is to blame an extremist group."

"Whoever the hell these people are, they're trying to start World War III," Owen said, anger coloring his voice. "Bloody bastards."

"So we're all in agreement?" Hannah asked. "The Consortium is planning to detonate a bomb at ground zero, quite possibly at eight-forty-six tomorrow morning. And more specifically, we're thinking that the exact location is tied to the girder cross. Does anyone know if it's still there?"

"I think it was moved to the front of St. Paul's, if I remember correctly," Harrison said, typing again on his computer to verify. "But if the setting is the same, then I'm guessing that means we're talking about the location, not the physical cross."

"How difficult is it going to be to get access to the site? There's quite a bit of construction there now, right?" Drake asked.

"You won't need to worry yourself with logistics,"

Logan said. "NSA will take it from here. I've already alerted the authorities in New York, and we'll mobilize national forces as quickly as possible." He held up his BlackBerry to underscore the words. "But I do want to thank you for all your hard work." He paused, his expression mocking.

"By what authority are you taking charge of this operation?" Avery asked, leaning over the table, his face inches from Logan's. The other man, to his credit, held his ground, but Tyler thought she could see him flinch.

"It comes from the top," Logan said, producing an official-looking document. "See for yourself. In light of your team's failures, it was decided that the endgame should be handled by someone with a little more expertise."

"You?" Avery asked, barely controlling his anger.

Logan smiled. "Yes, me. With Owen's help. He's the expert in nuclear weapons, after all."

"Hey, I didn't sign on for that," Owen said, exchanging a glance with Tyler.

Her emotions were running wild. Anger at being excluded on the one hand, fear for Owen on the other. Not to mention the horror at the possibility of something as cataclysmic as a nuclear bomb exploding in Lower Manhattan. A suitcase nuke had a lower yield than traditional nuclear weapons, but a one-kiloton explosion was more than enough to effectively destroy the city.

"You work for me," Logan said. "So you'll go where I tell you."

"And help you grandstand this into some kind of coup for NSA?" Owen snapped.

"No," Avery said, shaking his head, "you'd be helping prevent disaster."

"But he'll need help," Tyler said. "And I've got the right set of skills to assist him."

Owen opened his mouth to object, but Tyler shook her head. "I've got field experience you don't have. You need me." She turned her attention to Logan. "Both of you."

There was silence as Logan considered the option, the group waiting collectively for his decision. "Fine," he said, lifting his hands. "You're in. But there'll be no grandstanding. You'll do what I tell you to." His gaze locked with hers. "Understood?"

CHAPTER 27

There's still nothing," Owen said, handing Tyler a cup of coffee and joining her on the sidewalk bench. "The consensus seems to be that we've thwarted the attempt."

They'd been in Manhattan since the wee hours of the morning, complete with hazmat teams and representatives from pretty much every possible law enforcement agency. They'd covered ground zero from one end to the other without finding a bomb.

On the one hand, that seemed to signal success, at least if one listened to Logan Palmer and his endless parade of press conferences. He'd dismissed almost all personnel, deeming the crisis over. But Tyler wasn't buying it. And with the witching hour approaching, she still couldn't shake the idea that something was off.

"What if we're wrong? What if the bomb is somewhere else? Maybe Logan was right and Emmett was just trying to mislead us."

"No." Owen shook his head. "You said yourself he

wasn't involved for ideological reasons. He was in it for the money—right?"

"That's what he said," Tyler acknowledged. "But he also talked about being at 'war.' And that innocents had to be sacrificed for the greater good. So it was a bit of a mixed message."

"But you knew Emmett. And you knew how he operated. So what do you think the real truth is?"

Tyler sighed, running a hand through her hair. She was exhausted, and her body ached everywhere, the bruise on her cheek throbbing in time to the sound of a jackhammer off somewhere in the distance. "I'd have bet money that the riddle was real. But this just seems too easy. The Consortium's been ahead of us every step of the way."

"But they had no way of knowing we'd figure out Emmett was the mole or that he'd leave you a clue. Look, it took forethought to come up with that riddle and to hide it where he did. That implies that he had a plan. And if the plan was to throw us off, why not give you the riddle from the very beginning? Or better yet, make it easy for someone to find? But he didn't do that. In fact, he didn't mention it at all until he was dying. Which indicates to me that, whatever he was trying to tell you, it's valid."

"Then I think we got the riddle wrong. I just don't buy that we somehow cut these people off without so much as lifting a finger." She looked out across the open ground where the Twin Towers had once stood. Construction was everywhere, the new covering the old, but she could still remember what it had been like, the two buildings jutting into the air, a symbol of American enterprise.

She closed her eyes, her mind pulling forth more horrific memories. The plane slamming into the building, people screaming and running, debris falling everywhere, clouds of smoke obliterating the sky. But Americans had pulled together, and something wonderful had risen from the ashes. People reaching out to each other. Hospitals forming triage teams in nearby office buildings. Firefighters and policemen from all over the country coming to Manhattan's aid. Organizations serving food and offering shelter 24/7, manned by people from all walks of life. Ethnicity and religion trumped by citizenship.

She smiled, thinking that even in the most awful of times, there were always heroes. Across the way a church spire rose into the blue October sky, and Tyler flashed on a memory, a snippet from some forgotten news image.

"Hannah?" she said into her earpiece. "Are you still there?" Despite Logan's moratorium on A-Tac's involvement, Tyler and Owen had managed to maintain radio contact with Sunderland, Hannah manning the helm, as it were, updating the rest of the team as needed.

Owen frowned, adjusting his own earpiece, but Tyler shook her head, concentrating on the memory.

"I'm here," Hannah's voice crackled into her ear. "Have you got something new?"

"I'm not sure," Tyler said. "It's just a memory and I could be totally off-base. But I think there's a church somewhere around here that has some kind of important artwork. A statue maybe or a frieze or something?"

"You've just described half the churches in Manhattan." Owen shook his head, looking as frustrated as she felt.

"No. It's more than that. The artwork was important enough to have made the news. I remember seeing the news report. The church apparently sustained a great deal of damage. But the statue, or whatever it was, survived. It was heralded as a miracle. They made a huge deal out of it."

"Okay," Hannah said, "but I'm not sure I'm seeing how this fits in with a nuke at ground zero."

"Well, here's the thing. What I'm remembering is the name of the piece. *Divine Christ.*"

"*The divine still stands.*" Owen repeated. "Hannah, in the riddle, is the word 'divine' capitalized?"

"Yes," she said, the sound of typing echoing across the wires. "And you're right. It's a statue. *Divine Christ.* It was commissioned for St. Ann's Chapel in 1779 by Benjamin Franklin. A gift from France to celebrate America's victory in the Revolution." She paused a moment, clearly reading. "The altar and most of the sanctuary were severely damaged," she continued. "There were major fears that the statue had been destroyed. But after digging out the worst of the rubble, they found it." She released a whistle. "Undamaged—and still standing."

"That's got to be it," Owen said. "Is the statue still there?"

"Yes. The damage to the church was repaired, the statue put back in its niche to the right of the altar. And the chapel opened to services less than two months after 9/11. Tyler, I don't know how you came up with that, but I think you're right."

"Actually," she said, her stomach twisting as she remembered the day more clearly, "I'm certain of it. I know where I saw the report. It was a day or so after the attacks. I was in the war room watching the recovery efforts on television—with Emmett.

"Hannah, where's the chapel?" Tyler asked, glancing

down at her watch, her heart rate ratcheting up when she realized the time.

"Vesey Street near Church. That's quite a ways from where you are now."

"We'll manage," Owen said, jumping to his feet. "Look, Hannah, most everyone's gone from here. So I need you to take all of this to Avery. And tell him we're on our way now. He'll know what to do."

"But shouldn't we consult with Logan?" Tyler asked, looking across to where he was holding court with the media.

"There isn't time." Owen shook his head, slinging a small pack over his shoulder. "Avery will call in the necessary backup. But if we're right, and the bomb is at St. Ann's, it's set to blow in less than fifteen minutes."

St. Ann's Chapel was one of the oldest buildings in New York. Built in 1766, its simple brick façade was dwarfed by the towering skyscrapers of Lower Manhattan. Immediately after 9/11, the wrought-iron fence that surrounded the little church had been covered with fliers, photographs of people lost in the collapse. Now, fully restored, it spoke of better times.

"Hannah said the statue is near the altar," Tyler said as they moved into the chapel. A priest hurried down the center aisle, alarmed no doubt by their guns.

"Sorry to intrude, Father," Owen said, producing identification, "but we believe there may be a bomb inside the church. I'm going to need you to clear everyone out immediately."

"There's no one here but me," he said, accepting the news with the kind of calm only a New Yorker can muster.

"Is there time for me to get the Communion vessels? The chalice is quite valuable. It's in back in the sacristy."

"No. Better for you to just go out through the front," Owen said, checking his watch. "There's not much time."

The priest nodded, his eyes concerned as he made the sign of the cross. "Go with God." He turned and, moving as quickly as his robes would allow, strode into the vestibule and out the door.

"I hope he truly does have a direct line," Tyler said, as they made their way through the nave and up to the steps leading to the sanctuary.

The altar, like the church, was simple—a pink marble slab set on two carved mahogany posts. Above it, light streamed in through an oval stained-glass window. On the left there was a niche with a pedestal holding an elaborately illuminated Bible, and on the other side, an identical niche—this one with a beautifully rendered statue of Jesus, his arms lifted heavenward in supplication.

"The *Divine Christ*," Owen whispered, his voice full of reverence. "It's beautiful. I can see why people would have worried about its survival. Where do you think we should start?"

"I'm betting Christ himself," Tyler said. "If the bomb is here, it's probably tucked into the niche somehow. At least that would seem to fit with Emmett's riddle." She took a step toward the stairs, but Owen held a hand out to stop her.

"Go slowly. The area could be booby-trapped."

She shook her head, not bothering to slow her pace. "The priest was up there. So unless you think he planted the bomb, then I think we're clear as far as the floor being rigged."

This time Owen grabbed her arm, jerking her to a stop. "The priest was wearing robes."

"So what?" she asked, her foot on the first step, impatience making the words sound harsh.

"This is an Episcopal Chapel, Tyler. Priests only wear vestments during a service, and he told us himself, there's no one here."

"You think he was…"

"I don't think we can afford to take a chance." Owen knelt, his eyes scanning the floor and the walls for signs of tampering.

Tyler followed suit, studying the line of the stairs. "There," she said, pointing to a wire lying along the top of the step, just visible along the edge of the carpet. "Could be connected to the bomb, or some kind of secondary charge. We were meant to trip it when we ran up the stairs."

"So what do we do?" he asked. "Can we just step over it?"

"We can, but there's still a risk that it's motion-activated. So I think our best bet is to cut it."

"Isn't it also possible that we'll be setting off the explosion?"

"Possible," Tyler agreed, already working her way slowly up the steps, "but not probable. And to be honest, we're don't have time to debate the matter. There's only a few minutes left, and we still don't have the nuke."

Owen nodded, and she pulled the tool kit from her pocket, extracting a tiny pair of scissors. "You okay with this?" she asked, as she knelt beside the wire.

"I can't say that I'm thrilled with it. But you're right, we don't have the luxury of time." He nodded, and with a quick release of breath, she cut the wire.

Nothing happened, the chapel now seeming eerily quiet.

"All right, then. Chalk one up for the good guys." She

picked up the far end of the wire and carefully pulled it free of the carpet, following along as it ran the course between the altar stairs and the right-hand niche.

"Nice of Father Bombardier to leave us a trail," Owen said, using a flashlight from his pack to illuminate the thin filament.

"Let's see how you feel after we've located the nuke," she said. "How much more time?"

"We're down to six minutes, I'm afraid."

"Hannah?" she called into her microphone.

"You're not going to be able to raise her." Owen shook his head. "These old walls are really thick. Not much chance of getting reception in here."

"So we'll go it alone." She shrugged. "Two great minds and all that."

They stopped in front of the niche, the wire disappearing into a grouping of artfully potted lilies at the base of the statue. Together, they worked silently to move the potted plants, revealing a small metal suitcase lodged between the niche wall and the edge of the statue.

"I know this is going to sound stupid," Owen said, kneeling in front of the case, "but I didn't actually expect it to be in a suitcase." He slid it out from its cubbyhole, moving it carefully away from the statue. Tyler followed and knelt beside him, running her hands along the edges of the casing.

"I'm not feeling any kind of trigger. I could be wrong, but I think it should be safe to open it."

Owen flipped the latches, and despite her assurances, they both jumped as the case clicked open, the sound echoing in the soaring space. Owen counted to three and then lifted the lid, Tyler gasping as the internal workings were revealed. Up until now, the weapon had been purely hypothetical. But now, looking at the lethal reality, she felt a surge of panic.

"What do we do?" she whispered.

"First thing is to stop the timer." Owen nodded to the electronic box attached to the detonator. The green numerals glowed 4:58, the last digit decreasing every second. "According to Smitty's plans there's a start and stop code."

"Do we know what they are?" she asked, her eyes locked on the keypad at the base of the timer.

"No. They'd have been put in place by the developer, in this case somebody within the Consortium. But Harrison gave me a device that should be able to figure it out. He developed it going off the blueprints."

"But we have no idea if it will work."

"Have you got a better idea?"

She studied the bomb for a moment, watching the timer tick down. "Not at the moment, no. And there's no time to debate. Just do it."

Owen nodded and slid the device into a slot clearly meant for a key card of some kind. The timer beeped once, and Harrison's decoder glowed red, humming a little as it tried to calibrate the necessary sequence for disconnecting the timer.

"How long will it take?" Tyler asked.

"Theoretically, something like fifteen seconds."

"Theoretical being the operative word," she sighed, watching the numbers continue to decrease. Then with a triumphant buzz Harrison's device turned green and the numbers stopped.

"You did it," she said, relief making her dizzy, but then, just as suddenly as it had stopped, the timer started again. Only now the new setting was for less time, the declining numbers starting at three minutes.

"Bloody hell," Owen said, removing the box from the timer. "I've made it worse."

"Maybe, but my father always said that it's not over till it's over. So we just need to think. There's got to be another way around this. Something else we can do that will stop the bomb."

"I don't see what. If we try to move the explosives the whole thing will blow. And if we try to pick up the plutonium core, we could cause a compression that will set the damn thing off that way."

The glowing numbers had dropped to just under two minutes.

"What about trying to separate the two charges? The explosives from the plutonium? You know more about it than I do, but isn't the nuclear reaction triggered by the detonation of the explosives?"

"Yes." Owen nodded as Tyler studied the bomb.

It was amazingly simple in its composition. A lithium battery attached to the electronic timer and ignition switch, the stolen detonator connecting to a box with what looked to be some kind of IHE, the insensitive high explosive probably stolen from some government facility. The good thing about it was that although its detonation would trigger the nuke, sitting idle it was relatively stable.

At the other end of the box was the canister containing the plutonium core, the casing consisting of a jacket lined with uranium-238, the plates used to intensify the explosion and amplify the nuclear reaction.

"And the timer is only tied directly in to the explosives, right?" she asked, her mind turning over the possibilities.

Owen nodded, frowning as he considered what she was saying. "So you think that if we can break the circuit between the explosives and the plutonium, the bomb will blow, but the nuke will remain stable."

"It seems possible. We were in Pakistan once. On an undercover mission to try to recover a stolen nuclear warhead. We got it back, but before we could get out of the country the truck with the weapon was attacked. A mortar shell hit us and the back of the truck exploded, but the nuke didn't. It'd be the same principle, right?"

"In theory," Owen said, pulling a screwdriver from his pack. "But it's a long shot."

"And the only one we've got." She nodded at the timer, which had reached the one-minute mark.

Using the screwdriver, Owen pried one of the plates off the bomb, placing it carefully to the side. "If I can remove the trigger, it should stop the explosion from compressing the plutonium. But there's always a chance that we'll get blown sky-high in the process."

"It's going to happen either way," Tyler said. "I don't know about you, but I'd rather die trying."

"Well, to be honest, I was sort of hoping to avoid the whole dying thing," he said, gingerly tipping the bomb so that he could see the trigger. It was the size of a large gumball, but made of much deadlier stuff. "You see, I've only just discovered a reason to live."

Tyler lifted her gaze to his, her heart constricting at the love in his eyes. "Well then, I guess you'd better get on with it."

"First I want you to get the hell out of here," he said. "If this goes badly, there's no point in both of us getting blown to bits."

"Not a chance. We're in this together—all the way."

Owen paused for a second, nodded, and then after donning gloves, reached down through the opening he'd made with a pair of what looked to be oversized tweezers.

Tyler held her breath as the numbers reached thirty seconds.

"Almost there," he said. "When I say go, I want you to run for the door. If this works, there's still going to be a nasty explosion."

"Twenty seconds," she said.

"Damn the bugger. I can't quite get it." He twisted his hand, his face tightening as he concentrated.

"Fifteen seconds." Her heart seemed to be counting down along with the digital readout. "Twelve." She offered up a prayer. When in Rome... "Ten."

"I've got it," he said, pulling the trigger from the canister and dropping it into the bag. "Let's go."

They sprang to their feet and sprinted for the front of the church, everything momentarily seeming to move in slow motion. Tyler could see the saints in the stained glass above the vestibule, their peaceful faces oblivious to the reality playing out below them. Then suddenly the world burst into flame, the power of the explosion shattering the glass.

Owen drove his body into hers, propelling her forward into the vestibule, the church literally shaking as the blast rocketed through the little chapel. It lasted less than a minute. And then everything grew quiet, debris raining down on them, but the church still standing.

"Oh, my God," she whispered, as Owen rolled off her. "I think it worked. Are you okay?" She sat up, her hands reaching for him, even as he pulled her into his arms.

"I'm all right. You?" he asked, kissing her hair and then her eyebrows and nose.

"All in one piece." She tipped her head up, and he slanted his mouth over hers, their kiss a covenant. A promise of life and love.

Behind them sirens wailed, and a discreet cough pulled them apart.

"Logan," they said, almost in tandem. "Glad to see you got the message."

"I'd be furious," he said, eyeing the wreckage in the sanctuary, "but it looks as if the two of you have managed to save the day."

"We'll take that as a compliment," Owen said, his gaze still locked with hers, the emotion reflected there taking her breath away.

"The paramedics are on the way. Along with the bomb squad. I'm assuming there's still a nuke in there?"

"The pieces at least," Owen said, pushing to his feet, and then reaching down to help Tyler up as well. "It should be stable enough for transport now."

"Good." Logan nodded. "I'll put a call in to the mayor. Tell him this thing is really over." He walked out the front door, and Tyler turned back to look into the chapel.

There was debris everywhere, and most of the windows were shattered. A gaping hole yawned in the back wall, and one-half of the altar had toppled to the ground.

"Look at that," she whispered, as Owen came up behind her, his arms wrapping around her, pulling her close. On the right side of the church—the statue stood undamaged, Christ still resplendent in all his marble glory.

"It's a miracle," Owen said, his breath warm against her cheek. "Our own private miracle."

EPILOGUE

It was a perfect autumn day, the deep blue sky providing the perfect backdrop for the red-and-gold-tinted trees. The wind washed lazily through branches and across the pristine white markers of Arlington Cemetery. Tyler stood at her father's grave site, listening as the last of the rifle volleys faded into the first mournful notes of Taps, two-hundred-plus years of military tradition culminating in this last moment.

Mark stood on her left, her brother stoic as they watched the soldier fold the flag that had been draped over her father's casket. It had been a long week. First Della's funeral, then Jason's, and now their father's. Owen had been with her every step of the way. And he stood by her now, their fingers linked, his strength adding to hers.

In the aftermath of the aborted bombing attempt, the full extent of everything that had happened had hit hard. A-Tac would never be the same. They'd survive. And they'd move on. But there were wounds that would take time to heal. And though the immediate threat was gone, there was still the Consortium. There'd been no more clues to the identity of the group's leaders. Nothing that clarified their mission or their strength.

The priest at St. Ann's had in fact turned out to be an impostor, but he'd been found dead in his hotel room. Nothing there to link him to the Consortium. There were so many questions. And for now, at least, no answers. But Tyler knew that they'd find them. It might take years, but in the end, A-Tac would triumph and they'd emerge stronger because of their commitment to their country and to each other.

She smiled up at Owen and then at the rest of her friends. They were all here. Nash and Annie. Drake and Madeline. Avery, Hannah, and Lara. Even Harrison, who'd somehow become indispensable to the team. Everyone had come together to pay their respects and to offer their support.

Tyler felt blessed in so many ways.

The music faded, the bugler lowering his instrument. The grass whispered in the wind, echoing the voices of the countless men and women who had given their lives to protect a cherished way of life. It seemed a never-ending war. But at least, sometimes, they managed to win the day.

The officer in charge walked smartly from the casket, the now-folded flag held carefully in his gloved hands. He stopped in front of Mark and Tyler, offering this last honor. And Tyler accepted it with her chin held high.

"You know that wherever he is," Owen said, his hand tightening around hers, "he's proud of you."

She nodded, not trusting herself to words, and after a last long look at the grave, she turned and walked away, into the company of her friends.

Tomorrow was another day. And the fight would no doubt begin anew.

But for now, in this moment, life was for living.

Nash Brennon has spent eight years trying to forget Annie Gallagher. Now she's back and so is their passion— but can he trust her?

Please turn this page for an excerpt from

DARK DECEPTIONS

Available now.

PROLOGUE

Hotel Montague—Paris

S o do you think we're ever going to feel like a normal couple?" Annie asked as they stumbled back into their hotel room, Nash's hands cupping her breasts, his breath hot against her cheek.

"Trust me, angel, normal is overrated." He pushed her back against the wall, his thumbs rubbing heated circles through the soft silk of her halter top. "And anyway, I kind of like what we've got."

"Right," she sighed, shivering as he kissed her neck. "Sex on the run."

"Well, it's not like we have a lot of free time." His mouth slanted over hers, his tongue sending fire lacing through her belly. It was always like this. Combustible. Their desire heightened by the possibility that each time could be the last.

"Maybe we should adjourn to the bedroom?" She nodded toward the doorway of the suite, and then gasped as he pushed her skirt up around her thighs.

"What's wrong with right here? Right now?" He teased her with his fingers, the friction of satin against skin threatening instant explosion. She lifted her hips, but he pulled back, his slow smile taunting her. "Unless of course you've changed your mind?"

"Not on your life." She reached up to unbutton his shirt, her fingers tracing the scars that laced his chest. Twisted mementos of their life together. "Tell me what you want," she whispered, her breathing labored.

"You, Annie. All I ever want is you."

"So take me," she taunted, anticipation coiling inside her, hot and heavy. Sometimes she thought maybe she wanted something more. Something that resembled normalcy—commitment. But not now. Not in this moment. Right now all she wanted was Nash.

For a moment their passion stretched taut between them; and then, trembling with the sheer power of the feelings he evoked, she arched her back, welcoming his hands and mouth as he crushed her against him. This was what she craved. What she wanted. As long as she had Nash, she could endure anything.

Anything.

"The bed...I can't...please." She gasped the words as they stumbled backward, the need so intense now she thought she might die of it.

His dark eyes reflecting her passion, Nash swung her up into his arms and in two strides they were through the door and on the bed, the cool cotton sheets a counterpoint to the heat that pulsed between them.

Annie pressed against him, her eyes riveted for a moment on the mirror across from the bed and the image of their interlocked bodies moving in tandem. Two shattered souls desperately seeking release. She sighed, and then froze as something else in the mirror moved.

A shadow detached itself from the wall, and Annie dug her nails into Nash's back, instinct and training overriding passion in an instant. Nash's muscles tightened in response, and moving with a precision gained from years of working together, they sprang apart, a bullet smashing into the headboard between them. Annie rolled to the floor, reaching for the gun she kept strapped to her thigh. In her ardent haste she hadn't had time to remove her weapon.

But Nash had. He'd thrown his on the table as he'd carried her to bed.

Damn it all to hell.

From her vantage point beside the bed, she couldn't see Nash or their assailant. Which meant she needed to move. Popping up to fire a round in the direction of the shadow, she rolled out from the bed, diving for cover behind a chair as a bullet shattered a lamp just above her head.

Nash was cornered between the bed and the wall, the bed giving protection, at least for the moment, but the gunman had the advantage. He stood between them and the door, with a large wardrobe to his left blocking her from taking a clear shot.

"Well, isn't this a pickle," their assailant said, his accent a smooth blend of American and French. She should have known. Adrian Benoit. They'd only just been in his apartment. Looked like he was returning the favor.

"Seems we've got ourselves a Mexican standoff," he drawled.

"Except that none of us are Mexican," Nash quipped.

She could see him now reflected in the mirror. And when he smiled, she realized he could see her as well. Which meant he had a plan.

"Doesn't matter," Benoit continued. "I've clearly got the advantage."

"So what, you want us to come out with our hands up?" Nash queried, nodding almost imperceptibly toward his gun lying on the table about five feet in front of her.

"It would certainly make things easier. But what I really want are the files you stole from my computer."

"And then you'll let us go? Right. And I've got some swampland..." Nash's laugh was harsh as he tipped his head slightly, signaling for her to stand ready. Annie nodded, already shifting her position.

"Well now, there wouldn't be any fun in letting you live, would there?" Benoit responded, anger clouding his voice.

Annie drew a breath, rolled out from behind the chair, fired once, and then dove for the table, her hand closing around the butt of Nash's gun. "Two o'clock," she yelled, as she chunked the weapon overhand toward Nash, still shooting in Benoit's direction in an attempt to provide some modicum of cover. Her ploy worked, Benoit turning to return fire as Nash emerged from behind the bed in a flying leap, intercepting the gun as it tumbled through the air.

Two seconds later and it was over. Benoit lay dead in a pool of his own blood.

"Are you all right?" Nash asked, pushing to his feet.

"I'm fine," she said as they met halfway, Nash's arms closing around her.

"You sure?" He ran his hands down her now trembling

body, double-checking to ascertain if she'd told him the truth.

"Really. He didn't hurt me. You were the one without the gun."

"Evened the odds." He shrugged, his voice buoyed by adrenaline, his smile edged with a ruthlessness that had kept him alive more times than she cared to remember. "So where were we?"

"I think that ship has sailed," she said, her gaze falling on the body.

"I suppose you're right," Nash said, brushing a strand of hair from her face. "We've got to get out of here before someone starts asking questions. Benoit was using a silencer. But we weren't."

"I'll start wiping things down." She pulled away and reached for a pair of gloves, falling effortlessly into a pattern they'd perfected over countless operations.

"So what was it you said earlier?" Nash called from across the room where he was packing their gear, his tone teasing, the fact that they'd just survived death—again—already an afterthought. "Something about wondering if we'd ever be a normal couple?"

Despite the gravity of the situation, Annie smiled. She loved this man. With every ounce of her being. And the cold hard truth was that she wouldn't change a single thing about their life. "I think," she said, reaching down to retrieve Benoit's gun, "that I just answered my own question."

Drake Flynn knows how
to survive behind enemy
lines. But he's about to meet
one adversary he can't
subdue...or resist.

Please turn this page
for an excerpt from

DANGEROUS DESIRES

Available now.

PROLOGUE

San Mateo Prison—Serrania Del Baudo, Colombia

Madeline Reynard squinted in the bright light. After three days of total darkness, the dappled sunlight hurt her eyes. She flinched as the guard shoved her forward, losing her balance and careening into the exercise yard.

"I've got you," Andrés said, his voice raspy, his English heavily accented as he steadied her. "I've been worried."

"They put me in solitary," Madeline whispered. "I have no idea why."

"Sometimes there is no reason," Andrés shrugged. "The main thing is that you're out now. Are you all right?"

"I'm fine. It's getting easier." This was third time she'd been relegated to the dank, windowless cell in the far recesses of the prison. "I just try to think of somewhere else and let my mind carry me away." She'd spent a good portion of her childhood locked in a closet only slightly smaller than the solitary cell. Her father had clearly believed the adage "out of sight, out of mind." But the experience was not without value. If Madeline could survive living like that, she could survive anything. Even San Mateo.

A place for political prisoners, the prison lacked creature comforts. In point of fact, it lacked most everything. Which meant that days loomed long, the only bright spot the minutes spent outside under the canopy of trees. The surrounding jungle reminded her of the cypresses back home, their gnarled arms curving downward into gray-green umbrellas of whispering leaves. The bayou had meant safety. And now the Colombian jungle offered the same.

"It's best if you find a way to separate yourself from the reality here," Andrés was saying. He nodded toward the people scattered about the yard. It was nearly empty, this hour relegated to women and the infirm, her friend falling into the latter category. It had been a long time since she'd had a friend. There'd always been too much to hide. Too much to risk. But now—*here*—her past didn't matter.

"Are you sure they didn't hurt you?" Andrés asked, his voice colored with worry.

"I told you I'm fine," she reiterated as they walked slowly across the yard, her muscles protesting the movement even as her mind rejoiced in her newfound freedom. "I'm just a little stiff, that's all."

She'd met Andrés on her second day in the yard. At first, his matted hair and filthy clothes had been off-putting. But after almost a week in this hell hole, she'd been desperate for human contact.

When he'd spoken to her in his halting English, it had felt like a gift, as her Spanish was limited to schoolgirl verbs and useless nouns. Which didn't matter when she was alone in her cell, or being leered at by the guards. It didn't take a vocabulary to interpret their catcalls. But real conversation, without English, was impossible. And it was conversation that kept the mind sharp. She'd come to need Andrés as much as she needed food and water.

Madeline closed her eyes, shutting out the small, barren exercise yard, its occupants wretched in their filth.

"You need to keep moving," her friend said, his hand warm against her back. "It's important to stay strong."

"I know you're right, but sometimes when I think about spending the rest of my life here, it doesn't seem worth it."

"You won't be here forever," he said, his tone soothing. "Someone will come for you."

Madeline laughed, the sound harsh. "I killed a man. There's nothing anyone can do to change that."

"But there were extenuating circumstances." He frowned. "That should count for something."

"Maybe in a fair world." She shrugged, shivering as memories flooded through her. Her sister's screams, her fear cutting through the haze of the drugs. The big man pinning her to the wall of the flophouse in Bogotá, one hand gripping her wrist as he tore at her clothes. Madeline had acted without thinking, the gun in her hand an extension of her anger. She'd told Jenny to run, and then checked the body, cringing as she touched his lifeless skin. Then she'd tried to follow, but it was too late.

The Colombian police had found her. The man was a prominent politician. Jenny was a drug addict. No one believed Madeline's story. Her sister disappeared, and Madeline had wound up here at San Mateo. But if she had it to do over again, she'd do the same. Her mother had made her promise. With her last breath of life.

"Take care of your sister, Maddie. She's not strong like you."

Madeline had only been ten, but she'd promised. And

she'd kept her word. She sucked in a breath, pulling her thoughts from the past. Jenny was safe now. She had to believe that. It was the only thing that kept her going.

"Anyway, even if it would make a difference, there's no one to come," Madeline said. "What about you? You told me you have family. Why aren't they trying to help you?"

"They think I'm dead." Andrés shrugged.

"How horrible," she said, shuddering at the thought.

"Believe me, it's better this way." His expression was guarded. "For them. And for me. Sometimes the truth is better left buried."

"I suppose you're right." She nodded as they stopped by the far wall of the yard. "Anyway, we have each other now, right?"

His smile was gentle. "You have been a good friend. But I'm afraid all good things must come to an end."

"Why would you say that?"

"I'm a marked man," Andrés sighed. "My days are numbered."

Madeline dipped her head, tears filling her eyes. She'd heard the shots fired late at night.

"The only reason I was allowed out here with you is that I was so sick. But I am better now, and that means I will be returned to my original cell. I overheard the guards," he said. "I'm being moved back. Which means this is my last time in the yard."

"No. I won't accept that." She shook her head, panic mixing with dread. "Maybe you can pretend to be sick again. Something, anything that might keep you here—with me. I...I can't make it without you."

"Of course you can," Andrés said. "You're much stronger than you know."

"Señor?" A guard called from the doorway, his machine gun held at the ready. *"Ven conmigo ahora."*

Madeline turned to the guard, then back to Andrés, heart pounding. "What does he want?"

"He wants me to come with him." Andrés shrugged. "It's time."

"No. You can't go. I can't do this on my own." She waved at the yard, and the guards.

"Yes, you can." His smile was gentle, his teeth white against the dark growth of his beard. "You're a survivor. Never forget that."

The guard moved impatiently, his lips curled in a sneer. *"Apurate!"*

"Uno momento," Andrés said holding up a hand. "Here, I have something for you." He reached into his pocket and produced a grimy card. "Take this. It may be of help to you."

She took the card, the battered face of the Queen of Hearts staring up at her. "I don't understand."

"If you can get this to the American Embassy, they'll help you. No questions asked."

"But it's just a playing card." She shook her head.

"Trust me," Andrés said, closing her fingers around the card. "And keep it safe."

"But if this truly does have some kind of significance, shouldn't you be the one using it?"

"Señor, ahora," the guard called, his eyes narrowing with impatience.

Madeline ignored him, her gaze locked on her friend's. "Andrés, tell me. Why not use it yourself?"

"Because it is too late for me. I have accepted my fate. And it gives me pleasure to think that perhaps I can be of some service to you. No matter what you have done, you don't belong here."

"Neither do you," she whispered, her voice fierce now. "Keep the card."

"It is yours, my friend. I give it freely. Now I must go." He shook his head, waving a hand toward the guard. "Use the card to find your way home, Madeline. And then forget this place ever existed."

"I can't do that," she said. "Because if I did, that would mean forgetting you."

Tears slid down her face, the first she'd shed since landing at San Mateo. She wasn't the type to get sentimental. Andrés was right. She was a survivor. But something about the man had touched her heart. Reached a place she'd thought long dead.

And now they were taking him away.

When he reached the guard, Andrés stopped and turned, lifting a hand to say good-bye. Madeline's heart stuttered to a stop, her breathing labored as she clung to the wall, watching as her friend disappeared into the prison.

She sank to the ground, her back sliding against the rough-hewn stone of the wall, and opened her fingers, the mottled face of the Queen staring up at her. It was just a card. Unless of course she'd somehow fallen down the rabbit hole. A bubble of hysteria washed through her.

San Mateo wasn't Wonderland. And she was no Alice. She was simply a woman who'd run out of options. Life wasn't fair. It was as simple as that. Angrily, she dried her eyes. There were two kinds of people in this world. The ones who survived. And the ones who did not.

She'd learned that lesson long ago.

THE DISH

Where authors give you the inside scoop!

♥ ♥ ♥ ♥ ♥ ♥ ♥ ♥ ♥ ♥ ♥ ♥ ♥ ♥ ♥

From the desk of Cynthia Eden

Dear Reader,

I like to be afraid. No, let me qualify that—I like the *thrill* that comes from being afraid, but I also like to know that I am completely 100% safe.

As a teen, I was a horror movie addict. I jumped every time a killer popped out of the darkness on-screen, and I yelled each time the foolish/brave heroine walked into the woods by herself. I loved the rush that came from watching those movies—and that same rush got to me even more intently when I read scary books. (It still gets to me!)

Fear gives you a spike of adrenaline; it makes your heart race, your breath heave; and, for the villain in my new book, DEADLY FEAR—well, *fear* makes his life worth living. The killer in this tale has an intimate connection with fear. He feels truly alive only when he can see and hear the real fear of others. So he sets out to turn his victims' worst fears into reality. Oh, yes, this guy would have scared me as a teen.

But to give him a strong adversary, I created my heroine in the form of Special Agent Monica Davenport. Unlike the foolish/brave heroines from my past,

Monica keeps her gun close, and she doesn't let fear get to her. Instead, she gets into the killer's mind.

Getting into his mind is, after all, her job. Monica is the lead profiler for the SSD—the Serial Services Division at the FBI. Her job is to track and apprehend serial killers. Fear isn't an option for her.

But it is for me.

To learn more about DEADLY FEAR and to read an excerpt, visit my website: www.cynthiaeden.com.

Happy reading!

Cynthia Eden

♥ ♥ ♥ ♥ ♥ ♥ ♥ ♥ ♥ ♥ ♥ ♥ ♥ ♥ ♥ ♥

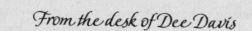

From the desk of Dee Davis

Dear Reader,

I read somewhere that "every character believes the story is about him." That really struck a chord with me because I've had characters hijack a book completely. In my first novel, a secondary character had too much to drink and in the course of a conversation revealed the entire plot—in Chapter 3. I took his tankard away, rewrote the scene, and lo and behold—he behaved. In my third novel, a character was supposed to have a one-line walk-on and wound up stealing the show with his dramatic death scene. So experience has taught me to always keep this in mind when I write, and I offer this same advice to any budding writers out there.

As a writer, I love all my characters equally. They're like children born from the murky depths of my imagination. But if I'm being really honest, some characters have a way of digging deeper into your heart. Tyler Hanson is one of those. Unlike some heroes and heroines I've written, who had to be dragged forcefully onto the page and compelled to reveal their secrets, Tyler sprang fully formed onto the computer screen almost from the minute I conceptualized her. She is strong, independent, and fiercely loyal. She isn't afraid of anything—except falling in love. And so I knew I was going to enjoy watching as she struggled with her growing feelings for Owen and, like all of us, the shadows that haunt her past.

One of the wonderful things about writing a series is that when the book ends, it isn't the end of the characters. They get to continue their journeys, albeit on the back burner, in future stories, and happily that means that I get to spend more time with characters like DARK DECEPTIONS's Nash and Annie and DARK DESIRES's Drake and Madeline.

And sometimes—because, after all, it's my world—I get to reintroduce someone from a previous book, someone I really hated saying good-bye to. Enter Harrison Blake. Harrison first appeared in my Last Chance series, and to date, he's gotten more mail than any other character I've ever written. So it's with great pleasure that I called on him to help Owen out in DESPERATE DEEDS. And I've got a feeling we haven't seen the last of him.

For more insight into Tyler and her romance with Owen, here are some songs I listened to while writing DESPERATE DEEDS:

"Blurry"—Puddle of Mudd

"Mad World"—Adam Lambert

"Kissed by a Rose"—Seal

I hope you're enjoying the A-Tac series. For more on the books and me, check out www.deedavis.com.

Happy Reading!

Dee Davis

♥ ♥ ♥ ♥ ♥ ♥ ♥ ♥ ♥ ♥ ♥ ♥ ♥ ♥ ♥

From the desk of Kira Morgan

Dear Reader,

I've heard that in order to write a good book, you have to take your perfectly nice characters and torture them mercilessly. Well, I'm afraid to tell you that's exactly what I've done to my poor heroine in CAPTURED BY DESIRE.

Florie Gilder is a 16th-century Scottish goldsmith's daughter with a mind of her own, a strong will, and a bright future. So what do I do with her? I confront her with an unfortunate misunderstanding, which deteriorates into a disastrous altercation, followed by a tragic accident that renders her utterly helpless. Worse, I thrust her into the path of Rane McAllister, a charming, assertive lady-killer of a huntsman who is used to getting his way, and then I leave her in his overbearing hands.

All her life, Florie has fought for respectability among her peers in the goldsmith's guild, but with a wicked twist of my pen, I upset her world and drag her down to the level of a common criminal, forcing her to claw her way back up. Knowing Florie prides herself on her independence, I strip that away from her too, leaving her completely reliant on a stranger.

Since Florie hates to be touched, Rane touches her all the time. Because she's accustomed to dining on roast capon, sweetmeats, and fine wine, Rane brings her coarse bread, hard cheese, and rough ale. Florie prefers velvet, and Rane dresses her in wool.

But I don't stop there.

Florie prefers to be alone, so naturally the hero is with her constantly. She doesn't like to be the center of attention, so I make a humiliating spectacle out of her. She's terrified of the enemy English, so they're a constant threat.

Then, when she thinks things can't get any worse, I make Florie, who has sworn on her mother's grave never to fall in love, fall in love.

Of course, I put a few thumbscrews to the hero, too.

Since Rane prefers compliant blondes, I throw him a spunky brunette. I obligate him to take care of Florie when he's supposed to be providing for starving peasants. I force him to choose between his loyalty to his lord and his love for Florie.

And because Rane is pretty much the village stud, I taunt him with women he can't have, all the while dangling the virgin Florie in front of him.

It's a cruel game, I suppose, making my characters suffer so much. But in the end, it really *does* make everyone's "happy ever after" that much happier! After all, what's pleasure without a little pain?

Enjoy!

Kira Morgan